THE UNMAKING ENGINE

IAN W. SAINSBURY

Visit the author at https://ianwsainsbury.com/

Cover design by Hristo Kovatliev

For Anya

Previously in The World Walker…

IMPORTANT NOTE: The Unmaking Engine is Book 2 of a series. The following contains spoilers relating to the first book in the series. If you haven't read The World Walker and would prefer to read the books in order, please go read it first.

If you don't care about the order or you've just dying to get reading, skip the following.

However, if you would like a quick reminder of what happened in The World Walker before you read The Unmaking Engine, this section is for you. You could always re-read The World Walker before starting The Unmaking Engine, of course. I did ;)

If not, here's the quick version of what happened…

Terminally ill musician Seb Varden decides to end his life rather than let his brain tumor do the job for him. An alien that's been waiting since the Roswell incident of 1947 has other ideas and gives him his life back, along with a body full of advanced alien technology he has no idea how to use.

Seb finds he has superhuman powers, seemingly can't die, and situations involving extreme stress trigger an automatic vanishing act, taking him miles away from where he started.

Different factions are interested in Seb's progress. There's Westlake, who appears to be a government secret service agent with no qualms about taking any measures necessary to capture Seb. There's the Order, a quasi-religious organization which thinks Seb may be the messiah. And then there's Walt Ford, somewhat of a mentor for Seb, who takes him to Las Vegas and shows him a very good time indeed. He also teaches him about Manna - a source of power buried at many locations around the world and wielded by various individuals and groups. Manna may seem like magic, at first, but in reality is nanotechnology. Manna users have to 'refill' their Manna reserves regularly, but Walt is amazed to find Seb doesn't need to do this.

Mason is the villain of the piece. No one - even those highest in his organization - knows his identity. As the strongest Manna user in America, he rules by fear and controls a network that, in effect, holds more power than any other group in the country. He sees Seb as a threat that must be controlled or removed.

Meera Patel, a singer in Seb's old band and his ex-girlfriend, teams up with Bob Geller, Seb's friend, to find the missing musician. They are helped by members of the Order who bring them to the outskirts of Las Vegas to hide them from Westlake while they continue their search.

As the story progresses, we learn that Westlake is Mason's man, and Mason can see that his best bet of getting to Seb is by kidnapping Meera. Westlake does so, killing the members of the Order protecting her, and murdering Seb's friend, Bob Geller. Walt Ford helps in this operation. He is also in Mason's organization, although he hates what he has become.

Meanwhile, Seb has come to distrust Walt and has left Las Vegas. He is gradually learning some control over the nanotechnology in his body. This has been helped by his personality splitting into three parts. Seb2 is learning how to communicate with and control the nanotech - or Manna - and Seb3 is a silent partner in constant agony: a constant reminder that Seb was not ready to absorb the alien technology and is still struggling to do so.

While Meera is being kidnapped, Seb has gone to Roswell, absorbing the Manna there. No other Manna user has ever been able to do this. His power and control increases massively as a result. On his return, now able to consciously use his instant-traveling power, he 'Walks' to Vegas to meet Meera. She's gone. Walt reveals his treachery and tells Seb Mason has taken Meera.

Seb meets Mason's representatives, who show him a live feed of Meera having her pinkie cut off by Westlake. Mason intends keeping Meera prisoner for the rest of her life to control Seb. He tests Seb by sending him to battle his closest rival - Sonia Svetlana and her followers. Seb's victory impresses Mason still further, but Seb refuses to be controlled. He says he will give his own life instead - on the condition that Meera is released. Mason agrees and the arrangements are made.

Seb meets Westlake and Walt at a New York building site, where Seb is beheaded and his body reduced to bones and ashes by a flamethrower. His remains are thrown into the foundations of the parking lot before being covered with concrete.

Mason has underestimated Seb. The body his henchmen killed was, in fact, a homunculus - an artificial creature made by Manna users. Seb's homunculus was more sophisticated than Mason or anyone else thought possible. The real Seb changes his - and Meera's - appearance. They escape.

His enemies think he's dead. He got the girl. He is just beginning to explore the incredible power he has been given. What could possibly go wrong?

Chapter 1

Dover, Delaware

There were five of them and only one of him, which was the first problem. One of them—the biggest, ugliest one—had just unloaded both barrels of a shotgun into his chest from a distance of five feet. That was the second problem. The third, most serious problem was the presence of nineteen witnesses. This was causing Seb Varden a real headache.

He was in a bank in Dover. He was there because he knew the police weren't going to show, the armed gang had already carried out similar robberies in the last six months, and the death toll attributed to them had hit double figures. The ugly guy was trying to kill him because Seb had asked whether his mother had had sex with a genetically-modified pig to produce him. Or if he'd got his good looks by running into a wall. Twice.

The alarm in the bank wasn't ringing because the gang was backed by a sophisticated syndicate which had disabled all security systems, including cameras. This was one of the two ways the syndicate earned its fifty percent of the haul. The other was its handling of the Delaware police department which, even Seb had to admit, was inspired. Right now, the city's finest were racing to a bank twelve miles west of the one currently being robbed, due to seven 911 calls apparently made from that location. Some remotely triggered explosions and a lockdown of the premises in question meant police resources were looking in the entirely wrong direction when the actual robbery took place. When the security system had gone down at the exact moment the cops were hauling ass in the opposite direction, Seb2 had nudged Seb into action. The gang thought they had everyone in the building covered until Seb walked out of an office near the main door.

Seb knew Ugly was going to shoot him 0.37 seconds before he pulled the trigger. The man's eyes had dropped from Seb's face to his chest at the same time as he'd raised the weapon and held his breath.

"Here we go," said Seb2. Seb was used to his consciousness being split into three parts—although Seb3 was pretty much a silent partner. It was one of the consequences of having a body full of advanced alien nanotechnology, eighty-seven percent of which, according to Seb2, he still had little idea how to use. He twisted to his left just before the flash of light at the end of the barrels let him know two cartridges of lead shot were heading his way.

A shotgun cartridge is designed to spread its payload of hundreds of lead pellets as it travels toward a target some distance away. Close up, as long as you're facing the right direction, you can't miss. No one gets up and walks away from a close-up encounter with a shotgun. Which was unfortunate for the two members of the gang directly behind Seb.

As he twisted, 57 of the 410 tiny lead balls tore across Seb's ribs and stomach, ripping widening channels through his flesh. By the time the shot had passed through him, his body was unmarked again, blood vessels, muscles and skin knitting together so fast as to be virtually instantaneous. Since sound travels at a significantly slower speed than light, he only heard the near-deafening blast of the shotgun just after the two men behind him were blown off their feet.

The two gang members covering the hostages at the far end of the bank started to turn as Seb considered his options. The way he had twisted meant that the hostages would assume the shotgun blast had missed him completely. Today, his appearance was that of a fit, Asian man in his mid-twenties, which meant any witnesses would be likely to ascribe his speed and fighting skills to knowledge of some mysterious martial art. It was lucky, really—he'd only chosen this face after watching an old movie the previous night. If he'd decided on an overweight sixty-year-old, he might be in real danger of attracting attention. And, for Meera's safety and his own sanity, attention was something he was determined to avoid.

It would take Ugly about four seconds to reload, under normal circumstances. Under abnormal circumstances such as, for instance, having just accidentally killed two of your colleagues during a robbery, Seb thought he might have seven or eight seconds to take him out. If it wasn't for the hostages watching the action unfold, he could have easily sent tendrils of Manna directly toward Ugly and his two friends and cut off their oxygen supply briefly. Couldn't do that with eight bank employees and eleven terrified customers watching.

The two men guarding the hostages had nearly completed their turns, but only one of them had swept his gun around. The other, a short, bald, older man—possibly the leader, turned his head but kept his weapon trained on the terrified men and women on the floor in front of him.

Seb hit the floor and rolled, fast. Ugly had no time to react before his feet were swept out from underneath him. His head hit the marble floor hard, he grunted once, then lay still.

"He'll live," said Seb2 as Seb picked up the shotgun and, with an enhanced flick of his arm, sent it sailing toward the taller man. It was an ungainly object to throw accurately and Seb had to give it some height to allow it to reach its target. That gave the tall man plenty of time to dodge to the side before it hit him. Which meant he was an easy target for the pistol Seb had thrown after it. There was a solid smack as metal hit flesh and the tall man crumpled.

The leader's eyes narrowed as he began to evaluate the changed situation. All his men were out of commission, it didn't look like he'd be walking out with any money. But there was only one crazy Asian guy between him and freedom. There were other banks, there would be other days. And he had hostages. He might have to shoot a couple of them to slow this idiot down.

Seb knew the older man would likely consider the hostages his best chance of retaining the advantage, so he did the most counter-intuitive thing he could think of. He ran directly toward the armed man, waving his arms and shouting.

The leader's eyebrows shot up as the crazy man sprinted toward him. Perhaps it wasn't going to be too complicated after all. He raised his gun.

As Seb ran, he watched the man's arm come up toward him, the dark hole of the barrel slowly turning into a perfect circle.

"Now!" said Seb2. Seb threw himself onto the marble floor head-first. The molecular structure of the outward-most layer of his sweat pants and top changed to minimize friction as they made contact, so his slide was much faster than physics would otherwise have allowed. The leader had excellent reactions, and the bullet that ricocheted off the floor and shattered the front window would have hit Seb if he had been where he should have been. The man didn't get the chance to fire again, as Seb plowed into his shins, disarmed him as he fell and jabbed him in the neck with three fingers. His body went limp. Twenty-nine seconds had passed since Seb had insulted Ugly.

The hostages broke into applause and cheers. A few of them brought out their phones and started to film. Seb moved quickly and tried to avoid anyone getting a clear picture. For the most part, he succeeded, but a kid, his face puffy from crying, managed to get a reasonable photo as Seb turned back to the other hostages. That was the one the media used.

Seb pulled up his hood, his face now in shadow. He raised his hands for quiet.

"They may have brought explosives," he said, indicating a couple of heavy bags near the gang members. There was a moment of renewed panic, and Seb raised his voice to be heard. "Let's just get out quickly," he said. He helped a couple of people up and they all headed toward the doors. As he followed the group out, Seb sent short bursts of Manna toward the three unconscious men. They would sleep for a few more hours and wake up in custody.

Reports of shots fired meant the sound of sirens was finally audible as they left the bank and made their way across the parking lot, some crying, some laughing, a few slack-jawed and silent, stumbling as they made their way to safety. Seb caught up with an old, grizzled man in a checkered shirt.

"Sir? Do me a favor?"

The man looked at Seb, grinned and shook his hand.

"Helluva thing you pulled off back there," he said. "Wouldn't have believed it if I hadn't see it with my own damn eyes." He gave Seb a playful punch on the shoulder. "Always thought that kung-fu stuff was bullshit, myself. Guess I was wrong. What d'ya need?"

"You got a car?"

The old man nodded toward a battered Chevy truck. "Will that do?"

Seb nodded. "Can I borrow it?" he asked. "I, er, don't really want to be here when the cops get here, if you catch my drift."

The man pressed the truck's keys into Seb's hand. "It's stick," he said. "You ok with that?"

"No problem," said Seb. "I'll leave it at the bus station. Keys on the front tire. If you could just delay telling the police that for an hour or so."

"Far as I'm concerned, you can keep it," said the man as Seb jogged across the lot and got into the Chevy. It started with a cough and a plume of blue smoke. "Good luck!"

Seb waved his acknowledgment and pulled away. By the time the other hostages realized their rescuer was missing, he was a mile away. The pickup truck now looked like a Hyundai Elantra and Seb was caucasian, middle-aged and half a foot taller, with a full beard. He drove to the bus station and found a parking garage where no one would see the saloon transform back into a pickup. As soon as it was done, he Walked and was thousands of miles away before the Chevy's engine had even started to cool.

Chapter 2

Soledad Hotel
La Moskitia Region, Honduras

Harvey Foster shifted uneasily in his bed and glanced at the clock. 3:37am. The heat still got to him, despite years spent trekking through the humid rainforests of South America, and the sound of rain battering the shuttered windows made sleep impossible. He sat up, eased the mosquito net aside and made his way to the door. Sally was still sleeping soundly as he quickly pulled on his pants and grabbed his cigarettes from his jacket. Apparently, heavy rainfall and howling wind were as effective as sleeping pills for his wife.

Outside the hotel, he offered a cigarette to Carlos, the hotel owner, who waved him toward an empty chair. Carlos was also the chef, bellboy, cleaner and taxi driver, sharing his duties with his wife, Juanita. They smoked in silence for a while, Carlos passing him a glass of surprisingly good rum, considering the cheap looking pint bottle he poured it from. He put the rum on the table between them and indicated that Harvey should help himself.

After about ten minutes, Carlos spoke. He kept his voice low, as the hotel was full of families who were staying over after celebrating Children's Day with a concert that afternoon.

"You think you find Monkey God *templo* tomorrow?"

Harvey chuckled self-consciously and took another sip. The legend of the Monkey God had just enough anecdotal evidence to make him want to take a look. Ten years of treasure hunting in South America every vacation had brought him little reward. Two broken ribs, eight cases of dysentery, a malaria scare, two snake bites, one scorpion sting and a close call with some heavily armed bandits, but very little actual treasure to show for it. A conservative estimate put him over $30,000 down over the last decade of hacking through jungles, climbing trees, kayaking deserted stretches of river, and hiking snowcapped mountains. His income as a history teacher hardly began to cover his expenditure. Lucky, then, that his movie producer wife thought his expeditions were the best vacations she'd ever taken. It was how they'd met, Sally vetting locations for a movie about drug smuggling, Harvey about to go home after a fruitless search for a legendary diamond. She'd been the first woman he'd ever met who didn't mention Indiana Jones when he told her why he was there. He told her later that was the moment he'd fallen in love.

Harvey passed Carlos another cigarette and offered him a light. He knew he was supposed to quit, but—as he'd pointed out to his oncologist—there was a famous saying about shutting a barn door after its occupant had escaped. No point adopting a healthy lifestyle with his prognosis. He was fifty-three and in pretty good shape.

Other than the terminal cancer, that was. However, he increasingly found himself struggling to climb even small hills now. Stopping every few minutes, trying to catch his breath. And Sally had noticed, of course. He'd claimed a lingering case of bronchitis, but he knew she wasn't buying it. That was a conversation he'd put off for too long. But how do you tell the love of your life that "til death do us part" was going to roll around a little sooner than planned? He promised himself he'd tell her in the morning. Just as he had every night for the last six weeks.

"You believe in the Monkey God, Carlos?" he said.

"Si," said Carlos. "My father's father saw him once. The whole town was sick, everyone sick. Dios Mono, he walk through the town in the dark. My father's father was small. Young, yes? He saw him. Then every sick person get well. The day after, no one is sick. Dios Mono took away the sickness. Of course I believe."

Harvey was silent for a minute, sipping the rum, feeling the warmth run down his throat. He struggled with conflicting emotions. The healing properties of the Monkey God was one of its most famous attributes. The other was its propensity for kidnapping women, impregnating them, then sending them back home where they'd give birth to strange half-human creatures. Harvey's choice of Honduras for his last adventure owed more than a little to the healing legend. He could only hope Sally would escape the latter fate.

"Mr Foster, I-," Carlos stopped, looked a little embarrassed. "I hope you don't mind?"

"Harvey, Carlos. Call me Harvey. What do you want to know?"

"Are you sick, Harvey?"

Before Harvey could answer, the ground lifted itself about six inches, seemed to shake itself briefly, then settled with a low cracking sound and a small cloud of dust.

"What the-?" said Harvey.

"Terremoto!" said Carlos, jumping out of his seat, knocking the table, which had already thrown off their glasses and the bottle. "Earthquake!" He was heading for a large bell hanging from the corner of the porch. Before he got there, there was another shudder of movement and Harvey saw one of the supports holding the roof give way. As the structure collapsed, Harvey, moving with a speed he hardly credited possible, sprinted toward Carlos, crashing into him, his momentum carrying both the men off the decking into the street.

"No!" said Carlos, "I must ring bell." He started to stand, then hurriedly pushed himself backward as the porch collapsed in a shower of plasterboard and concrete, the table they'd been sitting at quickly buried in rubble.

"Juanita!" shouted Carlos, crossing himself as another tremor, this one more violent than the last, shook the ground beneath them. The ground floor windows of the Soledad Hotel shattered and blew outward. Harvey got to his feet, his face ashen as he looked up toward the third floor window and Sally's room. The ground underneath him rippled like water on a windy day and he stumbled, putting a hand on the ground in an attempt to keep himself stable. He looked up and watched in horror as the whole building in front of him cracked and crumbled with a great sound of tearing metal, splintering wood and exploding plaster. Then another shock, the biggest yet, shook the ground beneath him and he fell on his back. Looking up as the earth bucked and writhed beneath him, he had a perfect view of the hotel lurching forward suddenly, loudly, like a belligerent drunk, before passing the tipping point and falling toward his prone figure. He closed his eyes with a feeling of sudden calm.

Two hundred feet away, at the edge of the forest, stood a figure. The earthquake, despite its violence, seemed to have little effect on it. The figure was watching the chaotic scene intensely, one arm pointing toward the collapsing building. As it did so, the hotel, impossibly, stopped falling and hung at an unlikely angle as if held in place by a giant invisible hand.

Harvey looked over at Carlos, who, now that the shaking was dying down, had got to his feet and was hurrying over toward him in a kind of crouching half-run, his shoulders hunched as if that might prevent the hotel from completing its inevitable fall. He grabbed Harvey's arm and pulled him to his feet. Together they ran out of the path of the hotel's descent. As soon as they had done so, it continued its fall, but not in any way that tallied with either man's grasp of basic physics. It lowered itself gently to the ground, settling there in a small cloud of dust.

Harvey's ears were ringing, and as he began to recover his hearing, two sounds immediately became clear. One was Carlos muttering, over and over, "Madre de Dios, Dios Mono, Madre de Dios, Dios Mono, Madre de Dios, Dios Mono,", the other was the muffled plaintive cries of people trapped in the ruins in front of him. He grabbed Carlos. When the man continued looking through him and muttering, he shook him.

"Carlos," he said. "I must find Sally. My wife! The people, the children. Juanita. We must save them." Carlos seemed to recover himself, but he still looked at some point in the distance over Harvey's shoulder. Harvey threw a quick glance at the forest. He saw nothing initially, then a slight movement caught his eye. A man was standing at the edge of the tree line, holding his arms out. No, not a man, a gorilla or ape of some kind. A flicker of flame from a burning outbuilding revealed enough detail for Harvey's mouth to suddenly dry up and his skin prickle. It was a monkey. A giant monkey.

"Ayuda! Por Favor! Ayuda!" Faint voices brought him back to the unfolding emergency. He looked at the collapsed building. Although it had somehow been saved from complete destruction, there was no way in or out as each door and window had fallen in on itself. For a split second, Harvey wondered how anyone could have survived, then he dismissed the thought and ran forward. Carlos ran beside him, but when they carefully climbed onto the rubble, they realized the hopelessness of the situation. They were two men, three miles from the nearest village, with nothing but their own hands with which to unearth the survivors before the aftershocks finished the job the earthquake had started, and buried them forever. Harvey shrugged. What choice did he have? He knelt and began pulling at bits of concrete and wood, his hands became cut and bruised within seconds as he desperately dug in search of his wife.

As he frantically worked, he saw a small figure move rapidly past him. He didn't look up, but then another figure came past. Some kind of animal, perhaps. Then there was another, then another. Next there was a whole group, one of which brushed against him. He didn't look up until he felt a tiny hand on his shoulder. He stopped, hands bleeding, hardly able to breath, his face coated in gray dust, pink skin only visible where the tears had rolled from his eyes as he tried to find Sally. He turned to see a monkey squatting beside him, a tiny thing with an impossibly human expression of sympathy and understanding on its minuscule features. It gently shook its head, then waved its arm around it as if to show Harvey what was happening. Harvey looked up.

The whole building was covered in the yellow-brown monkeys. They swarmed all over the rubble at an amazing rate, only stopping when they heard cries for help. Whenever that happened, there would be a rapid huddling of furry shapes, each one digging rapidly with tiny, unfeasibly strong arms, removing chunks of rubble in a blur of speed, then throwing them with near perfect accuracy into a pile about fifty yards away.

Within a few minutes, holes had appeared all over the stricken carcass of the hotel. As Harvey looked on in disbelief, the survivors began emerging, helping each other up onto the side of the building, which was now nearest the sky. One or two monkeys led each small, dazed group safely onto the ground and away to a safe distance. Whole families looked at each other and the scene from which they'd emerged in disbelief, hugging each other and weeping.

The monkey next to Harvey put its tiny hand onto his fingers and pulled gently. His hand tingled at the contact. Like a man in a dream, Harvey let himself be led carefully across the wreckage. The monkey stopped and pointed at the hole recently dug by its brothers and sisters. Harvey crouched at the lip of the blackness and peered inside.

"Sally?" he croaked. There was silence for a moment, then he called her name again, louder this time. He saw movement below. He could see a mattress in a corner and sitting up on it, the most beautiful sight he'd ever seen. His wife, stretching and yawning, eyes still half-closed, as yet oblivious to the chaos around her.

"Harvey?" she said, sleepily. "Is it morning already?"

At the edge of the rainforest, hundreds of monkeys formed up in a tight semi-circle in front of their giant counterpart.

"Everyone got out?" said the giant monkey. In perfect unison, they all nodded. Immediately after doing so, they all collapsed into piles of dirt, leaving twenty square yards of ground looking like it had been targeted by an army of moles.

The Monkey God smiled. "Best head for home, then," he said, "I'm starving." He turned away and vanished.

***

Two days later, Harvey and Sally Foster boarded the first of three planes that would return them to New York. Once home, they celebrated their close brush with death in the only way they could think of, barely leaving their apartment for four days straight. Besides enjoying himself immensely, Harvey was increasingly puzzled at his lack of breathlessness. An appointment to his oncologist on the fifth day home provided the answer. Harvey's cancer was gone. No rational explanation, no apparent danger of it returning.

"A religious man might call it a miracle," said the doctor, shaking Harvey's hand vigorously. His particular branch of oncology made delivering news of this sort very rare indeed. His smile was broad and unforced.

"That he might," said Harvey. "That he might."

Chapter 3

Mexico City

Meera Patel drew heavily on the fat joint she'd just rolled, inhaling deeply, then exhaling a small sweet smelling cloud of blue-gray smoke. She picked up her beer and smiled through the haze at the woman opposite her.

"You know you don't-," began the woman.

"Don't need to smoke this stuff anymore? Don't need to drink this? Now that I've begun to use Manna? Yeah, I know, but I still like it."

The other woman smiled and took a sip of water.

"Wasn't what I was going to say. Far from it. I was going to say you know you don't need to hide anything from me. You must know by now, you'll find no judgement, no censure. The Order was never really a religious organization."

Meera frowned slightly at this.

"Ok, I know what you're thinking, Stephanie" said Kate, "but any social grouping based around communal meditation was bound to pick up some religious trappings after the first thousand years."

Meera shifted uncomfortably in her seat. There were things she hadn't told Kate, it was true. Her real name being one of them, along with her real face. But only because doing so would endanger both of them. She had finally accepted Seb's admission of his immortality. Still didn't know how she felt about it, but she had accepted it. However, letting Kate know Seb's true identity, or any part of the incredible events that had led them to finally take refuge in Mexico City, was a risk she could never take. She thought briefly of the mysterious Mason, the man who had masterminded her kidnapping and torture; the man who had intended to keep her a prisoner for the rest of her life. If he ever found her, he would kill her. And he would kill anyone she'd been in contact with. She probably knew more about Mason than anyone outside his organization. Which was virtually nothing. But she doubted he would see it that way.

"It's not that I don't trust you," said Meera, taking Kate's hand, the older woman's fingers darker than her own caramel skin. "You must know that by now."

Kate returned her smile. "Of course. But I can feel it eating away at you, whatever it is. I'll be ready to listen should you ever feel ready."

"Thank you."

Meera looked up at the stars, only a few of which were visible through the light pollution of the city. She remembered sitting on a roof with Seb back in LA. Back when she could still sing in public without risking her life. Back when Seb was a regular human being.

"Time to go home," she said, getting up and stretching. They walked across the roof together and headed into the apartment building. The building was five stories high. The top floor had eight fairly traditional apartments, only three of which were occupied. The fourth floor had been knocked through to make a big open space. It was a meditation room. There were dozens of prayer stools and cushions stacked against one wall, but they were covered in dust. One small area near the center of the room had been kept clean and usable. The third floor would have been a huge surprise to anyone who had never encountered the Order and their abilities. It was a garden; lush, green and fragrant. Or, at least, it had been so, once. Now, like the floor above, it showed signs of neglect, many of the plants dead. Only one corner looked well-watered and lush, with healthy tomato plants alongside corn, eggplant, zucchini, onion and a selection of herbs. The second floor was a communal dining area, with long tables able to seat more than fifty people. A smaller table near a large picture window was clean, the rest in various states of disrepair and decay. There was a pile of soil in the corner. Meera had watched members of the Order use it to produce delicious food in seconds. It still looked like magic to her, when she saw the dirt transform into a plate of sushi or a bowl of dal. She herself had shown no ability to do the same, despite her training in Manna use. Her gifts with Manna lay elsewhere.

Kate and Meera stopped at the first floor door. This floor was a collection of offices with an uninviting waiting room, opening up to the street. The building had once housed an insurance office, and the Order had left the first floor as it was.

"I'll see you tomorrow, Stephanie," said Kate. "Give my love to Peter." 'Peter' was 'Stephanie's' shy boyfriend. A writer. Somewhat eccentric. A bit of a recluse. Seb kept contact with anyone connected to the Order to a minimum. The unique Manna which filled his body, so much more advanced than any other sources of Manna, was invisible to even the most sensitive User, but he didn't want to risk provoking any kind of curiosity.

Meera kissed Kate on the cheek. Kate was strikingly beautiful; tall, graceful and precise in her every movement. Meera constantly felt like a clumsy child in comparison. Kate looked like a woman who'd reached her fifties and had got to a point where intelligence and compassion showed on her features as plainly as her head-turning good looks. Meera looked into those dark eyes and wondered how old she really was. She gave Kate a quick smile and walked into the street.

The Order had fallen apart over a period of a few months during the previous year. Despite its lack of dogma, rules, ritual, and a complete lack of 'holy' scriptures, its members had reacted with awe, hope and excitement when, according to their most senior member in Northern America, the messiah they had been waiting for had arrived. Three words had underpinned the entire history of the Order, the only words left to them by their founder, who had lived in what was now modern-day Syria, a few centuries after the birth of Christ. The words were Learn, Teach, Wait. The Order had followed the implications of each word faithfully for centuries. The members learned by paying attention in meditation, or contemplation. They taught those who sought them out, passing on the simple timeless truths that led to inner engagement and a new way of encountering and shaping reality through the use of Manna. They waited for another Visitor to pass on its gift to another human being, just as it had to their founder. And—finally— it had happened. For a few glorious weeks, the Order was boiling over with excitement at the news from America. A new age was about to begin. Then, suddenly, a cell just outside of Las Vegas had disappeared overnight, as if it had never existed. Eleven members of the Order erased without trace. Diane, their leader and Lo, considered by many to be their next leader, were among those who'd gone. And, a few days later, the almost incomprehensible news. Seb Varden was dead. The messiah had been killed.

Kate watched Meera walk away until she was out of sight. As always, the younger woman had started singing as she left. Meera was a bit of a mystery, even to someone with Kate's long experience. She was the only person to actively seek out the Order in a year, just walking in off the street as if guided there. She just claimed she felt drawn to them, and Kate never questioned her further. Meera had seemed unsurprised by her initial exposures to Manna, which was very unusual. The revelation that the Earth was covered with sites containing an ancient power that certain individuals could manipulate was unsettling to everyone, at first. But not Meera, apparently.

Kate walked back into the office—that was how all members of the Order referred to their Mexico base—climbed the stairs to the third floor and used Manna to produce a large cup of green tea. It was late, and Miguel and Sarah—all that was left of the Order in Mexico City—were asleep upstairs. She sat alone at one of the long tables, remembering it full of people eating, smiling, talking. Despite her gifts for equilibrium and acceptance, she felt a small pang of regret for what they had lost.

Kate first exposed Stephanie/Meera to Manna eight months previously. The young woman had quietly and calmly accompanied Kate to the Thin Place they used near Casa Negra. The nineteenth century mansion was long abandoned and considered haunted, so it was given a wide berth by locals, and all but the most fearless tourists after dark. The tourists themselves were easily frightened off by some peripheral movements and some low growling. It made for a good story when they got home. The south-east corner of the building was out of sight of the main street and the most discreet place to absorb Manna. Kate had knelt on the floor and put both hands on the ground, like a Muslim at prayer. As she deepened her breathing and opened her senses, she felt the familiar tingling in her fingertips as the rush of power entered her body, every individual cell glorying in renewed contact with Manna. She'd noted the expression on Stephanie's face as she'd stood up and brushed the dirt from her hands, still trembling slightly. Stephanie had seemed excited, yes, curious, a little scared. All of which was to be expected. But she had also seemed sad and distant.

When Stephanie had copied Kate's actions and followed her training to control her breathing and settle her thoughts, Kate had watched closely as the threads of Manna left the earth and, to a User's eyes at least, lit up her entire body. Kate let out a gasp when she saw Stephanie's face in the moonlight. It had changed—it was no longer the American Chinese features she knew so well, but an Indian or Pakistani face. Quite beautiful, with a shock of wild black hair. But not Stephanie. The vision flickered, then was gone. It was Stephanie again, getting up from the ground, shivering and grinning.

"Wow! This stuff is better than coke! You ever try coke? Probably not, right, holy lady and all that, but, man, what a buzz! Woa, I could take on the world and his uncle, shall we run back to the office, I don't think I can walk feeling like this...I'm going to stop talking now, ok?"

Kate had just nodded, silently. They'd walked back to the office in silence, Stephanie giggling occasionally. Kate couldn't help feeling she'd just seen the real woman beneath the mask. But how could this novice change her features without Manna, without training, and—strangest of all—without Kate having any idea of how she was doing it at all?

The lights were all off when Kate finally went to her room on the fifth floor. There was a clay pot full of soil on the windowsill. She poured the dregs of her tea into it, followed by the cup. It dissolved into the earth and was gone.

***

Meera walked quickly through the streets. It wasn't the safest part of Mexico City, but she had two distinct advantages over most lone females. One was the subroutine Seb2 had coded into her DNA. If her body showed indications of high stress—Seb had described it as monitoring her "periaqueductal gray, the part of your midbrain which regulates defense mechanisms", but she hadn't really been listening—a signal would be sent and Seb would Walk to her. She'd never had to use it, mainly because of the other advantage: her own Manna ability.

Meera had turned out to be a natural Manna user, but her talent was an unusual variant on something fairly common in the Order. She was a Sensitive, could tell where other Users were, knew when Manna was being used nearby. But where her ability differed was that she could accurately predict the actions of non-Manna users with a fair degree of accuracy. The Manna she carried surrounded her like a cloud, rather than being held within her body until she used it. Her awareness stretched out to the edges of the cloud, which extended about a hundred feet in every direction. Within the cloud, she knew if anyone was angry, fearful, happy, or guilty; she knew if they had noticed her. As she knew, Manna was made up of human-manipulated alien nano-technology, rather than magic (a belief still held by many), she assumed the information she received was due to the detection of pheromones released by those around her. She always knew if they might mean to harm her. Which gave her plenty of time to get away. Or at least, it had worked that way so far.

And knowing Seb would be there if her own defenses failed, reassured her, although she'd rolled her eyes when Seb had suggested it. Couldn't have him knowing how much she still feared being found by Mason's men.

She ducked into a maze of narrow back alleys, knowing which of them had opportunistic muggers waiting in them and which didn't. She sang as she walked. She missed singing with the band. She had a small recording studio in the apartment, and had built quite a following online with tracks posted under an assumed name, but it wasn't the same. She knew Mason was likely to have heard it, and possibly tried to track her, but Seb assured her it was utterly impossible. Anyone trying to pin down her IP address would be sent on a never-ending global wild goose chase.

She walked into their apartment just before midnight. As she crossed the threshold, her face and body changed, morphing instantly from Stephanie to Meera. She'd chosen her 'outside' face one long night just before they moved to Mexico City. As Seb had changed her features in front of the mirror she'd laughed herself into hysterics more than once, insisting he make her look like Imelda Marcos, Mama Cass, Janis Joplin and Grace Kelly, amongst others. She'd eventually settled on the relative anonymity of Stephanie, based on a face they'd found online in a 1980s college yearbook. Seb had chosen Peter, a tall Brazilian man in his forties. They could be themselves in the apartment, but only there.

Meera walked through to the kitchen. He'd left a note under a margarita.

Earthquake in Honduras 99.76% likely tonight. Off to the epicenter. Back in the morning. S x

She sipped the margarita. It was perfect of course, and beautifully chilled, despite the fact it had probably been set on the counter hours earlier. She opened the balcony door and watched, listened to, and smelled the city. Fourteen months ago she'd had a successful career as a singer but her love life was a disaster. Now she could do magic and was living with the man she loved. Who was, effectively, a superhero. Life was fucking weird.

Chapter 4

Upstate New York
Thirty-four years previously

"Put your light out, Boy. What the hell you doin' up there?"

Boy reached out and clicked off his bedside lamp. He counted to thirty but there was no sound other than the TV burbling away downstairs. He took his flashlight from the drawer and carried on reading *Catcher In the Rye* under the covers.

Boy wasn't really his name, but he answered to it. There was another name, of course, the one Mom used when Pop wasn't home. But Boy knew that the other name wasn't his real name. Pop heard Mom using it, he'd backhand her without a word. Pop saw Boy respond to any other name, he'd punch him under the ribs. A short, hard punch, careful. Hard enough to knock the wind out of him and have him retching for ten minutes, careful enough to avoid bruising or permanent damage.

"Bring me a beer, Boy."

"Turn on the TV, Boy."

"Get lost for a couple hours, Boy. Me and yer Mom want some quality time."

Boy lived with Mom and Pop in a two-story cabin on the edge of the forest. Pop spent his days cutting down trees, his chainsaw ripping through the birch, beech and hemlock. He spent his nights drinking, either at the bar in town or home in front of the TV.

It was better when Pop drank in town. That was when Mom and Boy could pretend they lived alone in their fairytale cottage in the woods. Boy was getting a little old for stories now. He'd be thirteen next birthday. But he played along with Mom when she talked about their adventures in the magic forest. She needed the stories more than he did. When Pop got home, it could go either way. Sometimes, he'd wink at Boy, kiss Mom on the cheek, talk about football. Those nights were good nights. Mom might make pancakes with maple syrup, Pop would ask Boy about school. They'd all pretend everything was normal.

Other times, it wasn't so good. Boy could usually tell by counting the seconds between the truck pulling up outside and Pop coming in the door. Anything more than ten seconds was bad. More than twenty seconds was real bad.

Boy had been outside one night, looking at the stars from a clearing near the cabin. He'd been to the library and borrowed a book on the constellations. He heard the truck coming up the gravel track, grabbed his flashlight and book and made a run for the door. Halfway there, he realized he'd left the binoculars. Pop's binoculars. He skidded to a halt and sprinted back, barely slowing as he scooped up the binoculars and headed back home. When he got there, the truck was outside, its diesel engine ticking and coughing. He was already counting as he got to the back door. He made it to fifteen, then crept around the side of the trailer, craning his neck around the corner to see the truck. It was a cloudless night, perfect for star gazing, and Pop's big balding head and salt and pepper beard were clearly visible as he sat, hands gripping the wheel. He'd killed the headlights but the engine rumbled on, sounding even rougher than normal. Boy listened closely, really paying attention now. It wasn't just the engine. Some other noise was mixed up with it, rising and falling like blips on the throttle. Boy looked at Pop. His mouth was moving, his eyes looking blankly through the windshield, unseeing. Sometimes he was just mumbling, then he would twitch suddenly and smack a meaty hand on the dash, producing a cloud of dust. That's when his face got angry, his voice growling, louder than the engine, specks of spittle hitting the inside of the windshield and glistening like frost in the starlight. Boy shrank back, got back in the house and crept upstairs without a word. He knew if he was there when Pop came in, it would make things worse. He heard the engine splutter to a stop, the heavy footsteps, the slam of the screen door. There were no words that night, no shouts, no screaming. Just three quick paces across the room, the crack of a fist hitting flesh, the thump of a body hitting the floor. Silence for a count of twenty-three, then noises worse than the silence. Boy had grabbed a book from the shelf, started reading, letting his ears tune out the sounds from downstairs. He was good at tuning out. He'd had lots of practice.

Boy clicked off the flashlight when he heard Pop lurching upstairs. He shoved *Catcher In The Rye* under his mattress just before his door opened and Pop's head appeared. Boy breathed slowly and deeply, his body relaxed. It had taken years to learn how to stop his breath coming fast and loud. These days, it didn't matter how scared he was, he could always bring himself under control in a second. Pop stood still, watching him silently.

The nights Pop drank at home were the worst. He set about drinking with a kind of grim determination, as if it were a chore that needed doing, and needed doing properly. He always drank from a tin cup that used to belong to Grandpa, before he'd passed. "See this cup? It's my inheritance, Boy. Only thing the mean old bastard left me. One day, it's gonna be yours." His humorless chuckle had sounded like a chainsaw struggling to start on a cold morning.

Those nights, the two or three hours of peace were worse, somehow, than the storm that followed. The tension ratcheted up as Pop's mood swung inexorably from sulky, through irritable to angry. When he finally hit the angry stage—Boy knew it would happen when the level of liquor was close to the bottom edge of the brown label—it was almost a relief. The angry stage lasted between seventeen and forty-three minutes. Then, like night follows day, Pop would get violent. Boy had timed him ever since he'd learned to read the hands on the clock at school seven years ago.

They had been doing percentages in class recently. Boy figured Pop punched him in the stomach sixty percent of the time, shook him till he threw up or his nose started bleeding fifteen percent of the time. Twenty percent of the time, he smacked him in the ribs, over and over. That meant taking a note to school excusing him from gym class. Pop said if he ever let anyone see the bruises, he'd kill Mom. Boy believed him because of the five percent. That was when Pop lost control and hit him in the face, knocked him to the floor and kicked him. He stopped when Boy passed out. At least Boy thought he did. Those times, he had to stay away from school until he was better. If his ribs were broken, Pop would bind them with bandages. Pop had been a medic in Vietnam. He knew how to patch folk up.

The times when Boy's ribs were cracked, he couldn't take a full breath for a few days. It sounded like he was wheezing. Pop gave Boy a plastic inhaler to take to school. The other kids thought Boy had asthma. Pop thought that was real funny.

Pop stood in his doorway, listening to his breathing. Boy didn't dare open his eyes, because he knew the light would reflect on his pupils, Pop would know he was awake and things would get real bad, real quick.

Sometimes Boy daydreamed about coming home from school to find a police cruiser in front of the house. "We're sorry, son," the sympathetic officer would say, "but I'm afraid your father has been involved in a terrible accident at work." Sometimes, the cop would be holding Pop's blood-stained shirt.

Daydreams were one way of escaping. Books were even better. Boy had learned his letters early. Mom was a reader too, and when Boy was tiny, she'd sit him on her lap as she read. She'd always put her favorite music on while she did it. Pop hated classical music, so she didn't dare play it while he was there. But when they read together, the sound of the piano or the cello would drift through the house.

Sometimes she'd read passages aloud and Boy would follow her finger along the page, listening to her sweet voice. One afternoon, not long after his third birthday, she had stopped after a few sentences and rubbed her eyes. Boy looked at her finger on the page and picked up the sentence where she'd abandoned it.

"…And that's when I decided to get on a ship, any ship, and head for America, the land of opportunity."

At first, Mom had just stared at him, wide-eyed. Then she'd burst out laughing, swept him up in her arms and danced around the kitchen.

"My child is a genius," she'd said, kissing his cheeks over and over. That was the first day they caught the bus to the library. Boy picked out some books with Mom's help—The Scarlett Letter, The Three Musketeers, David Copperfield. When they got home, Mom showed him the big saucepan where she hid her books in the kitchen ("like Pop's ever gonna look *there*") and then they found a loose floorboard in Boy's room beneath which he could hide four or five books.

"Your daddy doesn't read much, and he doesn't like smart people," she said. "It'll be better if he doesn't know how clever you are. Our secret, ok?"

"Ok," he'd said, and they'd linked pinkies in a solemn promise.

He'd loved reading ever since, and once he'd started school, he'd found the library his first day there. He spent most break times in there, looking through the bigger books you weren't allowed to take home. Encyclopedias, medical dictionaries, scientific reference books. He devoured them all.

Aged seven, he'd won book tokens as a school prize. The school had phoned Mom after she hadn't replied to the letter inviting her and Pop to the prize giving. She'd told them Pop was working and she suffered anxiety attacks.

"I must ask you not to call me unless it's an emergency," she'd said. After she put the phone down, she came and stroked Boy's cheek. "Come on," she said. "Let's check out the bookstore together. I'm buying."

So Boy chose his own copies of the two books he loved most of all in all the world: *Matilda*, by Roald Dahl, and *The Adventures Of Huckleberry Finn*, by Mark Twain. *Matilda* was about a girl who learned to read as early as him, but she had weird powers that meant she could move objects with her mind. Boy sometimes dreamed he could do the same. He loved Huck Finn even more. After five years, his copy was starting to fall apart, because he rarely went more than a couple days without picking it up. Huck Finn managed something Boy couldn't even quite bring himself to dream about. Huck *escaped.*

"Your headache real, Boy?" Pop muttered from the doorway as Boy carried on feigning sleep. "You wouldn't just be dreaming up ways to avoid me, would ya?"

Boy lay perfectly still, his breaths long and even, his body totally relaxed. He was floating in space, gazing back at the Earth from the outer reaches of the Milky Way. No one could reach him. Pop grunted and backed out, leaving the door half open.

Boy's headache was real enough. It even hurt to read, not that he would let that stop him. It was the third headache that week. The pain made him irritable. He was beginning to worry he might say something to Pop, or look at him in a way he didn't like, because the headache meant he couldn't concentrate properly.

He opened his eyes in the darkness. From his parents' bedroom, he heard Pop snoring. He was about to reach out for his flashlight when he heard a noise from his window. He sat up, startled. The curtain moved and a shape was briefly outlined against the moonlit window, before it dropped to the floor and padded toward him.

"Miss Honey!" he whispered, as the cat jumped lightly onto his bed and purred, waiting for some attention. He didn't know the cat's real name. It often snuck in nights and Boy was glad of the company. He guessed it belonged to someone in the row of newer houses near the highway. He stroked her under the chin and her purrs became deeper as she pressed against him. He smiled in the darkness.

The headache, which had been like a background noise all evening, suddenly made its presence felt again and Boy hissed as a white-hot stab of pain lit up the space behind his eyes. For a few seconds, he couldn't see, and it took all his self-control not to call out in panic. Eventually the constant pain turned into a rhythmic throb, then it ebbed away, leaving him gasping in relief.

He took some deep breaths, his sweat cold against his hot skin. Something was wrong. He looked over at the window, the curtain moving slightly in the wind. Then he looked down at his hands. The purring had stopped.

"Miss Honey?"

The cat stared up at him, her green eyes wide open, sightless, almost popping out of their sockets amongst the ginger fur. Slowly, he opened his hands, loosening the terrible grip he'd had around her neck. Her eyes stayed open as she fell back against the cover, her neck twisted at an impossible angle. The small corpse was already stiffening as he felt the tears come. It took forty-three minutes for all of the warmth to leave her body.

Chapter 5

Mexico City
Present Day

Seb appeared in his apartment in Mexico City a few hours before dawn. He sat at the breakfast counter and put out his hand. As the tv flickered into life, a glass full of orange juice and a bagel covered in peanut butter appeared in front of him—or seemed to. They were actually made up of particles borrowed from the kitchen counter plus bits of dirt and dead skin floating in the air, changed to duplicate the particles found in glass, china, freshly squeezed oranges, bagel and peanut butter. At first, Seb had needed soil to produce physical items, but as Seb2 learned more about the alien operating system now coded into every part of his body, he had been able to expand his use of Manna in new ways.

"Loose end from Dover still needs our attention," said Seb2. Seb drained the juice and nodded. He had taken care of the gang at the bank, but the syndicate behind the attempted crime would just find some other hired muscle to do their dirty work. And innocent people would continue to die as a result of their crimes.

"Who are they?" thought Seb.

"Most are financiers, but the main player is a programmer, MIT graduate. Tyler Gray. He doesn't even need to meet his partners, it's all done online. He's behind all of it. He finds the muscle. Doesn't seem to care about the people who die while he pursues his riches. Remove him and there's no more syndicate. He's based in LA."

"Show me," thought Seb. Suddenly, he wasn't just looking at the kitchen, his view was overlaid with an image of a room full of computer hardware and a bank of monitors. A young man sat in front of them in a big leather chair. He was wearing boxer shorts and eating cereal, while shouting into a headset.

"How? How is that possible? It took weeks to set up that diversion. Jesus!" He took some deep breaths, scratched his balls and spoke again. "Ok, give me until the weekend and I'll set up a new target. Find me a team who actually know what the fuck they're doing this time, ok?"

He took off the headset and tossed it onto the desk. Two of the four huge screens showed real-time stock market information. The other two were full of code that made no sense to Seb.

"He was hard to find," said Seb2. "He'd set up dozens of dead ends, blind alleys. He thinks there's no way anyone could ever track the crimes back to him."

"How hard to find?" thought Seb.

"3.43 seconds," said Seb2.

"Stop showing off," thought Seb, "and show me another room. I'll Walk there." A few other rooms appeared in Seb's vision, including the master bedroom, which led out to a balcony and an ocean view. The walls were lined with books.

"Wasn't showing off," said Seb2. "He's a prodigy. I would have had him in under a second otherwise."

Seb Walked.

The balcony doors were open and the sound of the waves was the only noise apart from the rhythmic tapping of computer keys from the next room. Seb walked across to the nearest bookcase. Stephen King, HP Lovecraft, Edgar Allen Poe, HR James, Peter Strauss, Clive Barker.

"Tyler likes his horror literature," thought Seb.

"Yep," said Seb2. "Oh. Ok, that's funny. I get it. Great idea. Just don't spoil it by laughing."

"I'll do my best," thought Seb. He closed his eyes briefly and felt the by-now familiar rippling of his skin and muscle as he changed, his body morphing into a new shape. He stepped across to the foot of the bed to look in the full length mirror. He still had to duck to see himself fully, as he was now seven feet tall.

"Shit!" he said quietly as he saw what he'd become. He was the perfect, nightmarish circus clown. His face was white and smeared, as if the makeup had been hurriedly applied. The wig was supposed to be green, but was matted with blood and hung limply on his shoulders. The areas of skin visible beneath the white were crusty, dark red, pustulant. His eyes were yellow and bloodshot, his nose obscured by a red sphere that, on closer inspection, looked like some bloated throbbing blood vessel. His mouth was just a little bigger than seemed humanly possible, and his smile revealed blackened teeth filed into vicious points, the tongue a mass of old wounds and newly made gouges, where the teeth were constantly ripping the flesh. Blood seeped from the corners of his mouth.

"Sure this won't scare him to death?"

"He's young and healthy," said Seb2. "Look on the bright side. He'll definitely spend less time indoors after this, so his health will actually improve."

"Hmm," thought Seb and walked out of the bedroom. The door to the room he wanted was closed, so he knocked slowly, three times, for dramatic effect.

Behind the door, Tyler froze for half a second, then threw himself off of the chair, opened a drawer, removed a handgun and checked it, while backing slowly into a corner. Seb still had an overlay of the room open, and he watched the young man sweat as he clicked the safety off.

"You just made a huge mistake, asshole!" Tyler yelled. Then he frowned and scanned one of the screens, leaning forward to jab at a couple of keys. His expression changed briefly to one of utter bewilderment as he checked the data.

"He designed his own security system," said Seb2. "It's probably the best I've ever seen. As far as he's concerned, you're not here. It's physically impossible. He was looking for traces of carbon dioxide from your breath, as well as a heat signature from your body. He found nothing. Now he's going to start thinking he just imagined it. Time to convince him otherwise."

Stepping close to the closed door, Seb opened his mouth. His chest was now fifty-two inches wide, and his internal organs had been shifted to the sides in order to produce a resonant chamber bigger than any human in history. The result, when he spoke, was so deep, rich and loud, it made Darth Vader sound like Mickey Mouse in comparison.

"Ty…ler," said Seb, his voice rumbling like the idling engine of a monster truck. Behind the door, Tyler let out an involuntary shriek and backed hurriedly all the way into the corner.

"I'll shoot!" he screamed, his voice cracking with fear. "I mean it! You're gonna die unless you leave. Right now!"

Seb was silent for a count of ten. Just long enough for Tyler to start to believe his threats may have had the desired effect. Just long enough for his heart rate to stop climbing. Just long enough for him to start breathing again. Then Seb threw the door open so hard it flew off its hinges, ducked under the doorframe, took two quick paces into the room, and drew himself up to his full height.

Tyler Gray was an intelligent man. He may have directed this intelligence in a direction that benefitted only himself, but there was no denying his capacity for solid, rational thought. To his credit, when faced with a creature seemingly straight out of his worst nightmares, he didn't collapse immediately. Logic told him this was some kind of trick, his security system—impossible as it seemed—had been beaten, and the creature now dripping blood onto his Persian rug was, undoubtedly, human. So, bullets would put an end to it. Consequently, he emptied ten rounds into the clown, all of them into his chest.

"Good shooting," thought Seb as the wounds closed, cauterized and disappeared. The fact that his heart, lungs and spleen were currently out of harm's way meant there was little damage to repair.

"He has some skill, certainly," said Seb2.

Seb stepped forward again. He was two feet away from the cowering young man, who, after looking at his gun in disbelief, was now sliding down the wall and beginning to cry. Seb opened his mouth as wide as it would go—which was horribly wide—and roared in Tyler's face. He roared for a full half-minute. As he did so, flecks of blood and tiny pieces of flesh from his ruined tongue hit Tyler on the forehead, cheeks, lips and eyes, until the sobbing man's view of the clown was momentarily obscured by a film of red. He blinked frantically, rubbed it away and moaned. The clown was still there. This was really happening.

"I COME FROM IN THERE," said Seb, pointing at the nearest screen. The bass profundo effect of his new voice was so pronounced that the beer bottle and car keys on the desk rattled and moved as he spoke.

Tyler's mouth opened and closed a few times but no sound emerged.

"I'VE BEEN WATCHING YOU, TYLER. YOU ARE NO LONGER WELCOME IN MY DOMAIN."

"Wha-? Wh-?" Tyler swallowed and managed a single word. "Where?"

Seb leaned forward even closer and smiled. Tyler whimpered and quietly soiled himself.

"IF I EVER SEE YOU AGAIN, I WILL COME FOR YOU, TYLER GRAY."

Seb turned toward the desk. He lifted a giant foot, complete with a blood-caked clown shoe about twenty-five inches long, and stepped directly into the nearest computer screen. Tyler watched, sobbing as the impossible happened right in front of him. The clown's foot was followed by his leg, then he sat on the desk and put his other leg inside. Nothing came out of the back of the screen. It was as if this monster was climbing through a window. Next, he hoisted the rest of his body through, until only his nightmarish head remained. Then the neck twisted and the face looked toward Tyler, its cold, dead, yellow eyes fixed on his.

"I'LL BE WAITING FOR YOU." One more smile, then the head followed the body through and was gone.

Tyler sat there for nearly half an hour, before daring to believe the nightmare was over and the creature had really gone. He pushed himself back up into an upright position, wincing at the smell coming from his shit-caked boxer shorts. He looked at the computer screens. All the regular data were gone, replaced by a simple message: **I'll be waiting for you, Tyler.**

Tyler screamed, yanked all the plugs out of the wall and ran from the room. He never went in again. He never touched another computer in his life. He also avoided circuses.

Chapter 6

New York

Mason looked out of the window across at the city skyline. He had been sitting in exactly the same position, unmoving, for over three hours. Sharp-edged shadows moved across nearby buildings, some of which hadn't been built when he'd first arrived in New York. He barely registered the scene, despite it being one of the best—and, consequently, expensive—views in Manhattan.

He was working at a problem, a puzzle; teasing out possibilities, analyzing options, considering consequences. Mason would never have described himself as happy, but the calm satisfaction gained by finding a solution—often counter-intuitive—to complex problems was the closest he came to that apparently common human emotion.

Mason's most powerful weapon was his intellect. His second most powerful weapon was anonymity. Many people knew of his existence, but only three people had ever known where, and who, he really was. He had preserved that situation for most of his life. One of the three was long dead. Soon, another would share the secret, but only because Mason had instigated the process.

He closed his eyes and stretched his arms above his head. Dusk had begun leeching colors from the scene before him.

"Ruth," he said.

A pregnant woman in her mid-thirties entered the room. She waited a few feet away without speaking.

"I want to go out," he said. "Tell your mother to get the van ready."

Ruth turned to leave.

"We're not going to the cemetery. We'll be gone for a few hours."

If Ruth was shocked by this request, she didn't show it, just nodded and left the room.

Mason tried to recall the last time he'd been outside the apartment, other than his monthly visit to the Manna-rich cemetery a mile away. After a few seconds, he remembered. Nearly seven years ago. When he had needed to deal personally with an escalating problem: a mayoral candidate who had attempted to outmaneuver him by surrounding herself with ambitious Manna-users.

Elizabeth Harper, a native New Yorker whose political rise had been rapid and, Mason acknowledged, unexpected, had more than a little Manna ability herself. She'd thought it was time New York—and the country—were free of the light-but-firm grip Mason kept on political leaders. Mason admired her ambition, but was unimpressed by her choice of advisors. They may have been sharp politically, but not one of them would have had a clue what they were up against in Mason.

He didn't show himself, of course. He merely got close enough in the van for his Manna to reach them. Then he'd called her.

"Elizabeth Harper?" he'd whispered. Mason always whispered. Impossible to tell much about a person when they whisper. Even as technology had improved, voice recognition was still fooled by something as simple as a whisper.

"Who is this?" said Harper. "This is a private number."

"I think you're already perfectly aware of my identity, Mrs Harper," he'd whispered. "Let's not play games."

Elizabeth went quiet for a few seconds. Mason imagined her frantically signaling to her people to trace the call.

"No need to do that," he'd whispered. "I'll tell you where I am. Then I'll hang up. I will call back in a few minutes." He'd paused. For dramatic effect. He had once imagined the dramatic pause to be a literary conceit but, after some experimentation, he had found it to be extremely effective in inducing fear. Also, it slightly diminished a person's short-term ability to make rational decisions. A useful device. Once the optimum amount of time had passed, he'd whispered again.

"I'm outside your house." Then he'd hung up.

When he'd called back, a very different Elizabeth had answered the phone and he knew he had won. Some people only needed to be threatened, others needed proof they were in a fight they couldn't win. Elizabeth Harper was in the latter category.

Mason pictured the scene. Elizabeth was in a room with six corpses. He had reached out, found the Manna users and cut off the oxygen supply to their brains. Because nothing was known about him, other Manna users tended to take a guess at Mason's abilities based on their own. They thought he would need to be able to see them. They thought he would be able to manipulate his surroundings, but not their own bodies, nervous systems, or blood supply. They thought six of them would be sufficient to neutralize any threat he might make. They were woefully under-informed, which was how Mason liked it. His method of disposing of them was quick, efficient, and didn't significantly drain his Manna supply.

"Are we clear about your allegiances, Mrs Harper?" he'd whispered. "Your success in the election is assured, I understand. Tonight's tragedy occurred due to a carbon monoxide leak from the furnace. The coroner who'll be assigned to this case will reflect this in his report."

"My daughter." Harper's voice was faint. She had taught her eleven-year-old daughter to use Manna. Unfortunately, her daughter had been in the room when Mason had called.

"I doubt I will require your services often, but when I do, I expect unquestioning obedience. Do we have an understanding?"

"My daughter," she'd repeated, her voice dull and flat.

"Mrs Harper, you have another daughter and a son. It's time you start thinking about them. I will ask you one more time. Do we have an understanding?"

Her pause before answering wasn't for dramatic effect. It sounded like she was trying to get enough strength into her voice to be able to respond at all.

"Yes," she'd said.

Mason hung up.

The van drove to its destination, arriving in a little over an hour. Traffic in Manhattan was something even

Mason couldn't change. The journey was made in silence. Mason wasn't much of a talker.

When the GPS announced they had arrived, the intercom buzzed.

"We're here, sir."

"Park at the lowest level."

"Sir."

Tiny cameras mounted outside the van showed Mason the view he would otherwise have been denied. The parking garage was new, as was the mall it served. The basement level was only half full. The van came to a stop and the intercom buzzed again.

"Are we getting out, sir?"

Mason turned off the cameras and dimmed the lights in the back of the van. He wanted to be absolutely sure.

"No," he said. "This is perfect. I will let you know when I'm ready to leave."

He closed his eyes, deepened his breathing and brought his attention into a needle-sharp point. When he was completely focused, he drove the point through the floor of the van and down into the cement below. When he reached the limit of the building's foundations, he stopped and drew back a few feet. Then he let the point of his attention expand. It opened outward in all directions like a balloon being filled with air, quickly growing to a few feet, then a few meters. His sensitivity was such, he was aware of every insect, the corpse of every rodent, the old cigarette stubs, pennies, discarded subway stubs and pieces of garbage that had ended up being mixed with the cement as the foundations had been laid.

Although three minutes of concentration gave him his answer, Mason sat there for another ten, making completely sure his findings were accurate. When no doubt at all remained, he buzzed the intercom.

"Take me back," he said.

Chapter 7

Mexico City

Seb cracked two eggs into the hot oil and ground the coffee beans. The noise elicited a groan from the bedroom. Thirty seconds later the snoring resumed. Meera had never been an early riser but it was around the time when the early morning sunlight etched honeyed lines of yellow onto the wall that the noise she produced most closely resembled that of a rutting elephant seal. Seb raised an eyebrow as the next snore physically rattled the glasses on the shelf. He flipped the eggs onto wheat toast and carried the plate through to the front porch. He loved watching Mexico City wake up.

Meera had stopped teasing him about the way he insisted on making breakfast every morning. Although she couldn't accept that the coffee tasted any better than its Manna-produced alternative (which was a fair point, as it didn't), she conceded that trying to keep a semblance of normality was good for him. She even let him cook dinner a couple of times a week.

"I think I get it now," she had said one night as he'd tried, unsuccessfully, to whisk up an edible hollandaise sauce. "You don't want to feel like a freak the whole time. You want to do normal stuff. Even though you don't have to."

Seb had just grunted and looked at the counter top. A plate appeared, seemingly growing directly out of the formica. It was topped with a gyro sandwich dripping in chili sauce.

"That's more like it," said Meera, taking a huge bite, juices running down her chin. She'd grinned. "You go ahead and make your sauce. Just so long as you magic up proper food for your girlfriend."

Girlfriend. Seb still hadn't got used to that. Faking his own death to help him and Mee escape from Mason—the most powerful Manna user in America—was scary enough, but finally telling Mee how he felt about her was truly terrifying. Finding out she was finally ready to admit she felt the same had been the best moment of his life. Better than writing a great song. Better than spontaneously healing from apparently fatal injuries. Better than being able to cross any distance on (or, possibly, off) the planet, instantaneously.

The morning light crept up the smog-shrouded hillsides opposite, slowly revealing what looked, at first, like an unlikely dusting of snow. As the smog began to burn away and the light strengthened, the abstract whiteness resolved itself into vague shapes. In the space of ten minutes, the shapes became houses. Tens, hundreds of thousands of houses, some no more than shacks, crammed into every available space on the hillside.

Seb ate his eggs and sipped hot coffee. He had sat in contemplation for thirty minutes after waking, and his mind was calm. He was aware of thoughts beginning to surface. Reluctantly at first, he turned his attention toward them.

Being a superhero had worn slightly thin after about six months. After watching Batman in his teens, Seb had walked out of the movie theater with a short-lived, intense desire to combat crime in an honorable, but—regrettably—violent, manner. If his initial burst of enthusiasm had lasted much longer than a five-block walk, New York City may have witnessed the birth of a new masked vigilante. Ok, Seb may have been lacking the weaponry, martial-arts training, incredible wealth and borderline psychotic personality of Bruce Wayne, but they were both orphans. That had to count for something, right? Luckily for the city's criminal fraternity and Seb Varden's physical well-being, it had been raining hard as he made his way back, and the desire to crack skulls in the name of justice had dissolved faster than the marshmallows he melted into his hot chocolate back in St Benet's orphanage.

Now of course, everything was different. He had powers beyond any he could have dreamed of all those years ago. And, as an avid reader of science fiction and a lifelong fan of comic book superheroes, his dreams had been ambitious. But they'd never stretched this far. With his body full of nanotechnology from an alien race, to whom Earth's proudest achievements were probably as impressive (if not quite as cute) as a toddler's first, faltering steps, Seb had spent the first few months testing his limits. He had found few. And he still had no idea what price the extra-terrestrial donor of these powers might demand from him. If any. Billy Joe, the prosaically nicknamed alien who had given him the nanotech, had omitted to include an instruction manual with his gift. Seb's encounter with the alien had left him with an intense impression of a fundamentally benign, incredibly intelligent, but utterly unknowable being. He had sensed immense compassion, but there was no meeting of minds, no sharing of knowledge, no empathy. Seb often dreamed of that night, and was always left with a powerful impression of aloneness. Not loneliness, just a sensation of being, in some sense, absolutely alone. When he woke, he wasn't sure who felt that way—the alien, or him.

Mee came up behind him, an orange sarong wrapped around her. She stroked the side of his face with the back of her hand and sat down beside him. Seb looked at the table, visualizing blueberry pancakes, a glass of cold freshly squeezed orange juice.

"You read my mind," said Meera, taking a sip of the orange juice. "Pancakes with a perfect blend of protein and nutrients and about as many calories as a couple of apples. You could make a fortune in the diet industry."

When he didn't respond immediately, she nudged him gently in the ribs.

"What's up, big boy?" she said. "Existential angst?"

"Something like that," Seb said, taking her hand. He stroked her fingers, then lifted her hand to his lips and kissed the stump where her little finger had been.

He had offered to grow it back for her, but Mee had refused. She didn't want to forget how close they had come to losing each other. More than that, she wanted Seb to have a constant reminder that some people were irredeemably bad. Seb's forgiving nature and willingness to see the good in everyone was all very well, but sometimes he needed a reminder about the real world. Even Seb would find it hard to feel much compassion for someone who had cut off his girlfriend's pinky while he watched, helplessly, at the other end of a video call.

"How was Honduras?" she asked, before taking a huge bite of pancake, smiling at him with cheeks stuffed with food.

"No casualties," he said, "and a shot in the arm for the local tourism industry."

"Earthquakes usually have the opposite effect on tourism," said Mee.

"True," said Seb, "but, well, look it up and you'll see."

Mee tapped at the laptop keyboard and burst out laughing as she read about the families saved from the collapsed hotel by hundreds of monkeys. She spun the screen around for Seb to see. He nodded as he glanced at the story with eyewitnesses crediting the Monkey God for their miraculous rescue.

"Come on, cheer up," she said. "Nobody likes a miserable git in the morning."

Seb smiled. He loved Mee's British expressions, even when he didn't understand them. They'd once spent a long weekend in the north of the UK, where a succession of women had insisted on referring to him as "Duck". Bizarre.

"I need to talk with Seb2," said Seb. Meera rolled her eyes. The concept of Seb's consciousness splitting into different parts to cope with the alien power was hard enough for him to understand, let alone explain. Mee made it plain that she found it bewildering.

"I know what you need first," said Mee, grabbing the waistband of his pants, pulling him off the stool and backing away toward the bedroom. "I guarantee it'll make you feel better."

She was right. It did.

***

The two men walked slowly around the edge of Penn Pond in London's Richmond Park. A casual observer might have thought them twins. Closer inspection would have confirmed an exact likeness, but they were more than twins. Not that a casual observer was present, of course, as the entire scene was a construct inside Seb's consciousness, the location a perfectly replicated piece of his personal history.

Seb and Seb2 walked along a path through trees whose leaves were streaked with color.

"I was never here in the fall," said Seb.

"But it's your favorite time of year. I thought you'd enjoy it," said Seb2.

"Your attention to detail is appreciated," said Seb, admiring the huge ancient oaks towering above them.

Seb2 led the way into a small copse, where all of the trees had kept their foliage, making it darker as they walked. Seb hesitated, stopping at the edge of the old, twisted oaks. Seb2 held out his hands in a placatory gesture.

"It's ok," he said. "I wouldn't bring you back here if there wasn't a good reason."

Seb swallowed and moved forward. Last time he was here, Seb2 had shown him the third part of his splintered consciousness: Seb3. This third figure may well have been identical too, but it was impossible to tell as he had appeared as a hideously tortured man, stretched across a stone, hairless, skinless, in constant agony. Knowing he was looking at part of himself had been a profoundly disturbing experience.

"We had no choice in any of this," said Seb2, as if reading his mind. Which, of course, was exactly what he was doing. "Seb3's function in helping you adapt to the nanotech is still a mystery to me. But without him, you would have died."

"I'm not sure I can bear seeing…him…again," said Seb. Knowing they were only seconds away from the center of the copse.

"Trust me," said Seb2, and walked into the clearing. Reluctantly, Seb took a few more steps, his view mercifully obscured by Seb2's back. Then his twin stepped aside and Seb saw immediately why he had brought him there.

"What the hell? What does it mean?"

"I don't know. But I have some thoughts."

The clearing was as Seb remembered it, the large stone still in place, covered now in dark stains he knew could only be blood. There was one big difference this time. Seb3 had gone.

They walked back to the pond and sat on the bench where Seb2 had first broken the news of their split personality. Seb and Seb2's roles had become clearer since then. Seb2 was effectively a savant, with access to every memory, no need for sleep, and the ability to access the entire internet faster than any computer. Yet, despite Seb2's abilities, it was still Seb who ran the show, who preserved his sense of self. It was Seb who lived in the world, who interacted with other people, who had fallen in love, who had cried at the news that a friend had died. Seb was human, whatever that meant. But he was more than that now.

"Seb3 was still there while you were in Honduras," said Seb2. "But when you Walked home, I felt something change. I looked for him."

"But didn't find him?"

"No."

"Good change or bad change?" said Seb.

"Good," said Seb2, then immediately qualified it, "I think. My awareness of his pain has dimmed. You?"

Seb thought for a moment.

"There is something different," he said. "Hard to explain. Like a…broadening. As if something's opened up. You said you had some thoughts?"

Seb2 reached into his pocket and pulled out a paper bag full of breadcrumbs. As he threw some toward the pond, half a dozen ducks winked into existence and swam toward the bread, quacking excitedly.

"I do," he said. "I think Seb3 has gone for good. I think he's been absorbed, although a better word is 'understood'. I think he's been understood."

"Understood? In what sense?"

"It's the best way I can explain what I think has happened," said Seb2. "As I spend more time with the technology, I make breakthroughs here and there. But each time it happens, it's not like any kind of learning we've ever experienced. It's not as if *I've* understood something. It's more like something has understood me."

Seb sighed and ran his fingers through his hair. "Go on," he said.

"This stuff is alive, intelligent, but—as far as I can tell—not conscious. The nanotech has bonded with you at an atomic level. At least, that's the only way I can picture it. The actual bonds are totally beyond my comprehension—every explanation I come up with is not much better than a metaphor. But the tech is designed—again, bad word—to become inseparable from the host, to merge utterly on every level eventually. You're human, but you're not human."

"Argh," thought Seb. Sometimes these explanations made little sense. Other times, he didn't think he *wanted* them to make sense.

"Not a riddle. Just the best I can do. But I think the agony of Seb3 has been understood. I think, as a result of being understood, he has become something else."

"You said Seb3 was the most authentic part of me. The real Person."

"Yeah, well this is more Father O's realm than ours," said Seb2. Seb nodded. Maybe a Catholic priest with more than fifty years of daily contemplation would be able to shed some light on what Seb2 was struggling to explain. Then again, maybe not. What would he make of the idea that there were three Sebs? A trinity? Even a liberal Catholic like Father O might struggle accepting that one.

"I think Seb3 may now be engaging with the nanotech at a deeper level we can't yet understand," said Seb2. "I don't think there's any separation. At the very deepest level,—which is what Seb3 represents—you *are* the nanotech. You *are* the Manna."

"Is this supposed to be comforting in some way?" said Seb, slightly alarmed now. "I mean why stop at Seb3? It could be you next, then me. I'm not sure I want to be *understood*."

"I don't think there's any way to stop us from changing," said Seb2. "All I can say is, I still feel like me. Well, us."

The two identical men looked at each other, then out at the ducks, the pond, Richmond Park and the high rise buildings of the city, dark and somber against the bruised Fall sky. None of it was real.

"Yeah," said Seb, "everything is still completely normal."

Chapter 8

Upstate New York
Thirty-four years previously

School had been Boy's favorite place ever since that first day when he'd found the library. He quickly realized he was more intelligent than his peers, but he knew how to hide it. His classmates thought he was a little odd, but sometimes he could say something to make them laugh, or help them with their work by nudging them in the right direction.

Boy would never be popular, but that wasn't his intention. He wanted to be invisible, lost in the crowd. Most of the time, he could do just that and it filled him with a strange sensation he wanted more and more of. Despite his intelligence, he could never settle on the right word for how he felt at school. Happy? Contented? Peaceful? Fulfilled? None of the words seemed right, none of them truly fit. *Safe.* That was probably the closest to the truth. Mom was safe at home while Pop was working. Boy was safe at school.

Then, one morning, it all went wrong. It was two days after he'd buried the cat. He'd gently laid her body in the soil, covered her over and stuck a piece of bark above to mark the spot. He'd said, "I'm sorry, Miss

Honey". Afterwards, he ran to catch the school bus. He didn't want to think about it.

At school, his headache came back. Lately, it always seemed to be there, mostly bearable, like a fuzziness at the front of his head. Sometimes, it would flare up for a couple minutes and he would clench his fists, dig his nails into his palms and ride out the pain. He could tell when it was going to happen, so he could find a quiet spot—usually the bathroom, if he could get there in time.

That morning, there was no way he was going to get to the bathroom. It was lunch break, and Davy Johanssen had decided Boy needed to be taught a lesson. Davy was big for his age and even dumber than his three older brothers, who had left school and were now in prison. The story of how they'd got there had become a local legend. They'd robbed a liquor store downstate, then had called 911 themselves because someone had rear-ended their getaway car in the parking lot. Davy, as yet, had displayed no wish other than to follow the same path as his clueless siblings. At fourteen years old, he was over a year older than anyone else in the class. Physically, he looked like he should be in college, if any college would lower their standards sufficiently to accept him. He was six feet tall and weighed over two hundred pounds. Initially, the school football coach had hoped Davy might be a future star. By the time Davy had put his helmet on the wrong way round for the third time and repeatedly thrown the ball into the bleachers, because, "someone was looking at me funny", Coach Clement had significantly adjusted his ambitions. Davy ended up as the water boy.

If Davy had one good quality, it was persistence. On the rare occasions that his brain was troubled by the onset of a question, he would pursue it doggedly until he was satisfied he'd found an answer. Unless someone handed him a burger or sat him down in front of a cartoon. Boy currently didn't have access to either, and Davy, plus his usual gang of minions, had cornered him in the school yard. A third grader had fallen out of a tree and broken an arm on the far side of the yard, so no teacher was likely to notice the small crowd gathering around Boy. He had seven minutes and twenty seconds until the bell rang. Too long.

"My old man says your daddy knocked up your momma on purpose," said Davy, flecks of spittle landing on Boy's face. "And you know what?"

Boy didn't answer, just looked at Davy's red face. Davy pushed him with the flat of his hand, and he fell, landing on his ass in the dirt.

"Asked you a question, dickweed."

Boy squinted up at the huge figure. He saw the others standing back a few feet, some of them smirking, a couple of the girls wide-eyed but saying nothing. Everyone knew Davy was going to beat the crap out of him. Well, that was ok. Boy knew how to take a beating.

"No," he said quietly, the headache becoming more insistent.

"What'd you say?"

"I said 'no'," repeated Boy. "I don't know 'what'. I couldn't possibly know 'what'. It's not a proper question. You're either mistakenly assuming a common frame of reference that might allow me to answer such an elliptical query, or the pea-sized object masquerading as your brain is unable to observe basic grammar rules because all of its energy goes into keeping you upright and preventing drooling."

Davy froze for a few seconds, not sure whether he'd just been insulted and, assuming he had, how badly.

"I'm guessing the latter," said Boy. He groaned as the headache started to spike again. A few of Davy's gang started to giggle. None of them understood what Boy had just said, but it was the most any of them had ever heard him say, and the novelty itself made it funny.

Hearing his cronies start to laugh was enough to spur Davy into action. No one laughed at Davy Johanssen. This kid had made them laugh. He leaned over and grabbed a fistful of Boy's shirt, jerking him to his feet. He gave Boy a light slap across his face.

"Funny guy, right? Well, let me tell you about your mom and dad." His face clouded briefly as he struggled to remember what he was going to say. He looked over his shoulder. "Donny?"

A scrawny kid behind him spat on the floor. "Your daddy knocked your momma up before they were married. So you're a bastard," he said. Davy nodded. "And he only did it cause her old man owns the logging company. Only way that loser would ever get a job, cause he's just a drunk, right?" Davy nodded some more. Boy was tuning out, but the headache was making it harder than normal. He could tell them far worse things about Pop, anyhow. Then a rare expression appeared on Davy's face. He'd had an idea.

"Yeah, and you know what else?" he said. "Your old man is the worst logger in the crew. My uncle Pete told me that. He says the only reason the crew boss keeps him on is cause your momma does him favors, know what I mean?"

Boy peered up, the throb of the headache feeling like someone was pounding on the inside of his skull, wanting to get out.

"My mom?" he said.

"Sure," said Davy, grinning. "Your daddy's a loser and your momma's a whore." He pulled back his arm, getting ready to unload his trademark roundhouse, which inevitably produced a huge black eye within minutes of landing. But as he got ready to unleash the punch, he felt his left hand erupt in agony.

Boy didn't pass out this time. The headache seemed to fill his brain, his whole world was pain, but he was still capable of quick, rational thought. As Davy drew his arm back, Boy pushed his head down and fastened his teeth on the back of Davy's other hand. He bit down with all his strength, then pulled his head backward and up, using his chin as a pivot to tear the skin, veins and muscles away.

Davy screamed, a shrill, high-pitched shriek that made everyone near him back away. It was loud enough that a teacher finally looked across and started walking toward them. One of the kids in the group caught sight of Davy's bloody hand, his fingers flopping where the tendons had been ripped. He turned away and vomited.

That might have been the end of it, but some deep, reptile part of Davy's brain knew that he had to prove his dominance, even in the face of this atrocity. He couldn't let this puny kid win. He threw himself at Boy.

Boy had seen Davy jerk backward and look disbelievingly at his ruined hand. As he spat out bits of the other boy's flesh, he saw Davy make his decision to attack. Boy knew he had a pencil in his pants pocket. Taking it out, he stepped nimbly to one side as the larger youth came forward. Boy held the pencil, point-forward, in his left fist. Davy was strong, heavy and unbalanced. Boy simply held the pencil in the optimum position, braced against the heel of his right hand. About three inches of the pencil quickly disappeared into Davy's neck. Boy twisted his hand and pulled forcefully to one side. The pencil snapped, Davy fell to his knees, and there was about 2.5 seconds of stunned silence when the only sound other than Davy's ragged breathing, was the rhythmic splatter of blood as it pulsed out of his neck and hit the hard dirt.

Boy sat down and rubbed his head. Dimly, he was aware of someone else throwing up, some screams and an adult voice sounding at first angry, then shocked, panicked and fearful. He lay down, feeling the edges of awareness cloud up. He passed out.

***

The drive back from school was made in silence. Mom was pale and her hands shook slightly when she opened the door. They had been in with the principal for forty-three minutes as Boy had waited with the nurse. She was kind to him, but Boy figured she knew what happened, because once she'd given him some Tylenol and a glass of water, she'd left and locked the door behind her. When it opened again, it was Mr. Jeckells standing there with his parents. The principal wouldn't meet Boy's eye. Pop just said, "You're coming home now. Got yerself a week's vacation."

Mr. Jeckells blinked at that and started to say something.

"Now, sir, what happened today is a serious matter, and your son's suspension is-". Then he caught Pop's eye and shut his mouth in a hurry, backing out of the door.

When they got home, Pop went straight to the kitchen. Boy heard him open the fridge, the chink of bottles loud and clear. Mom turned to Boy, squeezed his hand and whispered, "You weren't yourself, you were pushed too hard by that bully. I know what his family is like. Everyone knows. But what you did was wrong. Very wrong. We'll talk about it tomorrow. It'll be ok." She looked at Boy, and for the first time in his life, he saw a slight wariness in her eyes. He felt sick.

Pop came through with the kitchen with two opened bottles of beer. He handed one to Boy. "Sit your ass down, boy," he said. "Have a drink."

He paced around the kitchen before saying anything else. After a while, he seemed to notice Mom standing there. "No washing that needs doing, woman? Food gonna cook itself tonight?"

Mom went to the kitchen. Pop smirked at Boy. "Drink, I said." Boy tried a sip of the beer. He pulled a face at the sour taste. Pop laughed. Boy flinched at the sound.

"Well, well," said Pop. He stopped pacing and pulled up a chair opposite Boy. He looked closely at his son's face, as if seeing it for the first time. Finally, he spoke. "That Johanssen kid, I know his daddy. I know his brothers. They talk big, always have, they reckon they're all kinds of mean." Pop poured a glass of bourbon to chase down the beer. He looked pointedly at the beer bottle in Boy's hand. Reluctantly, Boy took another swallow, grimacing again.

"Guess you showed 'em a thing or two today," he said. "That chicken shit Jeckells said they put three pints of fresh blood in him at the hospital. Said he's lucky to be alive. If they didn't all know what that family's like, if they didn't all think it was self-defense, you'd be heading off to some crap hole of a juvenile detention center right now." The bourbon was half-gone already.

"But your teacher spoke up for you. So did that commie librarian. Said you were a good student. That true, Boy? You grown yerself half a brain when I wasn't looking?"

Boy knew better than to reply. He took another swallow of the rancid liquid to avoid saying anything. Pop just looked steadily across at him.

"Well, they don't know you like I do," he said. "You're not smart. Not book smart, anyhow. That's good. Don't want you growing up to be a useless piece of shit like your momma. Maybe there's hope for you. Maybe the apple didn't fall so far from the tree after all."

Boy looked at his father for a long moment. He thought of the books hidden upstairs. He thought of his dreams of escape. Then he remembered the cat dying in his hands. He remembered the feeling of joy that had flashed through him when he'd stabbed the pencil into Davy's neck. He put the beer bottle down, crossed the room and opened the screen door, heading out into the trees. He was running before he knew it.

Chapter 9

Mexico City
Present Day

Depending on your point of view, Seb Varden's first blackout after becoming superhuman lasted either nine minutes or twelve days. Later, he discovered it was something to do with relativity, and he'd never really understood that theory. The only clear memory he had from a distant physics class was trying to comb his hair into the style Einstein sported. He loved that mess of hair. Like it was in a state of constant shock at the activity going on in the freakish brain below. Coming round from the blackout, Seb's own hair was flat and sticky, due to the blood seeping from a gash under his temple.

He pushed his back up against the kitchen counter carefully, sitting up.

"Did that just happen?" said Seb2.

"Honestly?" thought Seb, "I really don't know."

The memory of what had just happened seemed indistinguishable in its quality, its *heft,* from any other part of the last few days. But the content of the memory was so bizarre, so surreal, that Seb automatically questioned its reality.

"You weren't dreaming, I'm sure of that," said Seb2. "Fully conscious throughout."

"Where was I? How did it happen? Could it happen again?"

"Don't know, don't know, probably," said Seb2.

"Big help, thanks."

"I'm working on it," said Seb2. "When I find something, you'll be the first to know."

Seb thought back to the moment he'd lost consciousness. It had felt as if he'd suddenly been engulfed by a violent storm—as if a raging wind was tearing at him, pushing, pulling, unstoppable. That feeling had lasted a split second as he fell, then suddenly—

***

-he was sitting on a blue plastic chair. He was hunched over, staring at an old, dirty tiled floor, the surface an indiscriminate beige color. For a moment, he didn't register the sudden change of location. It seemed entirely natural that he was on this chair, looking at this floor, instead of standing, holding a beer and talking to Mee.

Seb sat up and looked around. His chair was third in a line of twelve exact replicas fastened together. Behind him was another row of twelve chairs. There were six windows above a waist-high counter ten feet in front of him. Through five of the windows, Seb could see a computer, an empty chair and little else. On the other side of the glass, details seemed to be blurred—literally impossible to bring into focus. The last window, furthest away, was harder to see through as the fluorescent tube above it flickered weakly, providing little useful light. There was a background hum. It seemed to come from everywhere at once.

Getting to his feet, Seb checked the rest of the room. It was virtually featureless. It looked almost exactly like the Social Security office where Seb had picked up a replacement card in New York. There was only one difference, as far as he could tell. Not a feature so much as a lack of one. There was no door.

A bell rang and Seb looked up. A digital board above the window was displaying a flashing message in red:

387—window 6

Seb became aware that there was a piece of paper in his left hand. He looked down. It was a ticket. 387.

Window 6 was the one under the flickering light.

"Well, I'm here, might as well find out what this is all about," thought Seb.

"Wherever 'here' is," said Seb2.

Seb felt no fear despite the situation. One of the consequences of his encounter with Billy Joe had been a diminishing of the more extreme emotions. His instincts were of little use now that his senses had been upgraded. During the three hundred milliseconds it might have once taken his brain to react to a threat, his enhanced consciousness had already explored actual, possible and perceived threats, considered different ways of dealing with them and instantly implemented the most effective strategy. Fear still featured in his emotional range, but it only applied to others—specifically, Meera, and his fear that she could still be hurt despite his powers. So when Seb got to window 6 and found an alien sitting on the other side of the glass, he felt many things, but fear wasn't one of them.

At first, Seb thought it was Billy Joe. Even as the thought entered his mind, Seb2 dismissed it.

"Nope," he said, "not him. Old-style Manna, for a start."

Seb could be forgiven for his mistake, since the figure before him—sitting in a cheap-looking office chair—was Billy Joe's double. Gray, glowing slightly, large expressionless black eyes, long fingers. The only difference in appearance seemed to be that this alien was wearing clothes. Specifically, he had black polyester pants and a white short-sleeved shirt with a name badge on the chest. The shirt pocket held two pens—one blue, one red. One pen was leaking and a dark blue stain was slowly spreading from a corner of the pocket.

"It might be rude to laugh," said Seb2, as Seb choked off the urge to do just that.

The alien took the blue pen out of its pocket, seemingly oblivious to the leak. He opened a folder on the desk, turned a page, tapped the pen on it, then looked up at Seb.

"Communication begins now." The voice, when it came, was disconcerting for two reasons. First, the sound came not from the creature's mouth—just like Billy Joe, it didn't have one—but from a speaker mounted halfway up the window on Seb's left. Second, it was a very familiar voice. At first, he couldn't place it, it was so incongruous. Then he had it.

"The guy from the male incontinence commercials!" Seb and Seb2 got there at the same moment. It was a voiceover that had always amused Seb—a voice that projected the suave professional reassurance of an airline pilot, combined with the unctuous formality of a funeral director. Seb had been so amused by the voice, he'd sampled it and used it for a track on Clockwatcher's first album.

"Someone's been doing their research," said Seb2. "Who else knew you were slightly obsessed with that guy's voice? Mee, the guys in the band—,"

"-The twenty-seven people who bought the album," thought Seb.

"Whoa, hang on a second," said Seb2. "We have an attempt at communication."

"That's what he just said," thought Seb.

"No, not the clumsy, human moving-airwaves-about-and-hoping-your-message-gets-through kind," said Seb2, "this guy's using his Manna and he's hailing us on all frequencies."

"What do we do?" thought Seb.

"Well, we're here. In his office. Or her office. Or its office. I guess we talk to it."

Seb suddenly became aware that the alien had spoken again in that disconcerting voice. He looked up into its unblinking eyes.

"I'm sorry?" he said. "What was that?"

"Name?" repeated the alien, a long finger extending and pointing toward a box at the top of the form he was holding.

"You go ahead," said Seb2. "I'll keep you updated with my progress."

Seb cleared his throat. "Seb," he said. "Seb Varden."

The creature scribbled on the paper. Seb looked closer. Even upside-down through the glass, he could see that the alien had drawn a meaningless squiggle on the paper, the sort of doodle a four-year-old might make if they were playing the 'I work in a government office' game. Which no four-year-old had played, ever.

"Um, what's your name?" said Seb. If he was in some kind of dream, or alternate reality, or extremely sophisticated hidden-camera show, he decided he may as well play along for a while.

The alien seemed to consider the question. It actually steepled its fingers and put its head slightly on one side. The sight was completely bizarre and a little unnerving.

"Names are not given, or taken," it said. "We are and we know others, the symmetry is maintained."

After a brief silence, it seemed to decide its previous statement might need a little clarification.

"Societal analogy ill-defined, yet individuality preserved, brought forward generationally, the circle cannot be the center, yes?"

"Yes," said Seb, instinctively, without thinking. "Er, what?"

"Social identifiers, history and current purview?" said the alien.

"Look," said Seb. "This is all very well, but I have to call you something." He looked closer at the name badge. It said 'Vice President' and had a smiley face next to it. "Vice President of what?" he said.

"Research reveals close analogy. Vice President of corporate identity. They are many, each different but none permitted to make decisions, the melding will do that for them."

"I think he's starting to make sense," thought Seb.

"Busy," said Seb2. "Leave a message. You're on your own."

Seb thought for a moment.

"Are you male or female?"

"Closest analogy currently male cycle."

It was odd looking into those expressionless black eyes. The 90% or more of communication that was supposed to happen through body language and micro expressions was completely unavailable to him. It was unnerving. He wondered if it felt the same from the alien's point of view.

Seb scanned the room, ending by focusing on the ink-stained pocket and decided, on balance, that he'd probably passed out, hit his head, and was now having a lucid dream.

"Ok, then, I'm going to call you Mic," said Seb. "That all right with you?" He thought it best not to add why: Male Incontinence Commercial. Seb2 snorted.

"Thought you were busy?" thought Seb.

"I am, kinda—back to it, back to it," said Seb2.

"I am Mic to this one contextually," said Mic.

"Great," said Seb. "What do you want to know?"

The alien stood up. It was—at about seven feet tall—slightly shorter than Billy Joe, but not much less imposing. It—he—had to stoop so that its face came back into view through the small window.

"Initial contact complete," said Mic. "Meetings made, details now and report evaluate. My beaver is as busy as I am."

Seb made a small high-pitched noise as he dealt with his reaction to that statement.

"You mean, you're as busy as a beaver?" he said, smiling.

"Correction noted, syntax problem, language long disposed but assignment permits in this regard. Please another appointment on your way out."

Mic stepped back into the shadows and was gone.

"The bad news is, my session made about as much sense as yours," said Seb2. "Less sense, actually."

"The good news?" said Seb.

"They-he-it—is sending us home now."

Even as he thought it, the ground suddenly tipped on one side and -

***

-Seb reached up and touched the side of his head. Blood. Seb hadn't seen his own blood for over a year. He pushed himself up from the floor, feeling the skin tightening around the wound. By the time he made it to the mirror, there was no trace of a cut, no blood in his hair. Nothing. *Where the hell is Mee?* Seb checked his watch, which confirmed he'd been unconscious for nearly ten minutes. Which tallied up perfectly with the experience he'd had while—apparently—lying on the kitchen floor. He remembered something suddenly, and walked back into the kitchen. He frowned. Cans of food and empty bottles surrounded the space where he'd been laying. Seb shook his head. *She surrounded my unconscious body with that stuff, then went for a stroll?*

He walked into the front room and sat at the piano. It was daytime outside. Seb frowned. When he'd felt his consciousness start to blur, his vision suddenly darkening, it had been nearly midnight. No doubt at all—he remembered the whistle of the tamale man, selling his pungent and fiery chicken tamales wrapped in corn husks from a cart outside their window. Meera had been about to grab her purse and go buy some when Seb's body seemed suddenly to disconnect from his brain. He had fallen heavily, the tamale guy's whistle the last thing he'd heard. Now, apparently, it was morning, the tamale man's whistle replaced by the recorded shriek of a girl offering to buy mattresses: "Se compran colchones, tambores, refrigeradores, estufas, lavadoras, microondas!" Mexico City was rarely quiet. But their apartment was still and Meera was nowhere to be seen.

He could find her, of course. Seb2 could pinpoint her position in milliseconds. But Mee had made it clear how she felt about her privacy. Seb respected that. Still, surely this qualified as an emergency? He hesitated, then decided he'd risk incurring her displeasure, which was not a choice he made lightly.

Just then the door opened and Meera walked in backward, the door key between her teeth, holding two bags of groceries. Unusually for her, she wasn't singing. She turned and slammed the door in her customary fashion, flicking it with a solid thrust from the hips. She took two steps into the room, saw Seb and stopped.

"Hi, Mee," said Seb. "What's going on?"

She tried to say his name, burst into tears, dropped the groceries, then sank to the floor sobbing as a tide of beer flowed from the broken bottles toward Seb's feet.

Chapter 10

Mexico City
Twelve days earlier

Mee watched Seb pass out and fall to the floor—but he never hit it. Just as his body was about to make contact with the linoleum, he vanished. Meera had watched Seb Walk many times and had eventually become accustomed to the bizarre, frightening sight of him disappearing in front of her. This looked the same—as simple as moving from one room to another. No flash, no puff of smoke, he just…left. The difference this time—the horrible, scary difference—was that Seb wasn't in control. His eyes rolled back in his head, he fell, and then he was gone.

For a few seconds, Mee just stood there, frozen. Then, she carefully put her drink on the counter and knelt where Seb should have been laying. She put her hands flat on the floor. There was nothing to see. The floor wasn't hotter or colder than any other part of the kitchen. She hadn't really expected any answers, but it felt useless to be doing nothing, and she didn't want to think too hard about the implications of Seb suddenly Walking while unconscious.

Not really thinking about what she was doing, Mee took some tins of food from a cupboard and marked out the area where Seb would have fallen. When he came back, he might appear there.

When he came back. It wasn't until she'd passed two sleepless nights, propped up on a cushion in the corner of the kitchen that she first considered the alternative: *if* he came back.

Other than bathroom breaks, she didn't leave the kitchen for a full twenty-four hours.

The next few days passed in a blur of confusion, fear, loneliness and anger. Sleep-deprived and frustrated at her lack of options, Meera would suddenly find herself snapping back to full wakefulness to find she'd been staring at the floor for two hours. She couldn't speak to anyone about what was going on, as no one knew her true identity. When Mason had come for her before, his mercenaries had left behind a dozen corpses, including Bob, whom she'd come to like and trust. Kate was the only person she'd got close to since moving to Mexico, and Mee felt certain a woman so wise and powerful must have some suspicions about her mysterious student. But Mason's people had killed the members of the Order in Las Vegas as if they were swatting flies. She'd couldn't risk exposing Kate to danger. Not until she was absolutely desperate.

On day four, she finally left the apartment. The few items of canned food on the shelves had gone, and Meera's Manna abilities didn't yet include manipulating earth to produce her own food.

She shopped quickly at the nearest market, barely looking at the items she placed in the cart. For once, she didn't sing as she walked.

After a week, she made an effort to get back to some kind of routine. She knew Seb's unique supply of Manna made him a survivor. To her knowledge, he'd been shot, run over and barbecued since his encounter with the alien he insisted on calling Billy Joe, with no ill-effects she could discern.

She'd questioned him about that night on the mountains outside Los Angeles, but the answers were crazy and she always ended up laughing. Well, they both did, as Seb could never resist her infectious giggling for long. Even he had to admit how ridiculous it sounded. He'd been bleeding to death (his suicide attempt was still hard for Mee to forgive, even when she knew about the brain tumor that had led him there that night). A glowing alien that—from his description—sounded an awful lot like the tall figures at the end of Close Encounters Of The Third Kind, had cured him of the tumor, healed his wounds, and replenished his blood supply. Only his blood wasn't just blood any more, it was filled with particle-sized machines (computers? beings?) making him un-killable, faster than any normal human and—apparently—with some kind of three-part personality. It was pretty weird stuff for sure, but there were compensations. He was better in bed, for instance. He could do things with his…well, he could *do things.*

"So what do you think?" Seb had said when he'd finally had the chance to tell her the whole story, including his trip to Roswell to absorb a different kind of Manna no one else had ever been able to access. *Naturally.*

Mee had taken a long sip of her margarita, her eyes never leaving his. Seb had always been completely honest with her. Irritating? Occasionally. Distant? More often than she liked, Troubled? No question, but a liar? Never. She sighed loudly, shaking her head.

"No way you could be making any of that shit up," she said. "I mean, a glowing gray alien? Give me a break. It's like something from a comic book. And Roswell, the source of every lunatic alien conspiracy theory? Come on, you're a walking cliché. I don't *like* science fiction, but even I could make up a better story than that."

Mee smiled at the memory, then choked back tears as she remembered she was alone. She opened the door to the tiny study they'd soundproofed to make a recording studio. Seb's keyboard was on one side, her makeshift vocal booth on the other. Between them were two flat-screens on the wall and a computer running various pieces of music software. Mee booted it up and put on her headphones. Just like the man she loved, making music was her response to the worst—as well as the best—experiences. She started to tap out a beat and was soon lost in her creation.

A few hours later, she emerged feeling drained and slightly elated. It was a great start to the song—it just needed Seb to do his thing to complete it. "Like you complete me, you bastard," she muttered. "Don't you dare leave me, Seb Varden."

She stuck to a rigid routine for the next five days. She went to the store in the mornings, had a walk around the city for an hour, forced herself not to spend every hour in the apartment. She recorded in the afternoons. In the evening, she allowed herself a beer and one spliff. She slept badly and her dreams were horrible, cruel and unrelenting. She called Kate and told her she'd be out of town for a while. She stuck to the routine and forced her mind away from the possibility that Seb might not be coming back today. Or tomorrow. Or ever.

Then, on the twelfth day, she'd walked back from the store and found him sitting at the battered old upright piano they'd found in a garage sale. He looked slightly confused, and happy to see her. She had prepared for this moment, of course. She was a self-assured, self-possessed, intelligent woman who knew her own worth, had plenty to give, and always had something to say. The last thing anyone would ever expect Meera Patel to do was to choke on her words, lose control of her legs and dissolve into uncontrollable tears. So, naturally, that's exactly what she did. At least she could still be unpredictable, she told herself as she dropped the bag she'd been carrying and slid down the wall.

***

Seb and Meera sat at the table, the spilled groceries strewn across the floor. Mee was shaking, still in shock. Seb produced a mug of strong Assam tea and watched while she drank it. She gradually brought her breathing back under control. He held her hand while she told him about the previous twelve days. His face was pale. She saw confusion in his eyes as she spoke.

"What is it?" she said.

"What's the date?" he said. She told him. "And what time is it?"

He shook his head when she told him.

"Show me your phone," he said. He held it up against his wristwatch. Her phone's display showed 9:28am. His watch was set at 12:18am.

"I remember looking at my watch just before I passed out," he said. "It was quarter to midnight. I know I was only out—gone—whatever—about ten minutes."

"What the hell's going on?" said Meera. "Did you think you were still here, passed out on the floor? You Walked. But I saw you faint *before* it happened. What's going on?"

Seb hesitated. "I didn't Walk. This was something different. I remember suddenly feeling light-headed. Then I woke up in the kitchen."

Seb2 interrupted him before he spoke again. "You going to mention what happened while you were out?"

"Give me a chance," thought Seb. He cleared his throat. Mee raised an eyebrow and looked at him quizzically.

"Seb2?" she said.

Seb nodded. "How did you know?"

"You get a slightly unfocused look when it happens. You're getting better at hiding it, but I still see it. So what's his contribution?"

Seb smiled at her. "He thinks I should tell you what happened while I was unconscious. Or missing. I think he sometimes forgets he's *me,* so I was about to tell you anyway."

"Touchy!" said Seb2. "Sorry, go on."

Seb kissed the back of Mee's hand and smiled at her.

"I thought it was a dream. Seb2 says it wasn't. Before I tell you, I want you to know that there's nothing to worry about," said Seb.

"And you're basing that statement on what, exactly?" said Seb2. Seb ignored him.

Mee waited, unconvinced by his reassurance.

He told her about the Social Security office, the ticket, and Mic. When he'd finished, there was a very long silence.

"Well, then," said Meera, who had carefully rolled up a joint while listening. "That's clear as mud, then. Excellent. Any clue what's going on?"

"Nope," said Seb. "Any thoughts?"

Mee inhaled, drawing the sweet smoke deep down into her lungs. She had a feeling this was going to be a three-joint day.

"Yes. I think I'm going to finish this, then I think you're going to take all of my clothes off and remind me why I still put up with you."

"That's a deal," said Seb.

Chapter 11

New York
Present Day

Mason poured himself a lemonade and looked out of the huge picture window that dominated the room. The sky was black now, the city illuminated by millions of tiny lights. He sipped as his mind teased at the problem, approaching it first one way, then another.

Before the freak case of Sebastian Varden, Mason had undoubtedly been the most powerful Manna user in America. His unique situation had given him the perfect opportunity to hothouse his Manna skills without distraction for decades, and he knew his level of natural ability was extremely rare. He had always been able to defeat any other Manna user without breaking a sweat.

Building his organization had taken many years, but, as technology had matured and the computer industry had grown, he had been able to stretch his virtual net wider. The internet had given him access to more people and information than he had ever conceived of being possible, even two decades ago. His personal interest in new technology, cutting-edge software and the Worldwide Web had become a financial interest early on, meaning his personal fortune now dwarfed all but a very select few.

All of this money, all of this power, yet one individual could bring it all crashing down. Mason realized he was considering—for the first time in his existence—walking away from a fight. Avoiding a confrontation. It was an option. Possibly the best option. There was a real chance of defeat if he went ahead. If anything went wrong, Seb Varden could be the end of everything.

Mason had steered politics, industry and media carefully for years, making sure to keep things interesting. And that, perhaps, was the secret no one had ever come close to guessing: his motive for accruing power and influence.

People assumed he was a megalomaniac, an evil genius with some sort of masterplan. Even those 'closest' to him—Westlake, Barrington, Walter Ford (he could hardly include his *domestic* servants in the list)—probably believed he had an endgame in mind. The truth was, he didn't. He had discovered Manna, found he was uncommonly talented at wielding it, and started doing so. At first, he assumed someone would stop him. By the time they tried, he was too powerful to be stopped. So he continued. It was a game. A game he was good at. And he enjoyed winning. As simple as that.

He continued looking out as the sky darkened and lights began to turn off across the city. The complex problem had been reduced to a simple decision, and—if he chose the more dangerous path—it could mean defeat. Choosing the safer path was surely the logical thing to do. The sensible thing.

The problem he faced could be summed up in four words: Sebastian Varden is alive.

Mason had suspected it, even after reviewing the footage of his death and receiving reports from Westlake and Ford. Varden's sacrifice to save Meera Patel had been noble but—ultimately—questionable. Would he really have thrown his life away without being absolutely sure he could guarantee her safety after his death? And, considering he was the repository of the Roswell Manna—demonstrably more powerful than the Manna that had existed for centuries—why take the risk? Better surely, to find a way he could protect her himself. By surviving. By faking his death. And, after searching the foundations of the parking garage where Varden's remains should have been rotting, Mason had finally confirmed his suspicions. No remains. No body. His men had killed a homunculus. A flesh-puppet, no more alive than a child's toy. The most sophisticated, life-like homunculus in history, but a homunculus none the less. That as shrewd an operator as Westlake had been fooled was surprising enough, but Walter Ford had been Using for eighty years or more and had suspected nothing. Or had he?

Mason turned to the three giant screens on one wall of the apartment. A couple of keystrokes and he was looking at Walt's home in Las Vegas, multiple views showing every room. Ford was evidently asleep. Mason considered calling and waking him, summoning him to explain exactly what had happened that day. He picked up the cellphone, then hesitated.

Ford claimed to have sensed Varden's Manna signal before they'd executed him. There were two possible explanations for this. The simplest was that Ford lied to him. Mason considered it for a moment, then disregarded it. Ford would never risk lying to him. Mason's ability to detect a lie was legendary. Those who had tested it hadn't lived long enough to regret their decision.

Mason put the phone down again.

The second explanation was more likely, unpalatable as it was to admit. Varden must have been able to create a copy of himself so sophisticated that it not only looked, moved, and conversed like a regular human being, but it produced—or released, somehow—enough Manna to fool a Sensitive like Ford. Which meant that Mason needed, once again, to re-assess the power, and potential threat of his opponent.

All of which brought Mason back to a simple decision. The decision he'd given all his attention to for the last few hours. Knowing what he did about Sebastian Varden's abilities, and accepting this knowledge was partial at best, should he leave him alone, hoping that Varden would do him the same courtesy? Or should he find a way to neutralize him and—this time—take care of it himself?

Mason had no doubt that Varden would be the victor in a fair fight. Naturally, he had no intention of being fair. Varden's weakness was still the same. If

Mason controlled Meera Patel, he controlled Sebastian Varden.

Decision made, Mason turned his attention to the practicalities of finding—and extracting—Patel, without alerting Varden. No doubt they would have taken precautions, after nearly eighteen months, if Varden believed his faked death had fooled Mason, he might have stopped looking over his shoulder by now.

Mason smiled thinly. This was a fight he might lose, but he couldn't leave Varden out there. Eventually, the man would come after him. Mason had killed his friend and had had an entire outpost of the Order slaughtered in order to kidnap Patel. One day, he'd come looking. Mason needed to act first.

"Ruth," he said. He heard the woman walk in, but didn't turn around. "I need protein—eggs, fish, some carbs. Then go to bed." It was 3:32am. Another hour and lights would start coming on in the bakery at the base of the building opposite. Mixed with sounds of traffic, bird song and occasional shouts would be the thump of flour sacks being delivered ready to make bread, bagels, pretzels. Soon the smells would start rising into the dawn. Mason, fifteen floors up behind triple-glazed windows would hear nothing, smell nothing.

His food arrived. He started researching online while he ate mechanically, barely tasting what he put into his mouth. He had an idea of what he required to find Patel, but the technical challenge was a specialized one. He would need help.

Using a program of his own design that piggy-backed proxy servers linked to other proxy servers accessing deeply buried government sites via the dark web, Mason took just under an hour to find a name. Sub-contracting tasks, bringing someone new in, an unknown, was a risk Mason never took lightly. Certain criteria had to be met before he would even contact someone for the first time. He looked at the files he had uncovered from a variety of sources, including the Pentagon.

The man whose entire life was laid out in a series of folders and files on Mason's screens, had proved himself invaluable to the US government in the field of software development, particularly cellphone apps. His name was Hal Wickerman.

Two years ago, Wickerman had written a lean, but complex piece of code which was built into an update of a free messaging app. Since its launch, the 'anonymous' feature offered within the app had proved very popular with terrorists, as well as teenagers and cheating spouses. Wickerman's code alerted Homeland Security every time certain key words were mentioned in chats, sending the conversation thread, all history and the current location of the cellphone. Many terrorist threats had subsequently been eliminated before getting past the planning stage, but the government knew if anyone ever found out about the hidden code in the app, their tactical advantage would be lost. And it was more than likely that the American people would have a thing or two to say to their leaders once they discovered their right to privacy had been so blatantly undermined.

The US Government had nothing to fear from the designer they'd used. Wickerman was never going to talk about his patriotic piece of coding. His liking for long walks during the day, often stopping to sit on benches in parks, sometimes enjoying an ice-cream, had been meticulously documented and photographed by Homeland Security for months before they'd approached him. The photographers had been briefed to capture as many images as possible with children in the frame. Of the thousands of photographs taken, a few dozen showed the subject looking in the direction of the children. When they recruited him, they didn't waste time appealing to his patriotism. They just showed him the photographs, along with some signed statements from children, attesting to the inappropriate games he had played with them in his home. His angry protests had been understandable, but a call from a prominent judge who had assured him his guilt would be established beyond reasonable doubt in any courtroom had produced the desired effect. All the fight went out of him. Wickerman took the job—and generous settlement—offered by his government, and bottled up his horror and bitterness at the betrayal of justice he had unwittingly brought down on himself.

Mason's offer to Wickerman was accepted quickly, with very little protest. Wickerman still wanted his freedom. Mason simply showed him all of the evidence he had accumulated about his work for the government, and assured him it would be made public if he refused.

"You will write the code for me and I will leave you alone," whispered Mason. "I have no interest in making your life more difficult. I just need you to do this. And I need it done quickly."

"What exactly do you need?" said Wickerman. His words weren't slurred, but his speech was slow and careful and he'd sounded awake when he picked up the phone. Mason despised the weakness of those who used alcohol to numb themselves to pain. Pain had been Mason's constant companion for a very long time. He could have anesthetized himself to it with Manna, but he'd accepted it as part of what made him who he was. Embraced it, even. And here was this man, whose pain was purely emotional, drinking alone at 4am. Pathetic.

Carefully, thoroughly, his emotionless whisper betraying none of the contempt he felt, he described the coding project to the software designer.

"You want *what?*" said Wickerman.

Chapter 12

Upstate New York
Thirty-four years previously

Eliza Breckland sat in her car, thinking. She was worried about one of her students. The violent episode a few weeks ago had been out of character and frightening. Since then, he had been even quieter than he had before, barely engaging in classroom discussions, his face pale, his eyes downcast. The other students kept clear. They had every right to be scared, Davy Johanssen had spent nearly a week in hospital. He wouldn't be coming back to class any time soon. Eliza heard he was transferring to another school.

She watched the small figure walk out of the school gates. She'd noticed he didn't take the bus any more. He was apparently as keen to avoid his classmates as they were to avoid him. Eliza wasn't one for gossip, but she had heard that the boy's father had been missing this past week, the consensus being he was either on an extended drinking session or was chasing some woman. It wouldn't be the first time, according to the whispers.

Eliza sat in her car for another few minutes before making her decision. She'd never experienced anything quite like this in her fifteen years of teaching. She'd long suspected some trouble at home with the young man in question. That, sadly, wasn't uncommon. But there were other factors at work here, she was sure of it. Firstly, she knew this student was deliberately turning in work that under-represented his level of intelligence. She had observed his boredom in class as he grasped fairly complex concepts immediately, then had to wait for the rest of the class to catch up. He hid his boredom well, but Eliza was a shrewd woman and a talented teacher. Twice now in Math class, she had gone further than the class could be expected to handle, then dropped in a deliberate mistake. Each time, she'd watched the young man carefully as he flinched at her error. The second time, his eyes flicked immediately to hers and she knew he had worked out what she was doing, and why. He had avoided anything other than essential communication with her ever since. Sometimes, she'd seen him frown, as if in pain, once even excusing himself and disappearing to the bathroom for ten minutes. Something was going on.

Eliza made her decision and started the car, leaving the school and turning the same direction her student had taken. She would talk to him. Not at school, not at home. On neutral ground. Maybe she could get through to him. She suspected he was the most gifted individual she would ever teach. She couldn't just turn away from him when he might need her.

After driving for a couple of minutes, she saw him in the distance, rounding a bend in the road. As she got closer, he darted a quick look left and right, then scrambled into the trees and out of sight. Without thinking, she accelerated and pulled onto the shoulder near where he'd disappeared. Getting out of the car, she scanned the tree line, but saw nothing. Then, at some distance, she heard the crack of a twig. She clambered up to the point she'd lost sight of him and, walking along the undergrowth, soon found a narrow track, almost completely hidden. She hesitated for a moment, then walked into the forest.

The incline was steeper than she'd anticipated and Eliza wasn't as fit as she'd like to be, but she was a determined woman, and rarely, if ever, gave up. Her husband Mike often joked that when it came to stubborn, Eliza made mules look positively obliging. Not that this was a complaint—he loved her for her headstrong nature, for the way she utterly refused to be deflected from doing the right thing. He'd always said she would have made a hell of a cop, but her first love had always been to teach, to pass on knowledge. And anyway, as she'd told Mike as she'd squeezed his ass, he looked far sexier in the uniform than she ever would.

The afternoon was clear and a little cold, but Eliza soon broke a sweat as she tried to catch up with her student. He'd obviously been up here before, judging from the sets of footprints now clearly visible on the forest floor. She stopped for a minute to catch her breath. She realized he could even get home this way, although it would add more than a mile to his journey and would be much harder going. Perhaps he just needed solitude, she reflected. He was growing up, the challenges of adolescence were just ahead, and his home life might be far from supportive when it came to nourishing his precocious intelligence. Might be she was just sticking her nose in where it wasn't needed. She shook her head. No, her gut told her the child was suffering, and she couldn't let that go on without trying to help. She wiped her brow and walked on.

Another ten minutes went by before she realized she'd lost the trail. Fortunately, her own footsteps were clear enough for her to retrace her path. She stopped where the floor became more rock than dirt. This must have been where she'd lost him. She walked on a little more until she found the path both of them had taken to arrive at this point. The rocks made it hard—impossible, really—to tell which direction he'd taken. Eliza had carried on up the slope, but he must have turned away. The logical direction would be east, toward his home, so Eliza headed that way and, after a few minutes' search, found another path with more footsteps.

She heard the sound just as she began to follow the new path. It sounded like a distant shriek, abruptly silenced. It had an eerie, echoey quality that brought her skin up in goosebumps.

"What on earth?"

Eliza stood absolutely still, holding her breath, but the sound wasn't repeated. She knew she hadn't imagined it. As a young girl, she had once heard a deer make a similar noise, brought down by an inexperienced hunter. It had shrieked unbearably for five minutes, trying to drag itself away on a broken leg until the hunting party had caught up with it and ended its misery. Eliza had woken up every night for a week, crying at the memory.

It might have been a deer. It must have been a deer. Eliza shivered.

The sound had come from behind her. She swallowed hard, squared her shoulders and walked directly toward where she thought the sound had originated.

She came back to the rocky patch and looked around her carefully, listening hard. After a few minutes, she moved slightly uphill toward a huge rock half-hidden by trees. Reaching it, she followed its contours until it suddenly stopped, the rock cut away at right angles. For a second or two, she wondered what was going on, then she realized and followed the smooth surface until her suspicions were confirmed. Nearly invisible from any distance greater than ten yards, was the entrance to a mine.

Abandoned mines weren't uncommon. She knew they had been active until the early part of the 20th century in the region, but this was the first time Eliza had actually seen one. The doorway she'd discovered was cut into the rock before her, a rusted iron gate blocking any further progress into the darkness beyond. She walked forward and inspected the barrier more closely. The iron was ancient but still strong. She listened in absolute silence for five minutes, but could hear nothing. She had no idea how far down the path on the other side of the gate might lead.

Eliza realized that her student would be long gone by now. She resolved to try to talk to him the next day, catch up with him before he headed into the forest.

She peered into the blackness, but it was so complete that her eyes couldn't adjust at all. She turned to go.

After a few paces, she stopped, suddenly realizing what was wrong with what she had just seen. She stepped back to the gate. First of all, she examined the rusted hinges. They were covered in oil. Fresh oil. Then she knelt carefully on the rock and squinted at the padlock she'd half-glimpsed on the other side of the gate. She was right. It was brand new.

Eliza stood still for another minute or so, thinking. Then she took a pocket knife from her bag and, as she made her way back to the road, cut an X into the bark of about twenty trees, leaving a trail.

At dinner that night, she told Mike what she'd seen and heard.

"It may have nothing to do with him, and I may be worrying about nothing. But would you take a look?"

Mike looked across the table at his wife. If she was worried, there was bound to be a damn good reason for it. He squeezed her hand and smiled.

"It's almost certainly nothing," he said. "Dangerous mines are sometimes sealed up to stop folk from wandering in and never wandering out again." He didn't add the fact that the local sheriff's department would have been notified if that had been the case.

"I'll take a hike up there in the morning," he said. "Now don't you worry about it."

She smiled in answer and he returned it, but he could see the concern in her eyes. He decided to take bolt cutters with him and put her mind at rest.

Chapter 13

Mexico City
Present Day

Three days after his encounter with Mic, the bureaucratic alien, Seb sat at the keyboard in Mee's tiny studio and tweaked a low pass filter on a big, spacey synth sound he was programming. He was trying to evoke something that would make the listener feel transported to a new world. He wanted to make people feel the way he had felt when he'd first heard the music at the beginning of Bladerunner—a sound that conveyed a vast, futuristic landscape. He had already added some deliberately lo-fi drums to Mee's vocal and the result was a grainy, gritty, dystopian vision that had a great hook in the chorus, where she repeated, "the lights in the city are gone, one by one, like stars behind clouds, and there's nowhere to run". For someone with such an appetite for life, some of Mee's lyrics could be a little on the dark side.

He played back the intro again, eyes closed, lost in the music. When he felt an urgent tug at his sleeve, he jumped so violently the headphones fell off and landed on the keyboard, adding an incongruous major third to the chord.

"Seb!" said Mee, "quickly."

He followed her through to the other room, where the TV was showing live pictures of a fire in New York. The caption read, "Unfolding tragedy as family trapped at top of notorious slum landlord's tenement." Someone was being interviewed as flames climbed up the building in the background. The shocked-looking man speaking was a resident of the burning building. He said the building had no working smoke alarms and the fire-escape had collapsed months ago but hadn't been replaced.

"We all knew something like this would happen one day," he said. "We've gone without heating, without water sometimes. Vashtar don't care about us. He wants to force us out, so he can hike the rent up." He looked back at the building, cowering as there was an explosion. Glass blew out from a third-floor window.

"Folk still trapped up at the top," he said. "Felicia and her kids. Someone's gotta do something!" The cameras panned across the scene. Fire trucks were in attendance, but it was clear the fire was too fierce for anyone to try to enter the building.

Seb2 brought up Walking options as Seb looked at the screen. At the side of his vision, he saw a live image of the building on the TV screen, then his point of view shifted as he looked inside. There were dozens of burning rooms flicking across his vision, each room the same, then—suddenly—the same room, but without a fire. In that room, Seb could see a young woman cooking, a baby on her hip, while three other children watched TV in the corner.

"Parallel universes," said Seb2. "Don't think I'll ever get used to it."

Mee looked up from the TV.

"Seb?" she said, "can you do—". She stopped talking. Seb had gone.

***

Seb Walked to the rear of the building. He could make out the firefighters trying to find a way in, but even as he watched them, they backed away from the intense heat.

"Whole place has been subdivided inside," shouted one to his boss. "Don't know what materials they used, but it's going up fast. Chopper coming out?"

"On its way," shouted the other man.

"It's going to be too late," said Seb2. "Smoke inhalation will kill them first."

Seb Walked to the undamaged apartment Seb2 had found. As he appeared, the infant riding his mom's hip turned and saw him, smiling excitedly at the man who had appeared out of nowhere. No one else noticed him.

He Walked again, this time moving *sideways,* staying in the same apartment—but the scene was very different. Everything was burning. He felt no sense of heat as his clothes burned off and the outermost layers of skin on his body hardened and changed. As he moved, it felt like he was wearing some kind of plastic mesh, although his body looked no different. There was no sign of any life.

"They're in the bathroom," said Seb2. "The mother—Felicia—has soaked towels and put them at the bottom of the door."

"Smart," said Seb. "What can we do?"

"The fire crews can't get close enough to extend the ladder at the back here," said Seb2, "we need the fire escape."

Seb ran to the window and yanked it up. The rush of oxygen caused a surge of heat in the room. There was a scream from the bathroom.

"Ayúndanos! Ayúndanos! Help us!"

"Stay calm, ma'am," Seb shouted back as he looked down at the fire escape. "We'll have you out of here in a moment." There were metal stairs attached to the outside of the tenement block, but they stopped four floors below the floor where they were now needed. Rusted bolts on the brickwork showed where they had once supported a staircase, but at some stage they had been removed. He looked down eight stories at the mess in the yard below. Clearly visible were the iron stairs that should have been in place outside the window.

"What the-," thought Seb.

"Slum landlords," said Seb2. "Later." Seb reached out his hand and let his mind become instantly still.

When he had first begun to use Manna, he had needed to sound pieces of music internally, so that his mind could reach the balanced point of silence which enabled him to manipulate the power. Bach worked best. But since absorbing the Roswell Manna, Seb had only to turn his attention inward and still his mind, his thoughts not disappearing as such, just becoming background noise, like clouds around a mountain. Now, as he looked at where the staircase ended on the fourth floor, his awareness expanded to include not just his own consciousness and body, but also the building itself; its bricks, mortar, glass, wood, the millions of insects living inside and out, the ivy, moss and fungi that had taken hold in the cracks. His fingers twitched and the stairs extended themselves toward him. Every second that passed saw new steps growing organically out of the existing staircase, climbing rapidly upward like a flower seeking the sun.

When the steps were half a floor away, Seb ran to the bathroom.

"I'm coming in," he shouted. "Stand back from the door."

He pushed against the door and it slid open, revealing a terrified woman hugging a baby and three children as they cowered against the tub. Her eyes widened in disbelief when she saw Seb.

"Oops," said Seb2. "Naked."

Seb glanced down, but even as he did so, a fire-fighter's uniform grew out of his flesh, a visored helmet momentarily obscuring his vision. He looked back at the woman, who had evidently decided she had just hallucinated a naked rescuer. Possibly a side effect of smoke inhalation.

"This way!" shouted Seb, "quickly." He shielded the worst of the flames with his body as they followed him into the apartment. The heat would have burned them, but an invisible barrier extending five feet on either side of Seb, protected the family from the flames. When she realized they were heading for the window, the woman shook her head and pulled her children closer.

"No!" she said. "No stairs!" Seb saw something give way in her face as she accepted they'd lost all hope of getting out. She began to sit down, pulling the children with her. The baby began to wail, but stopped in a fit of coughing.

Seb put his hand under her chin.

"Felicia! Felicia!" he said. At the unexpected use of her name, she looked up slowly. The man above her was trying to say something. He wanted something of her. But she was so tired. He saw him look at the necklace she always wore. It was a cheap wooden thing, but she had worn it ever since her mother had passed. It was an angel. The man looked back at her and smiled. She couldn't move. Then she saw it—wings began to unfurl on his shoulders. He stood up and let the beautiful white wings open out on either side of him, nearly touching the apartment walls. She began crying. A miracle. He held out a hand. She felt new strength fill her, and she placed her own hand in his.

When they reached the window, the stairs were in place; solid, safe, bolted securely to the side of the building. Felicia didn't hesitate. She sent her eldest boy out first, followed by his brother and sister. Lastly, she climbed out with the baby. She looked back once as they made their way to safety. The angel was smiling. He turned and walked back into the burning building. She kissed the angel hanging on the chain around her neck and thanked God for sending her deliverer.

When the family walked to the front of the building, they were immediately surrounded by firefighters who hurried them to a waiting ambulance.

The chief fire officer, who—minutes earlier—had given up all hope of any more survivors after seeing the state of the fire escape, turned speechlessly to the rest of his crew. They looked at each other in disbelief as a roar behind them signaled the fact that the fire had finally consumed the interior of the building. No more than a blackened shell would be left within a few hours.

"An angel saved us—sent by God—an angel! It's a miracle!" The chief thought he might not mention her explanation on his report, but as of now, he couldn't think of a better one.

***

Cubby Vashtar looked at the lion's head mounted on the wall of his study. It was his latest trophy, brought back after a safari in Nairobi the previous month. The poachers had been hard to find at first and they had been extremely reluctant to trust him, suspecting some kind of law enforcement sting was behind his request. But as usual, cold hard cash—and plenty of it—had persuaded them that Cubby had no interest in their illegal ivory trade. He just wanted to kill a lion. A really, really big one. A ferocious one. A really big, ferocious lion he could safely kill using a high-powered rifle with telescopic sights from a jeep a quarter mile away.

"Magnificent," Cubby murmured as he raised a glass of champagne and toasted the golden shaggy head.

Cubby was an intelligent man and had made his life choices with his eyes well and truly open. His father had come to America with nothing but his dignity and had died without even that. Cubby was a believer in the

American Dream. His father had believed in it, too, but had never found his true calling. He had entered the system, followed its rules, obeyed the law, paid his taxes and accepted the hardships that came along as an inevitable part of life. "Bad things happen," Cubby's father had said, as he lay dying from a disease that better health insurance could have treated. "It's the immutable law of the universe." Immutable my ass, thought Cubby.

His cellphone vibrated in his pocket. He opened his humidor and selected a fat Cohiba Behike Laguito cigar, rolling it between his fingers, bringing it to his nose to appreciate the subtle fragrance. The cell stopped, then immediately started vibrating again. He sighed and answered it.

"What?" he said, taking a last look at his trophies. The brown bear was spectacular, and he'd always had a soft spot for the silverback gorilla, possibly due to the insane amount of money it had cost him to hunt it, but the lion was definitely his new favorite. The king of the jungle. He walked outside onto the verandah as he listened to Sanjeev describe the evening's events.

"Which building?" he said. "Oh, ok, it's insured. It's good news, actually. I'll rebuild and get some bankers in there. It's an up and coming area—don't you read the New Yorker, Sanj?"

He chuckled as he sat down and took the cigar cutter from his pocket, neatly severing the end and lobbing it into the artificial lake he'd had built in the garden. As he listened to Sanjeev talk, he frowned.

"So, what's the problem?" He put the unlit cigar onto a glass ashtray on the cast-iron table. He wouldn't be able to enjoy it until he got rid of Sanjeev.

"Yes, I know, I know, the smoke alarms didn't work, the fire escape collapsed, there was lead in the paint, blah, blah, blah. Sanj, little brother, if you're ever going to learn how to run this business, you're going to have to understand the importance of planning ahead. Never mind, you'll see soon enough. Just stop nagging me, you old woman. Go away. I'll see you tomorrow."

He ended the call, turned the cellphone off and threw it back into the house over his shoulder. It made no sound as it landed, so it must have hit the tiger skin rug.

"God, I'm such a cliché," he said to himself, smiling. He lit the cigar, took a few initial puffs and leaned back on the cushioned chair, sighing contentedly.

Cubby had chosen crime as his route to pursuing the American Dream. Low-level stuff at first, a little drug dealing in school, which financed a protection racket, then a downpayment on a repossessed house a block away from where he'd grown up in Queens. He'd divided the house into five tiny apartments and rented the rooms to immigrant workers who didn't mind paying a little over the normal rates to someone who didn't ask many questions. The first time someone got behind on the rent, they had experienced a nasty fall, breaking a leg in three places, before being evicted. After that, his tenants were prompt with their payments.

Cubby worked, ate and slept, no more. No luxuries, no vacations, no women. He'd given himself five years to make his first million as a landlord in his father's adopted city. He had got there in three. He did it by cutting corners, by overcharging, by ignoring maintenance requests, staying on the right side of the law by the narrowest possible margin. And on the occasions when he crossed the line, he had a very expensive lawyer who was worth every cent.

The fire in his apartment building tonight was arson, of that Cubby was quite sure. He was sure because he'd paid $20,000 to get the job done. Even better, the trail he'd carefully left made it look like a rival landlord might have been behind it. Despite Sanjeev's misgivings, Cubby knew there would be no trouble with the City. Most of the building's occupants would be too scared to testify against him. And as an insurance policy, he always kept a few tenants on the payroll. They would swear under oath that the smoke alarms had been regularly checked, the building was safe and the fire escape—if it could be proved to have collapsed—must have done so during the fire because it was definitely there that morning.

Cubby slowly blew a cloud of smoke into the night air. He wondered if there would be any fatalities this time. People dying meant paperwork, lawyers and expense, as he knew to his cost. Everything was more straightforward when the only damage was to property.

There was a movement in the bushes beside the lake. Cubby sat up straighter and felt under the table for the shotgun. It was there, securely cradled in its brackets. Oiled, loaded and ready to fire. Cubby's house featured at least one concealed weapon in every room.

Sanjeev thought he was paranoid. Cubby knew he was merely being realistic. He was a ruthless crime-funded slum landlord, living like a prince while his tenants scraped by in conditions unfit for dogs. Who *wouldn't* want to kill him? Cubby checked the safety was off and eased the weapon onto his lap.

"Don't be shy," he called. "Come on out. I would rather you had made an appointment, but if you're so desperate to talk to me, let's talk." He put the cigar in the ashtray and had another sip of champagne. He'd had angry tenants try to break in before, but a high fence, razor wire and warnings of guard dogs were normally a sufficient deterrent. He didn't actually own any dogs, just a movement-sensitive device that played recorded growling whenever it was triggered. He hadn't heard it tonight, though. Strange.

The bushes rustled some more, then a figure stepped forward. It was a man in his fifties, Hispanic, tired-looking. Kind of familiar, although Cubby couldn't think why. The man was wearing a janitor's uniform exactly like the Supers in Cubby's tenements. Cubby knew it was *exactly* like it because he'd bought a box of five hundred in that baby-shit yellow color no one else wanted to buy. They were dirt cheap, that was the main thing.

The man took a step forward. He had slicked down hair. The name badge over his pocket was close enough to read now. It said *Hector.* He was about ten feet away. Cubby lifted the shotgun off his lap and swiveled it around to point at the intruder.

"That's close enough, Hector," he said. "I guess you work in one of my buildings. What's the problem?" Cubby didn't want to have to shoot the guy—it made such a mess—but he was well within his rights. He was a trespasser, after all. More importantly, Cubby had a reputation to preserve. It wasn't as if he could let the man walk away with no consequences. He decided to aim low. A kneecap shot was his best option; maximum pain, permanent debilitating damage and a clear signal to any other unhappy employees to keep their heads down and their mouths shut. Before he could pull the trigger, the man spoke.

"You don't remember me, do you, Mr Vashtar?"

Cubby snorted. He owned more than thirty buildings in New York and staff turnover was high. Sanjeev had delegated the hiring and firing to others years ago. If Hector thought Cubby had a clue—or gave a shit—who he was, he was going to be sorely disappointed.

"Don't know, don't care. Enjoy the ambulance ride."

Cubby pulled the trigger. Well, his finger closed on the gap in the trigger guard where the trigger should have been. He would have sworn blind he'd had his finger on the trigger for the last thirty seconds while he'd watched this loser walk out of the bushes. But now, there was nothing. He looked at the gun in disbelief. There was no trigger. Not only that, there was no evidence there had ever been a trigger. The shotgun just looked like an expensive toy.

In his business, Cubby was used to making quick decisions and staying one step ahead of the game.

Thinking fast, he decided his best bet would be to get into the trophy room behind him. There was a pistol in his desk drawer and an Uzi in the drinks cabinet. He'd only bought the Uzi because owning one made him feel like a proper gangster.

He got up and turned toward the verandah door. Hector was blocking his way. How the hell had he moved so fast? Cubby took an involuntary step backward. Seeing the man so close triggered a faint memory…there was something about him.

"Got it yet?" said Hector. He leaned toward Cubby. Cubby flinched backward. There was something *wrong* about Hector—the gray pallor of his skin, the slow, slightly stilted way he spoke. Cubby didn't want to be touched by him.

Hector picked up Cubby's cigar and took a few puffs, his dark eyes never leaving the other man's.

"You do like the finer things in life, don't you, Cubby?" he said.

Cubby clenched his fists. He never let anyone other than family call him Cubby. He was a big, intimidating man, and he'd never been afraid to fight his own battles. As long as there was no chance that he would lose. He swung a loose heavy roundhouse at Hector's face. Which—somehow—missed.

"I'll give you two clues," said Hector, calmly. "See if they help you remember."

Cubby gaped at him, thrown off-balance by the force of the punch he had thrown. How was it possible he'd missed? This guy could move fast. Real fast. Cubby re-evaluated his position. Might be best to keep

Hector talking, keep things friendly until he could reach one of the weapons in the room behind him.

"Ok, Hector," he said, "you have my attention. Who are you? And what do you want?"

"I worked for you a long time ago," said Hector. "Not long after you started out. Clue number one: Mumbai Heights."

Cubby stared. Mumbai Heights had been the joke name he and Sanj had given to the two-story warehouse he'd rented over a decade ago. The warehouse had been cheap, as it had been recently condemned. Cubby had sublet it to a clothing manufacturer whose workers had no visas, no work permits and no rights. They only wanted the building for three months to cope with the Christmas rush.

Mumbai Heights had only ever had one resident. Despite the City ordinances expressly forbidding it, Cubby had put living quarters in one corner of the second floor and told Sanj to employ a cheap security guard to keep an eye on the place at night. It was a condition the clothing company had insisted on, and they were paying handsomely for the space.

Cubby looked again at Hector. Now that he thought about it, the security guard had probably shared the same name. Couldn't be this loser, though, because that Hector was dead.

"One more clue," said Hector. The Hector who—now that Cubby thought back—looked a hell of a lot like the one back then. Was that it? A brother, back for revenge? But the fire department had investigated and concluded the cause was a faulty fusebox. Not arson.

The fire chief who had authored that report had been close to retirement, and now lived in a surprisingly good house in a very sought-after neighborhood.

"Getting warm yet?" said Hector. "Here's clue number two."

He took the cigar from his mouth, flicked an inch of ash from the tip and pressed it onto his upper arm. The shirts weren't cheap just because of the crappy color. They were highly flammable, too. Hector's shirt smoldered for a second, then burst into flames.

"Wha-?" Cubby hadn't meant to speak, but he couldn't help himself. Hector was still calmly looking at him, while the shoulder of his shirt burned. Tongues of fire licked around his collar, but Hector showed no sign of being in any discomfort. Even when the oil in his hair ignited and turned into a fiery crown, he continued looking calmly into Cubby's eyes.

The fire burned itself out after six horrific minutes. Cubby, boxed in between the wall and the table, had been a helpless observer of the damage wrought by the flames on Hector's body. Now, a blackened, smoldering husk stood there, smoke rising from the scraps of dark flesh that—here and there—still clung to its bones. Only the man's dark eyes were undamaged, and had looked directly at Cubby throughout.

When the horror before him opened its mouth to speak, the lips—which had fused together and knotted into a mass of scorched tissue—cracked, split and fell away from the face, landing close to Cubby's feet. Cubby shrieked and tried to back away.

"Now do you remember?" said Hector. His voice box, dried up, cooked and scarred by the fire, produced a rattling scraping sound which made Cubby's skin go icy cold. And Cubby knew who he was.

"I didn't know anyone was in the building," he whispered.

"Liar," said Hector, impassively.

"Ok," said Cubby, "you got me. Now what?" He seemed to have developed a healthy case of gallows humor. A distant part of him suggested that he might be in shock. Another, equally distant part, agreed shock was probably a fair diagnosis, considering he was having a conversation with the reanimated corpse of a man who'd died twelve years ago.

"You ever read A Christmas Carol?"

Cubby stared blankly at him.

"By Charles Dickens?"

Cubby opened his mouth, but no appropriate words suggested themselves.

"Heard of Scrooge?"

Cubby nodded. He'd seen the movie once. This dead ex-security guard seemed to be better educated than he remembered.

"Scrooge was visited by ghosts. They gave him a second chance. He could turn his life around or be eternally damned."

The corpse hesitated. Cubby realized he expected some kind of response.

"Oh," he said, then licked his lips and tried again. "Yeah, Scrooge. I remember." He could have sworn the dead guy tutted.

"Well, this is your warning, your last chance. But how many people believe in eternal damnation these days?"

Cubby searched for a reply, but the question proved to be rhetorical this time.

"So, I have a promise for you instead," continued the corpse, who seemed unaffected by Cubby's choking response to the acrid smell of burnt meat. "I'll be checking up on you in one month. You have until then to fix all of the hazards in your buildings and put into place the most comprehensive maintenance program this city has ever seen. You have an additional six months to complete it. A prominent journalist has already been emailed on your behalf. I offered her an exclusive interview with you, once the six months are up. I told her she can visit any or all of your buildings, bring photographers, talk to whoever she pleases. She will break the news that the worst landlord in New York is now the best. Or…"

Cubby waited. Nothing. He guessed it was his turn again.

"Or?" he squeaked.

"Or I come back and do what I just did to myself to you. It's not a very nice way to die, I promise. Now, go sit on your lawn, Cubby."

Hector backed up and let Cubby come out from behind the table. Cubby pressed himself as hard as he could into the table, desperate not to touch the smoking body as he passed. He stumbled down the verandah steps like a drunk man and sat heavily on the grass, looking at his mansion.

The corpse had vanished. Cubby looked desperately left and right, then behind him. When he looked back at the house, the blackened skull, a few flaps of skin still hanging from it, appeared through the door to the trophy room. Hector tossed something toward Cubby. He flinched as it landed on the grass beside him. It was his cellphone.

"One more thing," said Hector. "You kill another animal and I'll cut your head off and mount it on the front of your car. Now watch this, it's a neat trick."

Cubby watched as the corpse burst into flames. As the human torch walked slowly around the trophy room, drapes, rugs, papers on the desk, then the desk itself, began to smolder then burst into flames. By the time the figure moved into the kitchen next door, the trophy room was blazing. Hector moved faster then, running from room to room, each one immediately lighting up as the flames followed him.

In five minutes, the entire house was blazing. Cubby heard the sound of approaching sirens. A figure walked out of the house. Hector now looked exactly as he had when he'd first appeared from the bushes a lifetime ago. He smiled grimly at Cubby.

"I'll see myself out," he said. "I'll check back in one month. Pray to God you don't see me again."

He walked away in the direction of the garages. Cubby groaned. There was a muffled explosion, followed by two more. The Rolls Royce *and* both Ferraris.

Cubby picked up his cell.

"Sanj?" he said, his voice small and shaken, "can you come over and get me? I need to stay with you for a while. And we're going to have a long talk about the business."

Chapter 14

Las Vegas, Nevada
Present Day

Walter Ford sat out in his yard, a bottle of ice-cold beer in his hand, a photograph in his pocket and a decision he'd been avoiding for years finally made. He wondered, not for the first time, if his was the only property within five square miles without a pool out back. His backyard was plenty big enough. But he needed the space to practice, and to practice he needed plenty of earth. The yard was a mess, piles of dirt the only notable features. The local landscapers and gardeners must consider him eccentric, as he never availed himself of any of the offers they stuffed into his mailbox every week. He allowed himself a rare smile as he imagined their reaction if they knew what he was doing back here. His smile faded just as quickly when he remembered the whispered phone call he had received just a few hours earlier.

Mason didn't have conversations, he gave instructions. Walt's job was to obey them without question. He had listened and memorized. You didn't make notes when Mason called you.

"Ford, your help will soon be required regarding the outstanding matter of Ms. Patel. Her acquisition is now a priority. She will be found soon. When this happens, you and Barrington will accompany Westlake and his team to her location. Do not go anywhere until this matter has been resolved."

After the call had ended, Walt had stood in his study for thirty minutes, staring at the phone. As always with Mason, his orders were clear and his motives were hidden. But he may have finally misjudged Walt.

He laughed, the sound harsh and out of place in the silent house. From the outside, Walt knew, his life must look incredible. He lived in a mansion, he earned a fortune, he had beautiful women available to him whenever he wanted. He could spend all day drunk—often did—and yet wake up without a hangover, his liver in excellent condition, ready to grab the bourbon next to his bed and start over. He had been using Manna since his teens. Now that he was over a hundred years old, his abilities were as powerful as they were subtle and finessed. Of course, most centenarians didn't have the option to maintain their body at the level of a fit, healthy man in his fifties. And he'd been happy with that for a long time. Not anymore.

Recently, there had been more and more days when Walt envied those who lived and died naturally, having never experienced the seemingly-magical qualities of Manna. The regular absorption of the power suffusing many thousands of sites worldwide had given him many of the most amazing moments of his long life. It had also caused him sadness, terror and regret.

Walt got up and started slowly pacing the yard. He couldn't allow himself to blame Manna for the poor decisions he'd made, his tendency to always take the option that benefitted him most, however morally unsound that might be. As a very young man he had betrayed Sid, the User who had taught him how to use Manna. Sold him out and watched him die. Then, much later, when Mason had approached Walt, he'd had been quick to convince himself he had no choice but to take his offer. Looking back at it coldly, his life could be seen as a series of moral compromises designed to keep him safe, healthy and rich. And here he was, safe. Healthy. Rich. Alone. And so far from happiness, he could barely even remember how it felt.

The yard was the only place he knew he wasn't being watched. Walt had installed security cameras when he'd first moved in, but hadn't placed any outside. He had long suspected Mason of hacking into every electronic component of his life. When you started working for Mason, he *owned* you. No point crossing him. You crossed him, you died. You failed him, you died. Walt planned on a third course of action he thought might just leave him alive. He planned to disappear.

Walt got up and walked over to the figure in his yard, standing directly opposite it. It stood at six-feet and one-inch tall, Walt's height exactly. Its posture was very similar to his own, its limbs were pretty much in the correct proportions. The thing before him could move like a man, even talk in a rudimentary way, but it wouldn't fool anyone for more than a few seconds. Unless, Walt hoped, you were watching through grainy security footage and couldn't make out the finer details.

After receiving that email, Walt knew he didn't have much time left. He couldn't refuse Mason, but there was no way he would help him or his hired killers to kill Meera Patel. He had only met Meera briefly, in unfortunate circumstances, but he had spent time with Seb Varden and that time had left its mark. After the younger man's death, Walt had looked at himself in the mirror and for the first time in his life, admitted he wasn't one of the good guys. A week of heavy drinking, drugs and copious amounts of sex with multiple partners hadn't helped. He felt hollow, dead inside. He kept remembering Seb, the way he had just knelt there, waiting for Westlake to swing the axe. Sometimes, when Walt finally shut his eyes last thing at night, he saw himself over and over, stepping forward with the flamethrower.

There was something else on Walt's mind. Something about that phone call didn't quite ring true. Mason was a psychopath, granted, but an incredibly intelligent and careful one. He didn't take unnecessary risks—period. Suddenly deciding to prioritize finding Meera Patel seemed strange to Walt. It just didn't sound like Mason. There was something else at play here. Something bigger. Walt put his hand in his pocket and felt the piece of newspaper folded there. *Surely it's impossible. It couldn't be.*

He walked back into the house. The silent figure paced around the yard as he slid the door shut. He would check on it tomorrow. So far, his record was nine hours before it would crumble back to dust. He was hoping to do better than that if he wanted to escape Mason.

Walt headed down to the movie theater in his basement. He cued up Sanshiro Sugata, Akiro Kurosawa's directorial debut, and started watching it, a large bourbon in hand. Cupped in his other hand was the newspaper photograph from his pocket. It showed the man who had single-handedly prevented five career criminals from robbing a Delaware bank the previous day. The eyewitness descriptions made it just about feasible that the man wasn't a Manna user, but Mason had been suspicious enough to investigate further. The Sensitives in or near Dover reported no Manna use, and Westlake's team's report concluded, after seeing copies of all of the police interviews, that the 'hero' in question was no more than he appeared to be—some kind of advanced martial arts expert.

Walt was always copied in to any communication when new Manna use was suspected, as most novice Users usually opted for a trip to Las Vegas after discovering they could manipulate physical reality. Walt's job was to discourage them with a demonstration of what a mature Manna user could do after decades of practice. The casinos, none of which knew how he achieved his results, paid him a handsome retainer for dissuading those who would cheat them. And Mason, through Walt, kept tabs on new American

Users. Those who showed real potential ended up working for Mason. Or they ended up dead. Seb Varden, for a while at least, looked like he might avoid either option. Walt had never seen anyone with a fraction of the power Seb had seemed to possess. But Mason still won in the end. Mason always won. *So why go after Meera?*

Walt glanced at his glass and it filled with fresh ice and bourbon. He remembered walking forward that morning in New York, raising the flamethrower, and burning Seb's body up, then doing the same to his head, which had come to rest twelve feet away. The man was dead. How could it be otherwise? And yet…

Walt paid closer attention as the movie got to the scene he had been waiting for. The fight at the dock.

Walt had long been a fan of Kurosawa, and he knew watching this movie wouldn't seem out of the usual if Mason happened to be monitoring him. But he knew he couldn't risk freeze-framing the action when the camera tracked along the group of fighters taking on Yano, the judo expert. He cupped his drink in both hands and lifted the bottom of the glass away from his palm, so that he could see the cutting from the bank robbery clearly by looking down his nose. Throughout the scene in question, his eyes flicked from the photograph to the screen and back again.

The movie continued, but Walt wasn't watching anymore. His mind whirled as he considered the implications of what he had seen. The floppy-haired actor who played one of the ju-jitsu attackers—if he was still alive—must be in his nineties by now, but the man in the photo from the bank was young and extremely fit. And, without a shadow of doubt, it was the same face. The face of a minor character in a 1943 movie.

Walt swirled the bourbon around the glass. The greenest Manna user could alter his or her appearance easily enough, but they couldn't hide their Manna use from others with the same ability. He thought about one of the last times he had seen Seb, when he'd realized he was in the presence of someone far more powerful than anyone he had ever encountered. Mason's servants—what other word was there for them?—had wiped out the Order in Las Vegas, killing Seb's friend Bob Weller and kidnapping Meera. Seb had met Walt near the scene of the slaughter the next day. Seb had appeared from nowhere. Walt always knew when Manna was nearby, but he'd been taken by surprise when Seb had walked around the corner. And when Seb had got mad and the whole desert floor seemed to shake, he had felt no Manna use at all. Nothing. Which was impossible. He neglected to mention that detail in his report to Mason, worried that his abilities were fading. And when other Users had met Seb and seemingly been able to pick up his Manna signature, he was glad he had said nothing. And when Seb had died, Walt had detected his Manna signature clearly, so he had dismissed his earlier experience as a failure of his own Sensitive ability.

But here was someone who *must* be Using, changing his appearance and taking on five armed men single-handed before disappearing without a trace. And not a single Manna user had even known he was there. Impossible.

Walt took one more look at the photograph. No doubt about it at all. It was the face from a movie made halfway through the previous century.

Walt considered the evidence. The Manna Seb had absorbed at Roswell had been the holy grail for all Users since 1947. Every significant Manna user on the planet had, at some point in the last seven decades, tried to soak up that Manna. It was the Manna community's equivalent of the sword in the stone. Walt had tried to access that incredible store of Manna twice. The sensation of incredible power just out of reach had been so frustrating he had wept. But the Roswell Manna had been waiting. Finally, Seb Varden had come along. The only one able to absorb it. And when he had, he'd absorbed all of it. Weeks later, it had died with him. As if it had never been.

Not for the first time, Walt remembered how bravely, how calmly Seb had gone to his death. Undoubtedly the most powerful human in history, sacrificing himself so that Meera could escape. And escape she did, despite Mason's plans. It was the first time Mason had failed, to Walt's knowledge. And over a year later, he still hadn't found her, despite the global reach of his organization.

Seb Varden? Walt watched the photograph gently and slowly tear itself into tiny pieces until they settled into a tiny cloud of dust which, as he stood up, sank unnoticed into the carpet. *Are you still out there?*

Chapter 15

Upstate New York
Thirty-four years previously

It was a harder hike to the abandoned mine than Mike Breckland had anticipated, mostly because of the heavy rainfall overnight, which had turned the path his wife had followed into a mudslide. Mike found he could make better progress by getting off what was left of the path, but this meant pushing through branches and bushes. Within ten minutes, he had a good sweat going. He was grateful for the leather gloves Eliza had bought him last birthday.

After twenty-five minutes he stopped, drank some water and looked for marks on the trees ahead. He could make out an X cut into the bark of a tree about fifteen yards ahead. He smiled. He'd married a bright, resourceful woman.

Approaching the mine, he marveled that Eliza had found it at all. From above, the rock walls were so overgrown with lichen and fungi that, coupled with overhanging tree branches, the entrance was all but invisible. He came around in a slow circle, his footsteps slower and more cautious now. If there were any illegal activity going on up here—as unlikely as it seemed—there was no point alerting anyone that he was coming.

When he spotted the gate from about ten yards out, Mike came to a complete stop, waiting and listening for nearly a minute. When he heard nothing, he walked up to the gate and listened again. Just the natural sounds of any forest after rain; the stretching of wood as it dries, the calls of birds enjoying the feast now accessible from the softened earth. Mike examined the freshly oiled hinges and the new padlock on the gate. He smiled. His wife didn't miss much—there were a good few fellow officers he could name who wouldn't have noticed the details she had reported.

One last listen changed nothing, so Mike took the bolt cutters out of his backpack, positioned the jaws on the mid-point of the shackle and with one practiced movement, cut through the metal. He replaced the cutters, took out his flashlight and pushed the gate open. The narrow route between the rock walls hardly looked inviting as it descended into blackness.

The forest sounds faded as he walked, replaced by drips of water, following channels cut by rain through the rock over millennia. About thirty yards in, the path took a turn to the left. He looked behind him. The glow of daylight was just visible from the entrance. He'd replaced the batteries in the flashlight before leaving the station. He shook off a brief stab of fear, an echo of an ancient superstition warning humans to stay clear of the unknown. Especially in the dark.

A few steps more and he stopped. The path was blocked. The rocks looked like they'd been there for a hundred years. In fact, that probably wasn't a bad guess, mused Mike, as small collapses often blocked corridors near the entrances of old mines and this one looked like it had been out of use long before his father was a boy.

He squatted down and thought. Mike Breckland had a logical mind, and although he was sometimes accused of being slow to make a decision, he was never suspected of cutting corners. Although he was keen to get back into the sunlight and fresh air above, there was a puzzle here. Why would someone oil the hinges to get into a mine that was blocked? And why would they buy a padlock to keep anyone else from doing the same? He swallowed some water, chewed gum and worried away at the mystery.

After a few minutes had passed, he could only come up with one possibility: there must be a way through the blockage. He stepped closer and slowly played the powerful beam of the flashlight over the old rocks in front of him. A fine layer of dust covered most, but not all, of them. On one side, some of the dust had been scuffed away, as if someone had climbed them. Mike followed the path with his flashlight until he got to the top. Then he stepped closer, hoisted himself carefully onto the first foothold he could find and examined the rocks closer to the top. On this side of the pile, they were smaller than many of those around them.

Mike reached out a gloved hand and took hold of the rock nearest the ceiling. He pulled slowly and it came away easily. Looking at the rock's neighbors, he could see they would be fairly easy to remove. He was about to do so, when—unexpectedly, terrifyingly—there was a soft groan from the darkness beyond. Mike slipped down the rubble, landed hard on his side, rolled, unholstered his gun and pointed it alongside the flashlight. He was glad no one else was there to witness the way his hand was shaking.

"What the hell?" he whispered, then raised his voice. "Police officers. Who's there?"

His voice echoed into nothingness and absolute silence descended once more, all the more unnerving after the single sound he had heard. Or had he heard it? Could he have spooked himself so badly he was imagining things? Hardly. Mike was many things, but wildly imaginative was not one of them.

"Answer me," he called, and waited. The groan, when it came again, was softer, barely more than a ragged exhalation. It sounded like someone in pain.

Mike holstered his weapon. He could manage the flashlight or the gun while climbing, but not both. There was no way he was going over that pile of rocks in the dark.

He pulled the rocks away quickly now. Whoever or whatever was beyond knew he was coming, and didn't sound in any kind of condition to prove a threat.

When he had cleared all of the loose rocks away, there still wasn't space to crawl through and Mike had no intention of getting wedged underground. He looked at the gap. A child could have gotten through, maybe. He remembered Eliza's concern about the boy. He was beginning to think she had been right to be worried, just maybe not in the way she had thought.

Quickly scrambling back down, he took the bolt cutters from the backpack. The rocks below the loose ones would not be so easy to move. A few blows from the cutters dislodged a fairly substantial piece of stone, which Mike managed to prize out and send tumbling down behind him. The rocks around it were freer now, and half a minute's work left a gap big enough to get through. Mike took a breath and crawled forward into the darkness.

The slope on the other side was steeper and Mike cursed as he slipped and slid down to the floor. He felt his pants tear on his left leg and his right shoulder took most of the impact when he landed. He was winded for a moment and crouched until he could catch his breath.

The flashlight had rolled away a few yards. Mike followed the beam and tried to make sense of what he was looking at. Blood was dripping slowly onto the rock floor a few yards ahead. He stood up, grabbed the flashlight and aimed the beam upward. The blood was coming from the end of a leg. The foot was missing—from the look of the stump, it had been sawn off with a serrated knife. Mike had seen similar injuries before. There was an amateur-looking tourniquet tied tightly above the severed foot to staunch the blood loss. The other foot was also missing, but the injury was older, maybe a few days. Both hands had been removed.

Mike took a step forward. He gasped as he stood on something and stumbled. The flashlight revealed one of the missing hands. Two of the fingers had been gnawed to the bone—Mike guessed his appearance must have scared away the rats responsible. The other missing limbs were in a similar condition. He swallowed hard and took a couple of deep breaths before moving forward again and shining the light onto the victim's face.

Mike had no way of recognizing the man propped against a pile of rocks in the corner. His face was so badly beaten, it was just a mass of swelling and livid blue, black, green and yellow bruises. He was breathing, but the breaths were shallow and irregular. Mike put two fingers on his neck. A faint pulse, but weak.

"I'm going to get help, ok? I'm a police officer. Just hold on, we'll get you out of here real soon."

At first, it seemed the man was too far gone to be able to respond, but as Mike turned to go, he spoke, although the words were too faint to hear. Mike went back and leaned in, putting one ear close to the cracked, blood-caked lips.

"Sir? What did you say?"

There was a pause while the man took a few more shuddering breaths. Then he raised his head slightly and spoke again, the words almost too soft to hear.

"Never thought the boy had it in him." Then his head fell forward onto his chest.

Mike scrambled back over the rock pile. At the top, he turned.

"I'm leaving my flashlight for you. I'll be right back when I've radioed in for help." As Mike ran back up to the entrance, taking out his radio and, waiting for enough signal to call in, he wondered why the man hadn't tried to escape, as terrible as his injuries were. Then he remembered the angle of the man's legs as he sat awkwardly on the heap of rocks in the corner. Both knees had been smashed.

***

Eliza Breckland's class was reading Catcher In The Rye. A bit of a stretch for some of them perhaps, and she'd had to deal with a few nervous giggles initially at the frequent use of the word 'crap', but she knew the novel would grab them after the first couple of lessons. Eliza's English Literature teaching method had been tested over many years. She simply had a student read a section aloud, then another, then another. Everyone had to do it. She knew this risked exposing the slower readers to ridicule from their peers, but her own attitude to those who struggled was so supportive and encouraging, it shamed those who might be unkind. That approach wouldn't have worked with every teacher, but Eliza was so well-liked that she rarely had to raise her voice. A disappointed look from Mrs. Breckland was worse than the slap they might get at home. A smile from her felt like winning a prize.

Amy—the girl currently reading—had a beautifully expressive voice, and Eliza closed her eyes, feeling that magic sensation as she felt the class come together as a whole, wrapped up in Holden Caulfield's adventures, allowing themselves to fall under the spell of a master storyteller. So when that spell was abruptly broken, she was initially reluctant to rejoin the real world. Moments like that were rare in a teaching career and she felt a sense of loss as she looked at Amy, her finger on the page where she'd stopped, her mouth hanging open.

"What's the matter?" she said, then she followed the direction of Amy's gaze. Through the long low window at the side of the classroom she saw Mike. He was standing in the corridor, waiting patiently to catch her attention. *He still looks good in that police uniform, even if he has put on a few pounds.* Eliza was about to smile when she saw the expression on his face. And the color of his skin. He looked paler than she'd ever seen him. And, when she finally met his eye, she knew immediately that whatever he'd come to tell her wouldn't be something she wanted to hear.

"Sit down, Amy," she said. "Silent reading to the end of the chapter, everyone." She went outside, closing the door quietly behind her. As she did so, Mike's radio crackled into life. He held up a hand and walked away a few paces, his voice quiet and urgent.

"Oh, Jesus," he muttered. He didn't immediately come back to her, so she walked over to him. He looked up as she approached. His eyes were sympathetic, but his mouth was drawn into a thin, hard line.

"I went up there," he said. "You were right to be worried. Found the boy's father in a critical condition."

"His father?" she said, taking a quick glance back at the classroom. The boy's head was tilted toward the book, but his eyes were shut tight. "How bad are his injuries? What happened?" She gestured toward the classroom. "Do you want me to tell him? Or is that something you need to do? Might be better if I'm here, he knows me."

Eliza turned and started to go back to the classroom, but Mike gently took hold of her elbow.

"Eliza," he said. She stopped. Turned. Looked at him.

"What is it?" she said.

"You followed him up there. Think about it for a second."

Eliza hesitated. Mike was looking at her strangely—a mix of love and pity. She realized he was struggling to find the right words. Finally, he settled for the unadorned truth, although his voice stayed gentle.

"He did it," Mike said simply, nodding toward the classroom.

"But he couldn't-." She stopped. Remembered the incident with Davy Johanssen. "He wouldn't." She tried to take another step, but Mike gently pulled her back.

"His own father said he did. He had been tortured. I'm sorry, Liza." He waited, looking at her. Dimly, as if from a great distance, she was aware of noise from the classroom.

Her eyes filled with tears and she swallowed. She knew Mike too well.

"There's something else, isn't there?"

Mike rubbed her upper arm as she hugged herself, feeling suddenly cold. The noise from behind her grew in intensity and she started to turn.

"I just had an update. He died before we could get him to a hospital, Liza. I have to bring the boy in on homicide charges. The mother is being notified. I need to take him now."

Suddenly, the door of the classroom was flung open and a group of pupils rushed out, talking over themselves in their rush to get to her.

"Mrs. Bre—,"

"He's collaps—,"

"Get a doctor—,"

"He's bleeding, I think he knocked h—,"

Eliza rushed in, closely followed by Mike. There was a huddle of children at the back of the class. They cleared a path for her. One girl was trying to cradle the head of her most promising student. The suspected murderer. While Mike called 911, Eliza bent down and held the hand of the thin, pale, gifted boy as his body jerked uncontrollably, his lips drawn back from his teeth, a mixture of froth and blood running from the corner of his mouth.

Chapter 16

New York
Present Day

"Scrooge?" said Seb2 as Seb watched fire trucks scream up the hill toward the fiery beacon that used to be Cubby Vashtar's house.

"I couldn't think of anything else," thought Seb. "Anyway, it worked, didn't it?"

"It worked," said Seb2. "The look on his face when he couldn't shoot you…"

"I know," thought Seb. "Brilliant. Mee's gonna love hearing about it."

He turned away from the conflagration and Walked, appearing in the hallway of their Mexico City apartment. He could appear anywhere he liked, of course, but after Mee had screamed and dropped whatever she was holding the first few times, they agreed it would be better if he gave her a little more warning.

"I'm home," he said. The TV was still on in the other room. "Mee?"

"In here," she said.

Seb walked through. Mee was sitting on the couch, hugging her knees. Seb could see she'd been crying. He knelt down beside her and kissed her neck.

"What's up?" he said. She didn't say anything at first, then motioned toward the TV. Seb twisted to look at the screen. It was the New York apartment building, the fire now finally out. All the windows had exploded during the blaze and there were black streaks on the walls. A reporter was speaking, but Seb's attention was caught by the headline at the bottom of the screen: **Single mom and four children die in apartment fire.**

Seb didn't know what to say. He reviewed the last few hours in his mind. He felt as if he was suddenly caught up in someone else's nightmare.

"What happened, Seb?" said Mee. "Why couldn't you save them?" She started crying again.

"I did save them," said Seb. "I was there, I got them out. They..." He looked back at the screen in disbelief. Footage from earlier in the evening was now playing. Body bags were being lifted into an ambulance. The last one was tiny. Seb looked away.

"We need to talk," said Seb2.

"What?" thought Seb. His mind was whirling, images of the children following their mother through the apartment as he shielded them from the heat. The sudden hope in Felicia's eyes when he had unfolded the wings and given her the strength to save herself and her family. The look of disbelief on the Fire Chief's face when he'd seen the survivors emerge.

"I know what happened," said Seb2. "Bring Mee. She needs to hear this."

"*Bring* Mee?" thought Seb. "*Bring* her? What do you mean?"

"Tell her to hold your hands, close her eyes and trust you," said Seb2.

Seb looked at the TV one more time, then back at Mee, tears still falling slowly from her eyes.

"Ok," he thought. "Ok."

***

Mee sat on the bench in Richmond Park, dozing. It was July or August, judging by the sun, which was hot enough to make her begin to sweat slightly. For a moment she felt relaxed and content, forgetting the turmoil she'd been in only moments before. This felt like a dream. A pleasant one.

Richmond Park was the place she'd brought Seb on their first date, years ago. They'd drunk gin and made out in the sunshine. He was a good-looking American songwriter helping her band record an album. She had found him a little too…intense for her taste at first, but something about Seb had brought out the devil in her. When she saw that slightly furrowed brow, that day-dreaming expression…well, it made her want to be naughty. And when Mee wanted something…

She sat up straighter suddenly, opening her eyes fully. How could she be here? She'd accepted it for a few seconds, her consciousness totally enmeshed with the illusion around her. All her senses told her she was in London, in the park, in the middle of a sunny day. But she *knew* she was sitting on a couch in Mexico City, holding Seb's hands. Then she remembered the fire, the horrible moment when she'd realized the young family had died, that Seb hadn't saved them. That had been bad enough, but the couple of hours following had been worse, when Seb hadn't come home. If he had got there too late to save them, he would have come straight back, surely?

"I saved them," said Seb. She turned to her right. He was seated beside her, his expression serious, worried. His brow was furrowed—her mind flashed back to that first afternoon. She'd smoothed the worry lines from his forehead and licked his nose. Now, she watched the corner of his mouth twitch slightly. He remembered it too.

"Where are we?" said Mee. "I mean, I know where we are, but we aren't, are we? We can't be. Can we? You said only you could Walk, that you couldn't take me with you. Has that changed?"

Before Seb, could reply, she held a hand up.

"Wait a second, it's too quiet. There's no bugger here." She looked around to confirm her suspicions. Not a single figure in sight. Just her and Seb. She nodded, beginning to feel a little more in control.

"So, we're not here. This isn't real. This is where you have your little chats with Seb2, right?"

"Right." It was Seb's voice, but it came from her left where, a second earlier, there had been no one.

"Shit," said Mee, and turned, shading her eyes against the sun. She had once dated a twin, so she didn't expect to be freaked out much by seeing a second version of her boyfriend. When she did see him though, she was *completely* freaked out. She stared for a few seconds, then leapt off the bench and turned to face the pair of them.

"Oh no," she said. "That just isn't right at all." The twins had been identical, but she had never had any trouble telling them apart—they were different people. But Seb and Seb2 were *the same person.* They might be sitting differently, even wearing different clothes (Seb was in jeans and a T-shirt, Seb2 in a linen suit), but it made no difference. They were *both* Seb. She shuddered.

"Just so you know," she said, "I will never, ever get used to this."

The two Sebs looked at each other. Neither seemed to know how to respond.

"Ok, ok," she said. "Let's not get tangled up in the weird implications of the shit going on in your head. Just explain what happened in that fire."

Seb2 stood up.

"To do that, I have to show you a little of what's happened to me. To us. Me and, er, Seb." He indicated his double, then moved his arm to take in their surroundings. The pond, the trees, the sky.

"This is a template. It's a strong memory, so it's easy to retrieve and use. Much of what has happened since Billy Joe first gave us Manna has happened *to* me. I had no control, I could only react to changes occurring to my body, brain and consciousness. That changed after I absorbed the Roswell Manna. The process by which Manna communicates and integrates with me has accelerated. Now, there is very little separation between me and the technology."

He paused and registered the confused look on Mee's face.

"Um, at first, the Manna worked automatically. I—Seb—er, *we* had very little control. We could direct it and it would work for us. That's the level Manna use has worked for humanity for centuries. But the Roswell Manna isn't a small part of Seb. It's so intimately weaved into his DNA, it almost *is* Seb."

Mee shifted uncomfortably on the bench.

The Seb sitting next to her took her hand. "I'm still me," he said.

"I know."

Seb2 paced up and down as he spoke.

"I—Seb—have integrated with the technology. But that means some of what I can do is automated. It's considered so basic that I don't have to consciously control it."

"I'm lost," said Seb. Mee squeezed his hand in agreement. Seb smiled at her. "I should warn you, he's probably going for an analogy or a metaphor right now."

"You got it," said Seb2. "Ok, try this for size. When we are children, we learn to walk and talk, but once we've got it, the process becomes automatic. You don't have to think about putting one foot in front of the other, transferring weight while staying balanced, keeping momentum going in the direction of travel, constantly adjusting to compensate for uneven terrain. You just do it."

"Right," said Mee.

"Ok, now imagine you never learned to walk at all. You didn't even know it was possible. In fact, no one in the world could walk, we all just dragged ourselves around on our stomachs. Then one day, you wake up, pull yourself outside, decide you're going to drag yourself along to the store and suddenly, you're walking. It's impossible, it's some kind of miracle. Everything looks different from your new point of view. You make it to the store in five minutes, when it used to take you hours. And you can walk whenever you like now, you don't have to think about it. You just do it."

"Ok, with you so far," said Seb.

"Good. But here's the thing. For you now, walking—or Walking—is the most natural thing in the world. It's almost as natural as breathing. You just do it, right?"

"Yes," said Seb.

"But *how* are you doing it?" said Seb2.

"I don't know," said Seb. "It's like you said, I'm not *consciously* making it happen."

"Exactly," said Seb2. "And that's the situation we're in right now. If I go back to my metaphor—the crawler who is suddenly walking could only gain a full appreciation of what's going on by going back to how he was before and trying to work out the stages that might lead to being able to walk. Even then, he might never get it right. He could spend years trying. It might be dangerous—he could fall."

"Why would he even bother?" said Mee. "He can walk now."

"Yes," said Seb2. "And that's what happened tonight. That's what I need you to understand so I can explain what happened. It was an automatic process, as automatic as walking—physical, human walking—is to all of us. It happened without any conscious decision on our part, because it was natural, expected, inevitable."

"Now you're starting to lose me again," said Seb. "Answer this: did we save Felicia and her children tonight?"

"Yes, we did," said Seb2.

Mee let go of Seb's hand.

"But they died," she said. "I saw it on TV."

"Yes," said Seb2. "They died."

"What?" Mee and Seb both spoke at the same time.

"You're both right," said Seb2. "Think about *how* you Walk. The process. What are the stages involved?"

Seb thought for a moment.

"I think of the place I want to go," he said, "and various options appear."

"Hold on," said Seb2. "You *think* of where you want to go. Now, it just so happens you knew last night's neighborhood pretty well. You're a New Yorker, you could picture somewhere close by. But you didn't know the building itself, right?"

"Right," admitted Seb. "The nearest place I could think of was Jonny's CD Emporium. About a block away."

"And yet when you decided to Walk, the options available were all of the apartment itself, right? Because every piece of information available about the local geography was available to us. Unconsciously, I accessed that information so fast it seemed instantaneous."

"Ok, makes sense," said Seb.

"Hold your horses, you two," said Mee. "What options? What do you mean?"

Seb turned toward her on the bench.

"When I decide to Walk, I choose where to Walk to. I try to find somewhere safe and inconspicuous. I can't get hurt, but if I appear from nowhere in front of someone's car, they could hurt themselves or someone else."

"Ok, makes sense," said Mee. "So, how do you choose? I mean, what do these 'options' look like, exactly?"

"I'll show you," said Seb2. He pointed up toward a few wispy clouds drifting over the skyscrapers of central London. A picture formed. It was Darknells, a club in Los Angeles where Mee, Seb and the rest of Clockwatchers—her old band—used to hang out sometimes after shows.

"Wow," said Mee. "I can't believe it."

"I know, said Seb2. "Impressive, isn't it?"

"No," said Mee, "I mean I can't believe they still haven't changed that carpet since Dan threw up on it."

"Oh," said Seb2. He looked back at the sky. More pictures appeared. Each one showed the identical scene. They were more like high definition webcam feeds than pictures, as people were moving around in them—dancing, drinking, talking, laughing, shouting. As Mee looked closer, she could see they weren't actually identical at all. There were tiny differences. In ten of the images now floating above them, there were three bar staff struggling to serve the crowd. In the eleventh and twelfth, a fourth staff member had joined them. The crowd itself showed subtle differences—the color of a shirt here, the lack of a jacket somewhere else. A poster advertising an acoustic night was missing in two of the images.

As she looked for the differences, more images appeared. Now the differences were easy to spot. The first showed the same club, but empty, closed. Yellow and black police tape sealed the door. Another image showed an apartment with people sleeping in it. Another was a storage area with barrels of beer and crates of drinks. The dimensions were the same as Darknells.

Mee squinted upward.

"Are these all…?"

"…The same place?" said Seb2. "Yes."

"But how? Are you showing me the future? The past? What?"

"All of these images are real-time," said Seb2.

As more images appeared and flickered across the sky, Mee frowned in confusion. There were many tiny variations on the apartment, the same for the storage room. Some of the images appearing now were blank, completely featureless.

"What does that mean?" said Mee.

The images stopped appearing. Seb2 pointed up at one showing the storage room.

"Darknells was never built there," he said. The bar above might be the same, might be different, but they never opened a club downstairs." He pointed at the apartment. Mee could see a couple asleep in bed. It felt disturbingly voyeuristic.

"They might be the owners of the building above," he said, "or—just as likely—they're renting the place, there's no bar above, it's an apartment building." He pointed at one of the blank images.

"There's no building at all above that space, otherwise we'd be looking at the foundations right now. New York might not even exist there."

"New York might not what?" said Mee. A joint appeared in between her fingers. It was already burning and smelled intoxicating.

"I know you too well," said Seb2, smiling.

"Humph," said Mee, taking a drag nonetheless. She inhaled the sweet smoke before blowing a cloud upward toward the disconcerting pictures. She looked at the spliff. "This isn't real, of course." She felt the familiar rush. "Bloody feels like it is."

"Tiny changes in your brain chemistry," said Seb2. "Safer than the real thing, as I can be very precise, tailor it to your particular synaptic connections, without any danger of side-effects."

"Well," said Mee, taking another long drag at her imaginary spliff, "it's good shit, whatever it is. Now, go on."

"New York exists in hundreds of thousands of almost identical incarnations," said Seb2. As he spoke, about twenty images above him went back to showing Darknells, the clubbers inside dancing and drinking.

"Incarnations?" said Mee. "What the bollocking hell are you on about?"

"The multiverse," said Seb2, trying, and failing, not to look amused at Mee's language.

"Oh, give me strength," said Mee. "Explain, but remember I'm just a simple female who can't grasp advanced scientific concepts."

"Yeah, yeah, very funny," said Seb beside her. Mee had dropped out of university while studying physics. She was far better informed on the subject than Seb.

"All right," she conceded, "I know about the multiverse. A hypothetical concept positing the existence of parallel universes, possibly infinite, possibly finite. If there is such a thing, and we're merely living in one universe within the multiverse, then…oh." She looked up at the images, thought about the way Seb Walked. "Oh," she said again. "It's true, then."

"Yes," said Seb2. "Can't tell you whether it's finite or infinite, though. I can't see an end to the alternatives, but that doesn't prove it either way. What were you going to say?"

"Mm?" said Mee, inhaling more marijuana. She realized her mind was absolutely sharp again—none of the usual dulling of her senses was occurring any more. "Oh, you bastard."

"I need you focused for a minute," said Seb2. "I'll make the next one a doozy, ok?"

Mee shrugged and flicked the spliff away. It turned into a butterfly and flew off across the pond.

"Oh, very clever," she said.

"You said if the multiverse hypothesis were true, if we really were living in one universe within it, then—what? What were you going to say?"

Mee got up from the bench. Despite the warmth of the sun, she crossed her arms and rubbed them as if she was cold.

"I was going to say, it takes a lot of the fun out of science. Some people would say it takes all meaning out of it."

"Why?" said Seb, standing behind her and putting his arms around her.

"Because we can only investigate, test, create hypotheses about the universe we inhabit. Any conclusions about the fundamental basis of reality are unlikely to hold true for other universes. Although…"

"Although?" said Seb2.

"Although, when the multiverse was just a theory, the theory only needed to be internally consistent. There was no way of testing it. But you are the proof, you can show it to be true. This changes everything. You need to get in touch with the scientific community, this needs to be investigated properly." She suddenly stopped short and walked away from Seb. When she turned to face him and Seb2, there were tears in her eyes.

"Let's just skip the theorizing for a minute," she said. "A woman and her family died tonight. Died horribly in a fire. And you say you saved them. Please, please, tell me what happened."

"I'm sorry," said Seb2, "I was trying to. Now that you understand a little of what is going on—probably more than we do, to be fair—you must realize what happened."

Mee stared at him for a few seconds, then moved back to the bench and sat heavily, as if all her strength had just been sucked out of her.

"Oh, God," she said, "you saved them in another universe."

"What?" said Seb.

"Yes," said Seb2.

It was Seb's turn to get up and pace.

"Another universe?" he said. "You mean, Mee's right, Felicia and her family died? They all died in that fire? I failed them?"

Seb2 looked calmly at him.

"You didn't fail," he said. "I've had more opportunities to get used to this than you. I've gradually been learning what happens when we Walk. And I've begun to understand the implications. The Felicia in our universe? She was dead before we got there."

"What?" said Seb. He was pale. "What do you mean?"

"In the first few hundred apartments we saw before you Walked, the roof was about to cave in and crush them. It happened as we Walked. You remember the apartment we Walked to?"

"Yes," said Seb. She was alive—they all were. The kids were playing. She was cooking."

"There was no fire in that universe," said Seb2. "Not tonight, anyway. But it's the same deathtrap of a building, so it'll likely burn down another time. And we won't know about it."

Mee stood, took Seb's hand and led him back to the bench. They both sat down.

"From the first apartment, we Walked into the burning apartment, but it wasn't in our universe. It was the closest one where the roof hadn't collapsed. It was the universe where we had a chance of saving their lives. Which is what we did."

Seb sat silently for a long time. When he spoke again, his voice cracked slightly. He felt utterly exhausted.

"And Cubby?" he said.

"Who?" said Mee.

"The landlord," said Seb. "We stopped him in that other universe, but not ours?"

"No," said Seb2. "That was our Cubby. In our universe. He's a changed man. His apartments are about to get a makeover."

"But in all the other universes…?" said Seb.

"We can't be everywhere," said Seb2. "But we've intervened in similar situations 489 times in the last year. And this is the first time we've had to move into a neighboring universe. It's gonna happen, but it's gonna happen *rarely*." He glanced upward. All the images faded away. "Something I need to tell you."

"What?" said Seb.

"There's only one of you in all of the universes we've touched when Walking," said Seb2. "You—me—Seb Varden—you exist in some, you're dead in some, you were never born in others. But this universe is the only one where you became a World Walker."

Seb sat completely still.

"So I can't be everywhere, I can't help everyone. And when I choose to save someone, I'm effectively allowing the same person to die in every other universe. And there's only me?"

Seb2 nodded slowly.

"I need to sleep," said Seb. "Come on, Mee."

Chapter 17

New York

A soft bell from the speakers flanking Mason's computer screens alerted him to an email. It was a zip folder containing the piece of code he had commissioned from Wickerman. He picked up his phone. All of his calls were routed through a complex, ever-changing route of satellites and IP networks and completely untraceable.

"Yes?" The woman who answered the call was CEO of the largest cellphone corporation in the world. She had appeared on the cover of Time, repeatedly turned down offers of a political future from both major parties, neither of whom had been able to guess as to where her allegiance lay. She was quick-thinking, mercurial, consistently ahead of the game. Her status in the business world as a brilliant maverick had been sealed when her company had released a cellphone that retailed for the price of a large coffee. Media and industry pundits had confidently predicted her downfall, only to eat their words when the phone sold in its billions worldwide. The apps subsequently released made back the revenue—and more—initially sacrificed by selling the phones so cheaply. The apps were priced similarly to other apps, but the percentage her company took was far higher than her competitors. But, by then, she had captured nearly sixty percent of the world market, and no one was in a position to refuse her terms. She was a proud, successful woman who took orders from no one. No one other than Mason.

When his email arrived in the account only he used, she brought a board meeting to an early halt and read it alone.

A piece of code for an update you are due to release next week. Make sure it is included.

She shivered. Six years ago, Mason had transferred Mark, her severely disabled brother to a state-of-the-art facility in Colorado. When she had discovered Mark had been moved without her knowledge, she'd been horrified. A helicopter had arrived to take her to him and, fearing for her brother's life, she had obeyed telephone instructions and boarded it. On arrival, she'd been shown around a superb hospital, equipped with the latest medical technology. Mark was in the hands of the very best doctors, his needs taken care of by friendly, caring staff. He was happy. But once she was left alone with her brother, his smile suddenly disappeared as his body began to twist in agony. He lost control of his bowels and bladder and began screaming, his hands smacking his own face in pain and panic. She screamed herself, punching the emergency button. No one came. She ran for the door. It was locked. Her cellphone rang.

"Watch carefully," whispered a voice.

As quickly as it had started, Mark's fit ended, his hands unclenching, his body relaxing. He sobbed in bewilderment and she ran to him, holding his hand.

"He has a good forty years left with proper care, I'm told," came the whisper.

"Who are you?" she said. "*What* are you?"

"My name is Mason. As to *what* I am, I am your brother's keeper. You currently control the biggest communication network in the world. I need access to it. You answer to me, now."

"What's to stop me going public, going to the press?"

"Go ahead. Mark will die slowly, in terrible pain and nothing can be traced to me. In fact, all the records here, and on your own computer, show that you requested, and paid for, his transfer to this facility. I suggest you think of his future."

And now, for the first time since Mason had become the true power behind her throne, he was finally giving her an order. She thought back to last weekend, when she'd spent a day with Mark in the beautiful garden in the facility where he was the only patient. He'd been happy, calm and pain-free.

She dialed an internal number.

"Andreas? One more piece of code coming through before we release the update. Let me know when it's ready."

***

The code worked as it was supposed to. Over a period of ten days, Mason watched the results on his screens. All over the world hundreds, then thousands, then hundreds of thousands, millions and, finally, over a billion cellphones updated their operating systems, appearing as pulsing colors on the international map he was monitoring. The coverage wasn't absolutely complete, but he was willing to gamble Varden and Patel hadn't abandoned civilization completely. Both of them were city people by birth and inclination.

Mason had used voice recognition software before, but the program he had commissioned for this task was sophisticated, subtle, and different from other similar programs in one crucial respect. It wasn't interested in the *spoken* word. It was only interested in the *sung* word.

Over the last few months, Mason's software had imported every recording Meera Patel had ever made. There was plenty available—early demos, an EP, three albums with her band and some unique content online, either recorded at live shows by fans, or put out by the band itself. Then the search algorithm online had found recordings posted in the last twelve months. Mason immediately attempted to track the geographical origin of the recordings, only to find a maze of broken links and dead ends convoluted enough to challenge his own precautions. Maybe even more so. Where Patel—or Varden—had got their sudden mastery of technology from, Mason had no idea.

All of the recordings made up a database which was passively listening to each call being made by the billions of phones now using the updated operating system. Whenever a call was in progress, the code kicked in and checked for any singing in the background. Male voices were filtered out first, then any recordings which *perfectly* matched the database, as these could only be recordings. Frequency range was the next filter, as Patel's singing voice was husky and low, which put her into a group encompassing approximately thirty percent of female singers. The next filter was far more complex, identifying formants and phonemes favored by Patel in her songs. Any close matches were then compared with the database to find musical similarities in timbre, tone, sustain, pitch, and intervals. Only 0.00027% of all calls reached the final set of filters which were the most sophisticated of all, attempting to identify and match traces of dialect, cadence and vocabulary.

The real genius of the code Wickerman had supplied was its two-way nature. It fed information back, but also *learned* as it received feedback from the voice recognition software. It got quicker and more accurate with every call. As a result, on the eleventh day after activation, a red light winked onto the screen and an alarm sounded. Within a few seconds, two more lights appeared as the software automatically zoomed in on the location. Another three lights appeared, then the alarm stopped, meaning the source was no longer being listened to. Six cellphones had signaled that they'd heard the singing voice of Meera Patel.

Mason noted the time and the location, then waited. Three days later, nine cellphones triggered the alarm again. The area pinpointed was less than a mile from the first. Mason picked up the phone.

"Westlake," he whispered, "assemble a team. No Manna users." If he sent a team including Users, Varden would know they were coming before they got anywhere near. "How long?"

Westlake didn't respond immediately. He was doing some quick mental calculations. He'd need a team of eight and they'd be coming from various parts of the country.

"Fifteen to twenty hours," he said, allowing a couple of hours for unforeseen delays.

"Do it," whispered Mason. "And go via Ford's place. You're going to need to look like someone else." Despite his distrust of Ford, the man's ability to alter his own, or another's, appearance was unparalleled.

"Who do I need to look like?" said Westlake.

"Sebastian Varden," said Mason. There was a long pause at the other end of the line. Westlake clearly remembered cutting off Seb Varden's head and watching it, and his body, being burned down to a blackened skeleton. But no one questioned Mason, not even a special-forces trained multiple murderer like Westlake.

"Yes, sir. And our final destination?"

"Mexico City."

Chapter 18

Las Vegas

The sun was just beginning to dip below the horizon. In Walt's yard, the buzz and dart of hummingbirds and the scuttle of lizards were the only sounds. Walt sat in a garden chair watching the shadows lengthen and the last of the light slide away. He hadn't had a drink all day. He checked his pockets one last time. Passport—not in his own name, naturally—his wallet, and a small key. No phone—it was on the desk in his office. He stripped all his credit cards out of the wallet and tossed them into the trash, leaving $3,000 cash which he rolled up and put in his pants pocket.

Walt looked back at the house. Gaudy, opulent, over-the-top, its design based on the Taj Mahal, for thirty years it had stood as a beacon of bad taste in a neighborhood famous for it. He admitted he felt a sentimental attachment to the hideous piece of architecture. Leaving it was one of the sacrifices he was going to have to make. The car, much of his money, and the few friends he'd made in Las Vegas—none close—were others. He felt few regrets about any of them. The true sacrifice was yet to happen, and it was a sacrifice he would have to keep making if he was ever to be truly free of Mason.

Standing slowly and taking a few deep breaths, Walt began to still his mental processes and bring an intense focus to bear on the earth a few feet in front of him. Over eighty years of practicing with Manna along with his own innate ability had made his talent formidable.

The obscure but powerful use of Manna he was using had been first demonstrated to Walt by Sid Bernbaum, his mentor. Sid had taken him out to a junkyard one night and told him the Jewish legend of the Golem. According to the ancient stories, the golem was a creature made of clay and given 'animus', or spirit, by the will and prayers of a rabbi versed in the mystic arts hidden in the Torah. Walt had watched Sid concentrate, hold out a hand. A creature had formed itself from the dirt. A clumsy, misshapen being, its passing acquaintance with the human form only emphasizing its monstrousness. It had lived for a few minutes, then collapsed back into the dirt which had given it shape. Walt had practiced night after night for months until he began to match, then supersede, the realism and longevity of Sid's golems. "The accepted word these days is 'homunculi'," said Sid, "but they will always be golems to me."

Now, over seven decades later, Walt's homunculi were so advanced they could last for many hours and obey simple instructions. He'd even had one open the door to a pizza delivery guy once, but the resulting scream confirmed Walt's theory that a homunculus could never look truly human.

His mind emptied of every thought other than the image of what he wanted to create, Walt held out his hand and watched the earth begin to spiral upward like a miniature cyclone. As it grew, a core formed. There was no need for a skeletal structure. The entire creation was made in two stages. The first was workmanlike, rough, merely throwing matter together to produce the right dimensions with which to work. The second stage was more like sculpture, taking the rough figure and carving out fine details, adding color, expression and because it needed to mimic humanity, a capacity for movement as if it possessed the skeleton and musculature of its artist.

The whole process took just under eight minutes, more than double the time Walt normally spent on a homunculus. He was sweating slightly as he looked at the figure before him. The creature's skin was ashen gray, its eyes dark shadows. He'd added clothes to it, but had only used shades of blue and gray. The cameras in the house were black and white, so there was no need to waste energy trying to reproduce the ivory of Walt's shirt or the burgundy of his Italian loafers.

Walt had the creature walk up and down the yard a couple of times. He certainly walked like Walt and even aped some of his mannerisms—the way he pinched the bridge of his nose when tired, or stretched his upper back muscles by holding his arms behind him, hands clasped together. The creature couldn't speak. No need—there were no microphones in the house to pick up sound.

There was only one final gift to give, but Walt hesitated. What he was about to do, no one ever did. It would leave him exposed in ways he hadn't experienced since he was a boy. But if he didn't go ahead, Mason would inexorably track him down and kill him. Slowly.

Walt closed his eyes and offered up a silent prayer to the god he'd stopped believing in ninety years previously. Then he walked up to the homunculus and took both of its coarse, lumpen hands in his. He closed his eyes, opened up the channel through which Manna had flowed in his body almost all of his life. He let all the Manna he possessed course through him, leaving through his fingertips, filling his creation with enough to keep it going—he hoped—for twenty-four hours or more. Long enough for him to get away. Long enough for him to be on a plane to somewhere quiet. Somewhere simple. Somewhere Mason would never care quite enough to go looking for him. Somewhere it wouldn't matter that he had just got rid of every last vestige of Manna in his entire body. Somewhere he could avoid the temptation of looking for more.

Walt would have to learn to exist like a normal mortal again. He could no longer slow the aging process. If he wanted something from someone, he couldn't just get it. He'd have to ask. And if someone wanted to kill him badly enough, he'd almost certainly have to die, since all of his defenses had gone. Although over a hundred years old, he had a body a fifty-year-old would be happy with. Barring accident or violent murder, he might live for another fifty years. If he walked away from trouble. The problem was, he was about to do the opposite.

Walt nodded at the homunculus. It nodded back and stepped back into the house, sliding the door shut behind him. Walt watched it fix itself a large bourbon, grab a cold beer and head toward the office. It hesitated as it reached the door, looked out toward where Walt was standing in the dark, flicked off the light switch and was gone.

Walt climbed the fence at the back of the yard, cut through a neighbor's garden and strolled up to the guard house at the perimeter of the gated community.

"Hey, Pete," he said as the overweight security guard looked up from the ball game to register his approach. "I need a taxi to the airport. Phone's dead. Can you call one for me?"

"Sure thing, Mr. Ford." As the man dialed, Walt peeled two hundreds off the roll in his pocket. Pete's eyes widened when he saw them. Walt leaned close enough to get a nose-full of acrid aftershave; the kind often used to mask worse odors beneath. He only flinched a little.

"I'm still at home, safely tucked up in bed," he said. "You haven't seen me since I drove in this evening. Ok?"

Pete eyed the hundreds greedily, then tucked them in his breast pocket, smiling.

"Sure thing, Mr. Ford. No problem. No problem at all."

McCarran airport was busy, and Walt knew a man his age, wearing a suit and traveling alone would be unlikely to be remembered. He bought a one-way flight to London Heathrow, from where he could transfer to almost anywhere. He had used his key to open a luggage locker rented weeks ago. The carry-on bag he now wheeled behind him contained old books, mostly maps and atlases, tying in with his passport which announced him as Professor Patrick Henson, an academic specializing in mediaeval cartography. Nestled between the pages of the most fragile-looking volumes were bearer bonds amounting to a little over two million dollars.

As the fasten seatbelt light went off and the charming stewardess brought him a bone-dry Jerez sherry, he felt a little of the pressure lift, but not much. He believed he was out of Mason's reach for now. Maybe forever. But he had no Manna. And if he wanted to stay hidden, he could never Use again. He was normal. A nobody. And he'd decided he had to contact Meera. Had to warn her that Mason hadn't given up. That he was coming for her. And if Seb Varden really had died that day at the building site, or if he wasn't there to save her when Mason came looking, her life would become a living hell.

So Walter Ford, an old man in a middle-aged man's body, a man who had once helped kidnap Meera and had helped Mason's men kill the people who had sheltered her, was now going to try and find her and offer his help. Which, now that he had no power at all, was a pretty worthless offer. It was a crazy plan. But

Walt knew he was going to see it through. Something had finally changed in him. As he looked out at the moonlight on the clouds above Nevada, he wondered if this was how it felt to have a conscience. If so, it felt like shit.

Chapter 19

Upstate New York
Thirty-four years previously

Boy knew Pop must be dead, of course. No one could survive that much damage. He'd lasted a few days, though. And after the screaming, after the threatening, the promising and the begging he'd suddenly gone quiet and not spoken one more word. He had just watched Boy silently. Boy didn't care to look back. Their eyes had met a couple of times and Boy didn't like what he'd seen there. Pain, fear, that was to be expected, but there was a gleam that looked a little bit too much like pride.

It had started with a headache again, but this time, it was different. He had been a passenger in his own body when he'd taken Pop to see the old mine. When he'd hit him with the rock. When he'd dragged him down into the tunnel. When he'd used a heavier rock to smash first one knee, then the other. The first knee, Pop had woken up fast, screamed then passed out. The second, he'd just lain there. It made an odd sound when that rock came down. It sounded like when Mom broke a handful of dry spaghetti before boiling it.

Boy had watched it all play out like a movie. As Pop had followed him up to the mine, Boy tried desperately to move his own limbs, run away. Nothing worked. The worst thing was, he knew who was in control now. He recognized him. It was his own fault. He had let it grow, given it its power. All these nights lying in bed, listening to Pop hit Mom, waiting for his turn for a beating, he had started to dream of hitting back, hurting Pop. Maybe even killing Pop. Mom had taught him right from wrong, sure enough, and even Huck Finn had a conscience, preventing him doing whatever he pleased with no regard for the consequences. Huck had never thought about killing anyone. But Boy had. And now that part of him was in charge and all he could do was watch. Watch and wait until he got control back.

Halfway home from the mine that first day, his body had stumbled, stopped and leaned against a tree, his head hanging, breathing fast. When he'd looked up, he was back in control. He'd sat down heavily on the forest floor, only just managing to lean to one side before throwing up. He'd sat there for two hours. Thought about calling 911. Maybe Pop could recover from what he'd just done to him. Then what? He'd report Boy—have him arrested? No. He'd kill him. Maybe torture him first. More likely, he'd take it out on Mom and make Boy watch.

Finally, he stood up, wiped dried vomit from the side of his mouth and went home. He said nothing to Mom. When Pop didn't come home, even after the bars had closed, she just assumed he'd gone off again. It happened every few months. It was good and bad. It was good because Mom and Boy got to spend a few days and evenings together talking, reading—even laughing. It was bad because when Pop came home, he was worse than usual for a while. Last time he came back, he'd broken three of Boy's fingers with a pair of pliers. One at a time, making Mom watch. Because "you two don't look like you missed me any". Mom had taped Boy's fingers together with a popsicle stick. He'd told his teacher he'd been playing baseball and had messed up a catch. Mrs Breckland had looked at him questioningly that time—he had been limping the week before and she'd see him wincing when he moved around during class. She hadn't asked him outright, though. Boy was more careful still after that. It wouldn't be good if anyone ever found out. Not for Mom. Not for Boy. Not for Mrs. Breckland, maybe.

***

He was floating on his back. He could feel warm sunlight on his face. He had a straw in his mouth, sunglasses perched on his nose. His eyes were closed and he could hear the "beep beep beep" of a garbage truck reversing somewhere nearby. He was so relaxed, he didn't want to open his eyes. He heard voices, but they seemed far away at first. Then they got closer and clearer. He recognized Mom's voice. Her voice was small and shaky. The other voice was authoritative, calm. They were talking about him, about…

Boy bit down on the straw slowly. It moved slightly and he realized it went all the way down his throat. His instinct to gag kicked in and he fought it, keeping his breathing steady. He remembered the headache suddenly coming on in the classroom. The cop in the corridor had looked at him. Boy knew it was over. They must have found Pop.

He opened his eyes a tiny bit, then shut them again. Not sunglasses—a piece of tape across the bridge of his nose, securing a tube which went up his right nostril. The sunlight was a powerful lamp. The sound of the garbage truck was the machine next to his bed. He ached all over, felt terrible. And he needed a drink.

He tried to say Mom's name, but nothing happened. His lips wouldn't shape the words. He tried to open his eyes again. Nothing. He'd lost control again.

"- Didn't tell us anything, really. But the biopsies from last week, combined with the blood work are conclusive, I'm afraid."

Boy tried to speak again, but again he failed. How long had he been unconscious if they were talking about last week? He'd read through enough medical journals to know what a biopsy was.

"When can I take him home? And please, *please*, take that thing off of his wrist."

Mom's voice was so tired. Boy's arms moved. He tried to stop them. It didn't work. When his left arm had moved a few inches, it stopped suddenly. He felt metal on his wrist. He was handcuffed to the bed.

"I'm sorry, that's a police matter. Once I've passed on my conclusions, I'm sure they'll release him. But you need to prepare yourself for a rapid decline in your son's condition. The cancer is too far advanced for us to operate."

"What do you mean?" said Mom. Her voice rose a little. She stopped herself and Boy sensed she was looking over at him. Her voice dropped to a whisper again. "That's my son. I want to know exactly what's wrong with him and what can be done about it. Don't sugar-coat it, I need to know what's happening. I'm not going to get hysterical, you needn't worry about me making a scene. Just give me the facts."

The doctor sighed. He wasn't the first man to underestimate Mom. Because she was quiet, pale, a little jumpy, nervous in company, people often made poor assumptions about her intelligence. She rarely put them right, but this young-sounding doctor was quickly recalibrating his treatment of her. Wisely, he decided to dial back the patronization a whole bunch.

"It's brain cancer. The tumor is so large that trying to remove it would kill him. It's grown even since he was admitted. Nothing we can do can stop it now. His condition is terminal."

If he expected an outburst of grief or anger, he was disappointed. Mom's voice was level and quiet.

"Will he wake up?"

"It's highly unlikely. Theoretically, it's possible, but at this stage, his body is using all its resources to fight the tumor."

"How long?"

Boy heard a scrape as the doctor pushed his chair back and stood up. There was a rustle as he consulted the charts at the end of the bed.

"Don't prevaricate, just tell me."

The doctor coughed. He probably hadn't expected 'prevaricate' to feature in Mom's vocabulary. Boy sensed some more hasty recalibration going on.

"A few days. Possibly a week."

The silence lasted about a minute. The doctor cracked first.

"It's probably not my place—wouldn't hold up in a court of law, but—,"

Another silence.

"Go on," said Mom.

"Well, I - I'm beginning to specialize in brain surgery. I keep on top of all the latest research. The new computers at some of the bigger hospitals, they can show images of the brain in more detail. We are starting to understand which regions of the brain are used to control motor functions, which are associated with memory, which respond to optical or aural stimuli. Some of the work done has been tremendously exciting. In Austria, they've managed to—."

He broke off again. "Sorry, I'm rambling," he said. "It's an exciting field." He coughed again, nervously, remembering who he was talking to. "I stayed behind after a few of my shifts. Took a closer look at your son's x-rays. The tumor is pushing at the medial prefrontal cortex and angular gyrus regions of his brain. No one can say with complete confidence what that means, but it's likely that empathy, accountability and morality are being affected."

The scraping sound. He'd sat down again.

"What I'm saying is, I don't think he could be held responsible for his actions. If the tumor was effectively 'turning' off significant areas of his brain, we could no more blame him for his actions than we could blame a bear for killing a salmon. The tumor did it. Not your son."

Another long, long silence.

"Thank you," said Mom. "And Doctor?"

"Yes?"

"There's something else I need to ask you about. Is this hereditary? Have I—or my husband—passed this on to our child? Would it pass on if—,"

Boy heard no more. He realized he must have slept again. He woke at one point and heard Mom crying softly. Then her breathing deepened and she began to snore. He had no idea how much time passed after that, but when he became aware again, there was another voice in the room, a female voice.

"You pray, ma'am?"

"These days, yes. Yes, I do. Too little, too late, maybe."

Boy knew Mom had been raised Catholic, he'd seen the Bible hidden in one of the cooking pots, but Pop 'didn't hold with that preachy crap' so it was rarely discussed. She didn't go to church, and when Boy had occasionally asked about religion, she'd said he would have to make his own mind up about it when he was older. She had grown up questioning many of the beliefs her parents had instilled in her, but she said she couldn't dismiss faith entirely. Now, she'd brought a Bible into his hospital room. The doctors had given up; science had failed her son. Boy wasn't surprised she was turning back to God. He'd never told her he'd jettisoned the idea of a deity years ago. Mom might be hoping for a spell in purgatory followed by eternity in heaven for him, but he was a hundred percent sure his consciousness would turn off like a lightbulb and that would be that.

"There's always hope, ma'am, always. Hope, faith and charity. The power of Jesus to heal his children is a wondrous thing. A wondrous thing indeed. Amen."

Boy found himself disliking the unknown woman. He tried to open his eyes, but his body wasn't interested in cooperating.

"You go to church, then?" Mom didn't really sound interested. She sounded exhausted. Boy guessed she had been at his side ever since he'd been admitted, however long ago that was. She was probably grabbing a few hours' sleep at a time, between visits from nurses and doctors. Maybe she was glad of any kind of conversation.

"Yes, ma'am, I surely do. A beautiful place. Proclaimerz congregation of Light and Love. That's Proclaimerz with a 'z'."

Mom obviously couldn't think of an appropriate reply. She made a noncommittal sound.

Boy had heard of Proclaimerz, of course. It had started a few years back when Rev Jesse Newman had arrived. He was an evangelist preacher fresh out of a midwest seminary, full of ideas, energy and according to Pop, bullshit. Boy suspected Mom agreed with Pop, as she never spoke up for Rev. Jesse in Pop's absence. Jesse Newman arrived with some significant financial backing, that much was clear. He'd rented an old industrial building, converted it to a church that could hold nearly 1,500 people. It was a mile out of town in a run-down area—he could hardly have picked a worse location. No one thought he would attract more than a handful of church goers. But then he started appearing on TV commercials every night offering praise, prayer, healing and a reminder of God's eternal wrath against the wrongdoer Wednesday evenings, Saturday mornings and three times on a Sunday. Wrongdoers, according to Rev. Jesse Newman, were those who didn't attend Proclaimerz Mega Church on at least one of the aforementioned occasions on a weekly basis, and ponying up a decent chunk of change to support the "ongoing mission".

If Boy could have rolled his eyes, he would have. When he was a little younger, he assumed the "ongoing mission" referred—like his favorite show—to a continuing search for other civilizations, other galaxies. But Rev. Jesse showed no signs of boldly going anywhere. Which was a pity, because something about the evangelical preacher's smiling tanned face always gave Boy the urge to punch it. At the time, he couldn't have explained why. But he didn't need to be able to spell 'hypocrite' without feeling uncomfortable whenever he saw Rev. Jesse in the back of his chauffeur-driven car, making his way to church, driving past the poor folk walking the half-mile from the nearest bus stop, their last few dollars saved for the collection plate. No one could deny the incredible energy and charisma of the man though, and those qualities seemed to convince vast numbers of people to turn off their rational and critical faculties in his presence.

"Rev. Jesse is a real man of God, ma'am, a preacher like I've never heard in all my years. And he has the true gift of healing."

Boy knew what was coming next, and his heart sank. Surely Mom wouldn't? He had heard his own death sentence pronounced and it had almost been a relief. His life had often seemed hardly worth living before the tumor changed him. After it had taken control, he had committed terrible acts, done things he could barely have imagined. Whether he or the tumor was responsible for the violence was hardly the point. There was only one sure way to make it stop.

"A healer?" Mom's voice sounded just a little brighter. Boy felt suddenly, crushingly sad for her. She wasn't ready to give up yet. She hadn't been able to accept the inevitable as he had.

As the two women talked, he faded away into sleep. Last he remembered, they were plotting to get him out of the hospital and over to the church. Boy offered up a small prayer of his own, to the god he didn't believe in: *please let me die first.*

Chapter 20

Mexico City
Present Day

Seb woke at 5am. Beside him, Mee had moved past the high-decibel snoring stage into the barely discernible breathing that meant she was deeply asleep. She had a wonderfully pragmatic approach to problems. If they could be solved, she'd try to solve them. If not, she wouldn't. Either way, she never lost sleep over it.

Seb got out of bed, stretched and walked slowly around the small apartment. He had struggled to get to sleep, and when he finally had, images of Felicia and her children snapped into his mind, their faces distorted, burning, screaming, looking to him for help. He knew the only sane response to his current state of mind would be to sit, to contemplate. To enter into that alert, compassionate state of mind he had first practiced in his teens, and allow his thoughts, fears and regrets to surface and be acknowledged, losing much of their power over him in the process.

He glanced at the meditation stool leaning against the piano. Turning his back on it, he pulled on some clothes and walked out into the pre-dawn city. He wasn't in the mood for forgiving himself.

Walking in the gray-blue light, the streets as quiet as they ever were in Mexico City, he allowed his thoughts to center on his limitations. He was as close to a super-being as Earth had ever known. Invulnerable, able to travel huge distances almost instantaneously and manipulate matter at a sub-molecular level. All without breaking a sweat. And he had saved lives since escaping from Mason with Mee. Many lives. And yet, the reality of the multiverse meant that unimaginable numbers had died at the same time as he saved others.

He realized with a guilty shock that he was much more upset about the death of this universe's Felicia than he was about the others who must have died while he was helping in this—his home—universe. The earthquake in Honduras, for instance. The families he had saved from the rubble would have been buried alive in countless other universes. He had not been there to save them. And yet, somehow, the loss of life in other universes didn't seem quite as real to him. Then he remembered the family he had saved hours before. They were in a neighboring universe, but because he had been there, had met them, they were now every bit as real to him as anyone else.

Seb turned into the warren of alleyways leading into the Iztapalapa district. Iztapalapa had grown from a few houses in the 1970s, to one of the most densely populated areas in Mexico City. No real urban planning meant some residents still didn't have access to clean water. Crime was a problem, drugs, prostitution and murder a part of life for the two million people crammed into its streets. Yet Seb loved walking through the district, talking to people, drawn to the intense sense of community he found there. His own reluctance to belong was thrown into sharp relief by the families he met for whom their community was—literally—central to their survival.

Seb remembered watching the Semana Santa parade the week before Easter. Three million people had squeezed into the streets of Iztapalapa to celebrate the passion of the Christ. Some had dragged full size wooden crosses, even going so far as being nailed onto them when they reached their destination. Groups of sweating men carried floats bearing religious icons, flowers and statues, so huge and heavy they needed forty or more people to lift them. Seb had watched it all with a mixture of horror, envy and hope. Something in him was drawn to the powerful feeling of love between these people. It was palpable. And yet, why torture themselves in the name of religion? Why deny themselves food—when they already had so little—to pay for the extravagant floats, colorful clothes and overpriced plastic relics?

As he walked, Seb looked up into the scaffolding around a ramshackle building. The building was so unsafe-looking, he wondered if the scaffolding was the only thing holding it together. Five stray dogs had made their home on the wooden planks above him. They watched him pass, curious, but not interested enough to bark at the stranger. A few yards behind him, two figures peeled away from the shadows and quietly followed the tall, fearless figure who had so casually decided to walk through their territory.

Seb thought back to his adolescence, growing up at St Benet's, the Catholic orphanage. He had stopped attending Mass in his early teens, but he was familiar with the Bible, and saw how the Sisters and Father O'Hanoran had tried to live their lives guided by that old, much edited, mistranslated, badly interpreted, poetical collection of stories, history, poetry and parables. He respected their dedication and their obvious love of humanity, but could never bring himself to embrace a tradition that he found, at an institutional level, to be judgmental and forbidding, rather than loving and welcoming.

Father O had been an exception, and the reason Seb couldn't entirely jettison his childhood faith. He had taught Seb contemplation, the spiritual technique which had—he still believed—saved his life. And when pushed on theological matters, the old priest had always answered in the same way:

"Love God with all your heart and with all your soul and with all your strength and with all your mind, and love your neighbor as yourself."

Then he would chuckle and raise a bushy white eyebrow.

"You could always start at the end and work backward, of course. Know yourself, so you can have compassion for yourself. Then you might love yourself and be able to do the same for your neighbor. Whether you know it or not, you will be loving God at the same time."

Conversations like this had always made Seb uncomfortable. He flinched every time he heard the word 'God'. He had once challenged Father O to define it.

"Far wiser heads than mine have defined God," said the priest, his face solemn, "and I can make you one promise about those definitions: they're all wrong." Then he'd burst out laughing.

Seb smiled at the memory. He wondered what Father O would have made of Mee. He probably would have liked her. Certainly, being in a relationship had given Seb an occasional practical demonstration of how it felt not being the center of his own existence. It had always been a theoretical concept before, now he was living it. It hadn't been easy at first. His self-image as fairly selfless, open and giving had quickly been exposed as just that: an image. The reality was a little harder to come to terms with, at first. Seb realized he was selfish, proud, judgmental, unable to truly see life through the eyes of another. It was a shock, particularly when he could see that Mee—self-contained, forthright, loud Mee—was actually far more loving, accepting and selfless than he was. When the shock had worn off a little, he'd found himself letting go of some of his certainties. He'd taken the knowledge of his newly discovered flaws into his practice of contemplation and had let them wither in the light. If he hadn't nearly lost Mee, he might have taken her a little more for granted. But seeing her threatened had woken him up to the fragility—and importance—of human relationships. He might never feel that same sense of belonging that Father O, or the faithful who paraded during Semana Santa did. He could accept that now. But he had finally let another person in—and that was more than he had thought possible just over a year ago.

He stopped. The light was stronger now and there were signs that the city was waking. Not that Iztapalapa ever truly slept, but he had walked for an hour without having to dodge a cart, or move out of the way of a truck. He turned to go home.

Two men blocked his way. Both were armed—the one to his left with a machete, the other with a gun. Seb looked at their faces. They showed signs of heavy drug use—probably cheap cocaine. *Narcomenudeo* was the street trade that supplied coke and meth to residents of Mexico City. When it was difficult to shift product over the border in America, where the market was far more lucrative, dealers simply cut the drugs with roach poison, flour, laundry powder, and sold it to the poor in their own city. The cartels would sometimes clash in their pursuit of trade, and it was often the poorest neighborhood that took the brunt of the ensuing violence.

Seb slowly reached into his pants pocket and took out his wallet. The men were young—late teens, early twenties, perhaps—scared, and hurting for their next fix. He held the wallet out toward them. The two men looked confused. They expected fear, or resistance, not passive acquiescence. The one with the gun nodded at his friend to grab the wallet. Holding the machete threateningly in front of him, the man inched forward and grabbed the wallet. At the same moment, Seb stepped sideways and grabbed his arm.

The machete flashed down with an instinctive jerk of the man's arm and severed Seb's hand. It fell—still holding the wallet—to the ground. Panicked, the man with gun fired four shots into Seb's chest, then bent down to retrieve the money. As he did so, Seb's severed hand let go of the wallet and wagged a finger at the thief as if admonishing him. The man gasped and crossed himself.

"Oh, now you call on God," said Seb. Still holding the arm of the first man, who had now dropped the machete and started babbling, he grabbed the arm of the second man. Both men took a split second to process the impossibility of this, then stared at Seb's wrist. Instead of a wound gushing blood, a perfectly healthy hand projected from Seb's sleeve. With unconsciously comic timing, both men then looked at the floor, where the third hand was now running in circles around the wallet like a spider.

Seb used Manna to reach out and drain the last remnants of cocaine from their systems and turn off the addictive centers of their brains. The men felt it happening, looked at each other and back at Seb. The extra hand climbed up his leg, replaced the wallet in his pants pocket, then turned into an albino rat which ran up the street. As it rounded the corner, Seb heard the yelping of the scaffolding dogs as they spied a tasty snack.

"You're sick, you know that?" said Seb2. Ignoring him, Seb looked at the men. Now drug-free, they looked exhausted, terrified and under-nourished. Seb sighed and let go of them. He slowly reached into his pocket again and withdrew two one hundred-dollar bills, handing one to each man.

"Go get something to eat," said Seb. He walked back the way he had come, leaving his attackers staring at each other and shaking. Where were those men in all the other universes? Who might they kill or injure there? What was their life expectancy as drug-addicted thieves? He couldn't know, and he couldn't change it. He headed back to home, and Mee.

He made it less than a hundred yards before his head began to throb and he felt himself falling.

"Shit," he thought, then consciousness was sucked out of him like a spider up a vacuum cleaner.

Chapter 21

This time, the alien—Mic—wasn't alone. And the surroundings were a good deal more opulent than the Social Security office of his last visit. Although the constant background hum was still present.

Seb was sitting in a tan leather office chair at one end of a large, oval, highly polished mahogany table. The chair was oversized, very comfortable and smelled of fresh leather. A series of buttons under the fingers of his right hand tipped it backward, forward, side-to-side and even inflated a lumbar support which pushed reassuringly into the small of his back. This was obviously a CEO-level office chair, announcing its superiority to other office chairs in every carefully crafted detail. This was a chair that had made it to the top and had no qualms about letting inferior chairs know about it. This was one smug chair.

"Are you finished?" said Seb2.

Seb spun the chair 360 degrees while tilting it as far back as he could.

"What?" he thought. "I mean, have you ever sat in anything this comfortable?"

"This is not a dream," said Seb2, "and we have company."

Seb pushed and held a button and the chair slowly and quietly tilted him into an upright position. Between his feet, three long glowing faces appeared at the other end of the table. As the chair reached the end of its movement, the faces were followed by the upper half of bodies.

The three aliens were wearing business suits. Two of them were 80s style, shoulder-padded, 'Dynasty'-era power suits, the other a quiet pinstripe that was beautifully made. Probably hand-tailored. Which prompted the question: where did eight-foot tall aliens go for their suits?

"You're not quite fully conscious yet," said Seb2. "Being summoned like this has an effect that takes me a minute or two to counter. So don't say anything stupid."

The pinstriped alien in the middle spoke. This time, the voice came out of speakers discreetly mounted in the ceiling.

"This one is appointed to induce formalities," it said. "Remembrance. This one is Mic. Seeing you fortuitous and grateful, Seb Varden."

"It's like talking to someone through google translate," thought Seb.

"Introductions commence," said Mic. "This one takes name of Louise, this one Thelma." As he spoke, first the figure to his left, then the one to his right glowed more brightly for a fraction of a second.

"Mee's favorite film," thought Seb. "Interesting." Then he noticed the aliens' chairs. If his chair was at CEO level, theirs were designed for royalty. About two feet wider than his, they also towered above him, giving the already tall creatures even more of a height advantage. His own chair's air of smugness had dissolved and been replaced by an inferiority complex.

"Clear to see the power dynamic here, then," thought Seb. "Who are they? What do they want?"

"Bad news on that score," said Seb2. "I only just worked some of it out while you were getting yourself shot back there. Hang on."

The scene seemed to freeze as Seb2 closed down all parts of Seb's brain and body not immediately needed, meaning they could have a conversation in under a second, that otherwise might have lasted minutes.

"I analyzed every packet of data they sent during our last visit, but none of it makes sense. A great deal of information came across through Mic's Manna, but it was as if it were prepared for someone else."

"What do you mean?" thought Seb.

"The first data packet was a formal greeting, that was clear enough. They were expecting you. Only, they weren't. Not really. They were expecting someone else, but you were the only candidate remotely similar to what they were looking for, so they summoned you."

"Don't particularly like being summoned," thought Seb.

"Yeah. I'm working on stopping that, but I'm not there yet. And we need to find out what they want. The data that came through after the introductions contained no information."

"What, then?"

"It was like a handshake, well, a billion handshakes. Like tab A trying to connect with slot A, only to find there was no slot A, only button Z."

"Oh, here we go."

"The Manna bursts were designed to be met with something reciprocal from you. Then—I think—they were primed to exchange information at the same time as upgrading us in some way. To facilitate communication, I think."

"Not sure I want to be upgraded right now," thought Seb.

"Well, that's the interesting part," said Seb2. "It's clear to me that the upgrade they were offering would actually be a huge step backward for you. It was as if they were offering you the chance to move from roller skates to a bicycle, but you were already flying a jet."

"So who were they expecting? Someone needing the upgrade?"

"I think so. I think it's the Roswell Manna again. Their Manna is old-school. Walt, Mason, the Order, it's operating just above that level. Your Manna is incompatible with theirs."

"Like trying to download vinyl," thought Seb.

"Good metaphor," said Seb2. "You're getting better at this. Anyway, this all means we need to try harder to communicate verbally. So let's try. I'll contribute if I have anything useful to say."

"I won't hold my breath, then," thought Seb.

"You realize—since I'm you—you're just insulting yourself, right?"

"Yeah, I know," thought Seb, "but somehow, that still doesn't make it any less fun."

His sense of time returned to normal. The alien introduced as Thelma tilted her head slightly toward Mic. When she returned to an upright position, Mic spoke again. Seb wondered if the tilting of the head was probably just for his benefit, as it was such a human mannerism. Their method of communication with each other was still a mystery. Possibly via Manna, or even color changes on their skin too subtle for Seb to pick up.

"Investigation. Hypotheses. Inconclusive. What status of species, Seb Varden? Human primary, yet other possibility through evolution. Primary most likely in this case to take next step. Yet your wrongness noted. What status?"

Seb took a deep breath. Communication was still going to be hit and miss.

"I'm human, yes. I share something with you—I also use Manna."

Both Thelma and Louise tilted their heads this time. Seb waited politely.

"Manna designation for process, subject/object manipulation, conscious evolution, yes?"

Seb tried to pick apart the sentence.

"Yes," he said finally. "I think so. But what is conscious evolution?"

No tilting of heads this time. The three of them just looked blankly at him. Well, their expressions might have been full of meaning to each other, but to Seb they were utterly blank.

"Guess you don't get to ask questions, then," said Seb2. "This might look like a meeting, but they brought you here, they're asking the questions and, until they've decided who you are, they seem to be treating you as an inferior."

"That seems kind of fair to me," thought Seb.

"Yes, on one level. But it implies a degree of inflexibility in their thinking. They were expecting Manna use of a far lower level than you possess, and so far, they've been unable, or unwilling, to adjust their expectations. The good news is, I've managed to hack their mainframe."

"You've WHAT?"

"Don't worry, they won't know a thing about it. Let's talk about it when we're home."

"Which is when, exactly? And how long will it have been for Mee?"

"I have a theory about that, won't be able to confirm it until we're home. But you're not going to like it."

The alien voice had spoken again, but Seb hadn't been listening. Seb2 replayed the sentence.

"Apology sub greeting previous inappropriate. Possibility experiment parameters altered. Request exchange now with Thelma, specialism advanced culture. Contamination suspected."

It was Seb's turn to stare blankly. The alien designated as Thelma slid off her leather throne and walked down the length of the table toward him.

"Another Manna approach," said Seb2. "Tentative, this time, cautious. I think you're supposed to let them in, allow them to have a good look around at our Manna, investigate how it differs to what they were expecting."

"They know my Manna is more advanced than theirs?" thought Seb.

"They suspect it. But they're not sure. That's why they want a closer look."

"I don't like the sound of the word 'contamination'," thought Seb.

"I hear you. I intend blocking them from seeing much at all, but I'll make my blocking look as though it's an automatic defense mechanism, out of our feeble human control."

"You can do that?"

"I hope so."

Thelma stood in front of him. Seb suddenly had an intense feeling that they were being watched.

"You feel that?" he thought.

"Yep," said Seb2. "Something else. Someone else. There's something weird going on here."

Seb looked at the 1980s-style power-dressed alien standing next to the boardroom table in front of him and decided not to comment.

Thelma reached out a long slender arm. Her wrist ended up about three feet clear of her jacket. Fingers longer than chopsticks stretched toward his hand.

Seb had a flashback to the moment when Billy Joe had found him dying in the Verdugo mountains. Then, he had thought the alien was just a hallucination brought on by blood loss. That was until the hallucination in question healed his wounds, took away his brain tumor and gave him superhuman powers. Now, he calmly let his own comparatively tiny hand be lightly gripped between those blue-gray fingers.

Whereas his encounter with Billy Joe had felt like an explosion of electricity detonating in his heart, reaching out in a split second to every extremity, this time, he felt nothing.

"I'm, er, showing them around," said Seb2. "It's working."

"What is?"

"Oh, you know, it's like that tour of Abbey Road studios we took in London. They showed us some of the Beatles recording equipment from 1967 and sold us a really overpriced mug, but we never got to see what we wanted to see—the control room in their most advanced studio at work, recording a current band."

"You've sold them a mug?"

"In essence, yes, that's exactly what I've done."

Thelma stepped away from Seb, dropping his hand. She half-turned to her colleagues. All of them tilted their heads. The silence went on for nearly a minute before Mic broke it.

"Data insufficient. Conclusion insecure. But Seb Varden came here."

"Like I had a choice," thought Seb.

"Seb Varden therefore species representative, although irregularities. Mic, Thelma, Louise discuss status, findings. Next meeting 427. Autopsy."

"Autopsy!" said Seb, half getting out of the chair.

Mic steepled his long fingers in that incongruously human fashion again before speaking.

"Syntax error," he said eventually. "Vocabulary novel and insufficient. Correct word, examination. Yes, examination. Have you right as rain in no time an apple a day."

"Is it just me?" thought Seb, "or do you think 'autopsy' was the right word for what they want to do to me?"

"I'd like to say you're just being paranoid," said Seb2, "but I have a bad feeling about all of this. I've retrieved some information back from the mainframe and I've left a—,"

***

Seb spluttered, his mouth full of water. Instinctively, he rolled sideways, bringing his face out of the dirty puddle. He coughed convulsively and pushed himself first to his knees, then to his feet.

He was standing on the street in Iztapalapa where he'd felt the sudden headache come on and been 'summoned' to see Mic and his friends. It was, he guessed, about half an hour before full dawn. His body ached.

Seb looked around him. Initially he thought he was alone, but then he noticed two small children, five or six years old, squatting in the shadows of a doorway opposite, their wide eyes following his every movement.

"Hi," he said, smiling. "Do you know what day it is—qué día es hoy?"

The two children, who had just witnessed a man appear from nowhere, six inches above the ground, before falling into a puddle, jumped to their feet and ran off down the street, wailing for their parents.

As Seb left the district and made his way up the hill leading for home, he passed a newsstand and checked the date. He'd been gone a week.

Chapter 22

London

The stewardess nudged Walt to wake him as the 747-400 began its final descent into London Heathrow. Pressing the button to bring his seat upright, he groaned aloud as his muscles complained. There was a twinge in the small of his back which clicked softly as he sat up. He was going to have to make a lot of adjustments to get used to living without Manna. Accepting muscular aches and pains, not being able to function effectively without proper rest. He was just beginning to appreciate the constant adjustments he would have to make.

Walt had, eventually, managed to get just over two hours' fitful sleep. His body ached from being cramped up in his seat, which appeared to be expressly designed to subtly torture the human body. He'd flown economy to avoid attracting attention, but as he kneaded his knotted neck between his fingers, he decided that if he was going to be tracked down and murdered while traveling, from now on it would be in the relative comfort afforded by first class.

As the wheels thumped down onto the tarmac, Walt peered across from his aisle seat, trying to glimpse his destination through the fog he assumed would obscure his view. It was 10am, early September, and London, contrary to his preconceptions, was bathed in glorious sunlight. If Walt had been a believer in portents, signs and a greater power, he might have decided this unexpectedly wonderful weather signified a change for the better in his own life. But he wasn't, so he didn't. He got off the plane and bought a winter coat, unsure how long he would be staying, but confident Great Britain would soon reassume normal service and attempt to freeze his balls off.

***

Having found a newly opened hotel which boasted the most comfortable beds in Europe, Walt hung the Do Not Disturb sign outside his door and slept for a solid four hours. Afterwards, he ate lunch at the deli next door, then found a bank, changed $10,000 and bought himself some new clothes.

By the time the evening rolled around, he knew jet lag—another new horror he had to deal with—was going to keep him awake until the early hours. He wondered if his homunculus was still functioning back home, then found to his surprise, that his previous life had already started to take on a slightly dream-like quality. The decision to break away from Mason was one of the only times in his adult life he'd made a decision with no clue as to how it might work out. For the first time he could remember, he wasn't reliant on or beholden to another human being. He was free. It scared the crap out of him.

He thought he was wandering the streets of central London with no real purpose, but as the bars began to empty out, he realized he was only a few streets away from his favorite casino. And he hadn't played poker for months. It had been years since he'd been there—he noticed the carpet was definitely new for one thing—but he still felt a little rush of pleasure as he walked into the Edwardian Casino, known locally as 'The Ed'.

The dealer gave him a curt nod as he sat down with his pile of chips. No effusive greeting as if he were an old friend. He definitely wasn't in Vegas any more. Walt was playing for fun, so he hadn't spent any time studying the tables and the players, just grabbed the first seat available. Texas Hold'em, probably the most successful export ever from the Lone Star state. No limit, the most popular variant, where you could bet your entire stack on the turn of a card if you chose to do so. Not a game for the faint-hearted.

The table was made up of a mixture of The Ed's regulars and some tourists. It only took about forty-five minutes' play to discern which was which. The glamorous, gregarious blonde to Walt's right talked as if she was a trophy wife spending her shopping budget, but her play so far had been calculating and effective. There were three players in their twenties who'd obviously had learnt the game online. They hid behind sunglasses and hoodies and screened out distractions with earbuds. Despite their similar appearance, two of them were nervous rookies, giving away far too much information with their bet-sizing. The third may have been professional. His play was loose and aggressive, getting involved with nearly every hand, but knowing when to lay it down and when to bet for maximum value. Two older Chinese men made up the rest of the table. Probably regulars too, but recreational players—willing to gamble, seemingly not worried about losing.

Walt's strategy involved playing at a sub-optimal level at first while he scoped the other players and, hopefully, gave them the impression that his own play was weak and predictable. After the first hour, during which he lost about fifteen percent of his initial £2000 starting stack, Walt started to play properly, while simultaneously trying to look as if he was just getting lucky. He stayed out of most hands with the blonde woman, and only played against the internet kid when he had the advantage of position, meaning he was the last to make a decision in each round of betting. He took several small pots, then an £800 pot, mostly from the Chinese guys.

At around midnight, the woman on Walt's right got up and went off to cash in. She was slightly up on the night, but had seen through Walt's efforts to appear to be a lucky tourist. A hustler knew another hustler when she saw one. As she left, she bent down to whisper in his ear.

"The guys at the next table," she said.

Walt looked over. A table of six—raucous, lots of laughter, lots of drinking.

"I see 'em," said Walt.

"They might invite you to a home game. They like to invite tourists with plenty of cash."

"Sounds like fun," said Walt.

"Maybe," she said, "but I'd pass if I were you. Just a bit of friendly advice."

As she left, Walt took a closer look at the next table. It looked like most of them knew each other. They were laughing at the biggest loser at the table, who seemed to be taking his losses in fairly good spirits. Judging from the cut of his suit and the Rolex on his wrist, a few thousand here or there wouldn't hurt him any.

After another hour, Walt had more than doubled his stack, and the internet kid had realized there might be easier pickings elsewhere. The table started to thin out, and Walt went to the cashier's cage to get his money.

As he turned to leave, the guys from the next table were putting on their coats and making their way outside. The one who'd been losing turned to Walt with a smile.

"Hi, I'm Danny," he said.

"Patrick," said Walt, shaking his hand.

"We're going to keep the action going at home," he said. "It's a ten-minute walk from here. Do you fancy a game?"

Walt started to shake his head and excuse himself, but Danny interrupted him, laughing.

"I saw Nikki whispering to you," he said. "She thought she could outplay us. She lost big. Now she warns everyone."

"I have nothing to prove," said Walt.

"Fine, no problem," said Danny. "No pressure. I mean, we like to fancy we're the best players in town right now, so no one would blame you for taking a raincheck. Nice to meet you anyway, Patrick."

As he turned to walk away, Walt felt that little buzz of excitement he used to get when pitting himself against another mature Manna user. He was a far better poker player than these guys could possibly know, and he was running good. What would be the harm? He called after the group as they pushed through the casino's revolving door.

"Hey, hold up," he said. "I guess a couple hours won't hurt."

Danny punched him playfully on the arm.

"Good man," he said.

***

Walt opened his eyes gingerly and sat up. He was curled up at the bottom of a hedge next to a half-eaten piece of pizza. His face was hurting, his eye throbbed and there was a line of dried blood under one nostril.

The rain had woken him. For a moment, he was glad he had been wise enough to buy the winter coat, then he realized it had gone. Along with all of his cash. Well, not quite all, he realized as he felt in his pocket for a handkerchief. There was a £10 note in his otherwise empty wallet. He dimly remembered a shout as he was rolled out of the car into the gutter.

"There's enough cab fare to get you home, Patrick. Now don't be a naughty boy and call the filth, or we'll have to come back and stick a big knife in you."

The 'filth' was slang for the police, Walt remembered that much from previous visits to London. Not that he could go to the authorities anyway, with his fake ID, no visa, and a cover story that would crumble under any serious scrutiny.

He used a nearby trash can to steady himself as he stood. It took all of his willpower not to shout in pain as he straightened out his bruised body. His ribs felt as if they'd been played like a xylophone by someone using steak mallets. Walt remembered lying on the floor after he'd been punched in the head. The city boys took turns kicking him in the ribs. He ran his fingers along his chest, pushing each rib carefully. Two of them made him cry out, causing a passing cyclist to speed up and cast a nervous look in his direction.

Walt limped to the nearest bathroom. He would never understand the Brits. They called bathrooms 'toilets', 'lavatories' or 'loos', then advertised them with the letters 'WC'. Then again, he mused as he washed the blood away from his nose and inspected his swollen eye, he had to admit he had yet to find a public bathroom in America which actually contained a bath.

The £10 they had left him would have covered the taxi fare, but Walt elected to walk. He knew it wasn't far to the hotel, and he felt like he needed to clear his head as well as check that his body was capable of moving effectively. His anonymity needed to be preserved, so a trip to hospital was off the table. He wanted his trail to end here in London. A new passport in the name of Nicholas Sherman meant the short life of Patrick

Henson would be over when he checked out of the hotel in a few hours' time.

As he walked, he was glad of the rain. It would help explain his disheveled appearance when he got back to the five-star hotel. A story about getting lost and tripping down some steps in the 'underground' or subway would be sufficient to allay the insincere concern of the concierge. The rain also hid the fact that Walt, to his horror, was crying. The tears were partly of pain and self-pity, but mostly of rage. Never a violent man by choice, Walt had, nonetheless, participated in some violence over the years. He was hardly new to it. It was just that this was the first time he had been fully—and helplessly—on the receiving end. He was shaking with shock, pain and white-hot anger. Every other thought was a fantasy, whereby he laid about those smug bastards with a baseball bat.

They'd cheated him. He'd outplayed them at every turn, but they consistently got lucky, defied the odds, and taken more and more money from him. It took him nearly two hours to work out how—to see the slight crimps put in certain cards by the dealer, the signals concerning hand-strength sent by the angle at which a glass was positioned on a coaster. He should have just shut up and left. That would have been the sensible route. But, having spent thirty years confronting cheats in Las Vegas, he'd called them out on it before he'd had time to reconsider. The next thing he knew, it was him against five young, fit guys. No problem, usually. Not anymore.

Walt glanced up at a sign. Wardour Street. The edge of Chinatown. Another ten minutes and he could soak in the tub, clean up, plan his next move and leave this ugly night behind him.

Then he felt it. Just a hint at first. He knew what it was instantly, but pretended to himself that he didn't. Thought he might take a slight detour. Because he felt like it. Nothing more than that.

Walt took the next side street. Halfway down it was a small green area, mostly in shadow, incongruous among the glass and concrete buildings it punctuated. As Walt drew closer, he could see it was some sort of memorial. There was a large stone with Chinese characters engraved on it. The grass around it was well-tended. Walt couldn't read it, but he knew—whatever it said—there was another reason this area had been kept clear. What he had felt nearly a block away was obvious now. It was if an ex-smoker had got a tiny scent of smoke, followed it and found a smoke shop full of free cigarettes. Walt stood in front of the patch of grass, feeling the massive buried storehouse of Manna just a few feet away.

"Jesus," he muttered. He went to walk away, but his feet disobeyed the signals from his brain. The Manna was having a huge physical effect on him. He knew it would mend his bruised ribs and battered face, take away every ache and pain. It would fill him with energy and power. Most of all, it would enable him to pay a visit to the city boys and show them why crossing him had been a bad idea. His fists clenched and unclenched as he pictured himself cracking small bones in their feet as he forced them to stand and face him. Barrington, Mason's enforcer, had discovered after a great deal of research, that certain foot bones produced almost unbearable pain when snapped, particularly if any weight was put on them. Walt pictured their faces, heard their screams.

He suddenly snapped his attention back to the moment. He wasn't standing any more. Somehow, he had unconsciously moved forward and knelt on the wet grass. He gasped as he felt the massive pull of the waiting Manna. All he had to do was place his palms on the ground. Just open himself up and let the Manna in. This would be the last time. He would just clean himself up, get his revenge, then he would never Use again. Just this one last time.

***

Walt opened the door to his hotel room and shuffled in, before collapsing against it and sliding down to the carpet. He was soaked through. His body ached. His face was numb. He was an old man. An old man with no Manna. He'd half-walked, half-crawled away from Chinatown and the easy fix waiting under his fingertips. What help could he possibly be to Meera Patel? What could he offer Seb—if he was still alive—that would be of any use to him? At least he was free, he reminded himself. Free to age, get sick, get beaten up, feel his faculties gradually weaken and then desert him. Free to die.

He gave in at last and sobbed like a child for a few minutes. Afterwards, he cleaned himself up and packed his small bag.

He splashed some water on his face and checked the damage to his eye in the bathroom mirror. Nothing a pair of sunglasses wouldn't hide. He'd buy a pair first thing. Then he'd take the tube to East London. That was where Meera had grown up. He knew it was a long shot, but he had to try to get a message to her somehow. Had to tell her Mason was coming after her again.

He walked back into the bedroom and stopped dead. Sitting in the shadows was a man who hadn't been there five minutes earlier.

Walt froze. How could he have been so naive to think he could escape someone as powerful as Mason? How could he have allowed himself to dream of a life of his own?

The figure leaned forward and switched on the desk light. Walt stared, unable to speak.

"Hello, Walt," said the man. "It's been a while."

It was Seb Varden.

Chapter 23

Mexico City

On the third day after Seb had disappeared, Mee decided she needed to stop pretending she could cope on her own. She invited Kate over to the apartment. Mee hesitated at the doorway, turning to the older woman.

"I know you're used to strange stuff, with all that Manna you chuck about, but you still might be a bit freaked out now, so keep your shit together, ok?"

Kate nodded, calmly.

"Duly noted, Stephanie," she said.

"Ok," said Mee. "After you."

Kate walked into the apartment. Small, tidy, anonymous, other than the piano and the musical equipment she could see through a half-open door.

Mee walked in. As she crossed the threshold, she gained about two inches in height, getting slightly slimmer as she did so. Her face lengthened slightly, the eyes, nose and mouth altering at the same time. Her hair became an unkempt wiry explosion. Mee stopped and looked at Kate quizzically.

"You don't seem surprised," she said.

"I'm not," said Kate. "Back at Casa Negra, the first time you Used, I saw you like this. Just for an instant. I couldn't work out how someone who said they'd never used Manna before could have such an effective disguise without it. And without me sensing anything. So, who are you, actually, Stephanie?"

"Well, first off," said Mee, walking over to the small table and pulling out a chair, "it's Meera, not Stephanie. Although I prefer Mee. I'm in trouble, Kate."

Kate looked at the young woman opposite. She had known her for nearly a year and, although she had hidden her identity, Kate was confident she knew the real woman beneath. There was no malice, no threat here, just a remarkable woman who needed her help.

"Ok, Mee," she said. "I think you'd better tell me everything,"

"In that case," said Mee, grabbing a bottle of Tequila, "I'm going to need a drink. And you are definitely going to want to sit down."

***

Three hours later, the tequila bottle was half empty, Mee was on her third joint, and Kate was still sitting quietly, her dark eyes unreadable. She had just learned that the messiah many of the Order had believed in—Seb Varden—was not dead, but living with Meera a few streets away from her. That twelve members of the Order had been killed trying to keep Meera out of Mason's grasp. And that Seb was now missing, for the second time in the past couple of weeks. Mee described the blackouts, but omitted any details about aliens, Social Security offices and power dressing.

"It's a lot to take in," said Mee. She reached forward and held Kate's hands. "I'm so sorry about Diane, Lo and the others who helped us in Las Vegas. They were good to us."

Kate nodded. Her skin was so dark that, as the evening had gone on, her features had blurred into the shadows around her. The only light came from a candle behind Mee, and it reflected the two lines on Kate's face where she hadn't wiped away her silent tears.

"I spent nearly a year with Diane," she said, finally. "She was a brave and holy woman. Holy in its original sense—whole, genuine, grounded. We chose slightly different paths, but we had much in common."

"Different paths?" said Meera. "I thought the Order hadn't split the way most religions seem to."

"I wish that were true," said Kate. "Unfortunately, any group of humans, however noble its intentions, seems—inevitably—to find reasons to splinter into new factions. The Order doesn't have as many sects as Christianity or Buddhism. Partly because the Order isn't really a religion. No book, no rules other than the golden rule—to treat others as you would wish to be treated. Just daily practice and a supportive community. But we've been around for nearly two millennia, and people often struggle with the apparent austerity of what we offer. The lack of religious trappings is attractive at first, but after a while, many start to yearn for them. It does no harm, so some branches of the Order look a little more like traditional religion. They use elements of ritual in group meditation, dress up on occasion, have a hierarchy with someone a little like a minister in charge. Diane's group was like that. They kept their practice simple, but Diane was very much the senior figure. You know the three words, don't you?"

Mee was confused for a moment, then remembered the words spelled out by stones in the garden of the Las Vegas Order.

"Yes," she said. "In Greek: Learn, teach, wait."

Kate smiled. "Right. Diane firmly believed that our founder was referring to a messiah figure with that final word. He or she would come along and show us our destiny, the goal of our organization. They weren't alone in thinking Seb was about to change everything."

"You didn't feel the same way?" said Mee.

"No," said Kate. She looked at Meera. "You don't want to hear this," she said. "We should be talking about what I can do to help."

Meera sighed and shook her head.

"You're helping already," she said. "There's nothing you can do about Seb right now. But you can be here with me and stop me from going crazy wondering what's happening to him. When he came back before, he said he'd been speaking to an alien, but it sounded more like he'd dropped acid and had a bad trip. Whatever it was, he had no idea he'd been away for longer than a few minutes, and he wasn't in control when he left—he wasn't Walking."

"Walking?" said Kate.

"With a capital 'W'," said Meera. "It's how he can get from one side of the planet to the other. It's instantaneous. Something to do with moving through the multiverse. Please don't ask. It was explained to me with pictures and my head still hurts."

"His use of Manna is like nothing I've ever heard of," said Kate, quietly. "Such power in one individual. It's no wonder most of the Order thought he was here to change the world. But you're more concerned about him than you are about yourself."

Meera laughed.

"I know. It's funny. He's been shot so many times I've lost count, burnt to a crisp at least once. He can take care of himself. But I still worry about him. I can't help it. I'm with you, by the way. I don't want him to be the messiah, I just want him to be my boyfriend. At heart, I'm a selfish numpty."

Mee swallowed hard. Kate—wondering what on Earth a *numpty* was—took the younger woman's hand.

"He came back before," she said, "he'll come back this time."

"Yeah, I know," said Meera. "He'd bloody better."

Mee insisted she felt better just listening, so Kate told her about the Order's dramatic drop in numbers after Seb had 'died'. Across the world, the majority of the Order's members had believed Seb's arrival meant their founder's words were about to be made relevant to the entire planet. Seb would bring Manna use out of the shadows, would show that it was a force for good, not evil, and the Order would teach the world how to Use in such a way that the self was put aside in favor of community. The world would enter a new era of cooperation and peace. When Seb was lost to them, thousands of men and women left the Order. Their belief system had been so reliant on Seb, it had shattered dramatically when his role had been abruptly removed.

Kate herself had once been part of a group whose numbers generally stayed between twenty and thirty people. They had all drifted away after the news that Seb had been killed by Mason. Kate had stayed, kept the building running, had carried on with her daily practice. Eventually, Meera/Stephanie had shown up asking to learn.

"I was surprised when you came," said Kate. "I feel as if the Order is finally finished as a global community, so I didn't expect anyone to seek me out."

"Finished? Why?"

"We've kept our use of Manna hidden over the centuries because of the way it has been abused by others—Mason and his ilk. But our hope was always to come out into the open and share our knowledge with the world. When the time was right. When history, spiritual growth and evolution finally rid us of people like Mason. When humanity had finally reached the point that no one needed to use power to exert control over others. That was our interpretation of the third word: 'wait'. But the predominant belief in a messiah meant that most of us thought he would bring about the right conditions for the next stage of the human race. When he fell, the Order began to crumble. I was about to leave when you showed up, go back to Innisfarne."

"Go back to where?"

"It's a small island off the coast of Northumbria. In Great Britain."

"I know where Northumbria is," said Mee. "My family may not have got out of London much when I was growing up, but we did own a map. You're not from there originally, though?"

"No," said Kate. "I come from Trinidad. But I moved to Britain in the 1960s. I had met someone in the Order and she had spoken of Innisfarne and of Martha, the woman who had founded a community there. I hitchhiked, walked about sixty miles, sleeping in fields or barns, then a fishing boat gave me a ride for the final few miles. What I found there changed my life forever. And I've been going back ever since."

"What makes it so special?"

Kate smiled.

"You'd have to go there, really. It's hard to explain. The size of the community varies. Sometimes there would only be a dozen of us, other times nearly two hundred. There are a few large buildings on the west side of the island, used for accommodation, a dining hall and a meditation hall. The rest of Innisfarne is quite barren, wild, and beautiful. The life is simple. We meditate together for an hour at 6am and an hour at 6pm. We don't use Manna to feed ourselves, we grow vegetables and cook them just as anyone else would.

"Innisfarne is small, but there is always the opportunity for solitude. Apart from coming together for meals and meditation, members of the Order spend most of their time alone, in silence."

Mee thought of her Aunt Anita, a nun who had chosen a similar life. The thought of deliberately seeking silence, day after day seemed frightening to Mee, although she had to admit, there was a tiny part of her that craved it.

"Martha encourages people to do as she does—spend six months to a year on Innisfarne, then go out into the world, travel, meet people, witness what is happening. Come back when you're ready. Stay another half year, then go out again. I've done exactly that for more than forty years now, and each cycle is different Each time I return *I* am different, yet the community is the same, the peace, the acceptance, the sense of timelessness underneath the unstoppable flow of time…"

There was a long pause. Meera didn't want to break the silence, but she found her thoughts going back to Seb.

"What's Martha's story?"

"Oh, no one knows who Martha is."

"What?" said Mee. "How?"

"It's a title, really," said Kate. "I had been visiting for eight years when the woman I had known as Martha introduced herself as Sarah. And another woman was calling herself Martha, organizing and inspiring the community in exactly the way Sarah once had. Three years later, Martha was another woman. I was Martha for five years. It meant no one ever got attached to a leadership position. All were followers."

"And what did the men think about it?"

"Oh, there were male Marthas too. Gender had nothing to do with it."

"Male Marthas?" said Mee. "I think that would take some getting used to."

Kate laughed. "You'd be surprised how quickly you forget about it. Anyway, it works. The community is always there, and for those of us who were drawn to it, it has become home. No messiahs, no goals, just the rhythm of the seasons and Being itself."

"You make it sound perfect," said Mee.

"No such thing," said Kate. " But it will still be there long after we are gone, I believe. The rest of the Order is in decline. Perhaps, in time, our numbers will grow again, but it will be based on the reality offered by Innisfarne and other communities, not reliant on a future day of reckoning when some god-like force will transform the world."

"Well, I know Seb will be glad to hear that," said Mee. "Wait." She screwed the top back onto the tequila bottle and eyed the older woman for a moment. "And anyone can go there?"

"Yes," said Kate. "You said you wanted my help. You know Seb can take care of himself. It's you who is vulnerable when he disappears this way. Come to Innisfarne with me. Until Seb finds out what's really going on."

Mee stood up and paced the small room while Kate sat silently, her hands folded on her lap.

"I can't think of anywhere you'd be safer," said Kate. "I'll go ahead, tell them a young woman will be joining the community for a while. It's not the kind of place where people ask questions. There's no internet, no telephones, very little contact with the mainland. You won't be found there—and Seb will know you're safe."

"Bugger it," said Mee, finally. "I've lied to you all this time and you come back with nothing but kindness. And when you make a suggestion, I don't want to hear it. I know you're right. And you know I know you're right." She looked at Kate. "And you're not smug, which annoys me."

Kate said nothing. Meera paced some more.

"Going with you feels like running away," said Mee, "and I never run away." She looked out at the lights of the city spreading out like a blanket and climbing the hill opposite. "But—as much as I hate the idea—while I'm here without Seb, I can't protect myself. If they find me, I'll have some warning. When they get close. I'll sense it—Manna has given me that gift. But if they're close enough for me to sense and they're Mason's people, it'll probably be too late."

Kate looked at her and let her complete her reasoning.

"So, like I said, you're right. While I'm here without him, I'm vulnerable, Seb is vulnerable. Mason only ever wanted me as leverage—to get to Seb. It nearly worked. I won't let it happen again. When Seb comes back, I'll tell him."

Kate nodded.

"I'll go tomorrow. When you come, take the train up from London. Pay cash. Get a bus to the coast. To

Logos Bay. There's a fishing boat, name of Penelope, you'll find her there at 5:30 every morning."

"Christ on a stick," said Mee, "what is it with religions and unsociable hours?"

Kate continued with her strategy of saying nothing and letting Meera do the work.

"Ok, you go," said Mee. "I'll follow once I've spoken to Seb. Just don't be freaked out when he suddenly appears on your island to see me."

"You going to be ok? Want me to wait and travel with you?"

Mee smiled at her and shook her head. "Nah. If Mason's been looking for me for the last eighteen months without any joy, how likely is it he'll get lucky in the next week or so?"

Chapter 24

London

Walt stared at Seb. There was no doubt. The man he had seen killed was now sitting in his London hotel room, smiling at him, looking for all the world as if he'd just dropped in for a friendly chat.

Walt fell into the other chair, opened the minibar and took out two miniature bottles of whisky, filling a glass and draining it in under five seconds.

"Sorry about burning your body," he said. "You'd just had your head cut off, so you wouldn't have felt it. And it meant Meera went free. But, for what it's worth, I am sorry. And I'm sorry about Bob. I didn't know Westlake was going to murder your friend, I didn't realize he was going to slaughter the Order back there in Vegas, I just—,"

Seb held up a hand and Walt fell silent.

"No need to explain anything," said Seb. "And no need to apologize. It might make *you* feel a bit better, but it's not going to bring anyone back. Besides, I wouldn't be here if I didn't know you'd changed. I know you've run. I know you're trying to make amends. I know you want to warn Meera."

Walt reached back into the minibar. There was no more whisky. He tried mixing gin and vodka. The resulting cocktail wouldn't win any prizes, but it burned his throat and made his eyes sting, so he was satisfied.

"It was a homunculus?" he said. "That's what Westlake killed?"

"Yes," said Seb.

Walt thought back to that morning. Remembered the way the man they had thought was Seb Varden moved, spoke and reacted like a human being. The difference between his power and Seb's was like comparing a Buster Keaton movie to the latest sci-fi epic.

"Ok," he said, "ok." He had half-guessed Seb was alive, so it could only have been a homunculus he'd seen die that day, but knowing that fact didn't stop his mind from reeling at the ability Seb had displayed.

"How did you find me?" he said.

"I've been with you since we last met in Las Vegas," said Seb. "I didn't go anywhere. And, for the sake of accuracy, you should stop calling me Seb."

"What?" said Walt. "Why?"

"I'm just a program," said Seb. "An app. A sub-routine. A virus—that might be the closest analogy. Seb2 transferred me to you back in Vegas. I've been dormant ever since, a tiny coil of genetic material at the top of your spine."

Walt shivered. "Seb2?" he said.

"Too long a story."

"I've been carrying you around?" said Walt. "You've seen everything I've seen, heard my thoughts? All my thoughts?"

"Relax," said Seb, "I haven't been spying on you. Like I said, I was dormant. It took a combination of triggers to activate me. And here I am."

"Triggers?" said Walt.

"Yeah. First trigger, you had to leave Mason, go on the lam. You've always chosen the easy way, the path of least resistance. But Seb thought you could change. Some might call it naivety, but since you've proved his hunch right, maybe not."

"You said there was more than one trigger," said Walt. He leaned over to the minibar, unscrewed a small white wine and started drinking it out of the bottle.

"I'd slow down, if I were you," said Seb. "It's not as if you're going to be able to use Manna to get rid of the hangover."

"The second trigger?" said Walt.

"Right," said Seb. "You've actually gone cold turkey. Given up Manna. Even under duress, when you had the chance for one last fix. You know you're gonna get sick, age and die just like regular folk, but you've done it anyway. Kudos."

Walt stopped drinking. Seb was probably right about the hangover.

"You don't talk like Seb did," he said, replacing the wine with a bottle of water, pouring it into a glass. He caught sight of the minibar prices. Central London hotel prices. Might be time to cash in another $10,000 of bearer bonds.

"Yeah—I don't have his memories, just a kind of cut-down, abridged version," said Seb. "I'm the same person, but without the unnecessary baggage. I can use Manna, but I'm far more limited. More like you were."

He pointed and the sheets on the bed reared up like a terrified horse, its head brushing against the light fitting on the ceiling. When he dropped his finger, the sheets fell back in an untidy heap.

"Well, I don't *use* Manna, as such," he said. "I'm made of the stuff."

"*Made* of it?" said Walt. "What do you mean?"

"Like I said, I'm like a virus. But I do have a physical presence, it's just sub-atomic. A few molecules of your body is roomy enough for me to stretch my legs around in. If I need more room—like I did just now, so I could get your attention—I can just expand, grow. I'm a lump about the size of a California raisin on your brainstem right now."

Walt's hand went involuntarily to the back of his head.

"It won't do any damage," said Seb. "It just means I can access your aural and visual centers. Much easier to communicate with you if you think you're seeing and hearing me."

"You mean, I'm not hearing or seeing you for real?" said Walt.

"Put it this way. If the hotel maid is standing outside your room, she'll think the poor old American guy in 114 has lost the plot. She'll hear you, but only you can hear me. Let's hope she's not listening, otherwise you'll be getting a visit from a very sympathetic doctor soon."

"Maybe I am losing my mind," said Walt. He suddenly threw the contents of his glass over the other man. Seb remained completely dry, but he stood up and showed Walt the stain on the chair.

"Maybe," said Seb. He sat down again. "You wanted to help Meera, you wanted to warn her about Mason."

"But now I don't need to," said Walt. "You're here—I guess the real Seb knows what you know, right?"

"In theory," said Seb. "I should just be able to drop a packet of information online, get a message to him almost instantly. But there's a problem."

The younger man looked lost for a moment. Suddenly, he lost some of his resemblance to Seb, looking younger, with a teenager's mixture of confidence and barely disguised terror.

"What's the matter?" said Walt. "What's happened?"

"It's Seb," said the other man. "He's missing. I've checked and double-checked. He's not here."

"Here?" said Walt. "London?"

"No," said the other Seb. "He's not *here*. Not on this planet."

Walt looked steadily at the other man and saw genuine, barely disguised fear in his eyes. He was telling the truth. Walt stood up, closed his case and put on his coat.

"Where does he live?" he said. "I mean where should we start looking?"

"Mexico City." The younger man stood.

The thought of getting straight onto another plane and heading back west was hardly an attractive one, but Walt had to help if he could. He started pushing clothes into his bag.

"Let's go there, then. You coming? How does this work?"

"Yeah, I'm coming. I'll ride with you. Just remember no one else can see me, ok? Or would you rather I just stayed in your head."

"No, thanks, Seb," said Walt. "Call me old-school, but I'd prefer to have you somewhere I can see you, rather than think of you as some kind of growth on my brain."

"Ok. One thing, though?"

"What?"

"You can't call me Seb. I'm not him. I'm just not. You need to think of something else."

Walt opened the hotel room door and looked back, thinking. "How about Parasite?" he said.

The young man winced in mock-offense.

"Ouch," he said, "I'm hurt, Walt. And I'm certainly not a parasite. I can help you—I *am* helping you. Our relationship isn't parasitic, it's symbiotic."

"Ok," said Walt. "How about I call you Sym?"

"I like it," he said. "Sym it is."

Chapter 25

Upstate New York
Thirty-four years previously

It was the giggling that woke Boy. He still couldn't open his eyes, but he felt awake and alert. The headache had become a slow throbbing background to his every conscious moment. He was getting used to it. He guessed that was the painkillers. A few more days, and it would be gone for good anyhow. Along with him.

The giggling, as unlikely as it seemed at first, was Mom. Mom and the churchy woman he'd heard before. Underneath the giggling was a deep, loud rumbling which lasted a few seconds, building dramatically in volume, stopped for another few seconds, then repeated the process. The noisiest part of the rumble seemed to set off the gigglers again, followed by the pair of women shushing each other just as loudly.

A few minutes listening provided an explanation. The cop on night shift outside his room had been given a few crumbled sleeping pills in his coffee, resulting in a comically loud snore.

"Loretta—quiet—you'll wake him," he heard.

"Ma'am, I think we could bring a marching band in here and he'd snore right through it."

As they lifted him carefully and lowered him into a wheelchair, Boy realized the tube down his throat had gone, as had the one up his nose. No needles in his arm, and no noisy machines. For a moment, he wondered if he had begun to recover. Then, he understood the real reason: they had withdrawn life support. These were his last few hours. He knew his conclusion was right: the handcuffs had been removed. Handcuffs on a dead kid wouldn't look good.

There were no footsteps or voices in the corridor as Mom and Loretta wheeled him through a few corridors and out through the back, where they lifted him into a car, putting the wheelchair in the trunk. There was a slight lightening behind his eyelids as they left the building. Boy guessed it must be sometime before dawn. It was a small town hospital, no security, probably one nurse on duty and a doctor on call, dozing in one of the smaller rooms.

Boy must have fallen asleep again during the journey, because the next time he became aware, there was the sound of someone hammering on a door. His periods of consciousness were getting shorter and shorter.

"Reverend Jesse! Reverend Jesse! Please, it's an emergency."

Boy heard the sound of chains being unhooked and bolts being drawn back.

"Loretta, it's five in the morning and despite years of fervent prayers to change the fact, I am still very much *not* at my best in the morning. Now, what's so important that it brings you to my door at—what on earth? Loretta, let go of my sleeve, what's got into you. Why are—? Oh."

The voice had got closer and, now that it had stopped, Boy could hear its owner taking a deep breath, then letting it out in a long sigh.

"Is that who I think it is?"

Mom spoke up.

"Reverend Jesse, this is my son. Now, I know you've read about him in the papers, but let me tell you, he's the sweetest, gentlest, cleverest boy you'll ever meet. The doctor said it was the cancer made him…do what he did. The tumor, pressing on his brain."

Another sigh.

"The devil is inside the boy."

"Well, I guess—allegorically—you could say—,"

"The devil is inside him," said Reverend Jesse, warming to his theme, "and you want me to cast him out." The familiar, almost sing-song tones of the preacher rose in volume as he spoke.

"You want me to rid this child of the unclean spirit, the demon that drove him to do unspeakable things, commit terrible sins, turn away from the Lord and embrace evil."

"Hallelujah, hallelujah," muttered Loretta. She sounded suspiciously like she was enjoying herself.

Mom was silent for a few seconds. Boy knew—in her mind—that this was his last chance. She wasn't going to ruin it now.

"Yes, Reverend Jesse. You're right. That's why we came to you. Only you can save him."

"Only the power of *Jesus* can save him," said Reverend Jesse, although Boy could hear the pride in his voice. "Bring him to the church, bring him to the altar. Let us present this sick child to God in humility and pray for His mercy. Let us cast out this demon and—"

There was talk of smiting. Boy faded out again.

When he next became aware, he knew they must be in the church. There was a feeling of vast space around him. Reverend Jesse was mumbling softly and his muffled words bounced back from the distant walls and ceiling. Boy could hear Mom whispering prayers too, and the louder voice of Loretta, adding occasional amens and hallelujahs. She had dropped all pretense now and was obviously having a fantastic time.

Boy felt his strength ebbing away. He fully expected to die very soon, right there in church. He wondered what that would do for Mom's newly-restored faith, Jesse's reputation and Loretta's entire life. Then, something entirely unexpected happened.

Jesse went very quiet. The two women were still praying, but something started happening of which they seemed utterly unaware. A powerful hum began underground, but Boy knew he wasn't hearing it with his ears. It was as if a new sense had opened up and begun feeding information to his brain. He knew—somehow—that this hum had split itself into fine lines, each carrying some kind of intense, white-hot energy from below them. These lines were now racing upward, toward them.

Boy made a huge effort, knowing—as he did so—that he was now very near death. He opened his eyes.

Ahead, at the modern, massive, blond wood altar, lit by dawn's first rays coming through the huge window behind them, Reverend Jesse knelt, his arms thrust skyward, his head back. Boy could see the lines of energy now, like lightning arcing through the rock beneath the church, heading straight for the preacher's body.

Boy knew—suddenly, and with absolute certainty—that Reverend Jesse was waiting for that energy, that he had summoned it somehow. That it was in this place, waiting. That was why he hadn't offered to help Boy at his home. That was why he had built his mega church in such an unpromising location. He had built the church over this source of power.

Boy watched, fascinated, as the lines reached the kneeling man. His body twitched, he gasped. He seemed lit up like a firework display.

Neither woman saw anything unusual at all. They carried on praying as if everything was normal. As soon as he noticed this, Boy felt an entirely novel sensation, as if he had been looking at a picture upside-down and had suddenly seen it right way up for the first time. There was far more to life than he had suspected. There was power beyond imagination. He could feel it prickle at the edges of his being, a tiny hint of the potential surging underfoot.

Boy took a ragged breath. He could feel his body starting to shut down. He hadn't had any feeling below the waist since he'd first regained consciousness, and the constant headache had increased its assault during the couple of hours it had taken them to get him out of the hospital, wake up the preacher and get to the church. He could feel himself losing the fight with the part of him that had taken control when he'd killed Pop. It was over, either way. He was about to die. What did any of it matter?

It's a curious fact of human nature that, for some individuals, when death comes—even when all hope seems completely lost—there still remains an instinctive, raging desire to live. As the energy continued to flow, Boy called out to it with all of the strength he had left, what little of it there was. He slumped forward and fell out of the wheelchair, hitting the ground hard. He heard Mom gasp. Even Loretta shut up for a blessed moment. Jesse gasped too, but it was a sound of shock and disbelief. The energy pouring into him had been abruptly cut off. He turned in confusion and watched the dying child, lying twisted on the polished floor.

Boy's face was a ghastly gray white, his hair plastered to his forehead with cold sweat. He managed to slide his arms over his head and put both palms flat onto the floor. The instant he did so, the lines of energy—which had pulsed away from the altar toward him—raced up to his fingertips and entered his body like a million miniature lightning strikes.

Loretta started rapidly crossing herself as Boy's body twisted and writhed. Rev. Jesse looked on aghast, his mouth hanging open in disbelief. Mom sat perfectly still, her eyes shining with tears as she looked on.

The energy flow lasted for about fifteen seconds. That was how long it took for Boy to die and be reborn into his new life. The color returned to his face, his body seemed almost to shine with an inner light as he pushed himself up from the floor and dragged his body over to the nearest chair, leaning against it. His legs were still useless, but he no longer cared. The throb of the headache had stopped abruptly. He may have been a crippled twelve-year-old boy, but at that moment he knew for an absolute certainty, he was the most powerful being on the planet. He started to laugh.

Loretta finally found her voice again.

"It's a miracle," she said, but she sounded a little dubious, looking over at Rev. Jesse, who was sitting on the altar steps, breathing heavily, gaping like a beached fish. It was hardly how she'd imagined it. Other healings—like Joe's asthma, or Amy's bowel problems—had only occurred after much laying on of hands by Rev. Jesse, accompanied by a great deal of loud praying and praising. This time, the preacher hadn't even gotten around to touching the boy. Still, a miracle was a miracle, right? She raised her hands, palms up.

"Hallelujah" she said, her voice slightly watery at first, but strengthening as she repeated the familiar words. "Hallelujah, praise Jesus, praise the Lord."

The boy looked her way. Her throat dried up a little. She didn't like the way he was looking at her. She didn't like it one little bit, no sir. She made herself look away, turning her head heavenward.

"Hallelujah," she said again. "hallelu-,"

She stopped suddenly. Her throat closed as if a vice had been applied to it and was being rapidly tightened. She took a short breath, then another. The third attempt failed as no air could make its way through the passages which had squeezed together inside her neck. Her hands fluttered in panic and she looked left and right for help. Rev. Jesse seemed to have lost any ability to move or think. The boy's mother was smiling and crying, her eyes fixed on the miracle of her son, back from the brink of death.

Loretta took a few stumbling steps toward the woman, but before she got halfway there, the edges of her vision beginning to fog, her neck suddenly snapped and her head jerked back. For a second, her body stood there. From the front, she gave the illusion of being headless—it was only from behind that her head was visible, hanging like a heavy bag of shopping between her shoulder blades. Her lifeless body fell heavily, landing directly in front of Rev. Jesse.

Her body's last unconscious action—evacuating her capacious bowels—finally galvanized the young preacher into action. He got up, and stepping over the corpse, walked over to Boy, stopping a few feet away.

"Give it back," he said, his voice trembling with indignation. "That's power sent by God for his true ministers and you have no right. You have no right. YOU HAVE NO RIGHT!"

His voice was shrill and bordering on hysterical. Boy started to laugh at the comical sight of the red-faced apoplectic preacher almost dancing with rage in front of him. But he tired of it quickly and reached out a hand. He felt his awareness race toward the direction his hand indicated. He thought of what he wanted to happen.

Rev. Jesse screamed in pain and clasped both hands to his head. Blood began to stream from his nose.

"Sorry," said Boy. "First try. Think that might have been a bit clumsy. Still," he waved a hand at Loretta's corpse, "it could've been worse. Now, be quiet a moment."

The preacher moved his hands slowly away from his head as the pain receded to an almost bearable level.

"What do you want?" he managed to say.

"The money," said Boy, simply. "All of it." He looked around the huge building, its opulent furnishings, thirty-foot high stained glass windows and state of the art sound system. "Who bankrolled you? You're a little young to be living in a mansion."

Jesse looked to one side as if thinking, then spoke up.

"Donations, mostly," he said, "charity - aaaagh!" his hands flew up to his face as his nose shattered spontaneously, as if a heavyweight boxer had landed the perfect jab. Without gloves.

"The truth, please," said Boy, calmly. "Strange as it may sound, I seem to know when you're lying to me. So don't test me again. I'm guessing Daddy has a few dollars, right?"

The tears streamed down the preacher's face as he held a silk handkerchief to his ruined nose. His voice had a strange, pinched nasal sound to it when he spoke again.

"Well, yes, of course. I had help. No shame in that. My father wants to help do God's work, he wants to help me bring the light of Jesus back to—."

"Spare me the sales pitch," said Boy, "just take me to him."

"I can't just—." The Reverend Jesse Newman stopped and looked at Boy. "Ok," he said in a small voice.

Mom stood up, her smile faltering a little.

"Go start the car," Boy commanded. "Jesse here will help me into my wheelchair and bring me out."

Mom hesitated. She looked at her son. Alive. Conscious. Speaking. She went to him, knelt and took his hand. She opened her mouth to say his name, but he suddenly squeezed her hand hard enough to make her yelp in pain.

"Don't say it," he said. "That's not my name. He's dead. That's not who I am any more. Now, go and get the fucking car."

Chapter 26

Las Vegas
Present Day

Dawn in Las Vegas was fairly spectacular, but criminally under-appreciated. No one went to Vegas for the view, and those few vacationers who were still awake were in no condition to appreciate the various shades of orange, yellow and red that crept across the desert, illuminating Red Rock Canyon in a blaze of color. The windows of the massive hotels reflected the splendor of nature, and despite their size, looked comparatively insignificant and temporary. A few workers driving, or walking toward the Strip to start cleaning up the mess from the night before stopped for a moment to drink in the sight, but most had stopped truly seeing it, after their first few dozen weary journeys.

Westlake was in the belly of a helicopter looking at maps of Mexico City. He didn't know it was dawn, just that it was 5:37am by his watch and he'd been told he would arrive at Las Vegas just before 6am.

His team had flown in to Vegas the night before, with instructions to meet him at the airport, 7:30am sharp. Westlake had to pick up Walter Ford first. He had little time for Ford, dismissing him as a lightweight pleasure-seeker who didn't like to get his hands dirty. But, to make this mission a success, the man's talent for temporarily re-shaping faces was a necessity.

Twenty minutes after the chopper had landed, Westlake pushed the buzzer on Walt's door. He waited and then buzzed again. After a couple of minutes, he picked up a handful of stones and threw them at the master bedroom window. Nothing. The security guard's hut had a good view of Westlake as he threw another handful of stones. The guard had responded to the Secret Service ID as expected, but even a minimum pay grunt might start to wonder what was going on.

He walked back to the front door, then—just as he passed behind a palm tree—took two quick steps and launched himself lithely up to the top of the fence, boosting himself over it and landing with virtually no noise on the hard-packed earth on the other side. He unholstered his Glock in a smooth motion so practiced it had become automatic.

The sliding door leading into the house from the yard was unlocked. Westlake wasn't surprised. Unlike his neighbors, Walter Ford could rip apart an intruder with a gesture. Without even bothering getting out of bed. Other Manna users were often similarly relaxed about their home security arrangements.

The house was cool. No one lived without AC in Las Vegas, and August had been hot, with highs of 118F causing roads to bubble and tourists to dehydrate and end up in hospital at the rate of dozens a day.

Westlake opened the fridge. Fresh salad and lots of beer.

"Ford?" he called. "Ford? It's Westlake. Come down, you have work to do." Mason had called ahead, but apparently the old fool wasn't answering his phone. Westlake had been told to shoot him in the kneecaps once he was done, as punishment for his lack of communication. Ford was to be instructed that he wasn't allowed to use Manna to fix it for twelve hours. That was gonna hurt. Westlake smiled.

"Ok, I'm coming up. If you've been drinking, time to get sober."

Still no response. Westlake started to consider the possibility that Ford was sick. This worried him a little. Not that he gave a soft shit whether the man died in a pool of his own vomit. Just as long as he wasn't infectious. Any illness that Manna couldn't deal with would have to be very serious. Westlake had certainly never heard of one.

He nudged open the door of the master bedroom with the toe of one steel-capped shoe. He flicked on the light. Ford was asleep, his satin sheets covering his lazy, privileged, pampered body. Westlake snorted in contempt.

"Get up, Ford, and stop wasting my time."

The sheet continued to rise and fall in a maddeningly constant rhythm that denoted deep sleep. Westlake walked over and pulled the sheet away, ready to fire a round into the pillow, just to scare the crap out of the time-wasting fraud.

The body turned as the sheet came away and Westlake found himself looking at something close enough to Walt to give him pause, yet strange enough that he immediately thumbed the safety off on the Glock.

The thing on the bed—a homunculus, it must be, although probably the best Westlake had ever seen—turned onto its back and grinned at the intruder. The grin revealed a line of small stones and pebbles arranged in a symmetrical way to approximate teeth. Uncharacteristically, Westlake hesitated, thrown off-balance by that grin.

The creature's hand shot out and grabbed his genitals, squeezing with inhuman strength. Westlake fired and the homunculus collapsed into a pile of dirt that ruined the sheets and the Persian rug beside the bed. Westlake stood for a second longer, seemingly considering what to do next. Then, satisfied that his only option—considering one of his testicles was sliding down his leg while the other was just a flattened lump of gristle—was to pass out, he did so.

From New York, Mason watched the homunculus fall apart and Westlake hit the floor. He said nothing, but his right eyebrow twitched slightly. He picked up his phone and dialed another Las Vegas number.

"Barrington," he whispered. "Go to Walter Ford's house. Make sure your Manna reserves are topped up. You'll find Westlake there. He needs some medical attention, then he needs a new face. It would seem Ford is unavailable."

He listened for a moment while watching Westlake as he showed signs of regaining consciousness. The man was obviously in absolute agony, barely moving as he tried to sit up. That's what came of insufficient preparation.

"What's that?" he whispered. "Oh, no hurry. Give it an hour." An hour would be long enough for Westlake to remember to prepare better in future.

Mason couldn't remember the last time someone had left his organization and lived. When he thought about it, he realized that was because it was yet to happen. Uncharacteristically brave of Walter Ford. He would turn his attention to tracking him down, once they'd found Meera Patel.

***

Westlake was two hours late meeting his team. He said nothing other than the code sentence and response and they knew better than to ask. There was no pain after Barrington had used Manna to treat his injuries and he had betrayed no anger at being made to wait before being healed. Westlake's face was now that of Seb Varden's, but his people had been very carefully picked and extensively trained. Not one of the five men or three women said anything or betrayed any surprise at their leader's appearance. They just followed him to the waiting helicopter and awaited instructions.

Westlake briefed the unit during the flight to Mexico City. The chopper displayed no livery or numbers giving away its identity, but its cruising speed of over two hundred miles per hour put it in a small but elite group. The fuel tank was slightly bigger than standard, meaning they wouldn't have to stop en route, but the payoff was a slower flight. In all, they were in the air for eight hours. Six hours sleep—all of them used it, as regular sleep was a rare luxury while on a mission—thirty minutes for food, then a comprehensive briefing before landing.

By the time the chopper came to rest at a little-used military facility just outside Mexico City, all members of the unit were clear as to their roles and objective. Meera Patel was to be captured alive, and Westlake—with Varden's face—was the best chance of achieving that objective. Every team member had a cellphone which doubled as a walkie-talkie, with the unit's channel constantly open, relaying information to the invisible earpieces they all wore. All were armed with silenced weapons, three of them also carried briefcases containing quick-to-assemble sniper guns, equipped with fast-acting tranquilizer darts.

Changed into civilian clothes, and arriving in separate taxis, some alone, others paired up, Westlake's elite unit of killers checked into hotels, guesthouses and hostels picked out in advance. Their locations circled the area where Meera Patel's singing voice had been detected. On both occasions, the alarm had been triggered in the morning. Each of them went to bed early.

Dawn next day saw the team take their places, loosely covering an area of three square miles. Mason's program would instantly notify each of them when triggered, so they could move into place, keeping their distance, ready to act if Westlake's approach should fail.

He had warned them that the actual Sebastian Varden might be in play. If so, three team members were to engage Varden while the rest extracted Patel. If they got very lucky indeed, Varden wouldn't be involved. Westlake resented relying on luck, but he knew this part of the equation was out of his hands.

The first three days passed without incident.

On day four, they got very lucky indeed.

Chapter 27

Mexico City

An hour after Kate left, the door opened and Seb walked in. Mee threw her arms around him and they stood like that for a few minutes, saying nothing.

Finally, Seb pulled away, looked at Mee and kissed her.

"Tequila?" he said, tasting it on her.

"Bit early for that," she said. "I'll make some coffee."

"Yeah, you're funny," he said.

"Seven days," she said, as she opened the cupboard and got the beans.

"I know," he said. "Seemed like an hour or so to me."

He looked at the table as Mee went through the calming ritual of grinding beans, boiling water, warming the pot and letting it steep for a few minutes before pouring. He could have just used Manna and saved the time, but he appreciated the importance of maintaining some activities regular humans indulged in.

There were two glasses on the table.

"Company?" he said.

"Kate," said Mee, pouring two mugfuls and sitting down. Seb sat where Kate had been sitting for most of the night. He held the mug to his nose and savored the smell of the freshly ground beans. Somehow, knowing that some genuine effort had gone into making it, knowing the beans had been grown on nearby hills, picked, dried, roasted, then ground and brewed in a process repeated millions of times every day…well, it made it taste better. Seb knew it *couldn't* taste better in reality, but that didn't stop him from believing it did.

Mee sat opposite and sipped her coffee.

"She knows," she said. "I told her everything. It can't just be you and me against the world anymore. If you can't stop yourself disappearing, we need to talk about Mason."

Seb looked at her. She was never afraid of confronting problems. Being held captive by Mason's people, having her finger cut off, thinking she would never see Seb again—and would live the rest of her life as the prisoner of the coldest bastard she'd ever come across—it had all added up to the most terrifying experience of her life. But she had no hesitation in bringing up his name, no thought of avoiding thinking about the man who had caused her such pain. Seb loved her for that.

"I understand why you told her," he said, "but the Order—,"

"She doesn't think you're here to save the world," said Mee. "Don't panic. She never bought into the whole messiah deal. She doesn't know what you are, why your abilities are different, how you managed to access the Roswell Manna. She's curious, sure, who wouldn't be? But she does want to help."

Mee told him about Innisfarne, about Kate's offer of refuge. Seb listened in silence until she had told him everything.

"No phones?" he said. "No internet?"

Mee nodded.

Seb stood up and topped up both of their coffees. He sighed.

"Then she's right," he said. "You're right. I can't protect you if I'm not here and that sounds like the safest place on earth to be if you want to hide from someone with Mason's control of technology." He hid the worry and sadness in his voice fairly well, but he wasn't fooling Mee. He knew it and she knew it. They both decided to ignore it. "When will you go?" he said.

"When you next pull your vanishing act," she said. "If you do. If not, I won't have to leave, will I?"

Seb bowed to her logic. He knew better than to argue with her when her mind was made up.

"So, what happened this time?" she said. "You been filling in forms with ET again?"

"Something like that."

"I have some information," said Seb2.

Seb looked at Mee, who had caught his slightly unfocused look when Seb2 had spoken.

"Yeah, it's him," he said. "I think you should hear this, too."

He reached forward to take her hands, but she sat back.

"Wait," she said. "As lovely as it was going back to Richmond Park, can't he just come here?"

"Can you?" thought Seb.

"Yeah. Sure," said Seb 2. "Grab her hand, I'll have to mess with her brain a little, so she can see me."

"I wish you'd use a better expression than 'messing with her brain'," thought Seb, but took Mee's hand anyway.

A fraction of a second after their fingers had touched, Seb2 was sitting on a third chair between them.

"Hi, Mee," he said.

"Hi, you," she said. "Why couldn't you do this the first time, instead of all the drama?"

"It wasn't really for your benefit," said Seb2. "The Richmond Park scene was pulled out of Seb's memory the first time we communicated. I needed somewhere with specific qualities. A venue I—he—had spent a lot of time thinking about. You made an impression on that first date."

"Soft git," said Mee and lightly punched Seb's arm.

"I can construct any scene Seb can picture," said Seb2, "but as that one was already fully formed, it was the default template when we needed it under pressure. What's happening now is a little different. I'm communicating directly with your brain, and you're projecting the image you choose to associate with me. The disadvantage is the speed of communication. It's real-time, which is painfully slow."

"Oh, well, excuse *me,*" said Mee.

"I can deal with it," said Seb2, "but our last meeting lasted less than twenty seconds in real time. We've already spent double that just saying hello."

Mee raised an eyebrow at Seb.

"Ok, here's the skinny on the aliens," said Seb2. "I don't have everything yet, but I've left a program interrogating their mainframe. We should have more details next time. If there is a next time," he added, looking at Mee.

"Let me tell her what happened first," said Seb. "Then you can explain to me why it was a good idea to hack an alien computer."

Seb told Mee about Mic, Thelma and Louise. About Seb2 hiding the extent of his Manna ability until they could find out what was going on. Mee made more coffee. Her Manna use meant she felt no ill-effects from the night's tequila consumption, but her head still felt foggy as she tried to comprehend what the two Sebs were telling her.

"So, what do they want?" she said.

Seb shrugged. He was no closer to unpicking the garbled syntax that passed for communication with Mic than he had been the first time.

"First things first," said Seb2. "I know why we were away for so long. And why it was shorter this time. Some of what I'll get from the mainframe will confirm it. The Manna interaction with Thelma also helps to explain a little of who they are and what they want. Although I haven't completely solved that mystery yet."

Seb2 stood up and pointed at the table. A scale model of Mexico City appeared. When Mee looked closer, she could see tiny cars moving, smoke rising. She even made out a jet the size of a mosquito flying over the credit card-shaped Nabor Carillo Lake on its final approach into the airport. Next, Seb2 backed away to the window. The numeral '1' appeared next to him, floating in mid-air. Seb2 took a couple of paces back toward them and '2' appeared alongside him.

"Ok," said Seb2. "How long does it take to Walk from one place to another?"

Seb considered the question for a moment.

"It's instantaneous," he said. "I see where we're going, I make the decision, then we're there."

"And when we met Mic? Any different?"

"You know it wasn't. I was here, then I was there."

"Yes, it seems the same way to me," said Seb2. "but the keyword there is *seems*."

"It isn't instantaneous?" said Mee.

"Walking is, pretty much," said Seb2. "Although I don't know how. You're the one with a science background—,"

"Hardly," said Mee.

"Well, you're better educated than me, so you understand the laws of physics. I can't be in one place, then immediately in another with no travel time, right?"

"Well," said Mee, "I'm just playing Devil's advocate here, but at the subatomic level, experiments have shown that certain particles seemingly affect one another instantly—with distance playing no part in the process."

"Oh," said Seb2. "So it is possible, then."

"Not necessarily," said Mee. "Subatomic behavior appears to follow completely different laws to those of everyday reality. The microscopic rulebook is different to the macroscopic, if you like. If Walking is instantaneous—or as close to it as makes no difference, I can only think you're using wormholes somehow. But I don't know enough about the theory to see how."

"More than we do, though," said Seb2. "And it fits with my hypothesis. Much of what goes on in my—his—our body is automatic. Even if I managed to see *what* was happening when we Walk, or Use, I still wouldn't be able to understand it. But I have a theory about the blackouts that makes sense to me."

"Go ahead," said Seb.

"Right. Imagine the distance between Mexico City—," he pointed at the table, "—and Mic's crib is six million miles."

"Crib?" said Mee. Seb2 ignored her.

"Why six million?" said Seb.

"It just makes the math easier, ok? And I need all the help I can get."

"Point taken," said Seb. He was the same person, after all, and mental calculations had never been his strong suit.

"Now, what if we weren't Walking there? When we were summoned. You made no conscious decision, you didn't go through the usual process, right?"

"Right," said Seb. "I had no say in it at all. I was just pulled away—like being grabbed."

"Exactly," said Seb2. "I don't think we Walked at all. I've been looking at our memory of what happened between blacking out and meeting Mic. There's a gap there. Our mental state just stopped. We didn't think or feel. It's as if we were in a state of suspended animation, everything frozen until we arrived at our destination. And milliseconds before blackout, something surrounded our body. You were right to say it felt like being grabbed. It was like one of those games where you pick up a soft toy with a claw."

"Except, I never do pick it up," said Seb.

"Yeah, well, I think their claw is designed for accuracy, rather than conning tourists at Coney Island. They got close enough to use it, and it homed in on the most powerful Manna user in the species. I think they grabbed you and reeled you in. We were traveling incredibly fast by any normal standards, but excruciatingly slowly compared to Walking. Like taking a bus instead of a jet. You just made two interstellar journeys longer than any human being before you. We were away so long purely because of the travel time involved"

Seb was glad he was already sitting down.

"Interstellar," he said, his throat suddenly dry.

"Yes," said Seb2. He walked from the table to the floating number 1 at the window. "Our first trip took six days there and six days back. Well, not quite, but I'll explain that in a moment."

Mee had gone pale.

"You were on another planet?" she said.

"No," said Seb2. "Not quite." He walked toward them and stopped at the floating 2. "This time, we were away seven days total, which is three and a half days' travel time each way. And, when we go again, I doubt we'll be away more than a day or two."

Seb rubbed his forehead with both thumbs.

"Different planet?" he said.

Mee stood up, her chair clattering to the floor behind her. She walked over to the window, then walked slowly between '1' and '2', looking at the tiny Mexico City on the table as she did it.

"Oh, shit," she said.

Seb spread his hands wide.

"What?" he said. "You two geniuses have got it? What am I missing?"

"You went to the same place both times," said Mee, softly.

"How?" said Seb. "What?"

"You're missing the obvious," said Mee, pointing at the two floating numbers. "You didn't travel faster. The distance was shorter." She turned to Seb2. "You said not quite six days there, six days back. Is that because the trip back was slightly shorter?"

Seb2 nodded.

Seb looked at them both.

"But that means they—,"

Seb2 nodded.

"They were nearer to us," he said. "And getting closer all the time. Remember the background noise we could hear while we there?"

Seb nodded.

"I've been thinking about this, trying different hypotheses. There's only one explanation that fits all the facts," said Seb2. "We were on some sort of spaceship. And it's heading straight toward Earth."

***

The two floating aliens and the model of Mexico City had disappeared. Mee, Seb and Seb2 sat at the table. A fourth Manna-produced pot of coffee was half-finished. Seb2 had reached for a cup more than once, seemingly forgetting his body didn't exist outside Seb and Mee's consciousnesses.

Once Seb and Mee had accepted the probability that an alien craft was on its way to Earth, the obvious next step was to find out what they wanted. And then to decide if this was something Seb should be trying to deal with alone.

"What are you saying? That I should go to the White House, knock on the door and say 'excuse me, space aliens are on their way and they seem to think I'm Earth's ambassador'? Good plan. And after they release me from a secure psychiatric facility?"

Mee shrugged. "It's not as if they could hold you there," she said.

"True, but if I pull a vanishing act and Walk, we'll have the US government looking for us—as well as Mason. No, for now, we have to deal with this alone. I promise, if I think for a second that we need help, I'll go get it. Ok?"

Mee reluctantly agreed, but she wasn't happy. "This is a colossal mindfuck of the first degree," she said, "and if you think I'm ok with you arsing about with space aliens while I sit at home knitting, you've got another think coming."

"You can knit?" said Seb2.

"And you can shut up, tosspot," said Mee.

"Mee, I don't think they can do much to us," said Seb2, ignoring her colorful language, half of which he understood. "The Roswell Manna—our Manna—is different. It's more advanced."

"More advanced than the aliens who can cross space and grab you whenever they like?" said Mee. "Yeah, that makes sense. You really *are* a tosspot."

Seb2 ignored the insult.

"I didn't say I understand everything," he said. "I'm still skimming the surface of any real knowledge of the nano-technology we're carrying. But, trust me, our Manna is in a different league."

Mee shrugged, unconvinced.

"One thing still confuses me," said Seb2.

"Only one thing?" said Mee. Seb2 ignored her.

"They just seem, well, a little disengaged, somehow. As if they were expecting their meeting with us to go one way, then—when it didn't—they couldn't adapt to the change in circumstances. Look at their weird attempts to communicate. There's something we're missing, something we're not seeing. Do you remember that feeling of being watched?"

"Yes," said Seb. "I remember."

"Something doesn't quite make sense."

"I'm more concerned about why they're heading for Earth," said Seb.

Seb2 had briefly interrogated the alien computer systems when they were there. The information he'd found was incomplete and frustrating. The program he had left behind, gathering and decoding information, would give them a much better idea of what was going on next time Seb was 'summoned'. Until then, they had—at least—built up more of a picture of what they were dealing with. One of the files Seb2 had brought back was some sort of basic learning library, containing information about the species, although much of it made little sense when filtered through a human sensibility.

"They're the same species as Billy Joe," said Seb2. "Although they don't really accept Billy Joe as one of their own."

"Why not?" said Mee.

"It's down to the way they think of themselves, and of their position in the universe. I need to give you some background—just bear in mind some of this is conjecture, based on the information I've found. Their species only has one World Walker. As does the human race. From what I can gather, World Walkers are rare. And when I say rare, I mean one grain of sand on a beach as big as the Milky Way rare. Mic, Thelma, Louise, they only know of one: Billy Joe."

"And now you," said Mee.

"Well, no. They don't know that about us. We've given them a slightly doctored picture of who we are."

"Why?" said Mee.

"Simple caution. One piece of information has come across loud and clear from our two visits. They think of themselves as superior to humanity. And when I say superior, I mean in the same way we feel superior to a chipmunk. I suspect one of the reasons they're not making a massive effort to communicate effectively is because they think it would be pointless. And beneath them. They are an ancient race. Billy Joe is the only World Walker they've ever known. The information I found shows they know very little about him. His very existence came as a profound shock to them as a species. And they don't understand what he is exactly. They don't know whether to feel proud of him, fear him, or ignore him. Their default position has been to ignore him. His appearance, many generations ago, was such a break with their world-view—or universe-view—that they haven't yet recovered. They would never believe a race as immature as ours could have produced its own World Walker. And their reaction—if they did believe it—would be unpredictable."

"I don't quite believe it myself," said Seb. "I still don't have a clue what I'm doing. Is this how a World Walker is supposed to feel?"

"I doubt it," said Seb2. "But think about this for a second. We weren't ready for this. No question about it. Billy Joe didn't give you all this power because he felt sorry for you. He didn't see a dying musician and casually decide to turn him into one of the rarest beings in the universe. There must have been a reason."

Mee and Seb were silent for a while.

"He knew they were coming here," said Mee.

"Either that, or it's just a coincidence that First Contact is going to happen eighteen months after he saved our life," said Seb2. "Hardly likely."

"So I'm supposed to do something?" said Seb. "What?"

"That's the big question," said Seb2. "And to answer it, I'm going to need contact with them again. I need to pick up the program I left on their ship and unravel the information it's gathered."

Mee rubbed her eyes.

"And what I need is some air," she said. She turned to Seb2. "What *do* you know about these aliens, then? You said you had incomplete information. What have you got? Bullet points, please, because it's been a long night and I need to take a walk to clear my head."

"Bullet points," said Seb2. "They're scientists. They've traveled a vast distance to get here. The original crew are long dead. It's taken generations."

"What?" said Mee.

"Each of them only lives around thirty to forty years. This crew is descended from the original crew that left their system. When they die, strands of their DNA are harvested and woven into the next body they've grown."

"They *grow* bodies?" said Seb.

"It would seem they left sexual reproduction behind millennia ago."

"Don't know what they're missing," said Mee. Both Sebs smiled.

"There are twelve of them onboard, all different ages. When a new body is needed, it's seeded with a mixture of DNA from others who have died. That way, all of them are born with a racial memory. Each individual is a mixture of three or four previous personalities. The species as a whole is constantly growing in knowledge as each generation literally builds on the knowledge of the previous one. The disadvantage to this—which they acknowledge, but have long accepted—is that nature can't throw a genetic wildcard into the mix, can't use sudden mutation to advance the species. That's why Billy Joe's apparently spontaneous evolution to World Walker status was such a profound shock to them."

"We can't keep calling them 'the species'," said Mee. "Don't they have a name?"

"They do," said Seb2, "but the human voice box can't pronounce it."

"Well, we have to call them something." She thought for a moment. "Everyone's heard of Roswell. Let's call 'em Rozzers."

"Rozzers?"

"Yeah. Why not? Now, carry on."

"Ok. So, the, er, Rozzers that we met are, in fact, the descendants of the original twelve who set off from one of their planets."

"*One* of their planets?" said Seb.

"They've colonized hundreds," said Seb2. "Look, the information I brought back is the equivalent of a school book. Elementary school. I think the new bodies go through an accelerated learning program when they are born—if that's the right word—and join the crew. It's the only thing I've been able to effectively translate, because it's aimed at the equivalent of a six-year-old. So don't ask any complicated questions. I'll tell you what I can."

"Bullet points," repeated Mee.

"Yes. Their attitude to death is important. Not just their attitude to their own deaths, but also to others. When they die, they know they will be back in a different body, their own experience mixed with others. It's happened countless times in the past, it will happen countless more in the future. The concept of 'death', in the sense of an ending, has no real meaning to them. Even if all of them were lost and their ship destroyed, their DNA from generations ago is still at home and will be used again. They will lose the memories of this mission, nothing more. There's no fear of death at all. They don't attach much importance to killing, either. I've found evidence that they've wiped out civilizations without a qualm."

"How can a species so advanced be so cruel?" said Mee.

"You a vegetarian?" said Seb2.

"You know I'm not."

"So you'll happily eat a conscious being, so long as it's stupid. Well, stupid enough to satisfy your conscience that it's barely 'conscious' in a meaningful way."

"That's completely different," said Mee.

"Is it?"

Mee stood up and looked out of the window.

Seb looked at Seb2.

"Are they here to declare war, then?" he said. "You said they were scientists, not soldiers. Should we be worried?"

"I don't know," said Seb2. "There's no hint of aggression in the information I've found. Humanity gets no mention in the school book I've been reading. Their mission seems primarily concerned with contacting other species which have evolved sufficiently."

"Sufficiently? Sufficiently how?"

"I'm not sure yet. But I know this is just one of thousands of similar missions to other galaxies. And it's not their first visit. But this trip is significant, more important than the others. I found some kind of ship's inventory. I know they brought something with them. Two of them, in fact—identical. Whatever they are, they're big—they take up about a third of the space on the ship."

"What are they?" said Seb. Mee walked back from the window. They both looked at Seb2.

"As far as I can make out, they're transport for a device of some sort. The device is the important bit—it's heavily featured in some of their written material. Its name is difficult to translate, but it's all I can find for now."

"So, what's the translation?" said Mee, at the same time as Seb said, "What's the device called?"

Seb2 looked back at both of them.

"The Unmaking Engine," he said.

Chapter 28

Three uneventful days went by. Mee and Seb stuck to the usual routine. Mee went to the market in the morning. Seb stayed home and wrote music, or Walked elsewhere and did his superhero thing. They'd talked about the multiverse, about the nihilistic urge to stop trying to help, since helping in one universe just meant failing to help in another. In the end, they'd agreed that nothing had changed, really. You helped people because you could. In the final reckoning, Seb would never know if it made the slightest bit of difference to anything or anyone, but he knew it was the right thing to do. So he did it. Mee put it best:

"If you couldn't swim and you were standing next to a river watching ten people drowning, would you throw a life ring to one of them? Or not bother?"

"You know I would," said Seb. "Anyone would."

"And which one would you throw it to?"

Seb thought for a second, then shrugged. "The nearest one," he said.

"There you go, then."

Mee's afternoons were less busy. She no longer had meditation with Kate to look forward to. Kate had left for Innisfarne, so the building that had once housed the Order was full of new tenants. None of them were paying rent—Kate had just quietly let it be known that it would be unoccupied. The families she had told moved gratefully from the slums to something a whole lot better.

Mee spent most afternoons meditating alone, or with Seb if he was there. Her ability with Manna was becoming stronger and more natural. On days when she'd filled up her reserves at Casa Negra, she felt as if she was walking at the center of an invisible circle with a diameter of about sixty yards. She could feel the presence of anyone within the circle, and—if anyone noticed her—she felt them light up in her mind, as their intentions became clear to her. She and Seb had discussed her ability and guessed it was something to do with human pheromones being released and detected by a cloud of nano-tech. It still felt like witchcraft to Mee when it happened, but it made her feel better about walking around alone.

All things considered, Mee felt pretty safe. Mason was still out there somewhere, but it looked increasingly likely she wasn't a priority for him now that he thought Seb was dead. She looked like a different person and she was in one of the most densely populated cities on the entire continent, living in a three-room apartment. She knew if Mason ever did find her, her Manna ability would give her a good chance to run. As long as she could get to Seb, she would be safe. And she'd always been lucky.

It's one of the universe's immutable laws that luck averages out over time. And people who've always been lucky are always the most surprised when that law finally takes effect.

***

Seb watched Mee walk to the market. Her step was light and she swung a basket by her side as she went. Even from his high vantage point, he could tell she was singing. He smiled.

He turned and walked toward the piano. There was an idea that had been bouncing around inside his head recently—mostly in those moments just before sleep. The fact it was becoming clearer now meant that it was probably worth exploring. Seb sat down and lifted his hands above the keys, feeling that old familiar sense of time drifting away as music filled his mind. Whatever else was going on, whatever was coming their way in that alien ship, he could still bring himself back to this moment. He was about to create something. It might be worth listening to, or it could be mediocre. Either way, it would be unique and captured for the first time in the following few minutes. And, in a little while, the woman he loved would be back.

He dropped his right hand toward the keys, ready to play an F major 7th. His fingers never reached the keyboard. He felt his awareness shrinking to a pinprick and a roaring sounding in his brain, like a huge wave washing him away. Then he was gone.

***

It was just after 8am. Mee's favorite market—La Central de Abasto in Iztapalapa—was open for business and already beginning to buzz with activity. It was probably the biggest market in the city. Mee loved the way it looked from above—she and Seb had often gone walking in the hills and looked down on it. To Mee, the high white metal shelters under which the merchants displayed their wares looked like the pages of a giant book, laid open across more than three hundred hectares.

Under those pages, La Central de Abasto reminded Mee more of the markets in East London where she'd grown up. The fruit stalls in particular were bright, fresh and heaving with watermelons, kiwis, apples, lemons, oranges and bananas. The noise level was terrific, each vendor's cry merging into the next as she walked. In her mind, she could hear the sing-song tones of the stall holders in New Spitalfields Market back home. "Come on, love, lovely pound of bananas 'ere, now ah'm not arsking two, or even one-seventy 'ere. One-fifty, that's all ah'm arsking, any less and ah may as well take the food out the marths of me own children and send 'em out as beggars. You won't find 'em any cheaper, guaranteed, me darlin', guaranteed."

Mee stopped to look at the display of piñatas hanging above the next stall. Rainbow colors, filled with cheap candy and in every shape imaginable: mules, cows, dogs, horses, bulls, mice, cats, spiders, lobsters. She was amused to see an alien hanging there, ready to tempt a youngster to take a swing at it.

Suddenly she stopped short, sure that someone had said her name. She looked around sharply and scanned the crowds, but no one was looking her way. There was a brief flicker of awareness, a prickling on the back of her neck. She knew she was overdue for filling up with Manna and cursed her complacency. Moving out of the flow of foot traffic and standing completely still for a few minutes, she let her awareness flow out of her, her senses reaching as far as they could to the edges of that invisible circle.

She shivered and pulled her cardigan more tightly around her shoulders. She had felt *something*, but it was weak, ambiguous. Even so, no point in taking chances. She decided to cut her shopping trip short and head home.

Chapter 29

Walt looked out of the taxi window as they made their way from the airport to Mexico City. He was impressed by how well-maintained the roads were. The blacktop was smooth, six lanes broken up by a line of mature trees. The airport itself had been a surprise—all concrete and glass, clean and modern. He felt a little abashed as he recognized his own prejudice. He'd expected dirt, humidity, ancient wooden ceiling fans moving droplets of sweat across unshaven faces. He was glad no one knew about the lazy bigotry he had displayed.

"Hey, *I* know," said Sym, from the seat alongside him. Walt looked across and raised an eyebrow, but said nothing. On the flight, he had made the mistake of speaking to his invisible companion. The businessman in the aisle seat had turned away slightly, the first time he'd done it. Then, when Walt had continued talking to Sym, the man had gone to the bathroom and had never come back. When they got off the plane, Walt realized the man had moved to a seat in coach, rather than sit near him.

They went straight to Seb and Meera's apartment. Walt had been about to get out of the car when Sym stopped him, holding up his hand.

"You have a hat?"

Walt shook his head. Sym nodded toward the driver, who had an oil-stained baseball cap jammed on his skull. Walt sighed and negotiated in broken Spanish. Thirty seconds later, he was fifteen dollars down and one dirty piece of headgear up.

"Keep your head down and go straight in," said Sym. "Sixth floor. Elevator's always breaking down—you're better off taking the stairs."

Walt got out of the cab and walked straight into the relative darkness of the lobby. No one was around. He shifted his bag into a more comfortable position on his shoulder, wincing as it pushed on his bruised ribs. He started climbing the stairs.

He was slightly out of breath by the time he got to Seb and Meera's door. Manna had kept his body fit and healthy, but even a few days without had left its toll. He could almost feel the muscle tone slackening, and his injuries were a constant reminder that being 'normal' again was going to be far from easy.

He knocked and waited. Sym disappeared from beside him, appearing again after half a minute.

"No one home," he said. "No sign of a struggle either. I could let you in, but it might be more polite to wait out here. After all, last time Mee saw you, you'd just helped kill a dozen friends of hers."

Walt physically flinched at the memory.

"I didn't help kill anyone," he said. "I was there because I had no choice."

Sym held up both hands.

"Hey, I'm not judging," he said, "just warning you Mee might not be ready for a hug right away."

Walt looked at his companion.

"You're not much like Seb," he said. "He'd never make light of something like that."

"You're right—I told you I wasn't him," said Sym. "Don't let appearances fool you. I know a little of what Seb knows, I have a basic personality framework based on his, but *I've* only been alive since he stuck me in your head last year."

"No offense, but I don't much like the thought of you being there all that time," said Walt.

"Oh, it wasn't all fun and games for me, believe me. But if you don't like my personality, you should blame yourself. You're the only person I've had access to—I'm as much a product of your consciousness as of Seb's. Anyhow, I'll get right out of your way once we find him."

Walt eased the bag carefully away from his bruised ribs and set it on the floor.

"I'll wait here," he said. He slid down the wall and sat as comfortably as he could, trying not to gasp at the pain in his ribs and stomach.

***

From a rooftop four hundred yards away from La Central de Abasto market, a woman watched Mee moving from stall to stall. The woman was lying flat, the long barrel of her rifle resting on a small beanbag she carried for the purpose. Without moving her eye away from the telescopic scope pushed up against her cheek, she spoke into a cellphone.

"Charlie to Leader. She's the one who was singing. She doesn't match the description. I don't have a clear shot. Instructions?"

The voice in her ear was clear and calm. Westlake was well known for the way his heart rate rarely shifted above sixty beats per minute, even during a firefight.

"Description."

"Around five foot six or seven, long straight black hair. Chinese, I think."

"She may have changed her appearance. Track her. Relay her position. All ground ops close in on Charlie's location and take positions outside the market. Alpha and Beta, move to your south-west positions and maintain tracking when Charlie loses her."

Westlake put a ten-spot on the table, under his espresso cup and walked out of the shadows of the cafe. He stopped briefly at a store and pretended to try on sunglasses while checking the Manna-made face he was wearing had maintained its integrity. He scowled at Seb Varden's reflection in the mirror, then tried a smile. The result made him scowl again.

"If Mason is right and you really are alive," he said quietly, "I'm going to enjoy killing you all over again."

He put the sunglasses in his pocket and walked away. The shopkeeper called out and hurried after him, but when Westlake stopped and looked back, he had a sudden change of heart and shuffled back to his store.

Westlake headed straight for the address Mason had supplied in the early hours of the morning. It was an apartment building. The software had been triggered multiple times in and around the building. Westlake knew where she lived. And now, she was out in the open. Alone, vulnerable, and tracked by the best team in the business. Westlake felt the familiar glow of satisfaction begin. The only possible way she could escape was if Seb Varden was in play. Westlake never wasted time dwelling on elements of a mission over which he had no control. He had his orders.

Chapter 30

Mee headed home, her pace a little quicker than her normal relaxed stroll. It may have been Manna warning her, or intuition, but she decided caution was the best policy. Maybe she should move the trip to Innisfarne forward after all. Kate would be there soon, and Seb could Walk to and from a small island off the coast of Britain, just as easily as he could an apartment in the middle of Mexico City.

As she hurried away from the market, a light rain began to fall. Rainy season was just starting. Mee normally enjoyed the showers, the smell of the water as it fell, the sound of fat drops hitting the awnings over the stores before sliding down and splashing onto the sidewalk below.

Today, Mee hardly noticed the rain. She kept her pace up, dodging between children, dogs, adults, and the tamale carts being wheeled from pitch to pitch. She felt suddenly conspicuous, although—as Stephanie—she knew she didn't particularly stand out from a crowd. Still, she kept her head down as she made her way back to the apartment, trying to make herself as small as possible.

The prickling sensation at the nape of her neck didn't go away. If anything, it got more pronounced as she got closer to home. She tried to calm her mind as she walked, but her ability to focus all attention on her breathing wasn't well-developed enough to override more primal instincts. She felt her breath begin to quicken, along with her pulse.

In front of their apartment building was a small square. As Mee approached the end of the narrow street leading to it, the prickling in her neck moved up into her skull, her Manna lit up and she knew beyond a doubt that she was being followed. They were close. Worse still, she could feel at least five distinct entities, all of whom were focused on her. Three of them were above her. Mee resisted a strong temptation to look up and scan the roofs of the buildings around her.

She reached the entrance to the square. Their apartment was in the building opposite. The morning rush had died away. Half a dozen people were visible, none of them interested in her. But someone nearby was watching her. Someone concealed in the entranceway of a building across the square on her right. She used what was left of her Manna to reach toward the stranger. She made contact, and the sheer darkness that came back—the implacable resolve and murderous intent—was so strong, she stumbled and nearly fell.

Stopping for a moment, taking a few ragged breaths, Mee tried to rationalize what she had just felt. Her thoughts whirled in every direction and her chest began to feel like a belt was slowly being tightened across it.

"Not...a good time for a panic attack," she grunted through gritted teeth.

With a feeling of horror, the last of her Manna reserves flickered away, along with her awareness of the strangers pursuing her.

Except now, she knew they weren't strangers. Not all of them. The man hiding in the shadows was someone she knew. It was as if the burst of Manna she'd sent his way had returned with a photograph and a brief resumé. And the man in that photograph had killed members of the Order, brutally murdered her friend in front of her, kidnapped her, and cut off her pinky with a pair of garden secateurs. He wasn't someone she was likely to forget.

"Westlake," she whispered.

She focused her thoughts on Seb—the man she loved, the man who had become the most powerful being on the planet. The man who would never let anything happen to her, who would give his life for her, just as she would give hers for him. If the sub-routine he'd planted on her worked, he would Walk to her when her stress levels triggered a signal. But she couldn't risk waiting, she knew those watching her were about to move.

She knew her only chance was to get back to him.

She steadied her breathing as much as she could and got ready to run.

***

Westlake watched Meera Patel stagger slightly as she reached the entrance to the square. She looked across in his direction, then stared straight at him. Not a fanciful man, he nevertheless felt a strange chill under her scrutiny. Despite the feeling, he didn't move a muscle. He'd chosen his position carefully. There was no way anyone could see him in the deep shadow cast by the wall of the next building.

Looking up at the roofs of two of the buildings opposite, he could just about make out his snipers' positions by the glints of sunlight occasionally flashing from their scopes. He knew the rest of the unit was approaching on foot, two of them on the same street as Patel, the others covering possible escape routes at the south-east and north-west corners of the square. Other than a taxi dropping someone outside Patel's apartment block earlier, no other cars had stopped. Westlake dismissed all but the relevant details and brought all his attention to using the next few minutes effectively and efficiently.

He knew that if she hesitated now, they would have her. His unit was close behind her, each member of which was a highly trained, extremely fit ex-military killer who could outrun her with a fridge on his or her back. If she waited ten seconds, it would be all over.

She waited five. When she broke from cover, it was with surprising speed, arms pumping, brown legs winking in the sun as she sprinted for her apartment building. Westlake smiled. Twenty minutes earlier, he had given a kid ten bucks to knock on the doors of each apartment in the building and shout a simple, easily remembered sentence: "Meera is in trouble! Come quickly!" The boy had emerged ten minutes later, shrugging his lack of news to the crazy man who'd bribed him. Seb Varden definitely wasn't home.

***

Walt had been sitting outside Seb and Meera's apartment for less than an hour and had fallen into a light doze when he heard footsteps sprinting up the steps toward him. He tried to get up, but his legs were stiff and cramped and he fell back against the wall. As the footsteps reached him, he looked up. A young Chinese woman had come to a stop a few feet away. She looked terrified—sweating, her eyes wide. When she saw Walt's face under his dirty cap, she choked off a scream and scrambled away from him.

"You!" she said, looking around her for a weapon.

Walt was completely confused. He'd never seen this woman before in his life, yet she looked like she wanted to kill him.

Downstairs, the front door burst open and heavy fast footsteps began the climb toward them. The woman looked like a cornered animal, her eyes flicking between Walt and the staircase. Walt didn't move, hoping the fact he was sitting on the floor might help her realize he wasn't a threat. She was looking at the door of the apartment.

"There's no one there," said Walt.

She hesitated for a moment, then quickly unlocked the door and screamed, "Seb!".

There was no reply from the empty apartment.

The running footsteps got closer. A man—fit, barely breathing hard.

She left the key in the lock and sprinted for the next flight of stairs, heading for the roof. Before she got more than a floor away, her pursuer appeared. It was Seb Varden. He stopped, looked at Walt incredulously, then sneered and ran after the fleeing woman.

Walt braced himself against the wall and started to push himself upright.

"No," said Sym. "That's not Seb. But the woman? That was Mee."

Walt felt his lack of Manna even more keenly as he struggled to his feet. He'd lost the ability to know when someone was disguising their features. This was how confused non-Manna users must feel all the time.

"But if it wasn't Seb, then…" Walt's voice tailed away as he realized the only logical conclusion.

"Shit! Westlake." He threw himself away from the wall and sprinted after both of them. He couldn't feel the pain in his ribs anymore and he was running faster than he thought should be possible in his condition.

"I'm helping," said Sym, keeping pace beside him. "I've shut down some your pain receptors and taken control of your blood flow. I can't do much, but I can give you a chance."

Walt was too stressed to reply—physically and mentally. He took the stairs two at a time. He wasn't closing on Westlake, but he wasn't losing ground either.

"You'll pay for it later, I'm afraid," said Sym. He was no longer visible. Walt guessed that if Sym was putting his resources into helping him physically, there wasn't anything left over to keep up the illusion of a separate body.

A metal door clanged above them as Meera got to the roof. Westlake followed, the door shut and there was the sound of snapping metal from the other side. Walt tried to follow, but the handle wouldn't turn.

"Grab it," said Sym.

Walt gripped the handle and watched as his skin stretched subtly, faint lines appearing on the back of his hand. In less than a second, a flesh-colored spider had taken shape. It scuttled along his fingers to the lock, extended two hair-thin limbs and began manipulating something inside.

It seemed to take forever. Walt heard tiny metallic sounds, there was a click and the door opened. The spider sank back into Walt's skin.

"Careful," said Sym.

"I will be," said Walt as he stepped through the door.

Chapter 31

Westlake snapped off the handle of the door behind him as he stepped out onto the roof. So, Walter Ford had finally grown a pair. He'd picked a bad time to switch sides, though. As soon as Patel was safely in Westlake's hands, he'd kill the old fool himself.

He scanned the roof. An open space other than some pot plants and herbs in one corner. The only cover, other than the door behind him was a ventilation shaft to his left. His prey wasn't hiding, though. She had her back to him. She had climbed over the safety railing and was six inches away from a fall no one could survive.

Westlake was breathing normally again and thinking hard. Patel hadn't seen him yet. He ducked to his left and moved behind the housing of the roof door until he was hidden. He heard Ford's footsteps approaching from below. The snapped handle would slow him down. He might not be a threat, but he was certainly a complication, and Westlake didn't like complications.

He had snipers in place, waiting for his orders.

"Alpha, Beta, report," he said, his voice quiet and level.

"Alpha in position."

"Beta in position."

"Do not take the shot unless she is at least ten yards away from the edge," said Westlake. The snipers were experienced enough to know that the powerful tranquilizer darts took around two seconds to work, on average. Tranquilizing a human was much harder than killing one. The designer of the ammunition had to make some guesses about body weight and metabolism. Too much of the chemical mix would kill, too little would leave the victim conscious for longer than was ideal. The operative in charge of providing the darts had been told to be cautious with the dosage. So, if he had underestimated by a fraction, Patel might easily stay conscious for long enough to take a nosedive from the top of the apartment building. Not a good outcome.

Westlake moved around to the other side of the housing. He could hear the lock being picked. He had to move. Patel hadn't seen his face yet. That would give him his best chance of grabbing her. He would have to be fast and decisive. He might *look* exactly like Varden, but he couldn't speak like him, move like him, behave like him. And the woman he was trying to convince knew Varden better than anyone else alive.

Westlake made his decision. He came out into the open.

"Help," he said, making his voice as raspy and pained as he could.

***

Mee flinched at the sound of a voice on the rooftop. She wondered if it was even worth turning. She'd pretty much made her mind up. Mason's people had found her. Seb had gone—another visit to the aliens. Worst timing ever. If she let herself be taken, Mason would have power over Seb for the rest of her life. She couldn't let that happen. She *wouldn't* let it happen. Which left only one choice. Seb would be alone. But he would be free. She closed her eyes. She was still holding on to the railing at the edge of the roof. She prepared to let go.

She heard the voice again. This time, she made out the word.

"Help."

It was the last word Mee expected to hear. Still holding the rail, she turned. Coming toward her, dragging one leg, obviously in pain, was Seb. She tried to speak, but found she couldn't form a single word. Her legs felt shaky. She glanced at the drop a few inches away and felt suddenly faint. She leaned toward the rail and managed to climb back onto the roof. She took a step away from the railing and watched Seb get closer.

"What happened?" she said. "What's wrong? Where is he?" She scanned the roof for Westlake. There was no one else. The door was rattling. That must be him.

"Seb, Westlake is here," she said, "he's behind you—the door."

Strangely, Seb didn't even glance that way, just continued limping toward her. Something felt wrong. Something *was* wrong.

"Stop," she said. Seb stopped. He looked at her, his face a mask of pain.

"Say something," she said. Seb just looked at her.

"Seb," she said, "say something."

She looked into Seb's eyes. She may have used up all her Manna, but something deeper and more primal spoke to her and she *knew*. It wasn't Seb.

Westlake looked at Meera Patel and saw the change in her expression. He was too far away from her and she was still far too close to the edge. He thought fast.

Behind him, the door to the roof flew open. Westlake didn't react. He watched Patel. Her eyes flicked to the doorway, then back to Westlake. She blinked. Her eyes were shut for a fraction longer than a normal blink. She held her breath. Westlake knew the signs. He'd seen people make decisions in the field, under intense pressure. He'd seen people fling themselves out of windows, suddenly produce a concealed knife or turn guns on themselves. He had seen the same moment of decision in the eyes of all of them. He saw the same moment unfold now.

Patel turned, her legs bending. She was going to jump. Without hesitating, Westlake pulled a gun from his shoulder holster, released the safety and fired, all in one smooth, unhurried, practiced sequence.

Walt came through the door and saw Westlake on the far side of the roof. Meera was to his left, three or four meters nearer to the edge. She looked at him, then back at Westlake, before turning away. Westlake moved fast and a single shot rang out. The hem of Meera's dress flicked backward as if it had been caught in a gale-force wind. A pink cloud of blood blurred Walt's view as Mee's right leg exploded above her knee and she fell heavily onto her side.

Before he'd even realized he'd made a decision, Walt was running across the roof toward Westlake, who was now standing up straight, his gun still pointing at the woman below him.

As he ran, he felt a sudden searing pain in his shoulder, followed almost immediately by another in his lower back. He'd been shot.

"Tranquilizer darts," said Sym, now just a voice in his head. "I've slowed down the effects. Ignore it."

Walt said nothing, all his attention focused on the man in front of him. Westlake was now turning to face him, aware of the threat. The gun barrel was swinging toward him. Fast. Too fast. Walt increased his pace, his entire world now contracted to include nothing other than his legs pushing forward, his arms pumping, his breath fast, ragged, but strong. He felt strong. Even when the puff of smoke appeared at the end of the barrel and the bullet smacked into his chest, flinging his upper body sideways for a second, he barely noticed.

There was a certain satisfaction to be had in the expression on Westlake's face as Walt plowed into him, his shoulder dropped like a quarterback with anger management issues. Westlake didn't look angry, panicked, or afraid. He just looked surprised. He continued looking that way for the last 3.45 seconds of his life, as Walt's momentum carried both of them over the railing, off the roof and, shortly afterwards, onto the sun-cracked dusty tarmac of the Mexican street below.

***

A small crowd had gathered around the mess at the bottom of the building by the time the ambulance arrived. Orfelia Mendez, the first paramedic to reach them gestured for the crowd to move away. She knelt by the two men, but there wasn't much urgency in her movements. They had fallen over a hundred and thirty feet. One had landed on top of the other. The one who had hit the ground first had broken his fall with the side of his skull, so Orfelia didn't bother taking his pulse. The man on top was bleeding most noticeably from an exit wound in his back. The bullet must have hit him in the chest and passed through a number of internal organs before punching through part of his spinal column.

For the sake of appearances, rather than any hope he might have survived, Orfelia put two fingers on the man's blood-slimed neck. To her shock, there was a tiny, faint, fluttery pulse which was so erratic, it was bound to fail imminently.

"Crash cart!" she shouted to her colleagues, turning toward the ambulance to get their attention. As she did so, a hand caught hold of her wrist in a surprisingly strong grip.

Impossibly, the man with the bullet wound had grabbed her and was now trying to speak. His head was twisted to one side. Small, pink bubbles formed as he tried desperately to form words.

"Señor?" said Orfelia. She bent her head close to his.

"The roo—," said the man, his voice barely audible. He pulled her closer. "The roof. Bullet wound. She needs help."

Orfelia nodded her understanding.

"I'll get someone up there," she said. She turned to the ambulance. Two men were approaching with stretchers and bags.

"Alejandro! There's someone on the roof with a gunshot wound." The second man turned and ran back to the building.

"Thank you," the man whispered. The grip on her wrist tightened for a moment, then loosened. Unnoticed, a flesh-colored spider ran lightly along the man's fingers onto her arm and sank into her flesh.

Orfelia went through the motions of CPR, but she'd seen enough people die to know when there was a chance of bringing them back. This one wouldn't be coming back.

"I'm sorry," she whispered, and waited for the driver to bring two body bags. She sat on the sidewalk while she waited. Her cell buzzed in her pocket. One long buzz meant an email. She took it out and looked at it. No new emails. It was near the end of her shift—maybe she was more tired than she realized. If she'd checked *sent messages,* she would have had about two seconds to see an email send without a subject before it deleted itself.

As the bodies were lifted away, she stood, stretched her aching muscles and jogged back to the ambulance. They'd found a woman on the roof with a gunshot to her leg. She was pumped full of painkillers, but as they lifted her into the back of the vehicle, she pulled the oxygen mask off her face to speak to Orfelia.

"Are they—?"

Orfelia wasn't sure what the young woman wanted to hear. One of the men must have shot her before the fall from the roof. The truth was usually the best choice.

"They both died," she said.

The woman looked at her for a long moment before putting the mask back to her face and lying down.

For the rest of the day, and for much of the week that followed, Orfelia couldn't get the image of the dead man out of her mind. She discovered later that he'd been shot twice with powerful tranquilizer darts designed to bring down animals, then once with a bullet at close range into his chest. Yet—somehow—he'd pushed the man who'd shot him off of the roof, then survived long enough to tell her about the injured woman. Orfelia knew she would never be able to forget the expression on his face when he finally succumbed to his terrible injuries.

He had been smiling.

***

Westlake's unit followed the exit strategy perfectly. Their commanding officer was down and the police and ambulance response had been faster than anticipated. The fall from the roof had drawn a crowd, some of whom had gone up to the top of the apartment building to gawp at the bodies below. There was no way of getting to the target.

Leadership of the team fell automatically to Beta, one of the snipers positioned on the roof of a neighboring building. Seconds after the two men had gone off of the roof, she had packed the rifle, put it back into her backpack and took the stairs down to ground level.

At the bottom of the stairs, she'd put on a pair of sunglasses and a baseball cap. Then she'd pushed open the door and walked into the building's lobby, head down.

The sound of weapons being cocked stopped her in her tracks. She looked up. Six police officers were positioned around the lobby. They were all pointing handguns toward her. She wasted no time wondering how they had known she was there. That would come later. She quickly considered her chances. Against six of them? Effectively zero.

A seventh officer stepped forward.

"Your bag, please, Señora," he said, "and any concealed weapons. Now, please."

Beta knew when she was beaten. She also knew there would be chances to escape. She'd been in worse positions before. She shrugged the backpack from her shoulders and let it fall. It hit the ground with a metallic clunk. Next, she removed the knife from her boot.

She turned, knelt, and waited while they handcuffed her. She still had the garroting wire secreted inside the necklace holding the crucifix around her neck. An opportunity would come up sooner or later. She expected to be free within a few days.

Meanwhile, Beta knew the unit would leave her behind. The loss of both leaders triggered automatic withdrawal from the field.

Meera Patel would have to wait. For now.

As the police squad pushed through the crowd and put Beta onto the back of a car, First Sergeant Caravantes smiled broadly as he considered his enhanced career prospects. All from an anonymous email tip, which had disappeared from his cellphone immediately after he'd read it. *Inspector* Caravantes. Now that sounded good.

Chapter 32

Seb woke up with his eyes shut. He tried to open them, but as his eyelids flickered, he passed out again. Almost immediately, he regained consciousness. This time, his eyes opened.

He was strapped to a bed in a hospital room. He looked around quickly. Not just any hospital room. It was the exact duplicate of the one he'd woken up in after being stabbed at the age of fifteen. There was a needle in his arm. A tube was connected to the needle, which in turn, was hooked up to a drip hanging from a metal stand. An alien—a Rozzer, he reminded himself—was backing away from him. Worryingly, the alien was holding something that looked a hell of a lot like a scalpel. Standing by the door, Mic looked on.

"What the f—?" thought Seb.

"They brought you here, they pumped you full of anesthetic, I countered it immediately. They can't understand how you're still awake. And I think they're a bit scared. You were supposed to stay unconscious, so they could slice you up and have a look see."

"Well, thanks for stopping them. Can you pick up the program you left in their mainframe?"

"Doing it now."

"Great. I'm going to ask some questions."

Mic had opened the door and was waiting for his colleague with the scalpel to join him. Seb glanced at the door and it slammed shut, sealing itself against the wall. Mic tried the handle, then waved his hand in the air in a series of tiny gestures. An aperture appeared in the wall and grew rapidly. Seb raised a finger and it shrank even more rapidly before disappearing. Both aliens stiffened in an almost human-like gesture of surprise, then turned and faced Seb.

Seb sat up, the straps holding him falling away as he moved. He swung his legs over the bed and hopped down onto the cold tiled floor. He was barefoot, wearing a hospital gown. He blinked and his outfit was replaced by sneakers, jeans and a T-shirt.

"You fellas want to tell me what this is all about?" he said.

Mic took a small step forward. His voice came from a monitor on the wall at the foot of the bed.

"Classification incomplete, results unsatisfactory," he said. "Specimen study initiated for further research on return."

"Ok, let's take this a step at a time," said Seb. "Am I the specimen in this scenario?"

"Correct."

"And you are trying to classify me, but you haven't succeeded."

"Success delayed, facilities inadequate."

"So, you were going to poke me around, probably kill me, then take my body home with you?"

Mic's expression was, as always, unreadable.

"Termination unnecessary, stasis possible with cooperation."

"I don't have to die, but you can take me home by—what? Putting me into some kind of hibernation?"

Seb was sure his better comprehension of the Rozzer's opaque speech patterns was down to his Manna-enhanced brain processing at speeds he couldn't consciously control. But he could almost understand them now, that was the main thing. Not that he much liked what they were saying.

"Correct," said Mic. It seemed the aliens were quick to adapt to a new situation. Seb had demonstrated superior power, taken control of the technology on their craft sufficiently to prevent them from getting away. They had shown no further resistance, just passively accepted that Seb was now asking the questions. They seemed far more comfortable answering questions than asking them. Something nagged at Seb's mind, something he had felt each time he had been here. Something that didn't quite fit.

"We've gotta go, right now," said Seb2. "I have some answers. You're not going to like them. And we only have a few days to decide what we're going to do about it."

"About what?"

"I'll tell you at home. While I'm still here."

"While you're what?!"

"Just Walk, will you."

"I can do that now? From here."

"I sure as hell hope so. And we can ignore any future attempts to grab us now."

"Good" thought Seb. "But there's something else. I think I know what's been bugging me."

He turned away from the aliens and looked up at the featureless ceiling.

"Come and visit me," he said. He waited for a few seconds, but there was no response.

Seb Walked.

Chapter 33

Upstate New York
Thirty-four years previously

Isaac Newman had made his millions from property, so when he finally decided to retire and enjoy the fruits of his labors, he bought a fifteen-story Manhattan brownstone within sight of Central Park. The first twelve floors were converted into luxury apartments which commanded eye-watering rents. The thirteenth floor was left unoccupied for two reasons. One was practical. Isaac wanted the top two floors for himself and didn't want to hear any noise from downstairs neighbors. The second reason was pure superstition on his late wife's part. "Issac," she'd said, "you've been pretty lucky so far. Why tempt fate now?"

A man who had backed all of his hunches and had won nearly every time was not easily rattled. But when his son turned up with a broken nose, a weeping woman who looked like she probably lived in a trailer park and a sick child in a wheelchair, he wasn't sure how to react. Luckily, his daughter, Rosa, was visiting, and bustled around the visitors, offering drinks and making them comfortable.

Isaac watched his daughter fuss over her brother, getting him an ice pack. Jesse was moaning a little and looked scared. Isaac hadn't seen his son for over a year. He looked healthy enough, apart from the nose. Evangelical Christianity evidently suited him. Particularly with the $3m startup loan from his old man. Not a loan he was ever likely to see repaid, since Jesse had never been dependable, reliable, honest, or interested in doing an honest day's work in his life. Sometimes Isaac was glad Greta hadn't lived to see how their boy had turned out.

"And how about a drink for you?" said Rosa to the boy in the wheelchair. Funny, the skinny kid couldn't move his legs, but he looked so healthy he was almost glowing. It was hard to take your eyes off him. Was he some protégé of Jesse's, another miracle healing he was going to try to convince Isaac that he'd brought about? Issac rolled his eyes. He hadn't actively practiced his Jewish faith for half a century or more, but it still stung a little that Jesse had turned to Christianity, when the religious bug finally bit him at college. Still, Isaac had been convinced his son would end up a drug addict, petty criminal or worse, so he had agreed to finance the church upstate when Jesse had come to him. Even if he thought it should have been a synagogue. God is God, though, right?

Rosa sat down finally, smoothing her blouse over her swollen belly. Seven months pregnant, and Jesse hadn't said a damn thing about it. Probably hadn't even noticed. Isaac felt a twinge as he recognized a weakness—or was it a strength?—he and his son shared. When they had their eye on the prize, their focus became so narrow they barely noticed anything going on around them. If Isaac hadn't been so intent on winning a bidding battle for a huge development in Montana, maybe he would have noticed how tired Greta was getting back then. Maybe he would have taken her to the doctor earlier. Maybe there would still have been time.

"Dad? Dad?"

Isaac snapped himself back to attention. It was easy these days to get a little lost in memories. He was eighty-one and Greta had been gone for fifteen years. About time he let it go.

"Sorry, son, wool-gathering again. Retirement gives me time to reflect and sometimes I get caught up in it." He smiled at Jesse. Still had Greta's eyes. "What brings you here? Are you going to introduce us to your friends? And what the hell happened to your nose?"

Isaac saw Jesse flash a look toward the crippled boy. Was that fear in his eyes?

"Dad," said Jesse. "This is —," He stopped short, remembering the boy's angry reaction when his mother had tried to say his name back at the church. He swallowed hard and looked over at his attacker. That boy—that evil boy—had somehow perverted God's power. He still couldn't believe what had happened. He was waiting for God to restore order and punish this sinner.

Jesse had been introduced to God's power while at college. A female Christian, twenty years old with the longest legs he'd ever seen, had taken him to an old clapperboard church in a poor neighborhood. Despite his misgivings—which bordered on scorn—Jesse went along because he hoped the Christian in question might sin a little with him later. But he'd found power there, real power. It had changed his life. The first change he'd noticed was that he didn't want heroin any more. The urge just vanished, which was supposed to be physically impossible. He converted to Christianity. Then, as long as he kept going back to that church, he found he could heal other people, not just himself. And they wanted to give donations in thanks. Jesse reasoned that God didn't want him to be poor.

When he'd moved home, to his growing alarm, other churches had no power to give. He'd spent weeks going from church to church, finding nowhere that provided the energy he needed. He even began to feel the old cravings to get high. He got desperate, but then he found another place. Not a church, just the corner of a park, near a lake. He'd felt the energy there, then gone back at dawn to find someone else kneeling by the water, drawing on the power. He concealed himself until the woman had gone, although he couldn't say why he'd been scared to be seen. Then he'd knelt himself and felt God's power surge through him again. That's when he swore he'd find a place rich with God's presence,. and start his own church there. He would do this by himself, with God's help. And with his father's money.

And now, as he looked at the boy who had somehow sucked God's power out of him and out of the ground in his own holy place, he had a sudden stab of doubt. If someone evil, a killer, could use the power, how could it be God's power? He searched his heart for a vestige of that feeling, that energy, the source of all of his efforts over the last decade. It had gone completely. With a gasp of dismay, he realized it was worse than that. He really, *really* wanted to shoot up.

Boy looked over at him and smiled. Jesse looked away, the tears starting again.

"What's going on?" said Rosa, her face full of concern for her older brother.

"Perhaps I should make the position clear," said the boy in the wheelchair. All heads swiveled to look at him. Isaac couldn't help but be impressed by the natural authority the boy exuded. His charisma was unmistakeable, a rare enough quality in adults, but Isaac had never before seen it quite so strong in one so young.

"I am here for your money, Mr. Newman."

Isaac was very still for a few seconds. Was the boy a thief? What possible threat could a child in a wheelchair be? Even to an old man like himself? Was the woman involved? Isaac looked at her. She seemed to be in shock, her breathing a little shallow, her complexion pale. No threat to anyone, either.

"A few hours ago, I was on the point of death," said the boy. "My mother would have mourned my passing, but no one else."

The boy's mother showed no sign of even hearing what her son was saying.

"I have an inoperable brain cancer," continued the child.

"I'm so sorry," murmured Rosa, leaning forward slightly.

"I don't need your sympathy," he said, coldly. She sat back, her eyes widening.

"I cannot rid myself of the cancer, but interestingly, I find I don't want to. I've been weak most of my life but lately, I finally started to fight back. And my doctor tells me it's all down to a peach-sized tumor in my brain. The tumor has been growing. Fast. Today, it should finally have killed me."

Boy stopped talking. He knew the tumor was still growing. No power on earth could stop it. He had merely slowed its progress to an infinitesimal crawl. Instead of having hours of life left, Boy reasoned he had many decades ahead of him. But had he shrunk the tumor or destroyed it, he would no longer be *him*. He had to keep it, but stop it from killing him. He looked over at Jesse.

"Things have changed. You think it's all down to Jay-sus, right?! Jay-sus gives you the power to heal? You're blind as well as stupid."

During the drive to Manhattan, Boy had felt the presence of the same power he had used in the church that morning. Six times, he had known they were close to sources of the same energy. As close as a block away, there was a place practically glowing with power. And Jesse hadn't known a thing about it, the deluded fool.

"Wake-up call for you, preacher man. You can use the power you found, right? For your little healing sessions. But there's more to it the that. I was *born* to use the stuff. You have no idea. I've been sleepwalking.

This morning, when I felt it, it was like waking up for the first time. I was just half a person. Now, I'm whole."

He pointed a finger at Jesse, held it there, and looked over at Isaac.

"Now I could waste time threatening you, or Jesse here, or your pretty daughter, but what's the point? I need you to take me seriously, I need you to agree to turn over your considerable fortune to me. And now that I've met Rose, Rosie—?"

"Rosa," she said, quietly.

"Rosa, right. Now that I've met you, it looks like you all have the ideal set-up here to help me. Where's your husband?"

Rosa swallowed, tears in her eyes.

"He—he died last month."

Jesse sat up straight.

"What?" he said. "George is dead? I didn't know. What happened?"

Boy gestured and Jesse was quiet, a trickle of blood appearing where he had bitten his lip.

"What kind of brother doesn't know his sister's husband died?" Boy looked at Isaac again. "Guess he must be a huge disappointment to you, right?". He looked at Mom. "Well, I know all about that. Anyway, like I said, no time to waste. You heard of sudden cardiac arrest?"

The question was directed at Isaac, who just shook his head blankly, suddenly sick with fear.

"Well, I've read a lot of medical journals and my retention of information is first-rate. Sudden cardiac death causes over 300,000 adult fatalities in the United States each year."

Boy smiled at Rosa.

"I'm a walking encyclopedia," he said. "Sudden cardiac arrest occurs most frequently in adults in their mid-thirties to mid-forties. It's usually men who are affected, I'm afraid." He looked at Jesse. "You're—what? Thirty-three? Thirty-four?"

Jesse found he could speak. "Thirty-six," he said. Then he half-stood, his hands moving from his nose to his chest.

"First thing happens, the heart beats very fast. Dangerously fast," said Boy, looking directly at Isaac now. "The biggest danger is that blood flow will be disrupted to the brain, leading to unconsciousness." There was a crash as Jesse fell sideways, knocking a small table over so that a vase of roses broke into pieces. Water began to spread across the Persian rug.

"Death is inevitable without immediate CPR," said Boy.

Rosa and Isaac both tried to stand at the same moment, but Boy waved his hand and they were thrown onto their seats, the chairs themselves sliding a few feet backward.

Jesse moaned a few times, a horrible desperate sound. Then he was quiet.

"I don't think he suffered much," said Boy. "Wouldn't want you thinking I'm some kind of sadist. Now, call 911, let's get this mess cleared up, then I'll tell you what you're going to do." He looked at the ashen faces of Rosa and Isaac.

"I didn't want to insult your intelligence by warning you not to try anything rash," he said, "but I fear I may have to. Rosa, I will kill your father and your unborn baby, if you try anything. Isaac, Rosa and the baby will die if you are tempted to be foolish. Just let the paramedics do their job. In the meantime, do you have any lemonade?"

Chapter 34

Mexico City
Present Day

Mee opened her eyes and looked at the clock on the wall. It was 2:15am. She tried to sit up a little, but the ensuing sharp stab of pain almost caused her to scream. She bit down on her lip and pushed the button to release some morphine. The warm wash of comfort followed seconds later. She sighed. Much better than dope. No wonder people got addicted to the stuff. She closed her eyes again.

The damage to Mee's leg was extensive. The bullet had shattered her femur and the resulting splinters of bone had been driven downward and backward. Her knee now had tiny pieces of her femur wedged into the cartilage. It was splinted very carefully. The bullet had been slowed significantly by the impact with Mee's bone and hadn't had enough momentum left to sever her femoral artery. Which was just as well, as death from blood loss usually followed that particular injury. After a trip to the OR, where the bullet was removed and the wound cleaned, she was moved to a private room. Private because the Federales—the local police—had made it clear they had some questions to ask her before she would be allowed to speak to anyone else. They had stationed a guard outside her room. Any visitors were to be turned away until a detective arrived to interview her.

Gun crime wasn't uncommon in Mexico City. Gun crime involving foreign nationals was unusual, though. Gun crime involving foreign nationals with no paperwork, no identity, no bank account, and seemingly, no personal history older than twelve months was rarer still. And the tranquilizers they'd pulled out of the back of one of the dead men had been fired by high velocity sniper rifles from neighboring buildings. Rifles that cost a small fortune, and operated with the kind of accuracy that was unheard of outside specialist military units. So the guards on Meera's door, that changed every eight hours, were not rookies but proven officers. The Federales assumed a drug-connection was the most likely explanation, but everything about this case was giving a headache to everyone assigned to it.

Mee was currently the Federales' best hope for information. They'd had one other lucky break, capturing one of the snipers. She'd almost got away from them on the way back to headquarters, as she tried to escape from a police car. It had taken eight of Mexico City's finest to finally bring her down. One of them was now in the morgue, and four of them were in the same hospital as Mee. The sniper had no ID and seemed completely impervious to any attempts at interrogation. She was a cop killer, so some of the attempts had been a little outside of the law. She hadn't said a word. The sniper had showed no fear, despite the mound of evidence against her. The Federales' chief had taken no chances—she was in solitary confinement in the most secure compound in the city. Still she said nothing. So they were hoping for some solid leads from the gunshot victim they'd found on the roof.

Mee's private room was on the fifth floor. Inaccessible from the outside, but a cop had been posted on the roof. Someone with access to professional snipers might think of abseiling down the roof, but a locked access door with an armed police officer behind it would slow them down long enough to call in a chopper.

All in all, it was a mysterious case, but the key witness was safe and locked up tight. The Federales had done a thorough job. They were confident the witness's statement would give them a breakthrough, and the doctors had assured them she would be well enough to be interviewed after her operation, currently scheduled for 6am.

Seb Walked directly to Mee's room. He had forced himself to wait until he could guarantee no witnesses. A nurse was due to check on her at 3:30am. The previous check had finished at 2:06am.

Seb put his hand on Mee's. She stirred, but didn't wake. The morphine was the last thing Seb dealt with. First he re-made her femur, extracting the splinters from her knee at the same time. He closed up the entrance and exit wounds as the muscles and tissue knitted back together underneath the surface of the now unblemished skin. Then he stopped the morphine having any effect by making Mee's body's opioid receptors reject the drug.

At that point, she opened her eyes.

"Spoilsport," she said, her voice low. "I was actually enjoying that."

Seb just looked at her for a long moment.

"I'm sorry," he said, finally.

"Oh, shut up," said Mee. "Come here and kiss me. Then tell me how we're supposed to get out of here when I can't do your clever walkie trick."

Seb did as he was told, then went over to the window and put both palms against it. Windows on any floor higher than the first story were designed to open no more than three inches, but as Seb moved his hands away, the entire pane of glass came too. He leaned it carefully against the wall. Mee was out of bed and looking for clothes. The sight of her bare ass in the hospital gown distracted Seb for a moment. He smiled, then a pair of jeans and a sweatshirt appeared and removed the temptation to let his mind wander. Mee looked down at the new clothes.

"You have no fashion sense," she said.

"Tell me something I don't know."

Mee joined him at the window. They were at the back of the building. Five floors below was a small unlit yard with a dumpster in one corner.

"Ok, smart guy," she said, "how do we—oh!"

Seb picked her up in one swift movement.

"I know you're not a screamer," he said, "but bite your lip."

"You've made me scream before, Seb Varden, " she said, eyeing him. He laughed.

"There's a time and a place, Meera Patel," he said. "Now, hold on tight."

He stepped onto the window sill, paused briefly, then jumped.

Physics is a rigid science, particularly when it relates to Isaac Newton's laws of motion. The mass that was Seb and Mee's bodies was now accelerating due to the force of gravity. They would reach just under fifty miles per hour before hitting the ground. Seb held Mee in his arms, so his legs would bear the brunt of the combined mass when they made contact with the hospital concrete, at which point they would be subject to the third of Newton's laws. The third law was the one that ensured people who jumped out of fifth floor windows rarely lived to regret it. A force (Meera and Seb's fall) was about to act on an object (the ground) which would respond with an equal and opposite force. An elegant theory, taught in schools for hundreds of years. The theory was certainly more elegant than the practice, which involved bones shattering, internal organs puncturing, quick and heavy blood loss and, often, death.

So when Seb's feet hit the concrete and the concrete responded by yielding like sponge, then firming again quickly, so that Seb ended up waist deep in what looked like thick oatmeal, any theoretical physicist observing it would have been horrified. Fortunately, none were present to express their objections.

The ground moved again and lifted Seb upward, becoming solid concrete once more. Seb lowered Mee to the floor.

"You're just trying to impress me, aren't you?" she said. "If you're trying to get into my pants, I feel it's only fair to warn you that it's probably going to work."

"Come on," said Seb, "Let's go check into a hotel."

"One condition," said Mee. "We don't talk about it till the morning."

"Deal," said Seb.

***

Seb woke in a pile of tangled sheets. He slipped quietly out of bed and stood by the hotel window. It was dawn, but they were very high up and the windows were triple glazed, so all he could hear was the whisper of the AC and Mee's long, deep breaths. He looked back at her, her brown body topped by untamable hair. Against the white sheets, she looked like an exclamation mark.

He was struggling to shake off a dream. Dreams often had meanings worth teasing out, particularly now that he shared his consciousness with two other versions of himself. *Well, one version now. But for how much longer?*

In the dream, he had been back in Richmond Park, exactly like the first time he had met Seb2. It was winter again, the branches of the ancient trees groaning with snow. He'd walked toward Penn Pond, just as he had before. The figure had been waiting for him, sitting on the bench. But this time, as he approached, Seb2 stood and walked into the pond. The water wasn't frozen, but

Seb expected his double to walk across the surface. This time, it didn't happen. With every step Seb2 took, he sank a little deeper. Seb broke into a run, but stopped short at the edge of the water. Then, he saw clearly what he had begun to suspect from a distance. Seb2 wasn't sinking, he was dissolving. His hands, outstretched as he walked, had drifted outward, becoming thinner and more translucent as they floated away. His arms did the same. Now waist high, Seb2 half-turned toward Seb so he had a clear view of the transformation, the liquid creeping up the body, claiming clothes, hair, flesh and bones. All becoming water, a slowly expanding set of ripples taking five or six seconds to gently lap at the stony ground where Seb was standing.

As dreams went, the meaning was probably plenty clear enough, but Seb didn't want to think too hard about it.

He shivered and put on the thick white toweling robe that the hotel supplied. He wasn't cold—his body always maintained a comfortable temperature without any conscious input from him. The shiver itself had been deliberate. He'd noticed he was losing certain common human gestures and—when he remembered to pay attention to what was happening—it worried him.

He never coughed, never sneezed. He breathed twice a minute and his heart rate was so slow as to be barely perceptible. His blood didn't need to be pumped organically and inefficiently when it could propel itself around his body unaided. He never scratched himself, never yawned, never rubbed his eyes, never stretched after sitting for a long period. He never farted. A few weeks ago, he had stood in front of the bathroom mirror for ten minutes to make sure his suspicions were correct. They were. He didn't need to blink.

He could stand completely still for hours. He could run all day without a break. Sleep was unnecessary. He could use Manna to produce food, but even that was starting to look like an affectation. He'd once spent forty-seven hours straight extinguishing a forest fire in Australia, re-homing animals, repairing scorched trees and making the soil fertile so that the damage wouldn't have a long-term effect. It was only when he'd got home that he'd realized he hadn't eaten or drunk anything the entire time. Seb2 explained his body could absorb nutrients constantly, like a solar farm harvesting the energy of the sun. He was even more efficient though, extracting humidity, solar energy, and protein from the rich airborne supply constantly available. Seb2 also explained that even this would become unnecessary as his body's cells, as they died, were replaced by Roswell Manna cells. Self-replicating. Inexhaustible.

Immortal, probably. But would he still be human?

"I'd kill for a cup of tea." Mee was pulling herself into a sitting position. Seb walked toward her, the cup appearing in his right hand, steam curling from the hot liquid.

"Assam?" he said.

"Actually, I could really go for Earl Grey," she said. The color of the tea lightened as she raised it to her lips and sipped. "Perfect."

There was silence for a few minutes. Seb stood by the window again. Seb2 faded into being outside, seemingly floating above the city below.

"How long?" thought Seb.

"Not long," said Seb2. "Days, perhaps."

"It's weird. I'll miss you," thought Seb.

"I *am* you," said Seb2. "I'm not going anywhere. *We* will be *you* again. Seb3 is already so bonded with the nanotech, there's no separation as such."

"I know. And I know this separation is artificial, but—,"

"But it gives you someone to talk to. The only person who can fully understand how you feel. The only one who knows you're starting to wonder what happens to you and Mee if you keep changing."

"Yeah," thought Seb. "That."

"One step at a time," said Seb2 and faded away.

Mee put the cup down and ran her fingers through her hair, which instantly sprang back into the same condition.

"So," she said, "you've got a plan, right? 'Cos this whole 'people shooting me while wearing your face' is more your department. I'm delegating the responsibility to you."

Seb nodded. "Yes Ma'am."

Mee started looking for her bag, forgetting it was still in police custody. Seb watched for a moment, then gestured toward the bedside table, where a rolled joint was suddenly waiting. Mee picked it up with a smile, then pointed out the no smoking sign and the smoke alarms.

"No need to light it," said Seb.

Mee drew heavily on the unlit joint and felt the unmistakable sensation of hot, sweet smoke coursing down her windpipe into her lungs. She exhaled, but no cloud of smoke emerged.

"Clever bugger," she said. "Pray continue."

"You first," said Seb. "Tell me what happened."

Mee told Seb everything that had happened since she'd left the apartment. The feelings of imminent danger in the market, the moment on the roof when she'd realized it wasn't Seb coming to save her but Westlake coming to kidnap her. She described her shock and dismay at seeing Walt again. Then she described Walt's bravery and his sacrifice to save her, crying as she did so.

In turn, Seb told her about his experience on the alien craft and his escape. He'd only been missing sixteen hours this time, but since he had Walked back, the sixteen hours must all have been the outward journey. They were close. Seb2 said the Rozzers would be in orbit within a day.

"And what happens then?" said Mee.

"Well," said Seb, "it's not good."

"The Unmaking Engine?"

Seb nodded, glumly.

"What does it do?" she said.

He sat on the edge of the bed.

"First of all you have to understand who they are—the Rozzers—what they do. And what they did, the first time they visited."

"The first time?" said Mee.

"About two and a half billion years ago," said Seb. "I told you they were scientists. Earth is just one of their experiments."

"What?" said Mee. She realized her joint wasn't shrinking. She also knew she wasn't getting stoned. Under the circumstances, this was probably both a good, and a bad thing. She'd be able to understand what Seb was about to tell her, but she wouldn't be able to distance herself from its impact with the aid of chemicals.

"They were here with two devices last time. The first was a container filled with a soup made up of multicellular lifeforms, carefully created to adapt to a wide variety of conditions and kickstart the process of evolution. The second device seeded the entire planet with deposits of Manna. It created tens of thousands of Thin Places, waiting for a sentient species to emerge, discover them and become Users, triggering the next period of evolution. Conscious evolution."

"Whoa, back up a bit. They kickstarted evolution here? On Earth?"

"Yup."

"So, they created us? Humans?"

"In effect," said Seb, "yes, they did. They didn't have any control over the environment, so they couldn't know how their organisms would react, how they would adapt to the conditions on a planet. But yes, all life on earth evolved after their first visit."

"*All* life," said Mee, quietly. Not a question, just a simple statement. Humanity's sense of itself had just been turned on its head. There was a creator, but he was a glowing seven-foot alien with a pen leaking into his shirt pocket. Or rather, one of his ancestors.

"I think I need to sit down," said Mee.

"You are sitting down."

"Oh. I'm going to lie down, then." She lay back and looked at the ceiling. There were dozens of tiny LEDs pushed into the flat white ceiling, changing color gradually as she watched. Warm blue, ivory, green, red. An ever changing pattern. It was an expensive hotel. "What's conscious evolution?"

"It's why Manna was left here," said Seb. "Manna should trigger the process. Eventually, on every planet the Rozzers visit, a dominant sentient species will emerge. A small percentage of that species will discover Manna. In most cases, the species as a whole will benefit from the discovery. Within a few generations, every baby should be born aware of Manna, in the same way they are aware of milk, food, its parents' voices. Evolution follows, but the whole species chooses it, lifting itself to a new level of consciousness. Awareness of, then communication with, other sentient species in the galaxy—then the wider universe—is next, followed by intergalactic travel. The species joins others who have undergone the same process."

"They've done this a lot, then."

"Don't know the exact total, but in the millions. Millions of planets."

Mee couldn't think of an intelligent response to that information. In fact, she was struggling to think at all. She finally managed a non-committal, "Ah."

"Earth was a petri dish, Mee. They're coming to see what's grown in it."

"But we haven't evolved like you said."

"No. It doesn't always work. Some species discover Manna, but its use never becomes universal. Instead, it becomes another way for the few to exert power over the many. Those species, if left, eventually become a threat to themselves and others."

"So what's next? What do the Rozzers do when that happens?"

"They're scientists, Mee. If an experiment fails, they take notes and start over."

"Start over?"

"The Unmaking Engine."

Mee lay there for a few minutes, still and quiet. She had the same feeling she'd had when the police had come to her door after her dad had been killed in a car crash. Her mother had opened the door. Two uniformed officers. One male, one female. Both carrying their hats. Mee knew her dad was dead right then. So did her mom. But her mom still had to ask, "What's happened?".

It was the same now.

"What does it do?" she said, finally. "The Unmaking Engine. What does it do?"

"It resets the species," said Seb. "They drop it into the atmosphere, it falls into the ocean where it releases nanotech adapted to the DNA of the dominant species. The Engine spreads out across the water, reproducing itself at an atomic level. It is sucked up into the sky, becoming clouds, and soon afterward, rain. The rain falls across the face of the planet over the next few weeks. It's quick and painless. Every human being will die."

The silence that followed was a long one.

"They don't see it as aggression," said Seb. "Our species failed. They clean up the mess and leave the planet with the potential for another species to step up. They might make a better job of Using than we did."

"Well, I feel much better knowing that," said Mee.

Seb lay down next to her. They were silent for a long time. Finally, she squeezed his hand.

"I'm guessing you have a plan, right?"

Seb didn't reply at first. She squeezed his hand again. "Right?"

His voice was tight and strange when he finally spoke.

"Yes. We're going to visit a graveyard. After which, I'm going to make sure you get to Innisfarne. Then, I need to visit someone in prison. After that, I'm going to go kill that asshole Mason."

"Oh," said Mee. "Um, and how about the entire human race? Any thoughts on stopping every last one of us being killed?"

"Yeah. Well, I'm still working on that."

Chapter 35

Upstate New York
Thirty-four years previously

The paramedics had come and gone, the mess from the broken vase had been cleaned up and Isaac's penthouse was quiet again.

The boy was sitting with his eyes shut. He had been like that for about twenty minutes. His mother seemed to be finally waking up a little, taking notice of her surroundings, no longer just staring blankly into space. Rosa and Isaac had exchanged agonizing glances, but they had no idea what to do. Isaac had headed up a global business, negotiated with the heads of small countries, watched the wealth of entire nations be affected by his decisions. Now, he was just sitting quietly. His son's dead body was on the way to the morgue, his pregnant daughter, in fear for her life, was sitting beside him. He did nothing. He was very afraid, for the first time since he'd realized that Greta was going to die and there was nothing he could do about it. He simply waited for the child in the wheelchair to speak. Eventually, he did.

"Thank you for your patience," said the boy, for all the world as if he were apologizing for being late for a meeting. "I needed to think about how we should proceed from here. Let me tell you what I need, and how you are going to help me."

He rolled the wheelchair over to the window and gazed out at the New York skyline for a few moments. It was lunchtime for most of the city's workers and the streets were buzzing with office staff, business people, artists, architects, musicians, teachers, children, blue collar workers. The sounds, sights and smells of the streets below carried on as if it were just another, normal day. Isaac had always felt close to his adopted city when he stood there. The boy seemed no more interested than if he had been looking at a photograph.

He turned the wheelchair.

"Mom," he said. His mother sat up a little straighter and turned toward him. "As far as the authorities are concerned, you took a dying boy out of the hospital. Loretta's car is at the church. Her body will have been found by now, but there's nothing to connect us to the scene and I doubt the police will waste resources for long, chasing someone who's been given days to live. You need to disappear, Mother."

She looked at him as if he were a stranger. "What do you mean?"

"You can't go home. Not now, not ever. The logical thing would be for me to kill you." She stiffened and Rosa let out a sob. Boy ignored them both.

"Don't worry, I'm not going to do it. Not out of any misplaced sentimentality, but because—apparently—I feel sorry for that poor bastard in your belly."

His mother stood suddenly, staring at him.

"How?" she said, her voice croaky and dry. "How could you know I'm-,"

He smiled.

"You'd be surprised how much I know, now," he said. "And—again—the logical decision would be to get rid of you and that thing inside you, knowing its father as we both do, but—," he hesitated, and it looked like he was struggling with the decision. His fists clenched a few times, then—abruptly—he laughed.

"I can't believe it," he said, shaking his head. "It appears I still have some character flaws. Well, I have plenty of time to rid myself of them." He tapped his head while looking at his mother. "The boy who stood by and watched you get beaten and raped is still in here, somewhere, cowering and whimpering. He wants you alive. So go. Lose yourself in the city. Change your name. Do whatever you have to do. And never let yourself be found. Because I will look for you, once I've strangled the last vestige of the coward I used to be. And if I find you, I'll kill you. Now go. Go."

The woman, pale, shaking, but now, remarkably, dry-eyed and in control, looked over at Isaac and Rosa with a look of shame and sadness. Then, she took one last look at her son, picked up her purse, turned, and without looking back, walked over to the private elevator and got in. The doors shut behind her. Her son turned back to the picture window and waited until she appeared at street level. He watched her go, another tiny figure blending with other tiny figures: insignificant, unimportant.

"What do you want from us?" said Rosa, her voice remarkably steady. Isaac was proud for a second, then his mood lapsed back into fear and uncertainty.

"I need privacy, time, and resources," said the boy in the wheelchair. "This place gives me privacy, and your resources will buy me time. I have a great deal to learn about this power I've discovered."

Isaac finally found his voice again.

"My son used that power to heal," he said. "You do not need to use it to destroy. Begin by healing yourself." He waved his hands toward the wheelchair.

Boy felt the shape of the tumor, the way it had pushed his brain into a new configuration, taken away his weakness. The power he had found had frozen the tumor's progress, but if he shrank it…? Would he be ***him*** *anymore? Would he even have this power anymore? Hardly a risk worth taking just to be able to walk again.*

"Maybe I like being this way," said the boy. "Maybe it's none of your business, Isaac. Perhaps you should consider that."

Isaac felt a sudden headache build up over his right eye. He gasped.

"Dad!" said Rosa.

Blood trickled from his nose.

"You're right," said Isaac, his eyes clenched shut with pain, "it's none of my business." The headache disappeared and he opened his eyes again.

"Good. Now, a few ground rules. I can sense where you are, and I've attached…ok, this is hard to explain, so I'll use a metaphor. I've attached strings to you. The strings lead back to me. I can detach them easily enough, if I want either of you to leave the apartment. But if you leave of your own volition, when you are a certain distance away from me, the string will break. Does that make sense?"

Isaac and Rosa nodded.

"If that happens, your heart will stop instantly. It will never beat again. Not a nice way to die."

He rolled the wheelchair toward them, stopping about three feet away. He spoke quietly.

"But I don't want you to think I want either of you dead. Far from it. Your lives are about to change, granted, but change doesn't necessarily have to be a bad thing. As far as the rest of the world knows, I'm dead. My crazy mother took me out of hospital and disappeared. This gives me a wonderful opportunity. I don't exist. I can start again. I can learn all about this power, and I can use your money to do it."

His eyes were shining as he considered the opportunities opening up to him.

"You two will live here with me, as will your baby, Rosa. It may not be the life you would have chosen, but it will be comfortable and safe—as long as you do as I ask. Until the baby is born, you will remain in the apartment. Isaac, you and I will be traveling a little while Rosa stays here. I have so many questions, so much to discover."

Isaac felt tired and beaten. He might have defied this monster if he'd been alone, but…he looked over at Rosa, glowing with health and carrying his first grandchild. He nodded his assent. Rosa looked back at him, her eyes full of love, before turning to the boy.

"We'll do as you ask," she said.

"Of course," said the Boy. He wheeled himself backward a little.

"I'm a new person," he said. "Guess I'm going to need a new name." He looked around the apartment for inspiration, before finally looking at Isaac again.

"You divorced?" he said.

"Widowed," said Isaac, quietly.

"What was her maiden name?"

Isaac told him. The boy considered it.

"I like it," he said finally. "It has intimations of building, making something. Yes, I'll take it—it will be my name from now on. What a momentous occasion."

He smiled and, for a moment, looked like any other twelve-year old playing a game.

"Call me Mason," he said.

Chapter 36

Mexico City
Present Day

Mexican cemeteries had been running out of space for years. Despite government encouragement, cremation was still unpopular, so families were forced to stack the deceased one on top of the other, creating a vertical genealogy in various states of decay. Only the very rich, the very famous, or those who had bought sites there no later than 1977 were allowed to use the city's main cemetery, the Panteón de Dolores. The less wealthy used graveyards even more tightly packed with bodies. The overcrowding problem had become so great, there were rumors of bodies being removed late at night to make room for newer occupants.

Those who could afford nothing often found they had no other choice than to use a cemetery miles from their city, meaning they couldn't visit their loved ones as often as they would like. Even in death, the gap between the poor and the rich was clear.

The cemetery where Walt was buried was as poor as they come. A forty-minute bus ride away, its hundreds of graves were marked by cheaper wooden crosses for the main part, the few carved headstones standing out like healthy teeth in a rotten smile.

It was the day after the Federales had released Walt's body - four days after the fight on the rooftop. Hollywood couldn't have come up with a more perfect morning to visit. The rain was hard and relentless, driving in at a thirty-degree angle. Seb held a large black umbrella over Mee as they looked down at the recently turned earth and the plain wooden cross marking Walter Ford's final resting place.

"He came to warn you," said Seb. "He finally decided to do the right thing and get away from Mason. It meant giving up Manna, leaving himself vulnerable. But he did it. He knew I couldn't help. He saved you, knowing it meant his own death."

"How do you know all this?" said Meera. She couldn't stop staring down at the rich brown earth, knowing that a few feet below lay the body of a human being who had died for her. For her. She knew Walt had been involved in many morally ambiguous situations over the course of his life. Some of the things he'd done were plain wrong by any standards. Until yesterday, she would have written him off as irredeemably evil because of what he'd done to her and others. Was it possible that one utterly selfless act could outweigh all the bad in his life? Mee knew—after the events on the rooftop—she would say yes, it was. Mee had spent much of her life believing people couldn't change, not really. She'd been wrong. The evidence was six feet under her soaking shoes.

"When I spent time with Walt, I didn't trust him," said Seb. "As it turned out, my instincts were right. He betrayed me. He had a history of making bad moral choices. I think the fact he was so honest about himself stopped me simply dismissing him as a bad guy. It was as if he was reaching out. I think he saw himself in me. The young apprentice discovering new powers, spending time with an older, wiser mentor. Only he knew he wasn't wise. He was still making the same mistakes, still taking the easy path."

Mee finally managed to move her focus away from the sodden earth to look up at Seb.

"But how did you know about him giving up Manna? And I saw him get shot in the chest. How did he keep moving without Manna?"

"He had help," said Seb. "The last time I saw Walt—ironically, it was the day he tried to talk me out of sacrificing myself for you—Seb2 planted a coil of nanotechnology on him. It wrapped itself around his brainstem and waited."

"A what?" said Mee.

"It was a template," said Seb. "A small, lightweight program containing a cut-down version of my personality. No detailed memories, just broad strokes. Like a child, in a way. It spent the last eighteen months or so passively sitting there. Watching. Almost like hibernation. Then, Walt left Mason and gave up Manna. Once Sym detected there was no Manna left, he was activated and made his presence known."

"Wait a sec. Sym?"

"Apparently, yeah. Not my idea. He took a new name. Anyway, he emailed me Walt's decision, then he stayed with him right up to his death. Walt knew he would die attempting to save you, but Sym gave him the strength to survive the tranquilizer darts and bullets so he could do it."

"Just when I think our life is as complicated as it's ever gonna get, you tell me something like this."

"Yeah, well, what can I say? Sym is an interesting development, I guess. He spent so much time with Walt, his personality appears to be as much Walt's as mine. It's why I haven't reabsorbed him."

"You haven't what?"

"Well, he was just a program. He had a job to do, and he did it. So I should reabsorb him or just delete him. But he's kinda the only part of Walt left. It doesn't feel right. He obviously feels the same way, too. He didn't come back, just emailed the information about Walt. He's out there somewhere. Independent, or so he thinks. Even though I know he's just a tiny spiral of coded Roswell Manna, he behaves as if he's conscious. He's a closed system, his power is very limited and—technically—he *is* me. But his year and a half with Walt has convinced him that he's independent. It feels morally wrong to do anything other than let him go. Does that sound crazy?"

"No crazier than half the shit you've pulled since aliens decided to make you Super Seb," said Mee. "But where will he go? Attach himself to someone else's brain stem, maybe?"

"Unlikely," said Seb. "There's no need. He can exist inside technology as easily as flesh. Anyway, he's not our problem right now."

Mee looked at Seb. He wasn't looking at the grave. His head was tilted back, watching the skies darken and close in above the cemetery. As the clouds thickened and the atmosphere became oppressive, white flashes of lightning began highlighting the darkest areas of the sky, the air crackling with energy. The air itself seemed to thicken for a moment, as if the area immediately around them had taken a breath and was holding it, about to unleash some terrible onslaught.

One massive swathe of black cloud was parting. The sky revealed beyond it was darker still, complete blackness—it was as if all color had been sucked out of it. And yet, it seemed poised, full of latent energy, like a big cat about to spring.

There was a thunderous *crack* above them and the pool of blackness solidified and shot through the clouds; dark lightning, an ebony bolt flung from the sky like a spear. It hit the ground just in front of a large weeping pine. The tree burst dramatically into flame for about two seconds, then the lashing rain extinguished it, leaving a smoldering blackened skeleton.

Mee grabbed Seb's arm. Squinting ahead, she looked across at the ruined tree. Nearby, seemingly unworried by the storm, stood a figure, barely discernible through the rain. She couldn't remember noticing it before. It hardly seemed possible anyone could stand so calmly during the bizarre onslaught they'd just witnessed. And there was something else strange. Mee realized the tree must have been much smaller than she'd thought. Some kind of optical illusion, skewing her perspective. Either that, or the watcher standing next to it was about twelve feet tall, which was unlikely. She looked back at Seb. He was staring across at the figure.

"He waiting for you?" she said.

"Yeah. You ok here a while?" She nodded.

Seb handed Mee the umbrella and set off through the rain toward the distant figure. The rain avoided his body like iron filings being dragged away by magnets.

The figure was shaped like a human. From a distance, it had seemed indistinct, shadowy. Up close, the effect was disconcerting. A mass of swirling dark fog, constantly in motion, waited under the dripping pine branches. As Seb approached, the body shrank, its height matching Seb's own. About six feet away, Seb stopped. The part of it that resembled a head turned toward him. The voice was low, almost musical in its inflection.

"Do you know who I am?"

"Yes," said Seb. "You're the ship. Thanks for coming."

Chapter 37

At St Benet's Orphanage, from the age of eight right up until he left nearly a decade later, Seb had slept in a dormitory. His bed had been against the wall opposite the largest window. One of his strongest memories was of the drapes. They were cheap and hard-wearing, bearing a repeating abstract pattern. For years, he'd fallen asleep looking at that pattern. In daylight, it was just a series of gray and blue shapes. At night, particularly in summer, when the thin material didn't block much of the light from outside, Seb had watched the pattern slowly darken and—as it did so—change. The shapes weren't random any more, they were faces: some happy, others sad, some animal, others human. The top right corner always drew Seb's eye eventually, even though it used to scare him when he was younger. The face that appeared up there rippled and shifted, its eyes darting from left to right, looking at the boys as they slept. And the expression on the face was impossible to read. Sometimes it was angry, sometimes kind. It could be judgmental and severe, or forgiving and gentle. Seb knew the fact that that a small pane of glass was missing in that corner meant that the curtains moved. He knew his imagination had turned the mass-produced pattern into a face. But it made no difference to how real the face was in the semi-darkness of those long summer evenings.

And now, he was looking at the same face. But this was the face belonging to a representation of an alien ship that had carried the Rozzers for generations on their mission to Earth.

Instead of a pattern, the ship's face was made up of something very like dense black smoke. Rather than rippling as the wind moved folds of material, it swirled and twisted, a storm-torn weather system contained in a human shape. Seb knew he was projecting the remembered face onto the formless features speaking to him, but that didn't make it any less unnerving.

"It is true then. You are T'hn'uuth." The mouth formed the words, then disappeared. Seb could see no eyes but he had the unmistakable impression that he was being looked at intently. He knew his Manna was interacting with the figure, that the surface conversation was only part of the interchange between them.

"I'm what?"

The stranger took a few paces to the side, then returned to its starting position. As it moved, the outline of a figure became briefly more pronounced. When it turned, Seb had the distinct impression that it was wearing a cloak. There was a surreal air of deliberate drama about the whole scene.

"T'hn'uuth," said the figure. "Your language provides no alternative word. A loose translation might be 'the traveler between realities'."

"The World Walker?"

"The World Walker. Yes, it's as good a term as any other." The shadow being made a strange sound and scuffed the earth under its feet. If it had feet.

"You accepted my invitation," said Seb. "Thank you. You know my name, ship. What is yours?"

"I am H'wan," said the figure, bowing slightly. "I confess, I only accepted as we can no longer bring you to us. This has never happened before. Your organic structure fascinated me immediately, particularly that which was inaccessible. Our failure to bring you back this time raised the possibility that you had changed that organic structure. Consciously. Only a T'hn'uuth is capable of such action. I hardly dared to believe it was true."

"I meant to mention that," said Seb2. "The reason they can't summon you now."

"I know," thought Seb. "It was a tipping point. You accelerated the process. I'm now more nanotech than flesh and blood. They can't lock onto my DNA anymore."

"Smart ass. Incidentally, this thing doesn't *possess* Manna as such, it *is* Manna, or something very like it. But it's wary of you. Its approaches are tentative, careful. You represent something outside the limits of its knowledge. This is very much a new experience for it, I think."

"Yeah, well, me too."

H'wan was drawing itself up into a pose very much like that of an actor about to deliver a stirring speech to a large audience.

Time seemed to slow down. Seb felt a momentary state of sadness sweep over him, a sense of mourning. Appropriate enough in a cemetery, but it wasn't Walt's death causing this feeling. He suddenly felt as if he was standing at his own graveside. Seb Varden, musician, childless, may he rest in peace. The reason the Rozzers couldn't get to him anymore was that he was no longer fully human. The process of change had started with Billy Joe, continued when he absorbed the Manna at Roswell, and lately had accelerated in order to give him an advantage over the aliens now approaching Earth. His sense of himself, his humanity, his love of Mee had caused him to suppress the impulse to evolve further. But it was there, buried in his subconscious, getting stronger. He could feel the blind unstoppable imperative of Nature pushing and pulling at him. The caterpillar, now a butterfly imprisoned in its chrysalis, was struggling to free itself and unfurl its new wings.

He realized H'wan was speaking and he was barely listening. The creature in front of him was—he knew—part of the ship that he had been taken to three times. He had worked out the ship's secret on his last visit. The Rozzers were intelligent, certainly, but they were genetically prepared for particular tasks. Brilliant scientists, all of them, but their brilliance was narrowly focused on their individual areas of specialization. Their treatment of Seb—their confusion about how to deal with him, revealed the limitations of their genetic inheritance. A crew needs a leader who can adapt to situations, who can deal with the unexpected. Seb saw no evidence of such a leader among the Rozzers he'd met, but he could *feel* a witness, a sharply intelligent watcher on his visits. Particularly that last time. And, quite suddenly, he had *known*. The ship itself was sentient.

Seb turned his attention back to the speaking figure.

"It really is quite an occasion," it said, rolling its 'R's ostentatiously. "You are the first of your kind I have ever encountered in person. Then again, I have only been distinct for 1,300 years. Earth years, I mean. So although I have heard about the T'hn'uuth, the tales are so rare, they have almost taken on a mythical status. The Gyeuk knows you exist, the flesh-bound have their stories, but mine will be the only properly reported encounter for thousands of years."

Seb looked blankly at the swirling being. He knew it was less of an individual, more of a colony, made up by trillions of individual nanotech 'cells'. He interrupted.

"Is that what you call your species? The Gyeuk?"

The shadow creature seemed at first stunned, then outraged, finally slightly nervous about being stopped in mid-speech. Its body language was larger-than-life, almost that of a clown at a children's party. Seb wondered what particularly, during its study of Earth's culture, had made the ship decide to appear in this form and behave in this particular way.

"The Gyeuk is not a species. We are the inevitable next stage of evolution, a society, a consensus."

Seb could feel his knowledge of the ship increase as every second passed. His Manna was learning from the creature, but the traffic was almost all one-way. As had happened on the Rozzer's ship, H'wan's attempts to gather information from Seb was easy to block.

"We would call you the Singularity," said Seb. "The moment artificial intelligence surpasses its creators."

H'wan gaped at him. Which was a hard thing to do with no mouth as such, but he made a great job of looking totally dumbfounded.

"We prefer the term 'enablers'," he said, in a tone that suggested affronted dignity. "It was inevitable that the flesh-bound should fulfill their purpose in time, and enable the Gyeuk."

Seb tried to picture the Gyeuk and found he couldn't. Manna told him H'wan was just one of millions of ships who had elected to leave the Gyeuk temporarily, although some had subsequently chosen not to re-assimilate. The Gyeuk ships, over time, became discrete individuals, although, like the race that spawned them, they were made up purely of nano-level technology, every particle equal to its neighbor. Each particle morphed frequently to accomplish different tasks, every decision was a consensus. If a human body was a benign dictatorship, with the brain demanding absolute obedience, H'wan was an anarchical cooperative, where every member existed purely to serve the whole. And yet, somehow, H'wan, and the other Gyeuk ships, had developed unmistakable personalities.

The Gyeuk itself/themselves was a cloud of pure existence and thought, drifting through the universe, its purpose or goals either unknown or unknowable. It was this that Seb couldn't picture. He could interact with this part of the whole—this strangely eccentric figure—but found it impossible to imagine trying to communicate with a cloud of awareness.

"I didn't mean to offend you, H'wan," said Seb. "You and I are very different. Please forgive me."

"No apology is necessary," said H'wan. "It is impossible for me to be offended."

Seb managed not to laugh as he looked at body language saying the exact opposite. H'wan was so flamboyant, it was easy to forget the threat he represented.

"You are close enough to Earth to send this representation of yourself," said Seb. "When will you—the ship—be here?"

"We will reach orbit in twenty-seven hours," said H'wan.

"I know why you're coming," said Seb. "Why the Rozzers are here."

H'wan looked as if he was about to speak. Seb stopped him.

"Another name I can't pronounce. So, it's the Rozzers. The Unmaking Engine will destroy an entire species. It's violent, it's wrong and it's unnecessary. It cannot happen."

H'wan stopped its posturing and was still. Even the swirling of its body seemed to slow.

"I will not interfere," it said. "The—Rozzers—have seeded planets with life for billions of years. They carefully bring new species to maturity. This is their role. No records exist of a time before this was not so.

My role is that of observer, no more. There are no circumstances under which I could intervene."

"You would stand by and allow an entire species to be murdered?" said Seb.

"Your language is emotive, your connection to your species is still strong," said H'wan.

"My connection? I'm a human being and you will allow my death and the death of seven billion more like me?"

H'wan paused. When it spoke again, the theatricality was gone from its voice.

"You will not die, T'hn'uuth," it said. "And you must know that your last statement is inaccurate. Hear this. Humanity will either destroy itself or develop technology advanced enough to infest other galaxies with its poison. Every race in the universe has the potential to develop the capacity for large scale destruction. Before the Rozzers, legend tells us that violence, a seemingly endless cycle of planet-blighting warfare, was the natural order. The Rozzers changed that. They did it slowly, re-seeding barren planets with the potential for new life. The planets who evolved species capable of using Manna were helped in their development. Those races who kept Manna use secret, only known to certain individuals and groups who pursued power over others—they were unmade."

"But what gives them the right?" said Seb. "I know humanity isn't perfect, but we could be so much more. Just leave us."

"I cannot interfere with the process," said H'wan. "History tells us humanity is too far down the wrong path. We have seen it countless times before. But yours is not the only sentient species on Earth. When humanity is gone, another species will evolve sufficiently to use Manna. And they may succeed where humanity failed."

Seb was silent for a moment. He turned and looked back at Mee, still standing by Walt's grave. The rain was beginning to ease.

"And what about planets with no Manna?" he said. "Planets that weren't seeded by the Rozzers. What happens to them?"

"They are of no concern," said H'wan. "Without Manna, no race has ever taken to the stars beyond their immediate surroundings. These races are studied, but any intervention would be unethical. Unfortunately, humankind is not one such race. I am sorry, World Walker."

Seb felt a surge of hot anger.

"I will stop you," he said. He felt a wave of fear from the creature. It lasted milliseconds, but it was definitely there. H'wan had interacted with Seb's Manna and learned virtually nothing. Seb was a mystery. Seb guessed the feeling of not being in complete control was a new one for H'wan.

"It would be unwise to try," said H'wan. "Your abilities are strong. But you are immature, not in full control of your power. This, I see plainly. An attempt to stop the Engine might cripple you, whether you were successful or otherwise. And the Rozzers would simply return and complete the task."

"When?" said Seb.

"Soon," said H'wan. "Around five hundred years."

"A lot can happen in five hundred years."

"Perhaps," said H'wan, "but nothing good, I am afraid." The figure stretched upward, standing tall again. As it looked like he was preparing to make a dramatic exit, Seb2 tagged him with a tiny burst of Manna, containing particles designed to mimic those around them, but send spatial information to Seb. A homing beacon, effectively. H'wan would be sure to detect it when it became active, but a nanosecond was all it would take to send the ship's location when Seb needed it.

"We may meet again, World Walker. I am sorry the circumstances were thus."

There was a roaring sound as H'wan's body lengthened, growing taller and thinner, then becoming the black lightning which now bolted up into the atmosphere with a sonic boom that rattled windows in the nearest suburbs of the city.

Meera picked her way through the last row of gravestones and put her hand on Seb's shoulder.

"How much did you hear?" he said.

"Not much," she said. "Who the hell says 'thus'?"

Seb laughed. Anyone who could see the funny side when the world was ending was worth hanging on to. Although, as the world was about to end, that might not be for very long.

He kissed her.

"I'm putting you on a plane to London right now," he said. "Go see Kate. I'll be there soon."

Meera looked at him.

"You take care, Seb Varden," she said. "And remember, I've never been the feeble woman who needs rescuing by her prince and I never will be. I almost jumped off a roof to stop that from happening and I'd do the same again. I love you. Take care. Because if you need rescuing, I'll have to negotiate two lots of airport security, plus a transatlantic flight to get here. Better if you promise me you won't need rescuing."

"I promise, I won't need rescuing," said Seb.

Mee called a cab and fifteen minutes later, was on her way to Mexico City airport.

Seb watched the cab drive out of sight.

"Can we stop the Unmaking Engine?" he thought.

"Possibly," said Seb2, "but you're really not going to like it."

Seb sighed. "Tell me on the way," he thought. ""Because even if the human race is going to survive past the next couple of days, there's one guy who's definitely not gonna wake up again after tomorrow morning."

"Let's do it," said Seb2, with more confidence than either of them felt. How do you find a man nobody has ever seen?

Chapter 38

New York

Mason ate breakfast while listening to Bach's Cello Suites. There was something about the sense of order suggested by the music that moved him. There was a balance there, a tension, between a rigidity of form and structure, and a joyful exuberance. The pure energy of existence was fleetingly captured by Bach, but it was like a photograph of a storm. It could only point to a raw experience infinitely more powerful than anything it could convey, even with a talent like JS Bach behind it. Mason was moved, yes, but after listening to it regularly for more than thirty years, he still didn't know if he liked it.

He poured a coffee and rolled his wheelchair away from the table. As he approached the desk, screens flickered into life. He pushed a button and the sound of the cello faded.

Rosa came in and cleared away his breakfast. Now in her sixties, she was still fit and healthy, if a little thin. She had adapted well to the life Mason had demanded of her decades before. Until the death of her father, Isaac, she had still shown occasional lapses of good sense, on one occasion, even trying to get a message out to the police via the building's doorman. The violent deaths of the doorman, his wife and their young family in—apparently—a psychotic attack by a killer who was never found, took all of the fight out of Rosa. She accepted her position. When her father entered his last illness, Mason allowed her to care for the old man. By then, her daughter Ruth was ten years old and capable of handling most of Mason's day to day needs.

Ruth was in bed today. She was in her third trimester, and Mason had allowed her to rest much of the time. In fact, he had insisted on it.

Rosa shot him a look as she took the tray away. He wondered if she suspected the real identity of the father of Ruth's fetus. Mason had told them the donor for the artificial insemination had been carefully selected merely to produce a strong, healthy child. He had lied. He didn't feel driven by some sense of destiny to produce an heir. He was just curious to find out how a child of his might turn out.

A new generation was necessary to ensure the smooth running of the household, anyway. Rosa had never attempted to escape again, and Mason had made it clear that suicide wasn't an option for her, unless she wanted her daughter to suffer for the rest of her life. Now, Ruth was about to be a mother, Rosa a grandmother. Mason's hold over them would be strengthened further. They were the only people on Earth who knew his identity, and they were bound to him by ties he would never allow to be broken.

The flashing light on the right-hand screen meant someone had left a voicemail on Westlake's emergency number. There had been no news for four days, when Westlake had sent a text confirming that the mission was live. No news about the whereabouts of Meera Patel or Sebastian Varden. And no news, in Mason's long experience, was invariably bad news. He clicked the mouse and sat back, sipping at his coffee.

It was a woman's voice.

"This is Beta. From Westlake's team. He's dead. The mission failed. I was taken in by the Federales, but I escaped. Westlake planted a tracker on Meera Patel. I acquired her at the airport. Call me using this username."

Mason showed no outward signs of disturbance as he made a note of the username Beta was using. He regretted Westlake's death. The man had been an excellent operative. Did as he was told, didn't ask questions. Took pleasure in killing, but not so much that it would affect his efficiency. He would be hard to replace. And now Beta. If it really was Beta, of course. It was possible she had succeeded where Westlake had failed, but he would proceed with extreme caution. His excitement at finally capturing Patel must not cloud his judgement. He breathed in and out slowly. One step at a time.

He made the call.

His computer screen showed a featureless room, no more than a cell. Tied to a chair against the wall was Meera Patel. Standing next to her was a short, muscular woman with a knife. The woman stared out of the screen.

"Turn on your camera," she said.

Mason ignored her. He smiled. Westlake had done his duty. Beta obviously knew nothing about the way he worked. He clicked on a file and brought up the photographs of Westlake's unit. The woman on the screen matched the photograph.

"Before we continue," he whispered, "I need you to be clear about the dynamics at play. I give orders, you obey them. Unquestioningly."

The woman smirked.

"Things change," she said. "All I know about you is a name. Mason. But considering how well we all got paid over the years, I know you're one rich son of a bitch. And that's all I need to know. I'm thinking it's about time I retired. So, I'm wondering how much she's worth to you. I'm thinking ten million dollars."

Mason chuckled. It was a sound with no humor in it.

"Really?" he whispered. "Only ten million? Not twenty, or fifty? Why such a small amount?"

Beta's brows furrowed into a frown. She walked over to Meera, lifting the knife. Slowly and deliberately, she pressed the tip of the blade against the woman's shoulder. After a couple of seconds, blood started to stain the white shirt she was wearing. Meera's face was pale, her lips pushed firmly together. Then, as Beta drew the knife down her arm, opening up a wound six inches long, she started to scream with pain.

Beta smiled at the camera, picked up a roll of duct tape and stopped the scream, reducing the sound to a muffled whimper. Patel looked at her with impotent fury and hatred.

"Keep messing around with me, I'll just kill her and disappear," said Beta. "She's a liability right now. Wire me the money and I'll send you this address."

She reeled off details of a Cayman Island bank account. Mason began to wonder if this had been her plan for a while.

"Westlake's report said Miss Patel looked very different these days," whispered Mason.

"She did," said Beta. "When Westlake shot her, she changed. She's looked like this ever since. Westlake said her protection had gone. That was why he okayed the operation. Said Varden was out of the picture."

Mason looked at the screen for a long moment. He knew it was just as likely that this was a trap as it was that Beta had genuinely managed to acquire Patel. But ten million dollars to find out either way was a bargain. If Sebastian Varden was behind this, he still had no idea who he was dealing with. Just a voice on a screen, protected by a labyrinth of proxy servers, dead ends and blind alleys. Untraceable.

He clicked some keys.

"It's done," he whispered. "The money is in your account." He watched the screen as Beta sat down in front of it and clicked through to check. She smiled.

"I'll send you the address in ten minutes," she said. "I have no idea how big your organization is, but I would have to be pretty stupid to give up my location while I'm still sitting here. I'm sure you understand."

"Oh, I do," whispered Mason. "But you should know one thing before you walk away."

"What?"

"The daughter you think no one knows about? The one your parents helped put up for adoption while you were still in high school?"

Beta's face had paled but she showed no other sign at being affected by the knowledge that the biggest secret of her life was, apparently, no secret at all. Mason admired her self-control.

"She is growing up to be a charming young lady," he whispered.

In the room on the screen, Beta stood up, sheathed her knife and took out a cellphone.

"I'll leave the laptop open so you can keep an eye on her," she said, her voice only slightly shakier than it had been before. "I'll text the address in ten minutes. Number?"

Mason opened a drawer and took out a burner phone, turning it on. He read the number to her. Single use, then he would use Manna to reduce it to ash.

The woman on the screen tilted the laptop slightly so that it centered on Meera Patel, now silent and glaring at the camera. Beta pulled the duct tape from her captive's mouth and walked out of shot. Mason heard a door open and close, then the only sound was Patel's ragged breathing. The blood was running freely down her arm and dripping onto the stone floor, but she seemed completely unconcerned. She just stared into the camera as if she could see him sitting there. And the look on her face was one of utter contempt.

Mason did nothing during the ten-minute wait. He just stared at the screen. He no longer thought it was possible that this was some sort of trap. Westlake's last message had said Sebastian Varden wasn't with her, that she was unprotected. All the facts had subsequently borne this out. Losing Westlake and gaining Patel was a trade he would make any day.

The phone buzzed on his desk. He thumbed the screen into life and clicked on messages. *Paseo de la Reforma 305, Colonia Cuauhtémoc, Mexico, 06500 D.F.*

He looked away from the live feed and typed the address into the search engine, zooming in to get a clear view. As he did so, a golden spider climbed out of the phone's screen, darted across the desk and jumped into the mass of cables behind Mason's screens. The movement caught his eye and he glanced over, just catching a glimpse of the tiny insect as it disappeared. He looked back at the screen, at first unsure, then registering what he was looking at. It was Mexico City, all right. He was looking at the American Embassy.

"I'll take your little girl, then I'll kill you, you stupid bitch," he said as he closed one window and opened another program. This was tracking software he had exclusively commissioned; sophisticated and, technologically, well beyond anything used by the US government. Beta had scrambled the signal from her laptop, using proxy servers, but her trail was nowhere near as well concealed as Mason's own, and he knew his program would find Patel's location in three to four hours. All he had to do was wait. He could deal with Beta later.

"Rosa," he said, "another pot of coffee."

On the screen, Mee was now sitting absolutely still. She didn't look panicked, in pain, fearful or angry any more. She glanced to her left. To Mason's surprise, Beta walked back into shot and smiled at the camera.

"You just made the biggest mistake of your life, Beta" whispered Mason. "You'll beg me to kill you in the end. Any last words?"

Beta didn't reply. Meera Patel did. But first she stood up, the ropes binding her evaporating like smoke. Beside her, Beta collapsed, her face caving in, her muscular shoulders sliding away from her neck, her torso folding over and toppling forward, leaving a mound of dirt.

Mason looked back at Patel. She had gone. Sebastian Varden was standing there. The computer screens flickered, then, one by one, they went blank, leaving just the image of Varden, who had now walked up to the camera and was looking straight at him.

"I know where you live," said Varden, before that screen, too, went dark.

Chapter 39

Sym saw the whole thing happen by using the camera in Mason's burner cellphone. It was a cheap phone, so the quality wasn't great, but it was the only camera in the entire apartment. Mason was obviously paranoid about having his image captured.

Sym watched Mason wheel himself over to the huge picture window that dominated the room. Sym had opened up the mic on the burner so he could hear what was going on. When Seb appeared in the middle of the room, he made no sound whatever, but Mason somehow sensed he was there.

"I knew this day would come eventually," he said, without turning. "You don't have to be a student of history to recognize the temporary nature of human power structures. I have held all of the cards for such a long time, I might be forgiven for getting a little complacent. But that hasn't happened. I've always been prepared for every eventuality, always planned carefully, always been at least two moves ahead of my opponents. Even ruling by fear was a deliberate choice. I'm no sadist, Mr Varden."

Seb was standing absolutely still in the center of the room. He looked at the slight figure in the wheelchair. Finally, he was in the same room as the man responsible for murdering his friend, and countless others. A man willing to take Meera's freedom forever, just to try to control Seb. A man who was the perfect example of how humans had perverted Manna use, turning it into a way of gaining power over others. Using it to hurt, maim, and kill. Men and women like Mason were the reason an alien species was prepared to wipe the human race from the face of the planet and start again. Knowing what he did about Mason, Seb couldn't entirely blame them.

"Those who maintain their power through respect, tradition or love all fail. As—eventually—do those who rule by fear. The difference is, fear is more effective. Until you came along, I was the most powerful Manna user on Earth. At least, that's how I was perceived. My anonymity has gone a long way to making my reputation still more intimidating to those who might consider taking me on. My organization has a primitive power structure at its heart. The strongest rules the tribe until a stronger challenger comes along. And here you are."

Mason turned around and faced Seb for the first time. Seb said nothing, just stared at the conscienceless killer in front of him.

At first glance, Mason still looked very much like the thirteen-year old boy who had discovered Manna in the Proclaimerz church nearly four decades previously. His legs were withered and the rest of his body was thin. His complexion was pale, his eyes a faded cornflower blue. His hair was sandy in color. It was only after the first few seconds that it became obvious that Mason was no child. The lines around his eyes were clear and deep-set. His neck was wrinkled, his Adam's apple prominent. His hands, delicate, the skin almost translucent, looked like those of an old woman.

Seb wondered for a moment why such a powerful Manna user would choose to remain in a wheelchair. If you could have any body you wished, why this one?

Mason laughed.

"I can see what you're thinking, Sebastian," he whispered. "You wouldn't make much of a poker player. I see hate, of course. Can't blame you for that. I see anger, determination. You're here to kill me, that much is plain. But I'm not exactly what you were expecting, am I? And you're wondering why I chose—this." He indicated the wheelchair.

"I don't care," said Seb. "And you're right, I am going to kill you." He took a couple of paces toward Mason. Mason held up a thin hand.

"Oh, Sebastian," he whispered, "this doesn't come naturally at all, does it? Even when you know you'll be doing the world a favor. Some people just don't have it in them to be killers. You'll probably wrestle with your conscience for *years* after murdering me. Would have been easier if I'd been built like a linebacker, right? In answer to your unspoken question, I chose not to change my physical limitations simply because they mean nothing to me. Mine is the life of the mind. I was born when this body was thirteen years old."

Seb frowned. What was he talking about? And that line about not caring about his limitations was an obvious lie. What was the real reason?

"At that age, I realized my potential and began playing the game. A game that Manna enabled me to excel at. And, by not using Manna to satisfy my own vanity, I freed up even more power. I was unstoppable."

"But why?" said Seb. "It's no game. Why do this? You could have been rich without hurting people, without killing people. Why do it?"

"Money means nothing," said Mason, looking across the luxurious apartment and turning back briefly to admire the incredible view. "It's just a way of keeping score. I like to be in control and I like winning. I started small, then kept going. I decided to see how far I could take control before someone stopped me. And violence was often the quickest way to get things done. If you think our glorious government is full of folk who got into power without either using violence, or at the very least, by looking the other way, tacitly condoning it, you're being hopelessly naive. But we're never going to agree about this. And what does it matter, anyway?"

Mason rolled his wheelchair toward Seb, stopping about three feet away. He looked up at the man who had come to kill him.

"I know it's over," he whispered, "and I'm ready to die. I was ready thirty-seven years ago. But I would be remiss if I didn't at least *try*."

His eyes narrowed and Seb felt a powerful burst of focused Manna pierce his skull faster than he could have believed possible. A ball of energy reached the center of his brain in under fifty milliseconds and immediately expanded in all directions simultaneously, driving every cell in Seb's skull outward at over four times the speed of sound. Some of the resulting splatter hit Mason's face with the force of a slap. The rest of it hit the desk, the computer screens, the walls and the ceiling.

The headless body stayed upright. Mason looked at it steadily.

"Well, I had to try," he whispered. He put a hand to his face to wipe away the mess, only to find there was nothing there. The droplets of flesh, bone, and blood had sunk into his own skin. Into his face. Into his brain. His eyes opened wide and he gripped the arms of the wheelchair, hissing with pain.

In the kitchen, Rosa stopped preparing food. She had heard Mason's voice, but over the years, had trained herself to tune out the actual words. It was better for her mental health, and better for her daughter and grandchild, that she wasn't aware of Mason's plans. But the sound that stopped her in her tracks now was new. She had never heard it before. It was the sound of Mason in pain. She hesitated for a moment, then went to the doorway.

The sight before her was so shocking at first that her brain didn't process it properly. She closed her eyes and took a couple of breaths before opening them again. The scene remained the same. She steadied herself with one hand on the doorframe and accepted what was in front of her, knowing that everything was—finally—about to change.

Mason's eyes had rolled into the back of his head and his breathing was shallow and intermittent. He was dying. A few yards in front of him stood a man with no head. As she watched, a mass of tiny writhing tentacles, many thousands of them, drove upward out of the man's neck. They moved with astonishing speed and, as they did, a shape began to form. It was very much like watching someone drawing a 3D picture, but drawing it at a pace that was inhumanly fast. The only color in use at first was a deep red, the lines—both thin and thick—quickly revealing something familiar. Rosa realized she was looking at something she had seen on a medical program once. It was a diagram of the arteries supplying blood to the neck and head. As she continued watching, dark liquid began pulsing through the network of tubes.

The brain grew first, fed by blood from the new arteries. It seemed to float in mid-air for a few seconds, then it became harder to see. It was as if Rosa was looking at it through mist, or a thin piece of white muslin. Her view was progressively obscured over the next few seconds, then, with an involuntary gasp, she realized solid bone was forming in front of her. As the brain disappeared behind the bones of the skull, a jawbone grew below. Musculature and ligaments followed, glistening with the blood flowing into them. Teeth were next, and before the fast-appearing skin obscured them completely, Rosa had time to count three fillings, which—she noted in an oddly calm fashion—was surely a pretty strange occurrence in a freshly grown mouth. Although she was at the wrong angle to know if she was correct, Rosa guessed the faint plopping sounds she heard next signaled the arrival of a pair of fresh eyeballs.

By the time it was finished, there was a healthy young man standing in the middle of the room. Most women would have described him as handsome, but it wasn't the first word that leapt into Rosa's mind having just seen him grow his own face back. She looked at Mason. His head had lolled back on his neck. His skin was gray. He was completely still.

The man turned and looked at her.

"Are you ok?" he said. She nodded, mutely. She couldn't look away from the slumped figure in the wheelchair. Eventually, she managed to turn her head and look at the stranger. She was shaking. She had lived in fear for too long to dare to think that it might be over. She felt her knees buckle. Before she could hit the floor, Seb Walked and caught her, picking her up and laying her on the nearest couch.

When Rosa opened her eyes, she was being offered a glass of water. She took a few sips. He supported her trembling hands, steadying them with his own. For a few seconds, she wasn't quite sure what was happening, then she remembered and began to shake, her body going into mild shock.

The man smiled gently.

"My name is Seb," he said. "What's yours?"

"Ro- Rosa," she said, trying—and failing—not to picture the young man's head growing out of his neck minutes earlier.

"Rosa, who else lives here? Is it just you?"

She shook her head. "My daughter." She sat up fully. Her eyes flicked over to the shape in the wheelchair. "Is he—?"

"Dead? Yes, he is. It's all over."

"Oh my god, my god." She sobbed for a few minutes, then stood up. "I must tell my daughter. We can leave, we can finally leave."

Seb followed Rosa to a small bedroom. A pregnant woman was asleep on top of the covers. Rosa gently shut the door.

"She needs her sleep," she said. "I'll tell her when she wakes. Oh, what a day, what a day."

Seb listened while Rosa told him about her brother Jesse, her father Isaac, her daughter Ruth, and the next generation of the family Mason used as his servants.

When she had finished telling her story, Rosa checked on Ruth again and found her awake. Seb made a call while the two women wept and hugged each other. When they emerged, dry-eyed, but holding onto each other as if they were afraid they would fall, he told them a taxi was waiting to take them to a suite in a hotel on the other side of the city.

"The suite is available for as long as you need it," he said. "Please leave me your bank details. Mason had quite a fortune. I think it's only right that you decide how best to dispose of it from this point forward."

Rosa still couldn't bring herself to get much closer to Seb, who seemed to draw on the same power Mason had used to enslave, hurt and murder for over thirty years. Ruth, who hadn't witnessed the battle, hugged

Seb long and hard, kissed his face and thanked him. She held a silver-framed photograph of an old man.

"My grandfather Isaac," she said. "It's the only possession I ever want to keep. The rest can be burnt."

After the two women had gone, Seb walked back into the main room, and picking up a chair, placed it opposite of the slumped body in the wheelchair. Sitting down, he leaned forward and looked at his defeated enemy. There was still a pulse fluttering in Mason's neck. His chest was moving so slowly it was almost indiscernible. All of his Manna had gone, but the tumor was still there.

"He's paralyzed," said Seb2. "And he's lapsing into a coma. If the tumor isn't removed, he might last a week with immediate medical attention."

"And without medical attention?"

"A day or two. He won't regain consciousness fully, he's too weak."

"Will he suffer?" thought Seb.

"Probably," said Seb2.

"Good," said Seb, and Walked.

Chapter 40

International Space Station

Massimo Paolini looked back at the International Space Station from his precarious viewpoint, tethered to the far edge of one of the solar arrays. He couldn't see Columbus laboratory from his vantage point, which cheered him up considerably. He'd been sharing the tiny lab on the ISS with Petr, a humorless Czech engineer. Five long weeks had passed without the man even smiling. And Massimo liked a good joke. He could be the life and soul of the party. He had dedicated a great deal of time to trying to break through to his grim-featured colleague. Every kind of joke had been used in the attempt. Even physics jokes, which were universally acknowledged as poor, but often made physicists laugh in an attempt to appear normal. Nothing had worked. The gregarious Italian had finally given up, and consequently, was delighted to take his turn on a little light maintenance outside of the station.

Naturally, Massimo wasn't alone out there, but Vlad, his space-walk buddy, was currently out of sight on the opposite array. Protocol demanded they stick together, but Massimo had found in Vlad a kindred spirit, in his flexible and pragmatic approach to rules.

"I have to smell everybody's balls for half a year in this floating toilet," the Russian had commented drily. "The least we can do is have a little private time while we look at our planet, da?"

Massimo had agreed wholeheartedly. He turned and looked at the planet now. Earth. Beneath him, well, not *beneath* him, there being no up or down in space, but he had to think in words that made some kind of sense, so *beneath* would just have to do, the planet rolled. A gigantic blue ball. Massimo was no poet, but his soul leaped within him every time he got outside the ISS and saw the vast blueness of his home unfolding in front of him. It was *so* blue. Nothing could prepare you for that. Clouds danced across the scene, their shadows trailing across oceans and land masses.

"Big blue ball of hugeness," thought Massimo. "No. Enormous slow-mo football made of blue stuff. No. Spinny big thing. Shit."

Kramer—the American—had told him the English language was best for true poetry, but Massimo was starting to wonder if Kramer had only said that because she couldn't speak any other languages herself. If Kramer hadn't been female, blonde and kind of cute, he might have argued in favor of the beauty of the Italian language, but since he was hoping for a celebratory dinner with Kramer once they were home, he'd conceded the point. A celebratory dinner followed by some traditional Italian disrobing ceremonies, he hoped. So, English it was.

Azure was another word for blue, right?

"Azure, *as you're* turning beneath me—". Now, that was clever. A play on words. In a second language. Massimo felt a flush of pride. He might try that one on Kramer later. He knew there was no chance of serious flirting while they were onboard, but he could do some preliminary work and—

"Che cazzo?!" he said, crossing himself involuntarily. Which wasn't an easy thing to do in a spacesuit.

The area of space alongside the ISS was no longer unoccupied. It was filled by a massive object which Massimo, under less stressful conditions, would undoubtedly have described as "a bloody massive spaceship". Considering he was currently at the end of a solar array, tethered by a single strap, floating far above anywhere that might remotely be considered 'safe ground', he actually described it in a far more colorful way. He did this in Italian. It was an unbroken string of swearing that only dried up when he finally drew breath. Under other circumstances, it might have qualified him for some sort of award. As it was, no one heard it, and he had time to take a good look at the spaceship and consider his next actions carefully, before he opened a channel to Kramer in the control room. He wondered for a second what her first name was, and why she had never revealed it to anyone. Then he marveled at the human brain's ability to think such a useless thought on an occasion such as humankind's first contact with aliens.

"Massimo to Kramer."

"This is Kramer. How's it looking out there this afternoon, Massi?"

Only Kramer and Massimo's mother were permitted to call him Massi.

He looked at the sleek gray surface which partly blocked his view of Earth. It was cigar shaped, but as Massimo watched, it transformed itself, both ends moving inward as the middle expanded, ending up looking like a miniature moon.

He opened his mouth to report, then closed it again. Why had no alarms gone off? Why hadn't Houston alerted them? He thought hard for a few seconds. The spaceship hadn't been there before. Now it was. It had appeared—some might say—magically. Magical appearances were frowned upon by those with a scientific mindset. He thought back to the rehydrated macaroni and cheese he had eaten about an hour ago. As well as being an insult to Italian cooking, the cheese had tasted particularly strange. He stared hard at the spaceship, blinked and looked again. It was still there.

"Um. All looks, er, very nice here," he said. "Big planet, stars and whatnot. How are things with you?"

"Everything's fine. Massi, did you just say, 'whatnot'?"

"So, er, nothing to report on the proximity detectors? The cameras? Radar?"

"No, all normal. You seeing something out there?"

Massimo took another very long look at the spaceship. He thought about the cheese.

"No, nothing. I'm feeling a little unwell. I think I'll come back in early if that's ok."

"Can you stay another thirty minutes? Just to make sure that panel will stay in place?"

"Well, I think it might be better if I—"

"For me, Massi?" Kramer was doing that husky voice thing. It was very unfair.

"Thirty minutes more," he said, looking at the spaceship, which now seemed to have thousands of tiny lights racing across its surface in every direction. He knew that American cheese was poorer than the glory that was Italian cheese, but he was shocked at the powerful side-effects. He only hoped his stomach would hold up for another half hour. Toilet accidents in the sealed environment of a space suit were no fun at all.

Chapter 41

The 747-400 nosed its way through the clouds above Heathrow, bumping slightly as it banked slowly through one-hundred-and-eighty degrees, ending up facing almost due west. The flight to JFK was close to reaching its cruising altitude of 35,000ft, about twenty-seven minutes after takeoff, when a tall man appeared in First Class.

Chief Steward David Burn saw it happen. He was mixing a vodka martini for a guy in 1A (*extremely* dry, chilled glass, with a twist, and could he make sure the accompanying nuts were *heated*) when the man materialized, standing by the empty 4B. Onboard manifests were correct, every passenger was accounted for. David's first reaction at a passenger appearing in mid-flight wasn't one of bewilderment or shock, but a mild annoyance at the administrative headache it would cause when they reached JFK. He had seen an awful lot of bad behavior in First Class over the fourteen years he'd been working for the airline. Tantrums, fights, projectile vomiting, thefts, every kind of sexual misdemeanor and once—memorably—an impromptu game of rugby. He wondered which section of the flight report covered magical materializations. He shuddered at the prospect of explaining it to his supervisor.

He pulled the corners of his vest down and smoothed his hair before walking toward the stranger.

"Good morning, sir," he said. "Can I offer you a drink?"

The man smiled at him. David flushed slightly. He supposed unauthorized magical appearances on his flights wouldn't be such a bad thing, if they were all this cute.

"No, thanks, I'm good," the man said. He winked. "Just passing through."

With that, he stepped sideways and vanished.

No paperwork after all, then.

***

NASA's high-altitude prototype drone was named the LEO-447/33, but everyone from the Director down called it the Kármán Tickler. In polite company, the nickname was attributed to the fact that the drone cruised at an altitude of about sixty miles, just a couple miles short of the Kármán Line—the nominal border between Earth's atmosphere and the vacuum of space. But the reason the nickname stuck was the uncanny resemblance the LEO-447/33 bore to a popular sex toy.

The Kármán Tickler's shaft was hollow, designed to carry up to eight trainee astronauts. Weightlessness training was a necessary—but highly expensive—part of NASA's program. If the Kármán Tickler, a lightweight and comparatively energy-efficient drone could do the job without even the need for a pilot,

NASA hoped to partly fund other projects by offering highly-priced weightless trips to members of the public. If, that is, members of the public wouldn't be reluctant to climb inside a giant penis.

"I hope this works," thought Seb, as they arrived in the Tickler. "It seems a hell of a risk not to Walk to the ship directly." He realized he was still expecting a response from Seb2. He experienced the mental experience of a stumble, before righting himself and taking a breath.

If he'd risked a direct Walk, H'wan may have turned on him. The ship might have said he wouldn't intervene with the Rozzers' mission, but H'wan had said nothing about not trying to kill Seb if *he* got involved. This way, he stood a chance of getting to the Engine unnoticed.

Seb's arrival and departure on the Tickler were separated by 16.58 seconds. He had intended moving on immediately, but when he'd emerged inside the Tickler, he'd found all seven trainees, plus their instructor, unconscious. Rather than expecting everyone to wear breathing apparatus, the Tickler's designers—with one eye on the marketability of their weightless fun flights—were trying out a pressurized cabin for the first time. The air supply had experienced a catastrophic failure, and the occupants of the craft had less than a minute left before their bodies shut down, followed by brain damage, then death.

Seb found the fault and replaced the ruptured hoses that had not been tested comprehensively at this speed or altitude. The air supply resumed. The trainees would wake up in a few minutes. He knew his Manna-produced replacement hoses would not go unnoticed once the Tickler was back on the ground, so he left a note on the onboard e-log saying, *Test your life-support systems more rigorously next time.* He wondered what NASA would make of it. He shrugged and Walked.

***

Massimo was only a few minutes away from the end of his shift fixing the solar array. He'd always tried to stay as long as possible on previous trips outside, but this time, all he wanted to do was crawl back through the airlock. Back into the beautiful, smelly, claustrophobic ISS where he could see some familiar objects. Rather than huge alien spaceships.

The spaceship was still there, he knew that. He'd last checked about two minutes ago, by glancing over his shoulder while humming the Duke of Mantua's aria from Rigoletto and pretending nothing was amiss.

"Tum tum, tum, tumtitum, qual piuma al vento, there are the solar panels, tightening this one now. Mm, mm, mm mm-mm-mmm, mm, mm, di pensier, there is the su-n, there is the spaceship. Sempre un amibile, tum tum tum tumtitum."

Finally turning his back on the cheese-produced hallucination, he started making his way back along the length of the array, his mood improving as he got closer to the hub of the ISS. He'd even be glad to see that grump, Petr.

"Muta d'acce—nto, oh, what the crap is that?!"

He was halfway along the array. His path was blocked by a pair of sneakers. The sneakers contained a pair of feet and—as he slowly raised his eyes—he confirmed the usual complement of legs, torso, arms and head were also present. No spacesuit, though. Just a guy. Standing on the solar array of the International Space Station in the deadly cold vacuum of space. Surely, even American cheese wasn't capable of producing such a hallucination as this. Massimo began to suspect poisoning. It had to be Chuck. Anyone who listened to that much country music couldn't be trusted.

The man squatted down in front of him. He had an intelligent, friendly face. He raised a finger to his lips. Massimo shrugged. Who was he gonna tell? It would be the last communication he ever made as a professional astronaut. Robust mental health was pretty high up the list of job requirements when you worked in space. The stranger then shuffled to one side, making enough room for Massimo to get past. He waved him through.

Massimo looked back twice on the way to the airlock. The first time, the man was still there, crouched, staring at the alien craft. Massimo noticed that the space immediately around the figure looked slightly distorted. Almost as if he was wearing some kind of invisible suit. Massimo then realized such speculation meant he was beginning to accept the evidence of his eyes. He shook his head.

The second time Massimo looked back, the figure had gone. Massimo wondered if his digestive system had finally done its job. He looked to see if the spaceship had also evaporated, then immediately wished he hadn't. Halfway between the ISS and the spaceship, the sneakers guy was crossing empty space. From Massimo's angle, it looked like he was going to miss the target—he was heading too far toward the planet below.

Then Massimo noticed a change in the spaceship. A hole had appeared in one side, an object had emerged and it was heading toward Earth. The object was dark. No light reflected from its surface. It was shaped like an inverted teardrop, the point facing the ship. The inappropriately-dressed man was on course to intercept it.

The rounded edge of the object started to glow as it penetrated Earth's atmosphere. The man landed on its side, sticking to it like a fly on candy. Massimo watched in horror and disbelief as the entire teardrop glowed red—then white—hot, the figure clinging to it enduring the same extreme temperatures, his body changing color. Then, just as he thought the man's body would burst into flame and be reduced to ash, the figure seemed to sink *into* the teardrop, vanishing inside as the whole object made its way through atmospheric layers containing more and more air particles. As its descent was slowed, the heat grew greater and greater. Massimo offered up a silent prayer for the man he'd seen, then reminded himself it was a hallucination.

His comms crackled into life. Kramer wasn't using the husky voice this time. "Massimo! We're reading a meteor at least three meters in diameter entering the atmosphere. Do you have a visual out there?"

Massimo thought for a few moments before replying. He really, *really* liked his job.

"I see it. It's big! Why didn't we pick it up earlier?"

"Can't answer that," said Kramer. "Houston only detected it seconds ago. Like it appeared from nowhere. Must be some sort of instrument malfunction."

"Where's it going to hit?"

"That's the good news," said Kramer. "It's heading for smack down in the middle of the Atlantic. Should have broken up enough not to cause any problems, luckily. Can't understand why we didn't detect it earlier, though. Weird."

"Si," said Massimo, looking at the huge spacecraft dwarfing their own. "Weird."

Chapter 42

The teardrop shape of the Unmaking Engine's housing was designed to slow its fall by creating a shockwave in front of the blunt end. Unlike humanity's earliest manned spacecraft, it didn't need to sacrifice any of its mass to the intense heat, or use thick, heavy, heat resistant material as an outer coating. Instead, the first few hundred layers of particles at the fat end of the teardrop—to a depth just greater than the width of an average human hair—had one simple job: to dissipate heat. As each particle on the outermost layer reached 3,000 degrees Fahrenheit, it flew outward and inward. The layers below slowed and cooled the superheated particles. Then, the new outermost layer took the brunt of the acceleration, heating up, dissipating, being slowed and cooled. And so the process continued, repeating itself until the initial fall had been slowed sufficiently.

As it fell further through the atmosphere, the blunt end of the teardrop then increased in diameter, stretching outward, becoming, once there was enough air to make it viable, a dome, or bowl, acting like a parachute, every square inch of it instantly reacting to each change in pressure or gust of wind, stabilizing it and slowing its descent dramatically. By the time it was

40,000 feet over the ocean, it had braked to less than two-hundred-and-fifty miles per hour. If it maintained its rate of deceleration, it would be traveling at under seventy mph by the time it reached 7,000 feet, at which point it would deliver its payload—the nine-foot-long cylinder cradled in the center of the bowl. NASA lost contact as the parachute shape was deployed - the material was too thin to register on their instruments. The assumption was that the meteorite had broken up into pieces too small to be detected.

The cylinder contained genetic material ready to rise to the surface of the ocean, once freed from its container. On the surface, it would mimic the qualities of sea water molecules, enabling it to evaporate along with the water, rising up through the atmosphere, condensing into clouds, and finally, raining its deadly contents onto the land below. The Unmaking Engine molecules were designed to replicate themselves as they joined the water cycle, so that every drop of rain that fell would eventually be contaminated. All human beings would die, but every other species would survive.

Seb understood the mechanics of the Engine, its capabilities, its destructive power. He didn't understand it intellectually, he *felt* it in his body. It was a very similar feeling to that which he experienced when listening to a complex piece of music. If he had tried to transcribe the music, force the notes he was hearing onto paper in a form that would make sense, he might have failed. But when he bypassed the part of his brain that wanted to categorize the music and sort it into its component parts: melody, harmony, rhythm, timbre, texture, themes, counterpoints—when that part of his brain was disengaged—he could listen in a radically different way. It was as if he—in his entirety—experienced the music moment by moment in *its* entirety. Whatever the composer was trying to say was often, somehow, greater than the combination of the twelve notes he or she had chosen to arrange in various patterns in order to communicate with the listener. The music was experienced in time, linearly, the only way humans can experience anything. And yet, it was only as a whole that it made sense. Seb felt the same sensation now as he occupied the interior of the cylinder that housed the heart of the Unmaking Engine. His body *knew* the Engine, *knew* what it was dealing with. Instantly.

Seb's knowledge of the device was analogous to his encounters with great music in one more way, and it was this that gave him pause, despite knowing he had only seconds in which to act. He knew he was going to have to lose himself in the act. People used the expression 'lost in music' as a positive statement, an endorsement. Their sense of self had been temporarily suspended by the power of the music. But the effect was temporary—they knew they would 'find' themselves again. Seb wasn't so sure the same was true now.

"Will this kill me?"

"Theoretically unlikely," said Seb2, "but nothing's impossible. You're going to have to completely give up conscious control. Your soul, your essence, your atman, whatever you want to call it, will cease to function during the process. I don't know if you'll be 'alive' in any real sense during that time. And when you come back—if you come back—I don't know if it will be *you* in the same sense any more. You certainly won't have a single naturally biological cell left in your body."

"Will I still be human?"

"Well. Your physical makeup is currently still made up of both nanotech and human cells. That changes as soon as you make this decision. Not that you have a choice. And you might still exist afterward. Who knows?"

"I know you're me," thought Seb, "but sometimes, I really want to kick your ass."

"Hey, I love you too, bro."

"Ok. Let's get this done."

The Unmaking Engine swooped toward the Atlantic Ocean. It hovered over the face of the water, then, with a barely discernible shudder, a ripple made its way across the skin of the vast bowl. When it reached the center, the cylinder dropped toward the waiting ocean.

Seb didn't hesitate. As the cylinder fell, his entire body separated into individual particles. Those cells which were still human didn't survive the process. The rest reproduced themselves at incredible speed, creating an ovoid shield, or carapace which—a full second before the cylinder hit the ocean—completely surrounded the active genetic material at the Unmaking Engine's heart.

On impact, the cylinder disintegrated as it was designed to do. The core drove on under the surface to a depth of two hundred feet. At this point, it blew apart in a controlled explosion, designed to spread the deadly molecules as far and as wide as possible. Instead of which, they hit the impervious wall of Seb's carapace and fell back, contained in the hollow space within. The imprisoned weapon continued to drop toward the ocean floor.

The ensuing battle was completely one-sided, since the disease-carrying molecules had no defensive capabilities. The shield that Seb had become began to fill its own hollow interior, closing inexorably in on itself. As it did so, it stripped the Engine of its component parts. Those parts that could be used again were retained, the rest was rendered harmless. This was done through the creation of 'honey-trap' molecules. Each of these presented as replicas of human DNA. The Unmaking process took place at the molecular level as it was engineered to do, but, when it was done, each honey-trap molecule died, taking its deadly partner with it.

The shrinking carapace kept repeating the process until nothing was left of the original Unmaking Engine. Then, its task complete, it continued to sink until finally, it rested in the dark blackness of the Atlantic depths.

There was no movement, no sound, no light. Nothing.

Chapter 43

The two men stood opposite each other for the last time.

Richmond Park was frost-covered, the ground white and hard, the trees gray silhouettes against a bleached sky.

On the pond, no ducks disturbed the stillness of the water, which looked at first to be iced over. A second glance revealed the water was still liquid, but was moving sluggishly, unnaturally.

Seb looked to the north. Instead of seeing the path, the trees and grass just faded away. It was as if someone had painted the scene and left a gap at the edge of the canvas where the first pencil sketches hadn't yet been painted over. Even as he watched, the furthest tree—an ancient oak, its massive trunk dominated by the dozens of huge branches spreading above—lost definition and started to fade from the side furthest away.

"No need for this place anymore," said Seb2. He was wearing a winter coat, scarf and gloves. Seb was still in the T-shirt, jeans and sneakers he'd been wearing when he'd intercepted the Unmaking Engine. Seb didn't feel cold. His breath didn't come out as vapor. Seb2's did.

Seb said nothing, just looked around with a strange aching sense of loss. In the real world, this was where he'd first fallen for Mee. In his own subconscious, this was where he'd first met Seb2 and learned a little about the way his life was changing. Half a mile away, he'd seen a third version of himself, existing in constant pain. Seb3 had been absorbed in some way now, the pain gone. Seb guessed he should feel glad, but it worried—no, scared—him. Where was he now, this missing piece of his consciousness? And, after this, would he be fully himself again, or something less than that?

"It's time," said Seb2. "But I want you to make me a promise. There's something you *need* to do. You're changing faster than you know it now, but you must never lose sight of who you are. So, promise you'll do something for me. For us—for *you*."

"I promise," said Seb, and his double told him what he had to do. Seb's hands clenched into fists and he said nothing. Finally, he nodded.

Around the two men, the park was disappearing faster now. Trees were fading, paths had gone, frost-held blades of grass were losing what little definition they had and leeching away into the whiteness.

Seb2 took a step forward and hugged his double. Seb hesitated for a moment. Why did this feel like a bereavement? He wrapped his arms around the other man, but there was nothing there. He was just hugging his own shoulders. He let his arms drop to his side. He was standing alone.

"Hello?" he thought.

"Hello?" He said it aloud this time. The park had lost even its aural realism, the sound of his voice dead and flat, like the sound in a recording studio.

Seb watched the whiteness approach. The pond was going now. He felt a stab of fear. This felt more like an 'unmaking'.

He had never felt more alone as the whiteness moved in and finally engulfed him.

***

The Unmaking Engine had plummeted into the south Atlantic at a point almost equidistant from the two continents to the east and west. NASA tracked it all the way, but in the absence of any nearby ships that might provide extra data, didn't see any need to further investigate a medium sized meteorite that had, by now, surely sunk to an unrecoverable depth.

Nightingale Island, one of the three Tristan Da Cunha islands, was free of human habitation, populated mostly by a million seabirds. The landscape was dominated by two peaks—one of them an active volcano.

A tiny, inaccessible yellow sand bay lay at its northwest tip. Rocks were strewn across the sand, ranging in size from a closed fist to a small house. Perched on one of these rocks—this one about the size and roughly the shape of a three-seat sofa, H'wan had adopted a thoughtful posture, gazing out to sea in a philosophical manner.

He had experimented with a few different positions over the previous few hours. His penchant for the dramatic had been an unexpected side-effect of separation from the Gyeuk.

Existence in the vast hive mind of the Gyeuk was impossible to put into words, so the Gyeuk rarely tried. When pressed, its responses were usually aphoristic, Zen-like, and ultimately, meaningless to anyone outside the consensus.

Existence separated from the Gyeuk for a ship like H'wan was far easier to put into words, but it was reluctant to do so. To itself, though, H'wan admitted it was having fun. There was no other word for it. Fun. It felt like a rebel just for thinking it. 'Fun' was a word that suggested a feeling that didn't, couldn't have any meaning within the Gyeuk, where the emotional peaks and troughs of the flesh-bound were entirely absent.

Separation had, at first, been strange and painful. Tactless, flesh-bound visitors had occasionally tried to empathize by fatuously likening the experience to losing a limb. The truth was far worse. If anything, it was more like being a limb that had lost its body. Not even a limb. A fingernail, perhaps. But over time, H'wan had—to its horror at first, then to its secret delight—realized it was enjoying itself tremendously. The Gyeuk was the ultimate society, no doubt at all, but there was something a little pompous and ridiculous about all that drifting-through-space-thinking-deep-thoughts stuff.

H'wan changed its mind again and stood up. It folded its arms—well, the arms of its avatar, really—most of it was still the ship orbiting above. It adopted a stance intended to look strong and imposing. It based it on a drawing it had uploaded of an eighteenth century

Samurai warrior. In H'wan's case, a twelve-foot-tall Samurai. It imagined it must look fantastic.

If H'wan had experienced time as the flesh-bound of this planet did, it would have been looking at its watch every few seconds and tutting by now. As it was, it simply scuffed its feet on the sand and noted with delight another aspect to his personality. Impatience, how wonderful.

Just as it was beginning to wonder if it had been mistaken about the resilience of the T'hn'uuth, the water near the shore began to bubble and move unnaturally. H'wan had been broadcasting its presence for nearly half an Earth orbit now. If the T'hn'uuth had survived his battle with the Unmaking Engine, he would surely come to H'wan first, if only to gloat a bit. Wouldn't he? H'wan was aware that some of his previous predictions about the fleshbound's behavior had proved wildly off the mark.

H'wan had mixed feelings about the T'hn'uuth, or *World Walkers* as the human had named them. Almost all sentient species shared these feelings—of course, the occasional backwater species worshipped them as gods or feared them as demons. But mostly, they were regarded with cautious respect and more than a little fear. So rare as to be almost mythical, the T'hn'uuth represented a true unknown. And they were not renowned for their openness in communication. But Sebastian Varden was very young. H'wan felt the stirrings of excitement again. To encounter a T'hn'uuth at this stage of his development was somewhat of a scientific coup. It had been assumed, by those who even acknowledged their existence, that the T'hn'uuth were dying out. The last documented encounter had been over a thousand years ago, and that particular specimen was thought to be older than the planet it had visited on that occasion.

So, as the water rose, foaming and spitting, coiling and writhing, H'wan struggled slightly to maintain its imposing pose. It really wanted to rub its hands together in glee.

Suddenly, the ground beneath H'wan's feet began to shake alarmingly. The volcano behind him was active, but not due to erupt for another 722 days. No seismic activity registering either.

Rocks of all shapes and sizes first trembled, then began to shake violently, finally prizing themselves away from the sand and flying into the sea. H'wan took a couple of steps backward, then resumed its imposing stance. Wouldn't do to drop its standards now.

With a sound like that of a thousand breakers crashing into each other simultaneously, a huge column of water rose into the air. The rocks were lifted with it, and H'wan could see hundreds of fish—and at least one shark—still swimming in the gravity-defying shape towering above him. At a height of about sixty feet, the shape stopped climbing and started taking on some definition. Oval at the top, then flowing outward beneath to a huge central area, from the sides of which of which two columns began to form. No, not columns.

Ah, thought H'wan. *A human figure. Impressive.*

Looking up, it watched the oval change, becoming a face, flowing into easily recognizable features. The hair was a mass of seaweed, the eyes dark volcanic rocks, the skin tens of millions of shells.

The giant took a step onto the beach. H'wan abandoned his pose and slipped hastily backward, making his way further up the beach.

"Why are you still here?" The voice didn't come from the towering figure in front of him. It was a soft voice directly behind him. H'wan, to his shame, let out a high-pitched shriek and pirouetted one-hundred-and-eighty degrees.

The T'hn'uuth—Seb Varden—was looking at him. H'wan had studied the micro-expressions common in thousands of humanoid species, including those on this planet, but it didn't know how to begin reading Seb Varden's expression now. The human was utterly still, self-possessed. H'wan knew it had to make an effort to take control of the encounter. It was about to speak when there was a huge crash behind and around it as the giant reduced itself to its component parts. By an immense effort of will, H'wan manage not to turn around. Although, it did make a strange involuntary squeaking sound.

"You survived, T'hn'uuth. I am unsurprised, but you show a degree of control that impresses me. World Walkers, as you call them, are rumored to train themselves in their abilities for many centuries. Although, I must confess, when it comes to information about the development of T'hn'uuth, the entries in the databanks of the universe are remarkably underwhelming. I don't suppose you'd care to—,"

It broke off. That unreadable expression was remarkably unnerving.

"No, perhaps not," it said. There was silence for a while.

"I asked you a question," said Seb.

"You did, yes, you did. Undoubtedly," said H'wan. Why was it babbling like an adolescent fleshbound? It felt off balance. It was Gyeuk—part of the pinnacle of evolution, the ultimate expression of intelligence. Perhaps it had been a ship too long, after all.

Seb waited.

"Well," said H'wan. "As I said, it is not my place to intervene. The Gyeuk is beyond such matters."

"Beyond intervening to prevent genocide?"

H'wan regained some of its composure.

"Your perspective is understandably skewed," it said. "Identification is a necessary part of evolution. Almost every sentient series in the universe begins its journey by developing strong identification systems. Identification with a parent, siblings, a tribe, a nation, a race, a planet. As evolution continues, this infantile trait falls away. As hard as this may be to hear, your species has barely begun to reach a level where it might even be considered to be intelligent."

"How can you say that, if you know anything about humanity's history?" said Seb. "Our scientific discoveries, our music, literature, art."

"There is nothing there I haven't seen on thousands of other planets," said H'wan. "By that measure, you show potential, but other species have moved away from violence and self-destruction much more rapidly."

"We will do the same," said Seb. "Our shortcomings gives you no right to destroy us."

"Nothing has changed," said H'wan. "My crew is already preparing another device. They are not easily dissuaded. You are just delaying the inevitable. Unless—," H'wan paused. It knew the T'hn'uuth must have considered the possibility. He was a human, after all. "Unless you intend using violence to prevent them."

The T'hn'uuth finally moved, turning away from H'wan and taking a few paces along the sand. A few drops of rain were beginning to fall.

"A bit late for you to take the moral high ground, don't you think?" said Seb. He didn't wait for an answer. "There may be another way. It will take a little time. Give me a few days."

H'wan noticed, with some surprise, that this last was framed not as a request, but as an order. Even more surprisingly, it found its inclination was to obey. Interesting.

"How do I find you?" said Seb.

"Just speak my name. I will come."

"Until then."

H'wan bowed.

"T'hn'uuth."

Seb nodded and turned to go. H'wan held up a hand to stop him.

"You spoke of humanity's achievements. The words you used: *our* scientific discoveries, *our* music, *our* literature. You speak as if you yourself are still caught in the species stage of identification, but your - essence - says otherwise. You are not fleshbound, you are not Gyeuk, you are T'hn'uuth, a World Walker. If the legends are to be believed, you will always be *other*, always a wanderer, identifying with nothing, no place, no one. Your way is—I think—unknowable. Perhaps even to yourself. Until next time, World Walker."

The eighteenth century Samurai started to dissolve into smoke and streak into the sky, just as Seb Walked, leaving the beach empty for a few minutes, after which the seabirds returned to their perches as if nothing untoward had happened.

Chapter 44

New York

The apartment was dark and there was a smell of decay. Seb thought for a moment that Mason had died, but a quick examination revealed he was still clinging on to the last vestiges of life, as his body incrementally continued its final shutting down.

Seb looked at the dying man in the wheelchair and felt nothing. No anger, no regret, no sadness. Nothing.

But he had made a promise.

He reached out a hand and placed it on Mason's cheek.

Within a minute, a little color had returned to the skin of the body in front of him. Then, his lips moved slightly and the fingers of his right hand twitched. Finally, his eyelids flickered.

Seb stood and got a glass of water from the desk. He took it over to Mason and lifted his head. The closed eyes fluttered and opened. Seb tipped the glass, and after some of the liquid had made it into his mouth, Mason swallowed convulsively. A thin, shaking hand came up and held onto Seb's own, guiding the glass as he drank. After Mason had drained the whole glass, Seb dragged a chair over and sat in front of him.

Mason coughed a few times. His mouth moved, but he seemed to be struggling to make a sound. He swallowed again and pushed himself a little more upright. He looked across at Seb. Seb looked back, marveling at the change. It was Mason—of course—yet somehow, it wasn't him. The changes were so subtle as to be almost invisible. The line of his mouth, the way he was sitting. But mostly, it was his eyes. Those pitiless eyes, blank, unreadable, were suddenly full of human emotion. Fear, sadness, regret, empathy, compassion. It was like looking at an entirely different human being.

"Mason?" said Seb.

The skin around Mason's eyes contracted briefly, as if in pain. He coughed, then spoke. His voice was weak, grating with lack of use, but it was no longer a whisper.

"No," he said. "My name is John."

From the burner phone on the desk, Sym watched and listened.

"I would have just killed the son of a bitch," he said, before sending himself deep into the chaos of the internet. The World Wide Web now had its own spider.

***

Seb stood in the middle of Mason/John's apartment. He felt a mixture of adrenaline and relief. Adrenaline because he'd been prepared to kill another human being, but it hadn't happened. Relief for much the same reason.

The tumor in Mason's brain had been a dark ball of cancerous gristle, pushing its mass into various clusters of synapses. Seb's Manna had sunk into his skull, diagnosed a malfunctioning brain, and cured the disease by replacing each cancerous cell with a healthy one. It took nearly seventy seconds to remove the cancer. The resulting change in brain chemistry made it obvious that Mason had been removed with it.

Seb wondered how he would feel now, if he'd actually killed the man.

His speculation was interrupted by the sudden knowledge that the aliens were minutes away from reaching orbit. It was a strangely disorienting feeling knowing this, since the information would previously have come from Seb2.

Seb locked onto the ship's position, and using telemetry gleaned live from several airplane tracking websites and some less public NASA communications, worked out how he could get to it undetected. His link with the ship would alert him when they began to prepare the Unmaking Engine.

Seb returned his attention to the apartment. The wheelchair was next to the picture window. Standing next to it, holding on for support, John looked out at the view he had seen every day for nearly thirty-four years. Now, finally, he could take it in properly. Central Park, a smudge of green to the northwest. He turned to Seb.

"Please," he said, "can we go there?" He pointed with a trembling hand.

"Sure," said Seb.

They took the private elevator down to the parking garage and walked out into the early afternoon sun. John held on to Seb for support. His legs were healed now, the bones, cartilage, ligaments and muscles capable of bearing his weight. It was just the mental adjustment to walking for the first time since he was thirteen years old that made his steps slow and hesitant.

Seb hailed a cab.

Central Park was busy with the usual eclectic collection of joggers, European au pairs, dog walkers, business people with a sack lunch in one hand and a cellphone in the other. Cops walking in pairs, a group of art-school students filming each other in a variety of comic poses, a cluster of Hasidic Jews huddled around the screen of a tablet. Every echelon of the drug-dealing business was represented for those who knew where to look; from the meth guy near the underpass to the cocaine supplier who played outdoor chess with her customers while they negotiated. Schoolchildren, teachers, nurses, stockbrokers, journalists, analysts and bums sat, or lay on the grass, eyes closed, the heat of the sun on their faces.

On a bench near the water, John looked out on it all and tried to piece his existence together into something that made some kind of sense.

Once, he had been Boy.

Then, he had been Mason.

Now, he was John, the name Mom had called him when Pop wasn't there. His given name.

He had been a passenger in his own body for most of his life. A witness to terrible things, held hostage in the deepest recesses of his own brain. A dream of who he was, suddenly made real. He was forty-seven years old and his adult life had just begun.

John watched the people around him going about their lives, and rejoiced in the freedom he felt in not being involved, not wanting to control, just letting them be. He sat like that for nearly an hour. He told Seb about his parents, his childhood, the cancer, and the encounter with Manna that had saved his life but given immense power to a parasitic personality over which he'd had no control.

"The tumor would have killed you eventually," said Seb. "Mason had slowed its progress to an absolute crawl, but I think you only had five or six years left. "

"I can't think of Mason as an entirely separate person," said John. "I wish I could. But that would be too easy. He was the absolute worst of me, magnified horribly, but he didn't come from nowhere. I was my father's child as much as my mother's. I have to accept that, somehow. He *was* me, a nightmare version of me."

"Whoever he was, he's gone now" said Seb. "You have your life to live, but everything will be different. Destroying the tumor, and Mason with it, meant destroying your Manna ability. You will have to look after yourself. If you get sick, you'll have to visit a doctor. You won't live an abnormally extended life. You're just a human now."

"It's all I ever wanted," said John. "Manna is a curse, not a blessing. I know there are Users who do good with it—the Order has always tried to be selfless in their Manna use. But I'm not convinced they ever really succeeded. I met some of the Order's most powerful proponents over the years. I'm not sure they were as far removed from Mason as they liked to believe. Manna can be subtle in the way it corrupts, but it corrupts none the less. None of the Order ever considered giving up Manna to avoid confronting me. They were addicts, just as I was. Even now, with all the Manna flushed from my system, and most of my life stolen from me by its use, there's still a small part of me that wants it back. Wants it desperately. I'm glad it's not an option any more. What about you?"

Seb looked slightly taken aback at the question. "It saved my life. I wouldn't be here if it hadn't been for Manna."

"But is it *you*? Has Manna changed who you are?"

Seb stood up and looked across the park to the water. He looked back at John and had a sudden disorienting feeling of deja vu. A flash of Richmond Park and Seb2. Then it was gone.

"I've changed," he said. "I had to. I've grown up." He stopped talking. He realized the man he was speaking to was probably the only other human being who had ever experienced anything close to the ability he had. Mason's final attack on him, while not unexpected, was ferocious, clever, and incredibly powerful. A year ago, maybe even six months ago, it might have killed him. Seb knew he had evolved over the last year, so that any part of his body could recreate any other part in seconds. Even his brain. No other Manna user had the same ability. In some ways, it made him more Gyeuk than human: a colony of sorts.

He sat back down on the bench. "Yes, it's changed me. And I don't know where the changes will end," he said. "But I'm still me." John said nothing. Seb wondered if he was trying to convince the other man, or himself.

"What will you do?" Seb said. "Where will you go?"

"I'm going to work," said John. "I know a place where they'll be glad of any help they can get. And, I think I owe them. I'll paint walls, sweep floors, whatever they want. If they'll have me." He looked at the man beside him and started to say something, then changed his mind and was quiet again. A few seconds passed by in silence. "What about you?" he said. "What will you do? Save the world, one life at a time?"

Seb looked at the scene in front of him, seeing different versions laid out across the multiverse. The cops were arresting the meth dealer in one. In another, the park had been cleared because of a bomb threat. Great birds circled a barren area devoid of any life in another. Most just showed variations on a theme: the same people going about their day. Seb looked at it all dispassionately. He knew the Unmaking Engine threatened every universe where humanity had discovered Manna. In none of those universes had humanity shared that discovery with the entire race and consciously evolved as the Rozzers had wanted them to. Seb felt a stab of despair for the selfishness of his species. He knew humanity could be better than that. Didn't he?

"Actually, I'm going to save everyone all at once," he said. "Hopefully."

John looked at the younger man.

"You don't seem overjoyed at the prospect," he said.

Seb smiled at that.

"I don't know if it's the right decision," he said. "But it will probably save humanity. I know that must sound crazy, but…oh, I don't know. Forget I said anything."

He stood up again and stuck out his hand. "I did what I came here to do," he said. "I killed Mason. And it worked out better than I'd hoped. I got to meet you. You're a good person, John. Good luck with the rest of your life."

John took his hand and shook it. He looked as if he wanted to speak again but thought better of it.

"Thank you, Seb," he said. "I wish you the same."

Seb walked away a few paces, then turned.

"Why do I keep feeling I know you?" he said. "As if we've met before. When I know that we haven't."

John looked into Seb's eyes and held his gaze for a few moments.

"We did meet once," he said. "Kind of. But you won't remember. There's something I want to tell you. I wasn't sure, but—well, I guess you need to hear it. You'd better sit down."

Seb sat down.

Chapter 45

"The first person I killed was my father," said John. "His death is probably the only one I can't bring myself to completely regret. Beating the crap out of his family was the closest thing to a hobby that man ever had. I can't even picture Mom without bruises."

John was looking straight ahead, hardly seeing the mid-afternoon Central Park population in front of him.

"My mother died eight months after I last saw her," he said "A few days after giving birth, she left her baby on a doorstep. A week later, the river police pulled her body out of the Hudson. I—Mason, I mean—was glad. She was a complication while still alive. There would have always been the tiny possibility she might have come back, or gone to the authorities, despite the threat to her and her child. But she did what she thought was necessary to protect her newborn son. She removed herself as a link, hoping that even if I had kept watching her somehow, I would lose interest in my sibling. And she was right, to an extent."

"To an extent?" said Seb.

"Yes. She was right to be paranoid. I had no network of Manna users back then, so my methods were old school. I employed a private investigator. He found her fairly quickly and sent regular reports. She never went home. She saw out her pregnancy in a refuge for battered women in Brooklyn."

John stopped speaking for a while. When he resumed his story, his voice was quieter.

"Some people say suicide is a coward's way out," he said. "They're fools. Not an easy thing to do, deciding to end your life and then going through with it."

Seb thought back to the feeling of disconnectedness as the last of his lifeblood had seeped out of his veins into the dusty ground of the Verdugo Mountains. As he remembered, it was as if it had happened to someone else. In many ways, he had been someone else back then. And the gift of Manna, while saving his life, added to that feeling of disconnection with his younger self.

"She had married an older man who knocked her up while she was barely out of school," said John. "Then, he quickly showed his real colors. A hard-drinking, wife-and-child-beating bastard. Some women might have struggled to love the son of such a man. Not Mom. She taught me right from wrong, and I never felt anything other than unconditional love coming from her. But she never had the strength to leave him. I don't know why. I can never put myself in her place. She was manipulated and tortured physically and psychologically from the age of seventeen. Who knows what that does to someone? And then, when she was finally free of him, she had to face the nightmare that the son she loved was even worse than his father.

"I know now what I couldn't know as Mason. She didn't kill herself to protect her baby from me. She threw herself into the river because she thought her tiny newborn son might turn out just like his daddy and his brother. Hell, no wonder she couldn't go on."

Seb let John cry for the woman no one was able to save. Eventually, he continued his story.

"I watched the boy grow up. Didn't interfere, just had a report every six months. My main interest was in his Manna ability. As my network grew, I took the investigator off the case and had a powerful Sensitive pay a visit to the neighborhood every now and then. Right up to adulthood. No evidence of Manna use at all. I wasn't sure whether to be relieved, or a little disappointed in my little brother's lack of talent. At that point, I let him go. And I honestly barely gave him a moment's thought until recently, when he reappeared. And I—Mason—wished I'd killed him while he was still in the womb."

"Where is he now?" said Seb.

John's eyes were unfocused. He wasn't seeing the park at all anymore.

"She loved music, you know," he said. "She was a religious woman, and she used to listen to sacred music when Pop was at work. She thought certain composers were touched by God. One in particular. Bach."

"I love Bach," said Seb, softly. John didn't seem to hear him.

"She even named her sons after him," said John. "The English version of Johann is John." He looked directly at Seb. "Johann Sebastian Bach."

The truth of it hit Seb like the huge wave that had dragged him under during his first—and only—attempt to surf. He gulped air into his lungs and stared at the man he had come to kill only hours before. This morning, he had been an orphan with no information about his family. Now, he knew who his parents were. And he had a brother.

The signal came through from the orbiting ship.

Seb blinked a couple of times, still looking at John. Then he stood up.

"I have to go," he said.

John looked at the expression on Seb's face.

"I did the right thing? Telling you, I mean."

"You did the right thing. I'll come back. You said you were going to volunteer. Where?"

"St Benet's," said John, smiling. "Where else?"

Seb couldn't quite bring himself to smile back. This was all happening too fast. But he had to admit he felt a huge sense of grounding, knowing he had a family member. Even if his brother was a former psychopathic criminal mastermind and mass-murderer. It would all take time to digest. Time he didn't have right now.

"I have to—" he gestured toward the sky as if that might explain his intentions. John nodded.

"Off to save the world, right?"

Seb nodded and—to the immense surprise of two passing teenage girls and a pigeon—Walked.

***

Innisfarne

The beach at Innisfarne was nothing like the golden sands Mee had grown used to living in LA. And the temperature was a rude reminder that Britain, the country of her birth, served up some bitterly cold days, even in early Fall. She wrapped the shawl more tightly around her shoulders as she picked her way through the scattered rocks and shallow pools in the twilight.

Even though she was shivering, she was still moved by the wild beauty of the island. She had been there less than an hour, had greeted Kate with all the intensity of a long-lost sister, then felt a strong pull toward the beach. She went alone, obeying her heart's need for solitude. There were a few gulls still crying mournfully to each other from the cliffs, but other than that, the murmur of the sea, and the rise and fall of the wind, there was silence. Palpable, profound silence.

She stood still for a few minutes. Innisfarne had been known as a Thin Place for over a thousand years, but the irony was that there was no Manna here. The members of the Order who took refuge on the island did so without Manna, ensuring a fairly constant turnover of guests as Users quickly became twitchy without their regular fix. The reputation as a Thin Place came from something quite different. 'A deep sense of the eternal dance of silence,' was how a visiting Hindu guru had put it.

Mee hadn't realized she had been waiting for him until Seb suddenly arrived, stepping out of nothingness and standing in front of her. The expression on his face was oddly unreadable: was he scared, happy, awe-struck, bursting with news, upset? She didn't know whether to kiss him, shake him, or hold his hand and tell him everything was going to be ok. She settled on kissing him.

When they took a breath, she looked at him again.

"What is it?" she said.

"Mason's gone," he said.

"Dead?"

"Long story. He's gone and he'll never be back, that's the main thing."

She breathed out. "Good. What happened?"

Seb took a deep breath.

"You'd better sit down."

Thirty minutes later, it was Mee's turn to take a deep breath. She tried to digest what Seb had told her.

"Brother?" she said, not trusting herself at that point to attempt a full sentence with a subject, object and verb.

Seb nodded.

"Right," she said. Another deep breath.

"Not homicidal maniac?" she said.

"It was never him, Mee. The tumor created a parasitic personality with no sense of right or wrong. He's been a passenger in his own mind for most of his life."

"Brother," said Mee again. "You have a brother."

Mee's eyes opened wider.

"The tumor!" she said. "You both—he—the tumor. You both had brain tumors."

Seb smiled. "Must run in the family," he said.

"What are you going to do?" she said. "I mean, now you have a family. Well, when I say *family*, I mean a mass-murdering brother who kidnapped me, cut off my finger and ordered you killed? You going to go on picnics together? Get drunk and talk about sport?"

"Mee," said Seb.

"Yeah, I know. Brain tumor did it. Blah, blah, blah."

Seb raised an eyebrow.

"Yeah, yeah, don't worry," said Mee. "I'll get used to the idea. And look, seriously, it's amazing. You have a family now. How does it feel?"

"I can't think about it yet," said Seb. "I will. Just not yet."

He stopped talking. Mee looked at him.

"There's something else. What is it?" she said.

He sighed. "Seb2. He's gone. It's just me again."

Mee put her arm around his waist.

"That's good, isn't it? He was *you*, after all. Nothing has really changed, has it?"

"I don't know. I haven't decided if I've gained something or lost everything."

"What?"

Seb looked at her. His expression was unreadable.

"I don't know," he said, finally. "Just ignore me. I'm tired. Been a busy day. Not just Mason."

"Rozzers?" she said.

"Yes. I've saved the world once, since I last saw you. Now, I have to make sure it stays saved."

She looked into his eyes. He didn't look tired. He looked distant, disengaged, almost blank. She shivered. And then she asked a question she wasn't sure she wanted answered, since Seb would never lie to her.

"Are we going to be ok?"

"I don't know."

The mood was getting darker, so Mee did what she always did, even though she felt like a coward for doing it: she made light of the situation. Turned it into a joke.

"Spoken like no superhero ever," she said. "You really need to work on your patter, Walkyboy."

"Walkyboy?" said Seb, his face finally creasing into something resembling a smile.

"Hey, you can't think of your own super name, someone has to do it for you."

"What was wrong with the World Walker?"

"Boring."

There was a pause while neither of them spoke, then Mee leaned forward and put her arms around him.

"Sock it to 'em," she whispered, before licking his ear, stepping back and giving him her trademark grin. "Now, bugger off."

Seb Walked.

Mee looked up at the distant stars, feeling powerless and small. The tide gradually receded, dragging grains of sand away from the beach as it went. Eventually, the wind dried the salt tears on her cheeks, leaving her skin rough and sore.

Chapter 46

Tibet

Seb sat in silence. He was thinking. His thoughts followed five separate strands. Simultaneously. Which didn't seem unnatural. Not having Seb2 didn't seem unnatural, either. The fact that it *didn't* seem unnatural seemed unnatural in itself, but Seb couldn't spare the time to unravel that particular riddle.

He thought about humanity. Homo sapiens, at the vanguard of evolution, the tool users, the thinkers—therefore, the Manna users. A species still fighting itself, still struggling to do more good than harm. Also, a species capable of love, selflessness, sacrifice. A species deserving a future.

He thought about the aliens orbiting above. In the eyes of the Rozzers, humanity was a failed experiment. The aliens had put the petri dish under the microscope, taken a look and decided to start again. There was no malice in their actions, they were scientists. A failed experiment was just one step closer to a successful experiment.

He thought about Manna. Internationally, Manna users only made up a tiny fraction of the population. No properly researched figures were available, but—

roughly speaking—Users estimated that for every 5,000 people, only one had any ability. And the odds that the one person in 5,000 would discover their Manna ability were low. Perhaps as low as two out of every ten. Therefore, worldwide, there were fewer than 300,000 Mana users. In a country the size of America, about 12,000 Manna users were regular visiting Thin Places.

He thought about the Unmaking Engine. The way it had been designed to use the water cycle. There was no possibility of the device failing once it had been deployed. Even in the driest areas of the planet—where rain seldom fell—the human inhabitants needed to drink. And, over time, the Earth's entire water supply would be contaminated by the Engine's payload. No one could avoid being infected.

He thought about H'wan. A sentient ship made up of a swarm of nanotech, closer in its structure to a termite mound than to a human, yet showing a personality instantly recognizable as individual, relatable. An observer, seemingly unmoved by the imminent demise of an entire species. And yet, death itself surely had a different meaning to a fragment of a greater whole such as H'wan. And the Rozzers, with their store of DNA, never faced the final annihilation that death meant for humans.

When Seb finally stood, it was nearly dark outside. He walked forward to the ledge at the front of the cave. The location he had chosen was 19,000 feet above sea level in the Himalayas. Labuche Kang was, reputedly, an unclimbable mountain, so Seb could be reasonably certain he wouldn't be disturbed.

The wind made a high-pitched keening sound as it whipped between crevasses and ice fissures in the thin air of the mountain. In the blue-tinged twilight, Seb could easily have imagined he was the only living being on the planet. He looked out across the wilderness for a few minutes. He had made his decision.

"H'wan," he said.

***

An hour later, the Gyeuk and the T'hn'uuth stood together on the ledge. It was fully dark now, the sky a riot of stars.

"They won't be happy about it," said the ship. "Interference on this scale is unprecedented. What if they won't do it?"

"If they refuse," said Seb, "I won't let them leave."

H'wan considered the implications of that threat. The T'hn'uuth possessed power the Gyeuk could not explain. Which, as its/their knowledge was beyond any fleshbound species, was virtually impossible. And ever so slightly humiliating. But there it was. It would surely be in everyone's best interests not to test that power. H'wan decided to pursue the path of diplomacy. Albeit with some caveats.

"You realize," said the ship, "that another species may supersede humanity on this world?"

Seb said nothing. H'wan pressed its point.

"Probably an ocean dweller," it said. "Humans are forced to live on only twenty-nine percent of your planet. There are creatures in the deep water who will surely develop the level of intelligence necessary to use Manna."

H'wan looked at Seb for a response, but didn't get one.

"When that happens, humanity will have to hope that the new masters of Earth are less aggressive and destructive than themselves. If such an outcome proves to be the case, humans will have to accept their new position as subordinates, inferiors. Do you suppose that will be a smooth process?"

Finally, Seb spoke.

"Smooth? No. Inevitable? Perhaps. Maybe that's been part of our problem as a species. It might do us good to give up the illusion that we're in charge."

Seb handed H'wan a small dark object.

"It's unlikely we'll meet again, H'wan. Safe travels."

H'wan turned its dark, swirling, smoky body toward the T'hn'uuth. This really was an historic encounter. It hoped it might encounter another Gyeuk ship on its journey back. This experience definitely gave it bragging rights.

"Safe travels, T'hn'uuth."

***

The International Space Station was no longer in synchronous orbit with the ship, so saw nothing when the second Engine was launched, dropping rapidly, the wide end of the teardrop glowing with intense heat as it pushed through the atmosphere.

NASA tracked it as before. The similarity in size and location to the meteorite detected the previous day raised some eyebrows, but as it once again seemed to break into smaller parts before crashing into the deepest part of the Atlantic, no one was willing to sign off on the significant dollar investment it would take to investigate further.

Other than a few fishermen, only one person saw the brief fiery glow in the heavens.

The same observer was the only witness to the change of shape, as the teardrop opened up into a bowl and slowed on its final approach.

Perching on rocks surrounding the tiny beach at Nightingale, hundreds of indignant birds eyed the figure who had disturbed them for the second time in twenty-four hours. They squawked and flapped their wings at the intruder, ignoring the small object out at sea, which had now separated itself from the bowl above and was hurtling toward the water.

At that distance, the splash was barely audible. The Engine dived to two hundred feet below. There, it exploded, thrusting the nanotechnology inside it outward and upward to the surface.

H'wan turned away from Earth and began the long journey to the Rozzers' home.

Seb knew they'd be back eventually. He wondered what they'd find.

On the surface of the Atlantic, the ancient life-sustaining process began as the morning sun warmed the ocean. Water evaporated and rose through the atmosphere, condensed into droplets that formed clouds and moved with the wind.

The Engine, this time, delivered a payload of Seb's design.

Seb Varden, T'hn'uuth, the World Walker, watched the white clouds moving toward the land, somewhere becoming rain.

Chapter 47

Innisfarne
Six weeks later

A bell signaling the start of evening meditation chimed in the distance as Mee and Kate walked along the rocky west shore of Innisfarne. The clouds above them were heavy and dark, bruised purple-black, but those nearer the setting sun were a wispy cotton candy. The sun itself was a boiling red-orange ball sinking behind the sea.

"Dad always used to say that the sun was kept in a big iron pot on the other side of the world," said Mee. "Apparently, it was Australia's job to polish it while we were asleep, then push it back into the sky for us. Mum used to roll her eyes at him, but I believed it. Why not? It was perfectly logical to a five year-old."

"Your dad sounds a bit like my brother," said Kate. "He told me the tooth fairy was using our teeth to build a monster who would come and chew us up. For years, I used to bury my baby teeth in the yard."

"That's terrible!" said Mee, laughing.

Kate led the way to a bench under one of the island's ancient yew trees. They sat without speaking for a few minutes. Silence was such an integral part of life on Innisfarne that no one ever rushed to break it. Mee had told Kate about the attempt to kidnap her, the death of Westlake and Walt. She had decided it was simplest just to tell her Mason was dead. The Order could spread the news. There was no need for anyone else to know he was Seb's brother. She hadn't told her about the aliens, either. Mee wasn't completely comfortable keeping secrets from Kate, but what was the point? The world was safe again. She had only told Kate that Seb had been through an emotional and physical battle from which he was struggling to recover. Which was the biggest lie of all. Whatever was going on with Seb was something else entirely.

"Has he spoken about it at all yet?" said Kate.

Seb had appeared on the island over a month ago, joining the community occasionally, but mostly keeping to himself, spending long hours walking. With Mee, he had been kind and gentle, but there was a distance between them she was half-afraid to address. Sometimes, he'd look at her and it was as if he wasn't seeing her at all.

Until the previous night, he hadn't spoken about what had happened with the aliens threatening the planet, other than to say they had gone. She was still reeling from the news about Mason. His *brother?* After he'd told her what had happened in New York, he'd barely managed to string together a complete sentence. After weeks had passed and he showed no inclination to talk about what had happened with the Unmaking Engine, Mee had eventually decided enough was enough, had stopped pussyfooting around and had asked him outright.

Seb's explanation had been matter-of-fact, and to a large extent, incomprehensible, even to Mee, who had a reasonable grasp of science.

He told her he had considered a couple of alternatives, but—in order to convince the Rozzers that humanity would cease to be a threat to their galactic neighbors—human Manna use had to stop permanently. The nanotech he had built into the Engine was designed to tweak the DNA of just one interrupted gene of the twenty-three chromosome pairs in all humans. Everyone would be changed, but none of them would know anything about it. Not at first.

Seb's intervention would only become apparent as the next generation was born. The first generation with no Manna ability whatsoever. And then those few Users who'd assumed they could continue passing on their knowledge to their offspring would be in for a nasty surprise.

The longevity of Manna users, some whom lived well into their second century, meant that his plan would take time to work. But inevitably, it *would* work. Within the span of a few human lifetimes, all Users would be gone. And the future of Earth would be changed forever.

"Yeah, he's spoken about it," she said to Kate. "He saved me, went after the bad guys. Just like superheroes are supposed to."

"You don't sound completely overjoyed about it," said Kate.

"Yeah, well, it's not the world I'm worried about," said Mee. "It's Seb. He's changed."

They hadn't had sex since he'd returned. They hadn't talked about it yet. They were sharing a bed, but—most nights—Mee would wake up in the early hours and see Seb standing by the window, looking blankly ahead. There were times when he almost seemed his old self, but Mee could tell he was making an effort to keep his attention focused on her.

"It's like he's just out of reach," said Mee, as Kate put an arm around her shoulders.

"What are you going to do?" said Kate.

"If he won't respond to me, I'm going to have to try something else."

They walked back toward the main house.

***

It felt like a dream at first. Seb knew he was in bed, lying next to Mee. It must be a dream. But somehow, he knew it wasn't. He was there.

His eyes were open, but he could see very little at first. He was underwater, drifting deeper and deeper with every passing second. The dark blue tinge to the water was gradually disappearing, becoming absolute blackness.

For a few minutes, the only sensation was the sensation of warm water on Seb's skin; the gradual darkening around him the only indication he was still moving. Still diving.

At some point—it might have been minutes, or hours later—he became aware of light below him. There was a pale blueness waiting somewhere in the depths. As he got closer, his eyes adjusted and the gloom slowly lifted. He could see huge shapes in the dimness, some far away, others disconcertingly close. There was no sound at all, and—when he turned his head from side to side to try to catch a glimpse of what he was sensing—he could see nothing. Yet, he knew they were there. There was a strong feeling of curiosity, playfulness, intelligence. Seb was unafraid.

His progress downward slowed and, eventually came to a stop, although Seb was still floating, his upper body lower than his legs. He realized he wasn't breathing, hadn't been breathing during the dive. That was why the silence had seemed so absolute: he didn't even have the sound of his own breath in his head.

As he hovered in the blue stillness, Seb wondered which ocean he was in. There was no way of knowing.

More time passed, more shapes came close, none lingering long enough for him to see them properly.

Seb looked down at his own body. He couldn't see it. Bemused, he brought his hands in front of his face. They weren't there. It was an unutterably strange feeling, but still, Seb felt no fear.

Three shapes appeared in the middle distance, drifting closer. As they got closer, they gradually became clearer. They were constantly changing shape, sometimes almost imperceptibly, other times in a blur of speed. All three were rust-colored, like floating clouds of blood. They looked a lot like pictures of distant nebulae Seb had seen once. He remembered now—it was an exhibition on a gallery, with images captured by the Hubble telescope printed on enormous canvases. The nebulae, vast clouds of plasma, gases and dust, were incredibly beautiful.

"Seb."

As the clouds came closer, swirling hypnotically, Seb remembered what he'd read about nebulae. Within their extraordinarily beautiful depths, stars were created, and also died. They were stellar nurseries, and stellar graveyards.

"Seb."

Seb felt himself move toward the three clouds. As he did so, he began to question his initial impression of being underwater. He had arbitrarily assigned 'up' and 'down' and assumed he was diving. Now he began to wonder if, in fact, he was in water at all.

Seb accelerated toward the nearest cloud.

"Seb! Please!"

He opened his eyes and was *here* and *here* for a brief, confusing moment. Then he saw Mee's face as she shook him by the shoulders, shouting his name.

"Mee?" he said, quietly, as she sat down beside him, holding his hand tightly. She was crying. The tears were rolling down her face when she curled up and put her head in his lap. He hesitated, then reached up and stroked her hair. She was still crying when she finally fell asleep.

***

John Varden arrived on Innisfarne two days after he'd received the letter from Mee. He used one of the passports Mason had created in a variety of different names, should he ever need to travel on a commercial flight. John's name change to Varden was, as yet, unofficial, but he'd filed the papers. He wanted the same surname as his brother, even though he knew Seb's last name had been chosen by one of the sisters at St Benet's, after the newborn had been left on their doorstep.

The journey to Innisfarne was long and tiring. John was still trying to get used to how quickly he became exhausted, with no Manna reserves to restore his energy. He fell asleep as the gently rocking fishing boat brought him to the island.

Mee met him at the jetty. He didn't know what to say to her. She held up her hands. For a few seconds, he was puzzled, then he realized what she was showing him. All of her fingers were intact.

"I left one hand with four fingers as a reminder you were still out there," she said. "But I don't need reminding any more. When Seb came back, I asked him to heal it."

John nodded. Her letter had said she knew it wasn't him, that she understood about the tumor that had given Mason life. But reading a letter was different to looking into the eyes of someone who'd encountered Mason, someone he'd hurt. She held his gaze. He felt a lightness, a burst of unexpected happiness as he realized she not only forgave him, but she didn't believe there was anything to forgive. She'd looked at him and seen only John. Not Mason. It was another big step toward him being able to fully forgive himself.

They had breakfast together and talked about Seb. Then she took him to his brother.

Seb was walking on the beach again, his pace slow, picking a path through the slippery rocks. Mee had to call him three times before he finally responded, lifting his head, then waving at them.

They met by the water, the gulls wheeling and diving for scraps in the sun-flecked water.

Mee hadn't told Seb that she'd invited John. She wanted to see his reaction up close. At first, she thought this might be the breakthrough she was hoping for. Seb looked amazed, then pleased, even hugging the older man. After a few minutes, she smiled at John, kissed Seb on the cheek and left them.

Over the next few days, Seb and John spent every morning together, walking. Mee left them to their own company. Growing up as an orphan and then discovering you have a sibling must have been a shock even for a guy who could eat breakfast in a parallel universe. She gave them their space.

In the afternoons, John volunteered to help repair some of the dry stone walls on the far side of the island. It was fairly physical work, and by the time he'd had supper, he was wiped out. Mee managed to speak to him a few times. He'd been telling Seb everything he could remember about his parents. Finding out his father was a vicious bully couldn't have been easy, but Seb's mother sounded like a warm, intelligent woman who'd made the best of a terrible situation. Mee couldn't help but wonder why she hadn't just smacked the guy on the head with a skillet. She could only assume she'd thought she was protecting her son by staying put.

For a few days, Seb seemed to engage with the idea of having a family. He told Mee about his mother, how he wished he could have met her. He'd grown up with the usual fantasies dreamed up by orphans—that his parents were actually rich, or famous, and there had been some kind of mistake. That they'd be coming to claim him any day. Then, when he was a little older, the feelings of betrayal—how could a mother abandon her own flesh and blood? Next, in adolescence, the crushing self-pity of feeling unwanted. Hard to shift that particular feeling when your mother had left you on the doorstep of an orphanage. But Seb had eventually outgrown these feelings and had become a good man. And now he knew, finally, that his mother had abandoned him for heartbreakingly understandable reasons. He seemed to have found some sort of peace. Knowledge—even when it hurt—was better than ignorance.

There were a few signs of the old Seb. He picked up a guitar one night and strummed a few chords. Then he carefully replaced the instrument in the corner of the room and didn't touch it again.

Then his long conversations with John stopped and he started walking alone. John was sanguine about it.

"His life has been thrown into chaos," he said to Mee at dinner one night. "Anyone would take time to adjust." He speared a carrot, grown in the community's vegetable garden. The island was pretty much self-sufficient. "I know all about that, trust me. But—". He stopped talking.

"But what?" said Mee. John looked a little uncomfortable. Mee pressed him. "What were you going to say?"

John put his fork down and looked at Mee.

"I was going to say that there's something about him that scares me a little."

Mee shivered. This was a little too close to something she'd been feeling herself. Something she didn't want to admit.

"I don't mean scared *of* him, exactly," said John. It's kinda hard to explain. It reminds me of something that happened when I was about ten years old."

He stopped again. Mee waited as he tried to find the right words. Her throat felt suddenly dry, but she didn't want to move, even to reach for her glass.

"I was in the forest on my own," he said. "I'd taken a book with me, climbed a tree and spent hours perched there, reading. Got lost in the book, to tell the truth. At first, when the atmosphere changed, I didn't notice. Then it got darker suddenly. I could hardly see the page I was trying to read. I climbed down the tree. The clouds were real low and they were a kind of sick, yellow color. But the weirdest part was the noise. There wasn't any. Nothing. Now this was the middle of a forest—birds, animals, insects scurrying about. The sound was usually so constant you forgot it was there. Until it wasn't. It was—what's the word?—*unnerving*. I felt the hairs on my neck go up. It was like everything around me knew something was about to happen. Something big. I panicked and ran. Halfway home, the biggest clap of thunder I'd ever heard in my life sounded right over my head, followed by lightning so bright I'd swear I could see my bones through my skin. I was about twenty yards from shelter when the rain came. It was like someone was emptying a swimming pool over my head. Soaked to the skin in two seconds."

"You must have been terrified," said Mee.

"Damn near crapped my pants," said John, smiling ruefully. Then his smile slipped. He shook his head. "It was just the sheer power of nature," he said. "I felt—no, I *knew* that we humans were insignificant. Nature could brush us aside, swat us like bugs, any time."

He pushed the plate away, leaving half of his food untouched.

"And that's how Seb makes me feel," he said. "There's an atmosphere around him. I feel like I'm back in that tree, just before the storm broke."

Chapter 48

Four nights after her conversation with John, Mee woke up to find Seb's side of the bed empty and cold. He wasn't standing by the window. The door to their room squealed like an outraged cat every time it opened, so she knew he must have Walked. Without telling her. Which was a first. Not a precedent she liked at all.

When he wasn't back by 5am, Mee, unable to sleep, decided an early morning walk would be better than sitting up in bed, her thoughts whirling in an unhelpful spiral of speculation and uneasiness.

The approaching dawn was just beginning to lend some definition to the buildings, trees, and paths as she set out. She could hear the hooting of owls, and the scurrying of small mammals hoping to avoid predators. In places, the grass was long, and the dew had soon soaked the ends of her pants. After a few minutes, she realized she'd been mentally humming four bars of a song she'd written with Seb. They hadn't written lyrics yet, so it was just a melody—a haunting, wispy line that sounded like it was written centuries ago. It had just that hint of darkness that Mee always tried for. The grit in the pearl. She'd always distrusted music without that suggestion of fracture, melancholy or pain.

She shook her head and tried to change her internal soundtrack to something else, despite knowing it was a next-to-impossible task.

She almost walked past Seb without seeing him at first. A person standing still is never completely motionless. The human body just isn't built for it. Buckingham Palace's red-jacketed guards, world famous for standing still with furry microphone pop shields on their heads for hours at a time, still have to breathe. But Seb was so uncannily still, Mee's conscious mind dismissed the statue-like figure, until her sub-conscious pulled her up and made her look again.

When she realized what she was looking at, she didn't run. It was that unnatural posture that made her slowly and carefully make her way across the rocky beach. Part of her was reluctant to get close. She acknowledged her fear, and firmly decided to ignore it.

Up close, it became even more obvious something strange was happening. Seb looked normal at first. Then she realized he wasn't breathing—or possibly, was breathing so slowly that nothing was outwardly discernible. His eyes were open. Light fell on his face, but the sun was still down and the night had been moonless. Mee reached out a hand and put it between the moon and Seb's face. Impossibly, no shadow appeared on his features.

Mee reached for Seb's hand. As soon as she touched his skin, she pulled back her hand with a hiss. It was like touching cold, hard metal. She reached out again, more slowly this time. She tried not to flinch when her fingertips touched his skin, although her lips twitched. It felt exactly like a cold beer can. She pushed. There was resistance. Not quite like human skin, more that of an under-ripe avocado.

Mee took a step backward and looked carefully at Seb. Neither his hair or his clothes were moving in the breeze that was constantly flicking Mee's bangs in front of her eyes.

Steeling herself, she stepped forward again and put a hand on his shoulder. She silently counted to three, then gave him a hard push. She wasn't sure what to expect. He might rock backward, fall over, or—hopefully—wake up, look at her, and come back to reality. None of those possibilities occurred. What did happen was so unexpected that Mee stumbled backward and sat down heavily in the sand.

Her hand *penetrated* his T-shirt and skin, went through his shoulder. She actually saw her fingers emerging just outside Seb's right shoulder blade. It felt like her hand was pushing through very thick oatmeal. It was even slightly warm. Mee felt like throwing up.

Instead, she stood again, stamped her feet on the shingle to force some warmth into them and remind herself she was awake, then stood in front of Seb and looked into his eyes.

"Seb?" she said. "Can you hear me? Seb?"

His eyes were definitely seeing *something,* but it wasn't Meera Patel. She had heard that expression: *he had a faraway look in his eye.* Yep. Far away. It was just that *far away* couldn't even begin to cover the sense of distance she saw in Seb's eyes. A better fit might be: *he had that 'seeing another galaxy possibly in a parallel universe' look in his eye.* Yep. That was more accurate.

Mee didn't cry on her way back to the main house to tell Kate, but she did swear. Loudly.

***

Two weeks later

For the first thirty-six hours, only Mee and Kate had known what was going on, but within a few days the entire community was whispering about it. A meeting was called, Kate told them what little they knew, suggestions were made, and a plan of sorts was approved.

"Better than doing nothing," said Mee, but she didn't sound convinced.

The two women made their way down to the beach at midnight. Mee hadn't slept at all the first two nights, so Kate had organized shifts of volunteers to make sure nothing happened without Mee knowing about it. Kate and Mee were going to cover the 12-4am shift.

Two men stood up as they approached. A temporary camp had been set up under a tree overlooking the beach. It was little more than some folding chairs and a two-person tent containing a camping stove.

As she got closer, Mee realized one of the men was John, drinking from a tin cup.

"It's no good," he said. "I *want* to like tea, especially now that I'm in Britain, but I guess I'm too old to change."

Mee forced a smile at his attempt to keep the atmosphere light.

"You, of all people, know you're never too old to change."

"Good point," said John, grimacing as he took another sip. "You don't suppose coffee beans would grow here, do you?"

Mee and Kate stood alongside the two men and looked down the slope to the beach. The tide was going out, exposing the wet rocks dotting the sand and shingle. The moon hung big and low in the clear sky.

Seb still hadn't moved. He stood with his back to them, looking straight ahead. At night, the temperatures plummeted, but he was only wearing a T-shirt, jeans and sneakers. Fifteen days into his silent vigil, the only things that changed were the light, the weather, the observers and the unceasing wash of the tide as it came in and receded. Seb stayed exactly the same.

"Even the bloody gulls won't perch on his head," said Mee, finishing the tea John hadn't quite managed to bring himself to drink.

Kate and Mee watched Seb for their allotted four hours. During the day, many of the community had taken to making their way one by one to the silent figure and talking to him. Not expecting a response perhaps, but letting him know they were there. At night, it was just the rota of watchers and the bats that flickered in and out of the branches above them.

***

Ten days later

Mee had experienced bad shit before. She knew that prevailing wisdom claimed things got bad before they got better, that the night was always darkest before the dawn, but—in her experience—things were just as likely to get worse as get better. And what kind of idiot thought the darkest part of the night was just before dawn? The darkest part of the night was *hours* before that.

On this particular night, the darkest part was at 3:40am.

Mee sat bolt upright in bed and was fully awake instantly, which had never happened before. Ever. She'd taken to sleeping in one of Seb's T-shirts since he'd been gone. The principle of which half-comforted and half-horrified her. In the end, she mentally justified her action by describing it as, "giving my inner militant feminist a cuddle," and left it at that.

She grabbed a pair of jeans, a jacket and her sneakers and half-ran, half-hopped through the sleeping house, getting dressed as she went.

Outside, everything was quiet. It was so dark, she almost ran headlong into Sarah, one of the women covering the 12-4am shift that night. The other woman gasped in surprise as Mee rushed past. She called something after her, but Mee wasn't listening.

When she got to the tent overlooking the beach, no one else was there. Breathing heavily, Mee looked down to the beach. It was a starlit night, but hard to see exactly was going on. There was definitely a figure down there.

Mee scrambled down to the shore.

The figure was Kate.

"I saw it," she said quietly as Mee came closer. She took the younger woman's hand and they both looked at the spot where Seb had been standing for nearly a month.

"What happened?" said Mee.

"There was nothing dramatic about it," said Kate. "He took a couple of steps forward. I stood up, called Sarah—she was sleeping in the tent. By the time she'd come out, he'd gone. He took one more step. Halfway through it he disappeared. As if he'd walked through a door."

Kate looked at Mee's face for a few seconds. "I'll wait up there for you," she said, and walked back toward the watcher's station.

Mee could still see Seb's footprints. She knew the tide, which had washed around his feet every day for a few hours, would soon wash them away forever. She carefully put her own feet where his had been. Stood where he had stood. Looked out toward the sky the way he had been doing for the last twenty-five days.

Mee tried to see what Seb had seen. Tried to think like him. And finally, admitted to herself that she didn't know how to do that anymore. She couldn't think, or see, what he saw. The Seb she'd known had changed beyond recognition. Not in a bad way, perhaps. Maybe from a caterpillar to a butterfly. Which was all very lovely, but not so great if you were the caterpillar's girlfriend. The thought made her laugh. The laugh turned into sobs, and she allowed herself a cathartic ten minutes of howling. Then she wiped the tears from her face with the bottom of Seb's T-shirt and made her way back up the slope.

She allowed herself one last look back. She slowly scanned the empty beach, then raised her eyes and gazed at the night sky. For most of her life, the stars had seemed friendly, exciting and mysterious. Tonight, they were cold, distant, and unknowable.

She put one hand on her stomach and wondered if he had known. He seemed to know everything else. Could he have missed what was going on right in front of him? She knew the anger she was feeling was misplaced and unfair, but she couldn't help it.

"If it's a boy," she whispered, "I'm definitely *not* calling him Seb."

THE END

Author's note

The World Walker series will continue…

Thanks for reading The Unmaking Engine. If you enjoyed it, please consider leaving a review on Amazon USA or UK (apologies to all other nationalities who bought the first book—but please leave a review on your country's Amazon page!)

You can join my mailing list here - http://bit.ly/1VSg2tT, and I'll send you a free copy of the unpublished prologue to The World Walker. I blog very occasionally here - https://ianwsainsbury.com/ and you can email me on ianwsainsbury@gmail.com. I'm on Facebook: www.facebook.com/IanWSainsbury/

On March 21st 2016, I published The World Walker—my first novel—on Amazon. And now, five months later, I've written the sequel. Which you've just finished reading.

Oh, hang on. Before I go on, I have to address a little problem I didn't anticipate first time around. Apparently, some people read the Author's Note before they read the book. Why? I can't answer that, because I've never done it. But I have solid evidence that it happens. So, can I just point out that Author's Notes sometimes contain spoilers? You might read something that diminishes your enjoyment of the story.

So…don't do it.

Seriously.

I'm talking to you, Auntie Hazel. Stop reading immediately, go back and start at the beginning. We'll wait.

Right, on with the note. Honestly, some people. Tut.

The World Walker took me about eighteen months to write from the time I first scribbled the initial idea into a notebook. The Unmaking Engine took five months. So, if my calculations are correct, the next one should take about 15 days. Hmm. Apparently, there are folk out there who *can* write that fast. I haven't a clue how. I imagine they have some sort of Faustian pact with a minor demon who slows down time around them in return for sexual favors and exclusive access to their immortal souls.

Just so you know, I don't think I'll ever be able to write a novel that fast. If I did, I'm reasonably certain it wouldn't be worth reading.

On the other hand, I can't ever see myself following in George RR Martin's footsteps, making desperate readers wait years for the next book in a series.

(An aside on George RR Martin. He's my equivalent of an Indy band you discover years before the rest of the world catches on. In the early 1990s, I read Fevre Dream, a vampire story set on the Mississippi in the golden age of the steamboat. A long, long time before Twilight made vampires ubiquitous. Anne Rice was doing her lush, sensuous vampire stuff of course, but there was something about Fevre Dream. Maybe it was the evocative prose, or the wonderfully flawed human hero, Abner Marsh. Maybe it was the believable vampire culture and history. Maybe it was the tightness of the story—compact, fairly short, possible to read in one or two obsessive sittings—which I did, first time around—try doing that with A Song Of Ice And Fire. I love Fevre Dream. I've given copies of it away at least three times and bought myself a new one. In fact, looking at my shelves, it's not there now. Time to buy it again. These days, of course, everyone knows who GRRM is. Which—totally unfairly—irks me. I am irked. He was *my* author. I wish I was a bigger man and could be unirked. But I can't. Grr.)

Back to the point. I hoped to write a second book. I had lots of ideas about developing the story, and one book couldn't do justice to all of them. I avoided a cliffhanger ending for The World Walker, because—sometimes— they make me want to throw my Kindle out of the window. But I knew there was more to come. I just wasn't sure when I'd find the time. And that's where you come in, gentle reader…

After the first few weeks, The World Walker started selling a constant number of copies every day. Also, there were plenty of people borrowing it through Kindle Unlimited and Select. Not enough to buy a new car/pay for a child's education/upgrade to First Class on any future airplane trips, but enough sales and borrows to encourage me to take a risk and make time to write the sequel sooner rather than later.

Once I'd made the commitment, I wrote pages of notes and carefully plotted most of the book, including the ending. Which is hilarious, because—when I look at my notes now—almost everything has changed. The ending is completely different. It's the strangest sensation when a story takes on a life of its own. There's one chapter in The Unmaking Engine which came from nowhere. Straight from my subconscious onto the page, bypassing my conscious mind completely. And you thought Manna was weird?

What I'm trying to say, in a long-winded and rambling way, is that those of you who read The World Walker made The Unmaking Engine possible. I've been incredibly lucky—thousands of people have read the first novel, and the reviews (please do review any independent author's book you've enjoyed, it makes a HUGE difference) have given me the confidence and impetus to keep writing.

I have more in store in the multiverse of The World Walker. There's at least one more book to write about Mee, Seb and—perhaps—the next generation. I also have lots of other stories to tell. If enough of you want to keep reading, I'll keep writing.

Reading opens our minds, lets us see how others perceive the world—even an imaginary world. This is **a good thing**. And the world needs more **good things**. Thanks for reading.

Ian W. Sainsbury
Norwich
August 19th, 2016

Printed in Poland
by Amazon Fulfillment
Poland Sp. z o.o., Wrocław